Caroline Ander
armchair garden
and eater of lov
that order! What
friends. Reading. Writing contempor
stories. Hearing from readers. Walks by the sea with coffee/ice cream/cake thrown in! Torrential rain. Sunshine in spring/autumn. What Caroline hates: losing her pets. Fighting with her family. Cold weather. Hot weather. Computers. Clothes shopping. Caroline's plans: keep smiling and writing!

Lifelong romance addict **JC Harroway** took a break from her career as a junior doctor to raise a family and found her calling as a Mills & Boon author instead. She now lives in New Zealand and finds that writing feeds her very real obsession with happy endings and the endorphin rush they create. You can follow her at jcharroway.com, and on Facebook, X and Instagram.

Also by Caroline Anderson

Healing Her Emergency Doc
A Vet to Heal His Heart

Yoxburgh Park Hospital miniseries

The Midwife's Miracle Twins
Finding Their Forever Family

Also by JC Harroway

Mistletoe Baby Mix-Up

Sexy Surgeons in the City collection

Manhattan Marriage Reunion

Jet Set Docs collection

One Night to Sydney Wedding

Royally Tempted collection

One Night to Royal Baby

Discover more at millsandboon.co.uk.

FROM FRESH START TO FAMILY

CAROLINE ANDERSON

THE PARAMEDIC ROOMMATE PACT

JC HARROWAY

MILLS & BOON

First published in Great Britain 2026
by Mills & Boon, an imprint of HarperCollins*Publishers* Ltd,
1 London Bridge Street, London, SE1 9GF

www.harpercollins.co.uk

HarperCollins*Publishers* Macken House, 39/40 Mayor Street Upper,
Dublin 1, D01 C9W8, Ireland

ISBN: 978-0-263-41982-5

02/26

MIX
Paper | Supporting responsible forestry
FSC® C013604

Printed and Bound in the UK using 100% Renewable Electricity
at CPI Group (UK) Ltd, Croydon, CR0 4YY

FROM FRESH START TO FAMILY

CAROLINE ANDERSON

MILLS & BOON

Thanks to my family for their
(sometimes inadvertent) contributions:

My husband, John, for the first-hand experience
of a stroke caused by AF.

And our daughters: Sarah, who gave us terrifying
first-hand experience of a concussion, and Hannah,
who pointed out that nobody would forget something
so relevant just because they were in a hurry.

I love you all.

PROLOGUE

Mid-May

SHE'D DONE IT!

Landed the job she really, really wanted, and with it a fresh start, a new life here in this beautiful seaside town, and maybe now she could put everything behind her and move on.

She walked out of the interview room in Yoxburgh Park Hospital with a smile so wide you could probably see it from space, but she didn't care. She fumbled in her bag for her phone and pulled it out with shaking fingers.

'Mum, I got it! I got the job!'

Tears, laughter—and then she hung up and went to find Jake. Jake, who'd been given the task of showing her round the ED, who'd soothed her nerves and calmed her and bolstered her fragile confidence.

She found him at the desk, tall and rugged, and her heart did a little jig.

'I got it!' she told him, and he turned with a smile nearly as wide as hers.

'That's brilliant, well done!' he said, and wrapped her in a breath-stealing hug. He let her go, still smiling, and she couldn't speak for a second.

'I still can't quite believe it.'

'Believe it. You were streets ahead of the others. What are you doing now?'

'Oh—driving back to Southampton,' she said, wishing she didn't have to.

He frowned. 'That's a long way and it's after six on a Friday night. It'll be vile. Why don't you stay over, go in the morning—unless you're working tomorrow?'

She shook her head. 'No, I'm not working, but I asked as I was checking out and the hotel's full tonight.' She shrugged. 'I'll be fine,' she said, as much to convince herself as him.

'Will you? You've already told me you didn't sleep well last night. Try another hotel—or, look, my shift's finished and I've got a spare room doing nothing. Why don't you stay, get a decent night's sleep? Then we can go out for dinner tonight to celebrate and you can leave tomorrow when you're fresh.'

Stay with him? She searched his eyes, and saw nothing but concern. And he was right, the roads would be vile. She felt her shoulders drop with the release of tension. 'D'you know what? That would be amazing. Thank you.'

He smiled, that smile that did weird things to her insides and made her wonder if she was doing the right thing. 'Great. Give me ten seconds to change, and we're out of here.'

She drove them to his house in her car and pulled up outside.

'Is my car OK here?'

'Yes, it's fine till eight tomorrow morning. Come on in.'

His house was lovely—a classic Victorian semi, with a really nice spare room overlooking the garden.

'I need a shower first,' he said. 'Give me five minutes.'

She closed the door of her room, sat on the bed and sent her mother a text with the change of plan, then she put on her jeans and trainers and kept her simple white top on. Not that she had a choice. The only other top she had was the T-shirt she'd driven here in, and it had definitely seen better days. She wished she'd brought something rather more special, but then she told herself it wasn't a date, it was just a welcoming colleague wanting to share her moment, probably in a pub.

She heard him run downstairs, and took another look in the mirror. 'You're fine like that,' she told herself.

But she still dug out her lippy and gave her lips a quick swipe. Just to stop them feeling dry…

He was showered, dressed and in the hall by the time she came downstairs.

'Will I be OK like this?' she asked, and he ran his eyes over her and swallowed. Her interview suit had hidden her curves. The jeans and top showed them off just a tad too well, and he had to tell himself to get a grip.

'You'll be fine. Are you OK to walk? It's not far.'

'Sure. Where are we going?'

'A little place on the seafront.'

A place that by a miracle had had a late cancellation, because getting a table there was as rare as hen's teeth and he'd only tried on the off-chance.

They strolled down through the residential streets to the prom and from time to time their shoulders nudged, or their hands brushed, and he felt the touch like a live wire.

This was insane. He *really* needed to get a grip.

'Here we are.'

'*Zacharelli's?* I've read about this place. How on earth…?'

'Luck. Pure luck.'

She gave him a look. 'You're not paying.'

He felt his eyebrow climb. 'My idea, not yours, so yes, I am.'

He ushered her in and they were seated at a table by the window—another stroke of luck?—and handed the menu, which nearly made her drool.

'Oh, it all looks delicious. The *risotto con pollo* sounds lovely and I'm absolutely starving—oh, but they've got a seafood skewer! Now I'm really torn!'

'Me, too. Fancy sharing?'

'Absolutely, if you don't mind?'

'I don't mind. I'm torn, too.'

He ordered them both, and then, maybe to pass the time, he asked her to tell him about herself.

'There's not a lot to tell—apart from the fact that I've always wanted to be a doctor.'

'Nobody in your life? No boyfriend, husband, girlfriend, significant other?'

Pass the time? He was blatantly fishing. She tilted her head and met his eyes. 'Try unfaithful lying rat—and my ex.'

'Ouch. That sounds…'

'Unpleasant? It was, and I won't bore you with the details, but suffice to say Steve is a sub-human the planet could well do without and ditching him was the best thing I've ever done.'

'Sounds like you're well rid of him.'

'I am. Who needs someone without monogamy in their vocab? So how about you?' she asked, suddenly curious. Well, no, not suddenly, she'd been curious all day, but…

He shook his head. 'No other, significant or otherwise. Not for over two years now.'

He looked away, and that made her even more curious. How was a man so kind, decent and, to be utterly truthful, downright sexy as sin, living alone?

'What went wrong?' she asked softly, and he looked up at her again and shrugged.

'I was never there, and when I was, I was exhausted. You know how hard it is, how the stress builds up, how you can't put the patients out of your head. Did I make a mistake, did I miss something—it's not rocket science. And Claire wanted more. She deserved more, and she found it with someone else.'

'I'm sorry.'

'Yeah. Me, too.'

The light had gone out of his eyes, replaced by what looked like a deep-seated hurt, but before she could say anything more their food arrived. The risotto smelt every bit as delicious as she'd hoped, and his seafood skewer suspended over the plate looked divine, but before she could start to eat he lifted his glass of wine and she held hers up and they clinked, his eyes warm again and full of—pride?

'Congratulations, Lydia. I knew you'd do it.'

'Thank you. And thanks for showing me round and giving me all those useful interview tips.'

'Just following instructions from my clinical lead. He told me to do everything I could to get you to come.'

She watched him lift the glass to his lips and swallow, and she felt the breath stall in her chest and she squeezed her legs together. Get her to come? Right now, that wouldn't be difficult… No! He was going to be a work colleague! They couldn't let this be anything other than platonic.

Not that he'd suggested anything else, that was just her mind working overtime, but her body was telling her it wouldn't mind at all, and she had to drag her eyes off him and talk about something—anything—else!

She took a gulp of wine, a forkful of risotto, then looked up.

'I thought we were going to share?'

He smiled, a slow, lazy smile that teased all her senses, and he pulled a fat king prawn oozing with deliciousness off the skewer, stabbed it with his fork and held it up to her mouth.

She opened it, leant forward and pulled the prawn off with her teeth, and his eyes flared and he smiled and dug his fork into her risotto and put it in his mouth. She watched his lips close around it and had to look away, the breath jamming in her throat.

'That is really good,' he murmured, and came back for another forkful.

'Are you going to steal all of it?' she asked, hoping her voice wasn't as squeaky as she thought it was, and he chuckled and sucked his fork clean, pulled a scallop off the skewer and held it out for her, drawing the fork slowly away as her lips closed around it, his eyes on hers.

The intimacy of it stole her breath, and she had to look away.

She had to do something to defuse this! She dug her fork into her risotto and looked up again.

'So, if you were having a dinner party,' she said, hoping her voice didn't sound as breathless as she felt, 'who would you invite?'

She watched an eyebrow quirk upwards. 'Any categories?'

'Medical,' she said hurriedly, trying to drag herself out of the trance she was rapidly falling into. 'Dead or alive.'

He hesitated, his eyes thoughtful. 'You first.'

'Oh. Um—Florence Nightingale, for raising hygiene standards and making nursing a recognised profession? And Elizabeth Garrett Anderson, the first British woman to qualify as a physician and surgeon, and founder of the first medical school for women in this country. Oh, and Robert Winston, for his work with IVF. How about you?'

He studied her eyes, then frowned thoughtfully. 'Christiaan Barnard, for the first successful heart transplant? Alexander Fleming, for antibiotics. And Louis Pasteur, for vaccines and pasteurised milk. Your turn. And while you think, I'm going to steal more of your risotto.'

'Are you, indeed?' she said, and reached over and pinched a chunk of salmon off his skewer, trying and failing not to laugh.

She chewed and swallowed, then waved her fork.

'OK, non-medical now. Mother Teresa, and maybe Pope Francis—true humanitarians, and we could do with a few more of those in the world.'

He nodded slowly. 'OK, my turn. Nelson Mandela? And Barack Obama.'

'With or without Michelle?'

'Oh, with, they're a great couple,' he said, and his smile reeled her in again and made her heart do all kinds of weird things.

'They are.'

'I wonder what they'd all make of each other.'

She laughed. 'I think they'd get on well.'

There was a pause, then, 'I think we do, too,' he murmured slowly, and their eyes met and held and she had to look away because if she didn't she was going to catch fire.

She took a glug of wine and went back to her risotto, avoiding the dangling skewer that was going to get her into more trouble and mentally fanning herself to cool down the surge of—oh, good grief, she could only call it lust, and she'd never, *never* felt like that!

So she ate until she'd scraped up every last grain of rice, then she put her fork down and looked up and met his eyes.

'That was delicious. Thank you.'

'My pleasure,' he murmured, and his eyes showed he meant it, in every sense of the word. 'Fancy a dessert?'

Only you. She laughed breathlessly and shook her head. 'I couldn't eat another thing.'

'No, nor could I. Right, let's go. You need an early night, you've got a long drive tomorrow and I have to be at work at seven.'

They went out onto the prom, and there was a breeze off the sea that made her shiver.

'Here,' he said, and untied the sweater that was knotted over his shoulders and laid it over hers. She pulled it close, smelling the scent of his cologne, the warmth of his body heat wrapping around her and teasing her senses.

They walked back up the hill to his house in silence, and once they were inside she handed the soft sweater back to him.

'Thank you—for everything—for dinner, for being there for me today, for cheerleading, for offering me a room so I didn't have to drive—all of it.'

'You're welcome. Do you want anything to drink?'

She shook her head, then said, 'A glass of water for the night? I ought to turn in, really. Can I have a shower first?'

'Of course. I could do with an early night, too. You go first, you know where the bathroom is. I'll bring your water up.'

* * *

She was still in the bathroom when he went up. He put the glass down on her bedside table, turned on the lamp and walked out, just as she came out of the bathroom in lounge pants and a thin vest top that left very little to his imagination—and it was already running riot after that ridiculously sensuous food sharing. Stupid, stupid idea. And his choice of words…

He hauled his eyes up to her face. 'Find everything you needed?'

'Yes, thank you.'

'I've put the water by your bed.'

'Thanks—and thanks again for everything. You've been amazing.'

'My pleasure. Do you want a wake-up call at six?'

She smiled, her eyes soft and almost luminous. 'That would be great. Goodnight, Jake.'

'Goodnight, Lydia.'

He hesitated, then bent to kiss her cheek, but she turned her head at the last moment and their lips collided. They both froze, and he felt her breath drift out in a sigh against his face, and he let his lips soften against hers, sipping, tasting—and then his hands were cradling her face, her arms were around him, drawing him in against her body, and he was lost…

This wasn't supposed to happen! Why was she kissing him? It was crazy—but it felt so right, so good, so *necessary…* And then he pulled away, breathing hard and not looking her in the eye.

'We can't—we have to stop. I wasn't prepared for this, and I can't risk you getting pregnant. It's my unbreakable golden rule, not to be like my father.'

She held her breath for a second, then said softly, 'I'm on the pill,' and she felt his breath huff out against her hair, and his head lowered as he met her eyes again.

'We don't have to do this. We *can* stop.'

'Yes, we can. But we don't have to. Not if we don't want to. Your choice…'

His eyes closed, and when they opened she saw a burning need that echoed her own.

He caught her hand and led her into his bedroom, turning on the bedside light, closing the blinds.

And then his mouth found hers again, urgent now, his kisses, his hands, setting her body on fire—and hers were doing the same to him.

She could see it in his eyes, in his body as he stripped off his clothes and turned back to her, gloriously naked and definitely aroused, chest heaving, eyes intense, peeling her clothes away until at last they were together, skin to skin, heart to heart. They fell onto the bed in a tangle of lips and limbs, and he was there inside her, driving her over the edge as wave after wave of sensation swept through her and left her boneless.

He stiffened and a deep, guttural groan was torn from him, and then his head sagged against her shoulder, his chest heaving. For a long moment he stayed there as the echoes died away, and then he lifted his head and met her eyes and she wanted to cry.

'Hey… What's wrong? Did I hurt you?' His fingers were gentle, wiping away her tears, and she smiled at his worried frown.

'No—no, of course you didn't hurt me. I'm sorry—I think I've just been so wound up, and today's been so amazing, and that was…'

'That was incredible,' he said softly, his voice gruff,

and he kissed her tenderly and then rolled over, taking her with him, and kissed her again.

'Sleep now,' he murmured, and she snuggled into his side and closed her eyes and slept.

'Hey, sleepy-head, we need to get up.'

She felt his lips brush hers, then the bed shifted slightly and she heard the blind tilt, and she forced her eyes open and blinked at the unwelcome daylight. 'Really?'

He chuckled. 'Really. You wanted to get on the road early, and I need to go to work. You shower first.'

She slid out of bed, suddenly self-conscious, until he pulled her into his arms and dropped a kiss on her cheek, his body reacting instantly to the contact. And then he stepped away, holding her at arm's length.

'Go, shower, or we'll never get out of the bedroom.'

She went, still smiling, and stood under the pelting hot water, her face turned up to it, until she heard the door slide and he was there behind her, his soapy hands straying all over her body, setting fire to her all over again, turning and lifting her against him. She wrapped her legs around his waist, and he sank deep inside her, rocked his hips against her and took her over the edge again.

'Now I'm really going to be late,' she said, laughing and pushing him out of the shower so she could finish washing, then they swapped, and she towelled herself dry, cleaned her teeth and pulled out her pills from her washbag.

And froze.

She'd missed one. Yesterday's, before the interview, when she'd slept badly and had woken late in a rush. And now she'd spent the night making love with Jake however many times it had been. Two? Maybe, maybe more. And again, just now. And her body was still throbbing in the aftermath.

And in her head was his voice saying he wouldn't be like his father. Was that why he was in the world? Carelessness? She took that day's pill, vowing to get the morning after pill as soon as she got home, just to be on the safe side, and then she went back to her room, threw everything in her bag, zipped it up and walked out as he appeared, dressed only in jeans and looking so good she could hardly drag herself away.

'I'm off now.'

He nodded. 'Drive carefully. You've got my number. Let me know when you're home. And I'll come and see you—if you want me to?'

'Of course I do,' she said with a smile, and kissed him. 'Thank you—for everything. I'll see you soon?'

'Definitely. Drive carefully. And don't forget to ring.'

'I won't.' She kissed him again, then prised herself away, ran downstairs and drove off, a smile she couldn't seem to lose pinned on her face. She'd never felt so loved, so cherished, so happy in all her life.

Ten minutes later, it all went horribly wrong…

Ow...

Everything hurts. And those beeps—endless beeps. So noisy, and...a hospital blanket?

I'm in hospital?

Why?

What's happened to me?

I'm scared. Where am I?

She was waking up.

Jake let out a silent, shuddering sigh of relief, but it was tempered by dread. What if…?

Don't go there.

His heart, already pounding, picked up a beat. He watched her closely, saw her hands plucking the light blanket that covered her, feeling the texture, then scrunching it in her hands as if she were hanging on for dear life. He watched her chest, saw the rise and fall speed up, keeping pace with the monitor that registered her racing pulse. Pain? Fear?

Her eyelids flickered open, blinked shut, opened again.

'Hi,' he said softly, and she turned her head a fraction and looked at him, her eyes glazed and unfocused, the face he'd rained kisses on last night bruised and swollen, her lip bitten.

Oh, Lydia, what have I done...?

'Where am I?' Her voice was weak, a little shaky.

'Yoxburgh Park Hospital,' he said, keeping his voice calm and gentle. 'You had a car accident.'

'Oh.' She searched his face, frowning slightly. 'Do I know you? You look a bit...familiar?'

He sucked in a breath at the sharp stab of loss, which was ridiculous. OK, it had only been a little over twenty-four hours since they'd met, but...

If she'd lost all that, what else had she lost?

'Yes, you know me, Lydia,' he said calmly, even though he felt anything but. 'I'm Jake. We met yesterday, in the ED. I'm a doctor. I showed you round the department before your interview.' And then he'd failed to stick to the script—

She blinked, frowned again thoughtfully. 'Interview...'

Her voice tailed off, as if she was trying to make sense of that, and his heart kicked up another gear.

'You don't remember it?' he asked gently.

She shook her head, then winced and gave a tiny shrug.

'Maybe. Vaguely. Everything hurts and I've got a cracking headache.'

'I'm not surprised. Do you remember anything about the accident?'

She thought for a moment, then shook her head a fraction. 'No. No, nothing. What happened?'

'You swerved to avoid a motorbike and went off the road and hit a tree.'

Her eyes widened. 'I didn't hit the biker?'

'No, you didn't.'

'But—?'

No point in sugar-coating it, but he kept his voice soft, gentle. 'He lost control, went off the road and hit another tree. He wouldn't have known anything about it.'

'He died?' Her eyes searched his, finding the truth, her face stricken as she sucked in a breath. 'Oh, no… Was it my fault? Was I speeding?'

'No,' he said firmly. 'It definitely wasn't your fault. The police said he was doing well over the limit. They'd radioed ahead to set up a road block.'

'Oh…'

She paused, and he could almost hear the cogs whirring.

'So—not my fault, then?'

'No. Absolutely not your fault. You were not to blame in any way. All the witnesses said that.'

He saw the tension drain out of her, the relief, but if anyone had been to blame, it was him, because if he hadn't—

'So what happened to me?'

'You hit a tree and your car bounced off and slammed into another one and you hit your head on something. The airbags had opened, so it could have been a lot worse, but you've got a few seat belt injuries—bruises, abrasions, the usual—but no chest fractures or internal injuries that we could see on the CT or ultrasound. You were very lucky.'

'I don't feel lucky. I hurt all over.' She lifted a hand and touched her head, and winced. 'Ouch. That's really tender. Have I got a skull fracture?'

'No, but you'll have some fairly spectacular bruises and black eyes, probably. On the plus side, you haven't had a cranial bleed, but you do have concussion.'

He'd nearly said 'just', but there was no 'just' about concussion. It could do lasting damage, and that was all his fault. If he'd only let her go the night before—but she'd been tired, so maybe not a good idea, but he'd delayed her this morning and that was inexcusable. If he hadn't, she would have left earlier and she wouldn't be lying here now, bruised and battered and with a potentially serious head injury. And he'd have to live with that guilt for ever...

'So—where am I? What ward?'

'Neurology, under observation.'

'Oh.' She frowned, then looked back at him, her eyes searching for something. 'I got the job, didn't I?' she said slowly, as if she was picking up the scattered pieces of a jigsaw and trying to fit them together.

'Yes, you did,' he told her. 'You start in August.'

She looked up at him again, and he could see her mind dropping that one into place. 'What time is it?'

'Six-fifty.'

'I've slept all night?'

'No. It's the evening. You've been asleep for nearly ten hours, since they brought you up to the ward. You had the accident at six-thirty this morning.'

She frowned, the sort of frown when you're trying to work out what on earth is going on. As well she might be with all those jigsaw pieces flying round in her head. Not to mention the change of plan. Idiot. He should have let her go last night—

'Oh…' She closed her eyes again, then opened them, apparently giving up on the jigsaw. 'Has anyone told my mother?'

'Yes, she's on her way, she should be here soon.'

'Did you talk to her?'

'Not at first, the police did, but they gave us her number. I spoke to her later, told her I'd let her know when you woke up.'

'Oh. Thanks. What did you say your name was?' she asked, still trying to assimilate all the information, he guessed, but he felt another stab of pain at her words.

'Jake. Jacob Warren. I'm a doctor in the ED.'

'Jake…' Then she shook her head carefully and sighed. 'Sorry. I know I know you, but it's all so vague—'

'Don't worry about it. It doesn't matter. It'll come back, bit by bit, if you give it time.' He kept his voice gentle and reassuring, desperately hoping it wasn't a lie.

She met his eyes. 'Shouldn't you be at work?'

'No. My shift ended at five. Do you want to talk to your mother now? I promised her I'd ring when you woke up.'

She nodded, so he rang her on his phone, and after he'd given her the good news he passed the phone to Lydia and watched as her eyes filled with tears.

'Hi, Mum…'

He looked away, standing up and walking to the window, partly to give her privacy and partly for himself because he was hanging by a thread. He stood staring down into the car park below. It was thinning out now, all the clinics closed for the day.

Twenty-four hours ago he'd been showing her around Yoxburgh, taking her out for dinner and then—

You should have let her drive home yesterday instead of delaying her, and now look at her. This is all your fault—

'OK, Mum, I'll hand you back to Jake. I'll see you soon. Love you.'

He turned, taking his phone from her hand and replacing it with a tissue to mop up the tears.

'Hi, Mrs Fraser. Are you OK?'

'I'm better now I've spoken to her. At least she's coherent. Look, I'll be about half an hour. Can you stay with her till then? Please?'

'Of course I can, there's no hurry. Drive safely, and ring me when you get here and I'll come down and find you.'

'Thank you, Jake—' Her voice cracked, and she cut the call, and he put the phone back in his pocket and went to the door.

'I'll go and tell them you're awake. They'll want to know.'

'OK. Thanks.'

They did want to know, of course they did, but he needed space, needed to get out of that room where he'd sat for the past two hours watching her and wondering if she'd ever again be the same warm, funny, intelligent and responsive woman he'd met yesterday.

The woman he'd spent twelve hours getting to know all too intimately. The first woman in more than two years to break through his defences. The first woman that he'd dared to trust in those long, lonely years.

Surely not—not so quickly. It was only yesterday…

But it felt like a lifetime ago, and he'd been running on adrenaline for the last twelve hours. Still was. Lord knows what his blood pressure was.

She hardly remembers me. She doesn't remember last night. How could she forget that? Although maybe it would be good if she has. Less awkward.

He knew he'd never forget it. Not the slightest chance…

CHAPTER ONE

August

LYDIA PAUSED OUTSIDE the doors of Yoxburgh Park Hospital's Emergency Department and sucked in a long, slow breath.

So this is it. My first day here.

She was a mass of nerves. Would Jake be here today? She hoped so. He'd been so kind to her and her mother after the accident, and a familiar face would make a world of difference. And she wanted to thank him for so many things.

Time to find out.

She straightened up, walked through the doorway and headed to the reception desk, pinning a smile on her face. 'Hi, I'm Dr Fraser. Mr Slater's expecting me.'

'Oh, yes. I'll let them know you're here.'

A few moments later a door swished open, and a nurse came through it and smiled at her.

'Dr Fraser, hi, good to see you again, we're expecting you. I hope you're feeling better now?'

She pinned her smile on a little more firmly. 'Much better, thanks,' she said, although in some ways it was a lie, and she wondered if she'd met the woman before. No idea. Probably.

She was ushered through the security doors and into the

central hub of the ED, and there, to her relief, was Jake. He turned, those striking grey-blue eyes lighting up with that familiar smile as he strode towards her, and her heart did a little jiggle.

'Lydia! It's so good to see you again,' he said and then, instead of the handshake she was expecting, he reached out and folded her into a gentle hug, his warmth, his strength, the solid mass of his body so oddly reassuring that she wanted to stay there forever.

But then he dropped his arms and stepped back, taking all that lovely warmth with him, and she instantly felt cold and lonely. His eyes scanned her face, still with the warmth she remembered but with a touch of concern in amongst it. 'How are you? You look a lot better than you did the last time I saw you.'

Better for seeing him. She tried to smile, but it was a poor effort. She cranked up the smile. 'I am, thanks. I'm glad you're here today, though, it's good to see a familiar face and I wanted to thank you for staying with me until Mum arrived. And thank you for the flowers and card. That was so kind.'

'You're welcome. It was the least we could do.'

We, not I. She felt a tiny crush of disappointment, almost like loss. No, that was ridiculous—

'So—ready for the day?'

'Sort of. I'm a bit stressed—first day nerves and all that.'

'You'll be fine.' His smile didn't leave his eyes, and her heart did a little leap. 'You're going to be on light duties for a bit. Nice easy stuff till you find your feet, and I've printed you a plan of the unit so you know where everything is. James is tied up right now, but he's asked me to take you under my wing today, just to familiarise you with it all. I imagine you'd like another guided tour first?'

She felt a wash of relief and her smile this time was genuine. 'I'd love one, to be honest, if you've got time. It was a while ago and it's all still a little hazy.'

The frown was back, just a quick flicker of his brows. 'You don't remember any more?'

'Some. Bits and pieces, but of course I don't know what's missing anyway.' She met his eyes. 'Actually, when you have time, I think we could do with a conversation? Just some loose ends I need to clear up. Maybe you can help me fill in the blanks.'

He hesitated for a moment, then nodded, his smile a little crooked now. 'Sure. We're a bit pushed at the minute, but later, maybe?'

'Later would be fine. Thanks.'

'Good. Right, let's start here,' he said, and he walked her round the ED, showing her all the things she needed to know, introducing her to anyone who wasn't tied up, and then ending up in Resus, where two groups of people were working on patients.

She recognised it from her interview day, but now a cold shiver ran through her, as if her body remembered something she didn't. Something else…

'Was I treated in here?' she asked slowly, and he nodded.

'Yes. Yes, you were. Do you remember?'

She shook her head slowly. 'No, but I feel like there's something I ought to know, something I can't quite get hold of…'

'I can fill you in later, see if that helps. They look a bit busy so give me a moment, I'll have a quick word with James.'

He strode over to one of the groups, and a man looked up and then turned his head and met her eyes over his mask, his own eyes creasing in a smile. 'Hi, Lydia. Welcome back. Good to see you. You OK working with Jake today?' His voice was familiar, and she realised it was James Slater, the Clinical Lead.

'Yes, that's fine, absolutely,' she said, and he went back to work with a nod.

'Right,' Jake said, coming back to her and opening the door. 'I'll hand you back to someone who can give you your scrubs and name badge and security fob, then you can come and find me. I'm in cubicles today, so if you want to tag along?'

'Sure.'

She was, or she would be once she knew how they did things, but she was confident she'd get used to it and at least they hadn't chucked her in at the deep end as she'd feared. It was just the holes in her memory from the retrograde amnesia that were a worry, but they weren't clinical holes, just that short interval of time that had vanished without trace.

She'd had over a month off to recover fully before her old HR would let her go back to work, and she'd needed it. She'd been tired, a little queasy, with a constant niggling headache and her blood sugar all over the place, and so she'd used the time to rest and recover and get ready for her move before she returned to work.

For the last six weeks she'd been managing fine, although she'd been moved to Minors there as well, which had been less taxing because she'd still been feeling tired and queasy.

Now she just needed to find her feet here and she'd be able to get properly stuck in and stop fretting about the missing bits of her memory and give them time to come back on their own. If they ever did…

Jake did a bit of clinical hand-holding at first, but it didn't take long to realise she didn't need it. She might have gaps in her memory of that time, but she certainly remembered all the medicine.

If she'd lost that…

But she hadn't, to his relief, or he'd have the loss of her career on his conscience to go with all the other things. It was just the normal 'How do you do this here?' stuff that she had yet to learn, but they shared the cubicles for the rest of the morning and she managed perfectly well with those obvious questions answered.

He could hear her voice through the curtains, and she was lovely with the patients. Gentle, kind, firm, reassuring, and a good listener. She inspired confidence, and he very quickly realised he could let her get on with it. Just as well, as they were stacked up to the max and running flat out to keep pace with the arrivals.

Then at half past eleven things quietened down, and he grabbed the chance and went and found her. She was at the desk, writing up her latest patient, and he propped himself up beside her, breathing in the scent of her and resisting the urge to tuck an escaped strand of blonde hair back behind her ear.

'Everything OK?'

She threw him a quick smile. 'Good so far.'

'Great. Finish that and let's get out of here before anyone grabs us. I need a coffee and something to eat. I missed breakfast.'

She nodded, tapped in the last details and looked up. 'Right, I'm done. Let's go.'

He led her out of a side door and into the beautiful park that surrounded the hospital, following a path to a café set in the side of the building. She could see benches under some of the trees, and a group of bistro tables on some paving outside the café doors.

He went in and picked up a tray. 'We might as well grab lunch while we're here. We might not get another chance.'

She chose a sandwich and a banana, picked up a bottle of water and added it to the tray with his sandwich, blueberry muffin and coffee. He'd paid before she could offer, and they headed outside.

'Sun or shade?' he asked, and she saw a couple leaving a bench under a tree.

'Over there?' she suggested, because her head wasn't a fan of the sun since the accident, and he nodded and headed over to it, putting the tray down on the middle of the bench between them.

If she'd thought it might be a good time to talk, she was wrong, because he ripped open his sandwich and practically inhaled it. She ate hers more slowly, trying not to watch him, absurdly conscious of his every move—the flex of his arm, the muscle working in his jaw, the flick of his tongue to catch a crumb…

How am I so drawn to him? Why? Yes, he's hot, but—

'Are you ravenous, by any chance?' she asked to cut off her thoughts, and he threw her a grin that made her heart flip in her chest.

'Is it that obvious? I got called in early because of a pile-up, and I'm pretty sure I won't get a chance to eat again until at least seven tonight.'

He moved on to the muffin, peeling off the paper case and breaking off a chunk and offering it to her. She took it, their fingers brushing, and a strange quiver ran up her arm.

'So, tell me,' he said, breaking off another chunk, 'where are you living? Have you managed to find a place?'

'Yes, I'm renting a little Victorian house. HR put me

onto it. It belongs to one of the obstetricians, apparently, and it's lovely and it's only a ten-minute walk from the hospital.'

'That's handy. Where is it?'

She told him, and he nodded. 'I know it, it's a nice little street. It's not far from my house. Has it got parking?'

She smiled, but it felt a little off-kilter. 'Yes, it has, at the back, but that's irrelevant. I'm not driving at the moment.'

'Lost your confidence?' he asked, his look searching, and her smile faded.

'A bit. The insurance company sent me photos of my car, and when the police interviewed me they asked for footage from the dashcam for the coroner. I told them to help themselves. I haven't looked at it. I'm not sure I want to.'

'No, probably wise. The paramedics said it wasn't pretty.'

'I can believe that. The car was utterly trashed. I'm amazed the dashcam survived.'

'And you. You were very lucky.' He gave her another of those searching looks. 'So how are you now? Really?'

'Really?' She shrugged and smiled, but it felt a bit wonky so she gave up. 'I'm still a bit tired, the odd headache, and I've been a bit queasy. But yeah, I'm OK now, I think. I feel much better and it's good to be back at work. I'm enjoying it. And this morning's been good so far.'

He gave a little huff of laughter. 'Let's hope you're still saying that by the end of the shift.'

How prophetic.

They hadn't been back in the department long before there was a trauma call over the speakers.

He stuck his head round the curtain and shot her a quick look. 'Are you OK if I answer that?'

'Sure.'

He held her eyes for a moment, then gave a slight nod and went. She dealt with her patient, and while she was still filling in the notes there was another trauma call. And then another, a Code Red, just half an hour later, and she heard the sound of a helicopter coming in to land.

She was about to call another patient in when she was stopped by a nurse.

'Lydia, you're needed in Resus.'

She felt a shiver of apprehension. 'Me?'

'Yes, sorry, they've got two teams in there now and another one from the same crash site has just been brought in and everyone else is tied up.'

She went straight there, a little anxious but relieved to see that Jake was leading the team she was joining.

Until he spoke.

'OK, this is a complicated polytrauma, so we're going to need you all on top of your game. And we're going to be doing a lot of X-rays in here, so lead aprons, please.'

Hands shaking a little, she put on gloves and the heavy lead apron as the trolley was wheeled in by the air ambulance team and the patient was transferred to the bed and the blanket whisked away. Their doctor's handover was comprehensive and potentially devastating.

'This is Pete, thirty years old, his motorbike was in collision with a car that pulled out in front of him, he cartwheeled over it and travelled about fifty metres—'

She zoned out then, the blood draining from her head.

Why a biker? Of all things, why that?

Focus!

'—query fractures to cervical and thoracic spine, left flail chest, query splenic rupture, bilateral multiple fractures of both arms and hands, bilateral fractures of femur, tib and fib, conscious and breathing on arrival but GCS now nine. His family have been informed and are on their way. He's had tramadol and ketamine—'

She looked down at the man lying in front of her. He was thirty, the same age as her. She stared at him, at the splints, the blood, the distorted limbs, wondering if Ryan's body had been so badly broken. Wondering if this man—Pete—would survive—

Jake took over and she refocused on his voice, steady, firm, in control.

'OK, thanks, guys. Right, everybody, let's get a look at him and find out what we've got. Somebody, get another line in if you can, take bloods for group and save and let's start him on O neg and get Interventional Radiology and Orthopaedics down here now. Hi, Pete, my name's Jake, I'm going to be looking after you. Blink if you understand me— OK, no reaction. Right, Lydia, could you have a look at his legs? Emily, can you get the flail chest and check air entry please. I'll have a look at this abdomen.'

Lydia stared at the broken body in front of her, her heart pounding. She could feel her palms sweating in her gloves. Was he going to make it? How could he possibly survive?

Concentrate!

She felt for a pulse to his feet, her eyes scanning his legs. What a mess. *Please don't die—*

Jake's voice cut through her thoughts. 'Lydia, what have you got?'

'No pulse to the right foot, very weak pulse to the left. Toes are discoloured, the right metatarsal arch looks displaced. Bilateral distal compound fractures of tib and fib, displaced fracture of right femur just above the knee, or it could be a knee dislocation, left femur fracture in midshaft. And he might have a pelvic fracture on the right.

There's a lot of blue under the skin of his groin and his leg's rotating out, but that might be from the knee injury…'

She closed her eyes, saw a blinding light, then a violent jolt and darkness…

Her hands were shaking, and she took a step back.

'I'm sorry, I—I think I need some air.'

She glanced up and met Jake's eyes, and he held them briefly, swore under his breath then snapped into action.

'Right, can we get an image of that pelvis and knee please, and, James, Oliver, if you can spare someone, could they relieve Lydia asap? Someone, get her out of here now. And hustle Joe Baker, I don't like the feel of this abdomen.'

'I'm so sorry,' she said, but her whole body had started to shake, and James moved her gently aside and took over.

'Go, we've got this,' he said, his voice kind but firm, as another man arrived, striding swiftly in.

'OK, what have we got?'

A nurse lifted the lead apron off her and put an arm around her shoulders. She peeled the gloves off her shaking hands, and sucked in a deep, unsteady breath.

Please don't let him die…

'Let's get some fresh air,' the nurse said, and steered her out of Resus, through the doors into the park and over to the nearest tree. Her legs gave way as they reached it, and she slid down the trunk, leant back against it and closed her eyes, trying to slow her breathing.

The nurse crouched down beside her. 'Are you all right?'

'I will be. I don't know what happened there. A bit of *déjà vu*, perhaps, from my accident?'

'Maybe. Can I get you a drink?'

She shook her head. 'No, I'm OK. Seriously. You go back and carry on, you're needed in there and I'm fine now. I need to go back to cubicles, really. There'll be people waiting.'

'Only when you're ready. Don't rush it. Take your time.'

She smiled at the nurse, and realised she was the one who'd met her in Reception. 'I'll be fine in a minute. I'm sorry, I don't know your name.'

'I'm Julie.'

'And I'm Lydia—but you knew that already.' She tilted her head on one side. 'Were you there when I was brought in?'

She nodded. 'Yes, I was working on you with Jake.'

'Jake?' She frowned. 'I hadn't realised he was involved.'

'Yes, he was leading. He was quite concerned. I'm so glad you've made such a good recovery, and not just because we really need you here.'

They did, she'd seen enough evidence of it this morning, but what if this—this freaking out in Resus—wasn't a one-off? What if she wasn't ever going to be able to face working in there? Would they still be able to find a place for her in their team, or would she have to transfer to another department and leave them in the lurch? Another thing to ask Jake when they finally had time to talk…

'I'll just sit here a little longer and then I'll come back in. You go back to Pete, he needs you more than I do.'

'If you're sure?'

'Yes, really. I'm sure.'

She wasn't in the slightest bit sure, but she watched the nurse—Julie—go back through the doors and she closed her eyes and rested her head back against the tree, her thoughts tumbling.

What if she couldn't work again? What if they didn't want her here, so emotionally scarred by her accident that she was no use to them? Just because it didn't show didn't mean it wasn't real. What if she was going to fall apart every time she saw anyone who'd been in a bike accident? And Pete was so broken that she couldn't see how he could possibly survive…

Tears slid down her cheeks, a sob lodging in her throat and, pulling up her knees, she folded her arms, rested her head on them and cried.

'Hey…'

A familiar hand touched her shoulder and she felt Jake's body ease down beside her, a strong, safe arm coming round her shoulders and drawing her gently against his warm, solid chest. She let her head rest on it, grateful for its warmth, for the steady beat of the heart under her ear, calming her.

'Why are you here?' she asked, her voice cracking. 'Why aren't you with Pete? He needs you.'

'It's OK, James and Oliver have taken over and Joe Baker from IR is there too, so it's a bit crowded,' he said, his voice a low rumble under her ear. 'And anyway, I wanted to check on you, see how you were, because you shouldn't have been anywhere near that, and that's my fault. Are you OK now?'

She started to nod, then shook her head and blinked away another crop of tears. 'Sorry. It was just a bit close to home. I was looking at him, at the mess he was in, and wondering…'

She eased away and found a tissue pressed into her hand, Jake's voice soft beside her. '…if your biker was in the same mess?'

She nodded, and he squeezed her shoulder.

'He wasn't. He had an air-bag suit on so his body would have been largely protected, but his head injuries were unsurvivable.'

She winced. 'And Pete? Are his injuries unsurvivable?'

He shook his head slowly. 'I don't know. He's still alive, or he was when I left, but it's pretty touch and go. We've got the circulation back to his right foot, and they're taking him for a scan as soon as he's stable enough.' His eyes searched hers. 'Are you sure you're OK now?'

She nodded. 'Just about. I don't really know what happened there. Some kind of weird flashback—there was a blinding light, and then a thud, and then nothing… I'm sorry, I should have stayed.'

'No, *I'm* sorry. That was entirely my fault. I should never have let you work on him. I should have sent you straight back to cubicles and called for someone else. It was far too close to home and I owe you a huge apology for not protecting you from that.'

'Don't be sorry, it's not your fault. I need to get used to it again. I'm going to have to. You can't protect me forever.'

He gave a slightly disbelieving grunt and stood up, pulling her gently to her feet then looking searchingly down into her eyes, still looking for something she was pretty certain he wouldn't find.

'Are you sure you're all right now?'

'Jake, I'm fine, really,' she lied. 'I need to get back to work—and so do you. I'm fine, I promise.'

He nodded. 'OK. We'll talk later.'

It was much, much later when he found her at the central desk.

'How are you doing?'

She looked up and smiled, but it didn't quite reach her eyes and he wondered if the day had been too much for her.

Probably. And he hadn't helped any by letting her work on Pete. He was still kicking himself for that massive error.

'I'm OK. Tired, but then I'm always tired at the moment. How's Pete? Any news?'

'Still alive, not quite sure how. Good spot on the pelvis, by the way, it was fractured, and Joe Baker, our interventional radiologist, stopped the blood loss from that to buy him time, but I'm not sure it'll make any difference to the outcome. He's giving everyone a headache trying to keep him alive, but his aorta and spleen were all right, so that's one bit of good news. All down to the orthos now to pin him back together. Anyway, I'm done now for the day. Finish writing that up and go and change, and we can get out of here.'

'Can we talk then?'

He hesitated, but it had to be done. Not that he wanted to open that particular massive can of worms, but it was about time. 'Yes, sure. Why don't we go back to mine? I've got salad in the fridge that needs eating, we could have supper?'

She nodded slowly. 'That sounds good, but actually there's something I'd like to do first if we can. Is your car here?'

'No, I walked, but I'm right round the corner from you so it's not far away. Why?'

'Do you know where I had my accident?'

So that was it. 'Yes, I know. I've been there.' Been to see where it all happened, how it all happened, and how easily she could have died…

'I'd like to go—I feel I owe it to him. To Ryan.'

Of course she did. 'Sure, we can do that.'

She nodded again, finished entering the patient notes

and closed the file. 'Done. Give me two minutes to change.'

She went off to the locker room, and he watched her walk briskly away, then closed his eyes. She wanted to go to the crash site. Well, she was bound to. He already knew enough about her to know that she was meticulous in everything she did, and as far as her biker was concerned, she had unfinished business. He could only hope it would help her come to terms with it, to lay it to rest, because she certainly hadn't done that yet. And both he and James were concerned about her after the incident in Resus. They'd need to talk about that, too.

He heard the brisk tap of her shoes as she approached, and he opened his eyes and turned towards her.

'Good to go?'

'Ready when you are,' she said, and he nearly laughed.

She wanted to talk about the 'loose ends', and he wasn't sure he'd ever be ready to fill in some of those blanks. He'd been wrestling with his conscience for weeks, and here they were now, poised on the edge of a veritable minefield. He'd just have to navigate his way through it and hope they both came out unscathed.

CHAPTER TWO

HE WAS RIGHT, his house wasn't far from hers, and very like it, a typical Victorian semi, but wider, with a neat little garden in front of the bay window, the space beside it just large enough for the car that was parked there. She followed him up the short path to his front door.

'Let me go and grab the keys and I'll be with you,' he said, and he let himself in. She heard the rattle of keys on a hook and then he was back, locking the door behind him.

'OK, let's go,' he said, and as they set off she told herself to relax, but she couldn't. She'd been wanting to do this for so long, and now she was about to, she was having second thoughts.

No. She owed it to Ryan and it was the least she could do.

'Does that supermarket sell flowers?' she asked, spotting a sign ahead.

'Yes. Want me to stop?'

'Please, if you don't mind. I'd like to take some flowers.'

He shot her a quick glance, then turned in and parked.

'I'll wait in the car.'

The flowers were right by the door, and she stood in front of them, paralysed by indecision. Roses? No, they'd wilt in moments in this heat. Freesias? Sunflowers? Or a mixed bunch of flowers and foliage? Not lilies, with their heady scent and staining pollen. Gladioli? Except she wasn't glad, so they seemed wrong. But what, then? Should she even take any? Maybe it would be insensitive…

He found her standing in front of the flowers, arms wrapped round herself in a tight hug, and his heart ached for her.

'Need a hand?' he murmured, and she glanced quickly up at him and then away.

'I don't know what to get, or even if I should,' she said, and her voice seemed far away and uncertain. 'They all seem wrong, somehow. Maybe it was a stupid idea. What if his parents see them? What will they think? What if it upsets them even more? They sent me a card, apologising for him causing the accident. How could they bear to do that? And who wants flowers from the person who killed their son?'

He swallowed a lump in his throat. He really hadn't seen that coming, but he should have known better because in a way she was still blaming herself. Maybe always would. He could identify with that.

'You didn't kill him,' he said gently. 'It was his own fault. You know that.'

'Yes, I know, and I know it's irrational, but…'

'What was on the front of the card from his parents?'

'I don't know. Flowers of some sort, maybe? I've got it here.'

Of course she did. She delved into her bag and brought out a slightly dog-eared envelope, then pulled the card out slowly and held it up. A simple watercolour painting of flowers and foliage on a white background, above the words 'Thinking of you'. It brought a lump to his throat.

'How about these?' he suggested after a quick scan

along the rows of flowers. 'They're the same sort of colouring, a bit of foliage, soft blues and yellows—they won't offend anyone and I'm sure his parents will be very touched.'

She nodded slowly. 'Yes.' She sucked in a breath and blew it out slowly. 'Thank you, Jake. You're right, they'll be perfect.'

She took the delicate, pretty posy out of his hand, went over to a wall of cards, chose a very simple one, paid for them and then re-joined him at the doorway.

'Good to go?' he asked, and she nodded.

'As ready as I'll ever be.'

'You don't have to do this, Lydia.'

How wrong he was. 'I do, Jake. I really, really do.'

He drove for a short distance, then pulled up by the side of the road in a small layby, and she looked around. 'It was here?'

'No, it's a bit further on, but it's on a bend so not a good place to park. It isn't far.'

She pulled out a pen, hesitated, and then wrote inside the card: *I'm so sorry. I will never forget. Lydia x*

She tried to put it in the envelope but it jammed, and he took it gently out of her shaking fingers and slid it in, closed the flap and handed it back.

'Ready?'

No, and she never would be, but she nodded, and they got out of the car and walked the short distance to the crash site. She could see the right-hand bend he must have overtaken on, with a group of trees straight ahead.

She spotted one with the bark ripped off the trunk, the leaves on the branches above wilted and dead.

'Is that it?'

'That's the tree you hit. That one and the one to the right of it. His tree is over there.'

'Where?' she asked, looking round in surprise, and then off to her left she saw another tree, set well back away from the road, a patch of bark torn away, the flowers at its base, and her heart squeezed in her chest.

'Oh, Ryan,' she whispered under her breath, and she walked over to the tree, knelt down and sat back on her heels and stared at the flowers lying there wilted. It seemed unfair to remove them, even more unfair to add hers to them. She had no right to mourn his death, she didn't know anything about him.

She laid her posy gently down a little apart from the others, on the ground where he might have fallen, where his parents had come and grieved for him, where passers-by would look and see the flowers and maybe slow down a little.

She kissed the card and tucked it in beside the flowers, then got to her feet, resting a hand against the scarred trunk as she stood there, eyes closed.

He wouldn't have known anything about it.

She hoped Jake was right. What if he'd known? What kind of terror had he felt? Did he know he was going to die? He was only nineteen…

She felt a gentle hand on her shoulder, and she turned and pressed her face against that safe, solid chest as his arms closed around her and held her. She wouldn't cry. She'd done enough of that already and surely her tears had run dry.

How wrong she was.

Jake held her close, cradling her against his chest, his lips pressed to her head, aching to be able to take away her pain. But he couldn't, any more than he could take away his own.

She knew it wasn't her fault, but what she didn't know was the blame he carried for convincing her to stay that night. If he hadn't done that, if he'd let her go, then she might never have been injured, Ryan might still be alive—

Or else he could have hit something or someone else. He was an accident waiting to happen, Jake knew that, but guilt wasn't always rational.

And then she lifted her head, fished about in her jeans for a tissue and blew her nose, turning away from him while she pulled herself together. And then she turned back and gave him a teary, brave little smile that made him want to hug her and make it all better. But he couldn't. It wasn't in his gift.

'Thank you. For bringing me here, for being so kind.'

If she only knew the truth...

'You're welcome. Are you ready to go?' he asked gently, and she nodded.

'Yes, I think so. I've done what I needed to do.'

And maybe she'd be better able to live with it now. He wished he could say the same for himself.

He reversed into his narrow driveway, cut the engine and threw her a smile.

'Come on, let's go and have something to eat.'

She climbed out of the car, careful not to hit the door on the wall beside her, and followed him into the house.

It was a lot like hers, with the typical Victorian layout of stairs straight ahead, a room to the right and another beyond it off the passage that led through to the kitchen, with a window at the end overlooking the garden.

So not entirely like hers, because the wall between her

stairs and the dining room had been taken out to open it all up, and she didn't have a window at the end of the kitchen, but a conservatory on the side. And his was bigger.

So not like hers at all, really, and yet for some reason it felt familiar, almost as if she knew it.

He went straight to the kitchen and opened the fridge, and she followed him thoughtfully and hitched herself up on a stool at the little breakfast bar at the end and looked out at his garden. Small, but big enough to sit out in, with a pretty tree at the end and a lawn bordered by neat little shrubs.

'I love your garden,' she said to fill the silence.

'Really? I don't, but it does the job. What would you like to drink?' he asked, and she swivelled round and met his eyes.

'Whatever,' she said, not knowing what he meant by 'drink', but quietly relieved when he pulled out a bottle of nicely chilled white.

'Pinot Grigio OK? I know it's a school night, but we can have a small one?'

'Lovely. Thank you.' And maybe it would settle her nerves.

Why do I feel nervous? What is there to be afraid of?

She had no idea, but her body was thrumming with tension. Did it know something she didn't?

He handed her a glass, their fingers brushing lightly and sending a strange tingle through her arm.

'Garden?' he asked, and she nodded.

'Garden would be lovely. I don't know why you don't like it.'

His smile was wry. 'It's just dull—too tidy. I'd rather have a tumbling mass of scent and colour, but I don't have the time so I've kept it manageable. It's a bit soulless, though. Come on out.'

She followed him, and they sat down at the little bistro table on a small paved area skilfully placed to catch the last of the evening sun before it dropped behind the rooftops.

'So how was your first day?' he asked, leaning back with his legs stretched out and studying her. 'Apart from our biker, which was a serious error on my part. I'm really sorry you got called to that. I should have sent you straight out.'

She shrugged. 'No, I have to do it. It's not rare, and they're normally in a mess. It was just knowing that in my case I'd been the cause of it—'

'No, you weren't, you know that. Even his parents know that. It was entirely his fault.'

'I know. They said so in their card, and the police told me he'd been clocked doing over eighty miles an hour and they were waiting for him, so they were on the scene almost immediately. They knew exactly what had happened. But at the end of the day, it was my car he swerved to avoid, and there's nothing I can do to change that.'

'Which doesn't make it your fault. His airbag suit probably made him feel invincible, but that all falls apart when you hit a tree trunk at that speed. You were lucky he didn't hit you side-on or you might not be here now. The man who pulled out in front of Pete has serious injuries, and Pete wasn't going anything like as fast as Ryan. You were lucky to get off so lightly, really.'

'Yes, I know I was. But I don't know why I was even there then, and I can't remember anything leading up to it. There's just this hole, like a little time capsule that's gone missing.'

He frowned and glanced away. 'You remembered you'd got the job. Nothing more come back?'

'A bit, here and there. Maybe a flashback today to the accident? I don't know. The feeling that I'd been in Resus? But there are all sorts of things—tiny snatches of stuff, like when you wake from a dream which was really intense and you can hardly remember it, just odd bits here and there, and it doesn't make sense. Where had I been? Apparently, I'd told my mother I was staying over because it was too late to drive back, but I've got no hotel bill on my bank or credit card statements, only the one for the night before my interview, so where was I? Obviously, I stayed in Yoxburgh, because I had the accident on the road out, but as for where and why, I have no idea. I don't suppose you know?'

He was silent, and she searched his face—difficult, when he was looking away, but she could see his jaw working, the tight set of his lips as if he was holding something in, and then at last he turned back towards her and met her eyes.

'You were here.'

That was the last thing she'd expected him to say, and her heart skipped a beat, then thudded against her ribcage.

'Here? In your house?' *No wonder it seems familiar...*

His eyes held hers, but there was something in them she couldn't read, something he still wasn't telling her. Surely they…

No. It couldn't be that.

'You were going to leave and drive home, but it was after six by the time you'd finished with the interview panel and you hadn't had anything to eat. You were dreading the drive, but the hotel you'd stayed in was full, and you said you'd hardly slept the night before the interview.

I was worried about you being safe to drive, so I offered you my spare room for the night. We came back here and changed, then walked down to the seafront, went to a restaurant overlooking the sea, had dinner to celebrate your new job, then walked back.'

And then?

I offered you my spare room...

Did she take it? Or—

He looked away again. 'My shift started at seven the next morning and you wanted to get on the road before the rush, so you left before half six, said you'd stop on the way for breakfast, and I left a few minutes later. By the time I arrived at work you'd already had your accident, and you were brought in almost immediately.'

'Julie said you led the team.'

'Yes.'

'How was I?'

He gave a small, humourless huff of what could have been laughter. 'Raving a bit—kicking the blanket off, fighting the collar, whacked me when I tried to feel your head, told me off when I flashed the light in your eyes. Typical head injury reaction. Drowsy, feisty, you couldn't see—I didn't know at that stage how bad you were or how bad you were going to get. I just knew it was my fault, because if I'd done the sensible thing and said, "Drive carefully and we'll celebrate when you come back," then it wouldn't have happened, because you would have left the day before.

'But I didn't. I took you out, you stayed, and then you could have died. So, yeah, you have guilt about Ryan, but boy, do I have guilt about what happened to you. When you woke up and you were coherent, I could have cried with relief.'

'You were very calm.'

'No, I wasn't. I was in doctor mode. I was a mess inside.'

She felt her mouth tilt in a smile, and she reached out and laid her hand briefly over his. 'Thank you—for being there, for answering my questions and filling in the gaps—and for taking me out for dinner. That was very kind of you. I just wish I could remember it. Was it nice?'

His mouth tipped up at one side and his eyes softened. 'Yes, it was. It was very nice. We should do it again some time.'

She searched his eyes, and something in them triggered a wash of warmth all through her body. She was on the point of asking him to tell her more when he drained his wine glass and stood up.

'I'll go and knock us up a salad. You stay here, enjoy the last of the sun.'

She watched him go, watched him moving around in the kitchen, taking things out of the fridge, lifting something down from a cupboard, bending out of sight, coming back up with plates…

It wasn't just guilt he was feeling, she was sure, but what else could it be? He'd already told her he felt guilty about encouraging her not to leave that evening, so it had to be more than that, because he was still hiding something. But what?

What wasn't he telling her? And why?

She picked up her wine and followed him inside, putting the glass down by the sink, unfinished.

He was standing with his back to her, and he turned his head and studied her for a moment. 'Are you OK?'

'Sort of. Not sure. I feel like there's something else missing. I just wish I could remember it.'

He sucked in a long, slow breath and then put the knife

down on the chopping board and wiped his hands before he turned.

'It'll come back. Give it time.'

He wrapped his arms round her in a gentle hug, and she laid her head on his chest, listened to the steady beat of his heart under her ear, and the feel of his body against hers triggered something that set her heart thudding against her ribs. Something warm and wonderful that made her whole body come alive.

It wasn't a dream. I've done this before, I know I have...

She lifted her head and looked up into his face. It was guarded still, his eyes telling her nothing.

'What if it doesn't come back, Jake? What if I never know what really happened between us, because something's missing and I don't know what, but I know it's important…'

Her voice cracked, and he dropped his arms and stepped back, his smile a little crooked, his eyes wary as he propped himself against the worktop, long legs crossed at the ankle, arms folded. It was a defensive posture if ever she'd seen one, and she braced herself for what was coming.

He swallowed and looked away, then with a heavy sigh he met her eyes again, and this time she could read them loud and clear.

'I kissed you goodnight. I didn't mean to. You were coming out of the bathroom, I'd just put a glass of water in your room, and I bent my head to give you a peck on the cheek, and you turned your head and our lips brushed and—I kissed you.'

'And that's all?'

His huff of laughter told her everything.

'No. No, Lydia, that's not all, not by a long way. I tried to stop, told myself it was madness, told myself it was every kind of a bad idea. It was obvious where it was leading, and then I realised it couldn't, because I didn't have any condoms in the house because I just don't do this, and especially not with someone I really don't know—and I would have stopped, I swear, but—'

'—you didn't.'

'No. I didn't, because you told me you were on the pill. You didn't have to tell me that, we could have stopped then, I would have stopped if you'd asked me to, but you said you were on it, implying that that made it OK, and that was that.'

She stared at him, the eyes holding hers honest and unveiled and filled with—with what? Regret? Remorse? Or—longing?

Her heart thudded against her ribs, and she took a step forward, laid her hand against his cheek, felt the soft graze of stubble against her palm, the flex of his jaw, the beat of his racing heart under her little finger where it rested against his carotid artery.

She stroked her thumb over his lips, and his eyes closed and he swallowed, his hands lifting to her shoulders to hold her away.

'Don't. Please don't.'

'Why?'

His eyes opened, held hers, and she could feel the heat of his breath against her face.

'Because we can't do this. We have to work together, we don't know each other—'

'Apparently we knew each other well enough in May.'

He looked away and shook his head, his sigh filled with disgust—for himself? For her? She had no idea.

'May was a fluke,' he said, the words dragged out of him. 'We should never have done what we did. I should have stopped long before. Should never have let it start.'

'What *did* we do, Jake? What exactly did we do? Please tell me, because I need to know. I need to understand exactly what happened that night.'

His eyes met hers again, filled with something she didn't quite read before he blanked them again.

'You're right. You do need to know.' He looked away, looked back again, and this time she could read everything in his eyes.

'We spent the night together, and we made love. Several times.'

Made love. Not 'had sex' but 'made love'.

Her heart turned over, and she sucked in a breath, put her arms around him again and rested her head against his chest.

'Thank you.'

His laugh was startled and she felt it under her ear.

'What on earth for?'

'Telling me the truth. I know you didn't want to.'

She felt the brush of his lips on her hair, the warmth of his mouth against her scalp making it tingle.

'No, I didn't. I wanted you to remember it for yourself, and if you didn't, then I thought maybe it was better to leave it forgotten.'

'Let sleeping dogs lie and all that?'

'Something like that.'

She shifted so she could look up at him, so close, his mouth just there. She went up on tiptoe and kissed him, just a fleeting touch to those firm, sculpted lips.

Or at least it was meant to be…

He tried.

He tried really hard to pull away, but the warm, soft lips yielded under his, and his resolve crumpled like a wet tissue. He wanted her so much. She'd been in his dreams, in every waking moment, haunting him for months.

He'd told himself it couldn't possibly have been as good as he'd remembered, but it was. The feel of her body against his, strong and toned and yet soft where it mattered. The tiny whimper as he deepened the kiss, his tongue tangling with hers.

He pulled away, chased kisses over her cheek, her throat, down to the hollow where he could feel the rapid beat of her heart against his lips. Then up again, up the side of her neck, his teeth teasing her earlobe, making her whimper again and squirm against his body.

He wanted her. He wanted her so much, but he couldn't do this. Not now, not when they were going to have to work together. What if it all went wrong? And anyway, he was too tired and strung out. He'd hardly slept last night, worrying about what, if anything, she'd remembered and how she would be with him, and then it had been a hellish day from the pre-six start right through to the finish.

And this, this was madness. He'd been there before with Claire, too tired to function, too tired and stressed to make the necessary effort—and look where that had got him. He wasn't doing that to himself again, or to Lydia.

He straightened up, cradled her face in his hands and kissed her tenderly.

'We need to stop,' he said gently, and she pulled away and looked up at him, her eyes like deep pools.

'Do we? Really?'

He closed his eyes and let out a soft laugh.

'Yes, Lydia, we really do. Your emotions are all over the place at the moment, and I'm exhausted, I won't do you justice, and anyway, besides all that, it's not a good idea.'

He waited for the protest, for her to argue with him, to

try and convince him—and, to be fair, it wouldn't have taken much, but she didn't.

She just nodded and laid her head on his shoulder.

'You're probably right. I'm sorry, I shouldn't have started it, but I…'

'You what?'

'I wanted to know if it was a dream, or if it really had been good enough to…'

'To…?'

She shrugged and pulled away, looking up at him with a tender, tentative smile, her cheeks warming. 'To convince me to abandon my principles and sleep with someone I didn't know. That is just so not me.'

The words sounded as if they'd been dragged out of her against her better judgement. He knew all about that. He'd felt exactly the same.

'And was it?' he asked, his mouth and his ego taking over from his common sense.

She tilted her head and met his eyes, and her own were soft and luminous.

'Yes. Yes, it was.' She moved a little further away, out of reach, where she probably always should have been. 'I think I ought to go home now.'

He shook his head, knowing she was right but reluctant to let her go. 'Not yet. We haven't eaten and it's ready. Stay, Lydia. Eat with me, and I'll walk you home, but I really need to eat, and so do you. This won't go any further, I promise.'

She hesitated, as if she didn't trust herself. Or him? Maybe both. And probably wise, because he still wanted her. And then she nodded and gave him a tentative little smile.

'OK.'

* * *

He insisted on walking her home, waiting while she put the key in the lock and opened the door, and then he bent his head and kissed her goodnight.

Just a touch, a brush of his lips against hers, the warmth of them sending tiny sparkles of joy flickering through her. And then he turned on his heel and walked away, and she went in, closed the door and leant against it.

We made love. Several times.

She couldn't sleep.

Partly because she was tired after her first and quite difficult day, and partly because some of the gaps in her patchy memory of that time were now filled.

But only in her imagination, and it was running wild.

She made some camomile tea, took it back to bed and lay sipping it and thinking about what he'd told her. All she had to go on were facts, and without that kiss she would have struggled to understand how she could possibly have ended up in the bed of a man who'd been a total stranger until that day. Or any man, come to that, after Steve.

But not now. Now she knew what it was like to kiss Jake, to be kissed by him, and her body throbbed and ached with longing and a weird kind of loss.

She put her cup down, turned out her light and closed her eyes, and then the dreams came, but this time with more detail—his touch, the feel of his body on hers, in hers—

She woke, startled, not sure where she was for a moment, her body throbbing, and then his words came back to her, and she closed her eyes again and rolled onto her side, curling up under the duvet, his voice echoing in her head.

We made love. Several times.

How could she have forgotten that?

Her brain might have done, but her body hadn't. It had known better than her fragile memory what had taken place, and it wanted more. An awful lot more. It wanted him again…

'Not happening,' she said firmly, and rolled over to the other side, punched the pillow into shape and finally, eventually, she went back to sleep.

CHAPTER THREE

HER SECOND DAY started off a bit calmer, to her relief.

She was working alongside Laura Stryker, not Jake, but that was fine, she'd found her feet and Laura was lovely—and anyway, it was probably easier than working with him, after his revelations of the night before and the way her dreams had filled in the gaps.

She was still finding it hard to process what he'd told her, and the kiss had done nothing to make it easier—although in a way it had explained her totally uncharacteristic behaviour. And she needed to stop thinking about it and concentrate on doing her job.

But then James Slater came and found her between patients.

'Can we have a quiet word?' he murmured, and her heart picked up a notch. Was this about yesterday in Resus? Bound to be.

'Sure.'

'We'll go in my office,' he said, and she followed him, her heart pounding.

Was he going to tell her she couldn't work on the unit? Or tell her to get counselling? Probably not a bad idea. Restrict her to Minors indefinitely?

Please not that. She'd rather retrain than die of boredom—

The door of his office clicked shut, and she turned to face him. 'Is this about yesterday?'

'In a way. Have a seat, Lydia.'

She sat, her hands shaking a little, but he smiled.

'Firstly, I need to apologise. We shouldn't have called you into Resus, it's too soon after your accident, and it was a particularly unfortunate case for you to be involved in under the circumstances, so I'm sorry we didn't protect you better.'

Well, she hadn't expected that, but it was too soon to be reassured. Still, she was going to fight her corner.

'Thank you, but you honestly don't need to apologise.'

'I do. I'm Clinical Lead, and I didn't lead. I should have been all over it, so I really am sorry, and so is Jake. Can you tell me what happened in there?'

She gave a little shrug and shook her head. 'I don't know. I had what I can only assume was some kind of strange flashback to the accident—maybe a scrap of memory from the accident, maybe from being in there myself, I don't know, and it just overwhelmed me, but please don't treat me with kid gloves, I need to be able to be a fully active member of this department, and that means being able to work in Resus. So I should be apologising to you for letting the team down.'

He shook his head. 'You've got nothing to apologise for, Lydia, and we aren't going to treat you with kid gloves, but we do think it might be an idea for you to have some counselling.'

We? You and who else? Jake again?

He went on, 'What you were showing was signs of PTSD, which isn't surprising after what you've been through, but the last thing we want to do is make it worse.'

'It won't. Honestly, I can do it, it was just—it was too

close to home, I guess, and I couldn't see how Pete could survive.'

'Well, if it helps you, he's still alive, he's conscious and coherent with no spinal injuries, but he's got a long way to go and a lot of surgeries to get through, and there's a good chance he won't ever be back to full fitness. You were right, by the way, it was a lateral dislocation of his knee, not a femoral fracture. But he's talking to his wife, asking about his kids, and he's still very definitely here.'

She let out a breath she hadn't known she was holding, and blinked away sudden tears of relief. 'He's a father—I didn't know that, but I'm so glad to hear he's still alive, and at least he's got a chance to see his children grow up. My biker never had that chance. He was only nineteen, and he threw his whole life away.'

James nodded slowly. 'Yes, he did.' He searched her eyes. 'Jake told me that he took you to the crash site yesterday evening.'

She nodded. 'I had to know where he died. To be there to acknowledge that, and my part in it.'

'You do know it wasn't your fault?'

Him as well as Jake? She let out a shaky sigh. 'My mind knows that. My...soul, if you like...will always have him on its conscience.'

He nodded slowly. 'I can understand that. As doctors we face it all the time. It's there in your head going round and round. Was it my fault? Did I do something wrong, or miss something? Could I have saved them? You do your best, and that's all we can ever do, which is why I want to make sure that we never put you in a position where you're going to blame yourself for the death of a patient because you froze or were overwhelmed by the enormity of it. We can't let that happen to you. It's not fair, to you or to the patients.'

Oh, no. Not that...

'Mr Slater, please don't confine me to Minors for the rest of my rotation.'

'I have no intention of doing that. I know from your references that you have a huge amount to offer, which was why we wanted you, and why we're going to make sure you aren't asked to work on a case that's going to trigger you. We just want to protect that ability until you've had time to process fully all the things that have happened to you.'

Not to mention that missing night…

She closed her eyes and nodded. 'OK. Thank you.'

'Don't thank me, it's the least we can do. How are you feeling now? Jake said you still get headaches.'

What else is he telling James?

'Only now and then. It doesn't interfere with my work. I get tired by the end of the shift, but I'm sure that'll get better with time as well.'

'Good. So this is what I propose. No night duty for at least another month or until you're feeling stronger, only part of the day in Majors, carefully monitored time in Resus on vetted cases—we want you to get better, not worse, and if at times it feels like we're overstretching you, then you have to say so straight away. We'll take it at your pace. Any questions?'

She shook her head. 'No, not really. I'm so sorry—'

'Don't be. I'll sort out some counselling for you. Oh, and for what it's worth, everyone seems to think you're a very good doctor. I'm glad you decided to join us. You're going to be a real asset, Lydia.'

'Thank you, Mr Slater.'

He got to his feet with a smile. 'You're welcome. And for goodness' sake, call me James.'

She swallowed, dredged up a smile and got to her feet. 'Thank you, James.'

'You'll be fine.' He gave her a quick, reassuring smile as he ushered her out, and she went back to work partially relieved that he didn't intend to mothball her in Minors indefinitely, and partially a little concerned that she'd let him down if she freaked out again.

No. Think positive! And you'll have counselling—would have had it already if you hadn't turned it down. So stupid...

There was no sign of Jake, and it wasn't until later that she ran into him. She wasn't sure how he'd be with her, but he was just his usual self—kind, considerate, but keeping a fraction more physical distance than before, which was probably wise after their somewhat apocalyptic conversation of the night before. Never mind the kiss…

No! She wasn't going to think about the kiss!

She worked her way steadily through the waiting patients, treating some, admitting others, and she got through the rest of that day and the next without any hiccups.

Until mid-afternoon on her fourth day, when she called in a young woman who'd been vomiting profusely for days. She'd been getting steadily worse over the last two weeks and had no idea why, and when Lydia pinched the skin on the back of her hand it didn't retract immediately, indicating severe dehydration, so, to eliminate the obvious, Lydia asked her if she could be pregnant.

She shrugged, shook her head, mumbled, 'I don't know. Don't think so. But my bra's tight even though I've lost weight, so maybe—'

She broke off and retched again, so Lydia asked a nurse

to set up a glucose saline drip and do a pregnancy test while she treated another patient, and then when she went back there was a positive test lying in the kidney dish by the bed.

Bingo. Hyperemesis gravidarum. She referred her to Gynae, who admitted her, but for the rest of the afternoon something the woman had said was niggling in the back of her mind.

Weight loss, tight bra—she'd definitely lost weight since the accident, and yet this morning her jeans had felt tight around the waist. And were her breasts perhaps a little fuller?

She felt suddenly dizzy and lightheaded.

No. Please, no. I can't be. Surely not.

Only apparently she could, if Jake was to be believed.

'We made love. Several times.'

Did they? She had only his word for that, but now it seemed as if it was all too real. If only her memory would come back…

The rest of her shift passed in a daze, and as soon as she'd finished, she walked home via the nearest supermarket, bought a pregnancy test and headed back to her house.

Please, no, please, no, please, no...

Positive.

She sat there staring at it, wondering if it could be wrong, if maybe because she was on the pill it had screwed up the test, but logic told her she was clutching at straws. There was no such thing as a false positive except in vanishingly rare cases for a good reason. A false negative, yes, especially if it was too early. But it wasn't too early, and it wasn't negative.

It was positive, and she was pregnant. End of.

Except it wasn't the end, it was the beginning, and her

hand slid down and lay over the bowl of her pelvis. Was it imagination, or was there the tiniest suggestion of a bump?

She closed her eyes, swamped by emotion. A baby. How could that have happened? She was on the pill!

Except somewhere along the line she'd missed one. She hadn't realised until she got to the end of the blister sheet the week after her accident, and it didn't end on a Sunday. She always started a new sheet on a Monday, so at some point she'd forgotten one.

She'd assumed it was after the accident, but could it have happened the morning of her interview, when she'd woken late, flustered and stressed and hurrying to check out of the hotel and get to the hospital on time for her interview? Or maybe the following morning, after she and Jake had apparently spent the night together and she'd got up early and set off for home, right before the accident?

Had she been in such a hurry to beat the traffic that morning that she'd rushed out without thinking and failed to take it?

No, not after a night like that. Even if she'd been in a tearing hurry there was no way she would have forgotten her contraception. But the morning before, because she'd been exhausted from lack of sleep and nerves? That seemed more likely.

And if she *had* slept better that night, then she would have taken her pill on the morning of her interview, she would have gone home after the interview and not stayed with Jake, so she wouldn't have been involved in the accident, and she wouldn't be pregnant now.

She'd have to tell Jake, but how? How could she tell him that on the night she couldn't remember, they'd made a baby?

A baby, for heaven's sake!

Her hand slid down again, cradling protectively over the tiny life inside her—the tiny life that was going to change her own life beyond recognition.

Her life, and Jake's.

She needed to talk to him, but not yet. First, she was going to buy another pregnancy test, and check again. Just in case…

It's pointless. You know you're pregnant.

She ignored the voice in her head, walked to a different supermarket, the bigger one where she'd got the flowers for Ryan, and bought one of the tests that said how many weeks pregnant. She went home, drank a glass of water, cooked herself an omelette and poked it around on the plate until it was cold, then did the test.

Pregnant 3 weeks

So, no false positive, then. No faulty test. Her last glimmer of hope dashed.

How on earth am I going to tell Jake?

He was staring at the contents of his virtually empty fridge when his phone rang.

Lydia. Why was she calling him? She'd been avoiding him since Monday—or had he been avoiding her? He swiped answer.

'Hi, how are things?'

'Not great. We need to talk.'

About what? Probably the chat she'd had with James on Tuesday. 'Sure. Yours or mine?'

'Yours, I think, please. If you don't mind.'

She sounded a bit weird, shaky, and he frowned.

'Of course I don't mind. Come whenever you're ready.'

'I'll come now if that's OK?'

'It's fine. I'll leave the door on the latch.'

He walked to the front door, unlocked it and then went and stood in the sitting room, hands shoved into his pockets, eyes on the road, his mind whirling.

What's going on? Is it because of something James said to her? Or is it something else? Is she going to quit? Surely not. So—what...?

He closed his eyes. She'd be here soon enough, no point in worrying and overthinking it. It was bound to be something James had said, and no doubt she'd tell him.

He looked up the road again, and there she was, walking briskly towards the house. She looked like someone on a mission, and as she got closer he could see her face and she didn't look happy. Far from it.

He opened the door, and she walked in past him and stood in the hall, hands twisting together, looking really uncomfortable.

'Sitting room or garden?' he asked.

'Sitting room. If that's OK?'

'Sure. Glass of wine?'

'No. No, thank you. Perhaps a glass of water?'

'Fizzy or still?'

'Fizzy, please, if you have it.'

'Have a seat, I won't be long.'

What on earth is going on?

She didn't stay there, of course. He might have known she wouldn't, but when he'd poured the drinks and picked them up and turned, she was standing in the doorway, her arms wrapped around her waist, and he put their drinks down and stood in front of her, his hands on her shoulders.

She stiffened as he touched her, and he dropped his hands and searched her face.

'What's up, Lydia?' he asked gently, but she still wouldn't look at him, so he tried again. 'Lydia, talk to me. Please. Tell me what's happened.'

She looked up at him then, finally meeting his eyes, and her words took the wind right out of his sails.

'I'm pregnant.'

'*What?*' The breath left his body in a great rush, and for a moment he felt sick with shock, disorientated.

No! She can't be. Surely not. She said...

'How?' he asked, but his voice was a hoarse croak.

She gave a short, humourless laugh. 'It's no good asking me that, Jake, I don't *remember* it. You tell me how.'

Her voice was taut, tinged with—sarcasm? Or fear?

He let out a short sigh and rammed his hand through his hair. 'I don't mean *that* how, I mean how could it have happened—you said you were on the pill?'

'I was. I am.'

And then a hideous thought occurred to him and he spoke without thinking.

'Are you absolutely sure it's mine?'

She felt her eyes widen, and she stared at him, her mouth falling slightly open in shock.

'*What?* Are you *kidding* me? I don't even know what happened that night, so unless something really weird was going on, I'm pretty sure you were the only other person there, so who the hell else's *could* it be?'

'Steve's?'

She froze, her breath jamming in her throat, searching his face. *How on earth...?* 'Have you been talking to my mother?'

He looked shocked. Even more shocked. 'No, of course not! You told me about him over dinner that night. Told me what a lying rat he was and the planet would be better off without him, so I can't imagine why you would want to see him, but if there was some kind of reconciliation—'

'No! Absolutely not! No way on earth would I let that man within a mile of me ever again. I haven't seen him for months, and he's one reason why I was so keen to get the job here, to get right away from him.' She shook her head. 'I can't believe I told you about him—and I can't believe, if I did tell you, which I obviously did, that you could imagine for a single second that I'd get back with him.'

He shrugged, his whole body echoing his confusion. 'People do odd things sometimes. We aren't always logical or rational. Take that night. If we'd been thinking clearly, we wouldn't have done what we did. But we did.'

She swallowed hard. 'So you regret it?'

Was that a sigh, or a tiny huff of laughter? 'Now I know I've got you pregnant, absolutely, because it's the one thing I've always sworn would never be because of my failure, but until now, not for a second have I regretted making love to you.'

Those words again, and his eyes look so sincere…

'But now?'

He looked away, staring up at the ceiling, giving a helpless shrug before he met her eyes again. 'Now, of course, I bitterly regret it. I shouldn't have relied on your contraception. I should have taken responsibility—'

'But I told you the truth. I was—I am—on the pill.'

'So how? How are you pregnant, Lydia? I don't understand—unless you didn't take it regularly, in which case, why would you rely on it? Why would you expect me to rely on it?'

His eyes searched hers, and she swallowed. 'I do take it regularly, without fail, but I know that somewhere along the line, I missed one. No idea when, really, because I am so meticulous about it, but I know I didn't sleep well the night before the interview and then, when I finally did nod off, I overslept and had to rush, so I might have missed it that morning. Or the following morning, after we...'

'—had spent the night together.'

She swallowed. 'Did I leave in a rush?'

'Yes. Yes, you did, and that was my fault again, but I know you took it that morning. I watched you take it, right before you left.'

She closed her eyes, drew in a long, slow breath and then opened them.

'So—how...? If I only missed one, surely that wouldn't be enough?'

'It could be,' he said slowly, 'if you were sick after the accident, which would have been very soon after you'd taken it. That would make it two days running, and that would be enough.'

'So why would I throw up? Would that have been from the concussion? Surely it's too quick?'

'Shock, or just from being flung against the seatbelt? It's not uncommon.'

'Would it be in my notes?'

He shrugged. 'Probably, but it's pretty irrelevant now.'

'Not to me. Because if it was my fault, if I'd failed to take it, I'd be blaming myself.'

'What, instead of blaming me for not having the common sense and self-discipline to stop before we did anything so rash and spontaneous and downright stupid?'

'I can't blame you for that, Jake, it takes two. And I think I must have missed it the day before. You didn't know that and neither did I, and if I hadn't hit the tree, if I'd realised I'd missed one, I'm pretty sure I would have taken the morning after pill to be on the safe side. It might have been too late for that, anyway, but now…'

'Now you're pregnant,' he said softly, and closed his eyes, squeezing them shut as if to chase away the possibility.

If only it were that easy...

Then he opened them and looked into her eyes, his own bewildered and sincere. 'I'm so, so sorry, Lydia. I never meant this to happen.'

'No, I'm sure you didn't, and I certainly didn't, but we are where we are, and we have to deal with it. And I have no idea where to start.'

He held her eyes for a long time, then turned away, bracing himself on the edge of the worktop, staring blankly at the wall while his heart thrashed in his chest. He had no idea where to start either. He'd never been here before, never imagined he would be as careless and inconsiderate as his father. But he had. And now she was pregnant. With his child.

He felt a little leap of joy, and crushed it.

Don't count on it. It's up to her what happens now. It's her life that's going to change, not yours, not in the same way.

But—a baby? Really? He had no idea how to be a father—he'd never known his own, never had a role model—and the enormity of it all engulfed him, but one thing he knew, he was going to be an active part in his child's life, and a better man than his father had been. For starters, he wouldn't do something totally irresponsible and end up dead before his baby was born…

She stared at his back, his whole body radiating tension. What was going through his mind? What did he feel—

really, really feel? And how was he going to react when she told him what she wanted to do? She had absolutely no idea, because she didn't even really know who he was, far less be able to read his mind.

Time to find out more about the father of her child.

'Talk to me,' she said, and he straightened up and turned back to face her, his expression carefully neutral.

'What do you want me to say? Apart from sorry.'

'I want you to tell me about yourself. You know about my past. What about yours? Are you divorced? Resolutely single? In an open relationship? Do you have kids?'

He frowned and did a mild double-take. 'Kids? What kind of a question is that?'

'A valid one, because it occurs to me that you're the father of my baby and I know *nothing* about you—nothing at all except that you're a doctor and you were kind to me and my mother after my accident. And that's it. Who are you, Jake? And where have you been? You're—what? Thirty-one? Thirty-two? So you must have a past.'

'Thirty-two—and yes, of course I have a past, and if there were any children in it, I'd have pictures of them up all over the place like anyone else.'

'So, no children, then. What about relationships?'

He folded his arms defensively across his chest. 'Nothing currently. I had a long-term relationship with Claire, which ended over two years ago—I told you about her that night, over dinner—'

'Which I don't remember.'

'No. No, I know that. I'm sorry. So—Claire. She's a graphic artist, she illustrates children's books. We'd been together for three years, I thought we were good, so I asked her to marry me.'

'And?' she prompted.

'She said no.'

He looked away so she couldn't read his eyes, and she could tell the words were being dragged out of him.

'I was—well, stunned probably isn't too strong a word, but she pointed out that whenever she wanted us to do anything together as a couple, I was working, or too tired, too busy studying—and she was right. I was tired all the time and our sex life had become non-existent.

'She told me she'd met someone else, someone who had the time and the energy to do her justice, which I didn't. We hardly ever made love, and when we did I sometimes couldn't follow through because I was just so damn tired and stressed, running the day back through my mind, seeing the face of a patient I'd lost, the anguish of their parents, their partners… Sex was the last thing I was interested in, and weeks would go by in between, but it reached the point that I really didn't care any more one way or the other, because there was no joy left in our relationship, and I'd probably only proposed to try and make it better.'

'Which is why you stopped kissing me on Monday night, and why you walked me home and left,' she said slowly, his reaction then falling into place. *Oh, Jake.* 'You said you wouldn't do me justice.'

He nodded slowly. 'Her words.' He glanced down. 'Because I was afraid it would happen all over again. It had been a hell of a day, fighting to save Pete, worried that we hadn't done enough soon enough, your reaction in Resus— My head was all over the place, and my ego just doesn't need that kind of battering.' He sighed and rammed a hand through his hair again, leaving it tousled and messy, before he looked up again and met her eyes. 'Plus, if I'm honest, there's a bit of me that wants to keep the memory of our night intact.'

She laughed, a short humourless huff that almost choked her. She'd started to feel sorry for him, but the loss of that memory was too raw, too painful, so she ripped into him.

'Well, that's lovely for you, but let me remind you I don't have that memory, Jake, and I may never have it. And we made a *baby* that night. You should be able to remember monumental stuff like that, but I can't—'

Her voice cracked and she turned away, her arms wrapped tightly round herself, trying to hang on to her emotions, but they were spilling over, running down her face with her tears, breaking out of her body in huge, racking sobs.

She felt his hands on her shoulders turning her towards him, cradling her against his chest.

'I'm sorry,' he said, his voice a gruff murmur. 'Sorry I asked if it was mine, sorry I asked if you could have got back with Steve, sorry I got you pregnant, but please don't be angry with me. I never meant to hurt you, and I'm so, so sorry that you can't remember that night. I swear that you were with me all the way, and it was just—it was beautiful. Wild and raw and yet so tender…'

She felt his chest heave, and she had an inexplicable urge to comfort him. Her arms freed themselves from her waist and slid round him, hanging onto him until her tears had stopped, drawing on his strength. And then she let go and moved away, hunting in her pockets for a tissue.

'Here.' He put one in her hand, and she blew her nose and blotted her eyes.

'I don't know what it is about you—you turn me into a watering can.'

He tried to laugh, but it sounded more like a sob and he tilted his head back, dragging in a shuddering breath and blinking away his own tears before he drew her back into his arms.

'I'm sorry, Lydia, I really am. So, so sorry, for all of it. And you're right, we do need to talk. It affects both of us, and it isn't going to go away.'

She nodded against his chest. 'No, it isn't.' She sniffed and wiped her nose. 'Sorry. Messy crying seems to be my speciality.'

She felt the huff of his laughter, then the touch of his lips, warm against her head. 'Don't be sorry. You've got nothing to be sorry about. This is my fault.'

'You can't hog all the blame.'

He laughed again, let her go and ran a hand down her arm, threading his fingers through hers. 'Come on, let's go and sit down. It's more comfortable and I get the feeling this is going to take a long, long time.'

They picked up their drinks and went back to the sitting room, and he sat on the sofa and gently tugged her down beside him. She kicked off her shoes and curled up in the other corner with her legs tucked under her, keeping a little distance between them, but their fingers were still entwined and she could feel the rhythmic sweep of his thumb over hers, keeping the connection between them.

'So,' he said, and she could tell he was searching for the right words—if such a thing existed in such circumstances. She doubted it. 'Have you had any thoughts about what you're going to do?'

'What I'm going to do?' She felt her heart thud. Surely he wasn't going to suggest—

'Yes. Because you do have options, Lydia, and whatever you decide, I'll respect that. It's not my body that's going to carry this child, it's not my career that'll be put on hold. The impact of this on you is going to be massive, whatever you decide, and I'm well aware of that. But this has to be your decision and, whatever it is, I'll support you in every way I can.'

She watched his face carefully. 'And if I don't want it?' she asked, and he flinched and looked away, his throat working.

'Then I'll respect that,' he said, his voice a little forced, as if the words were being dragged out of his body.

'But it's not what you want.'

He looked back at her, his eyes raw with emotion. 'It's not about what I want, Lydia. It's about what's right for you.'

She gave a tiny, quiet huff of laughter and retrieved her hand. 'It's a bit late for what's right for me, Jake. As you've pointed out, it's my body, my career that I've spent years working towards that's going to be put on hold, my life that's going to be turned upside down—and no, that's not right for me, not now, not in my current situation, but that's what I've got to work with and it's all I've got to work with.

'And no, it's not going to be the five-year plan of getting fully qualified and then maybe getting married and having a family, it's going to be now, and I'm going to be a single mum, and my career plan has gone up in flames, but—at the end of the day, that's not what matters. All that matters is the baby, who didn't ask for any of this and had no say in it whatsoever.'

She looked back at him, and he held her eyes for the longest moment.

And then he said quietly, 'We could get married.'

CHAPTER FOUR

SHE STARED AT HIM, SPEECHLESS.

For a moment there she'd thought he said 'married', but—he couldn't have. Could he? Her heart skipped a beat.

'That's jumping the gun a bit.'

He shrugged. 'I thought it might be an option.'

'Why?'

He shrugged again. 'Why not?'

'Because I don't know you! And anyway, getting married because you're having a baby is archaic.'

'No, it's not, it's practical. There are all sorts of practical reasons why it could be a good idea—financial security, legal issues with custody, with access, authorising medical treatment, legal responsibility, pension, inheritance—'

'*Inheritance?* Are you planning on dying or something?'

He shook his head, a wry smile on his face, but it didn't reach his eyes. 'No, I'm not planning on dying, any more than Ryan was. But it happens. It's why we have Accident and Emergency departments, because there are all sorts of things we don't expect ever to happen to us, but they do. They happen every day to someone.'

'So we need to get married in case one of us dies way down the line? What happened to love? And anyway, we don't even *have* a baby yet.'

He opened his mouth, shut it again and looked away. 'OK, it was just an idea. Forget it.'

But she couldn't, because it was lodged there in her brain now, and it didn't seem to want to budge. It had always been part of her five-year plan. Finish her training, fall in love, get married, have a baby. Except she was doing it all backwards, and the enormity of her situation was suddenly overwhelming.

She closed her eyes and looked away, and she felt his hand on her shoulder, warm, gentle, reassuring.

'We'll work it out, Lydia. Whatever you want, we'll find a way to make it work. Just don't rule anything out yet, not till we've thought it all through. And the first thing you need is to see a midwife. You must be—what, nearly fourteen weeks?'

'I… I don't know. I haven't worked it out. I only did the test when I got home. Then I did another one to be sure—you know, just in case…'

'I don't think there's such a thing as a false positive—or only very, very rarely, but that's so unlikely. You need a scan.'

'I do,' she said, and her voice sounded hollow to her ears. Probably because she felt hollow inside—although she was anything but. There was a baby growing inside her—a baby, for goodness' sake, a tiny human being in the making. *How?*

'Hey…'

She heard his gentle murmur, then his arm slipped around her shoulders and he drew her against his chest, and she rested her head on his shoulder and let him hold her.

'It's OK, Lydia. It'll be all right.'

But she couldn't see how. Maybe it would, maybe it wouldn't. The only thing she knew was that it would never be the same again.

* * *

He held her for an age, just resting against him, her breathing a little uneven, and he could feel the tension in her body.

'Have you eaten?' he asked, and she shook her head.

'I'm not sure I can.'

'Yes, you can. Stay here and rest and I'll go and cook us something simple.'

He eased away from her, and she rolled down into the space where he'd been, curling into a ball, her face buried in the cushion. There was a light throw over the arm of the sofa, and he laid it over her and left her while he went to see what he could pull together for her to eat.

Assuming there was anything worth having in the fridge. He'd already had a look and hadn't found anything that excited his taste buds, but maybe it needed to be something plain. What did she like?

She'd had *risotto con pollo* that night, he'd had the seafood skewer, and they'd shared them. His idea, and what a stupid one, because it had been too intimate, too sensual.

He dug around and found a couple of large potatoes, stabbed them a few times and threw them in the microwave to soften while the oven heated. If nothing else, they'd fill a hole and get some carbs into her.

He left them cooking and went back to see how she was and found her asleep, her cheek rested on her hand, her other hand fisted in the soft fleecy throw that she'd snuggled up under her chin. She'd held the hospital blanket like that, too, clenched in her hand.

Insecurity? Fear? Hanging on for dear life?

He sat on the chair, propped his elbows on his knees and watched her sleeping. The mother of his unborn child.

How had he let this happen? *What an idiot.*

He was awash with emotion, his protective instinct roaring to the fore, his worry over how this would all pan out bubbling in the background. And work. How about work? And how on earth did they tell James? Never mind everyone else.

James had spoken to her on Tuesday about what had happened in Resus, he knew that much, but he had no idea how it had gone.

At least she'd had a lead apron on while they were assessing Pete, so hopefully the baby would be all right, but she needed a dating scan.

Or was it him who needed proof that her baby had been conceived that night?

No. He was pretty sure she wouldn't lie about something that important. She was a useless liar anyway, nearly as bad as him. But she still needed a scan.

He went back to the kitchen, poked the potatoes and moved them to the oven to finish cooking. And then what? Should he wake her? Or let her sleep?

He had no idea. No idea about that, or about where they went from there. Only one thing was sure. He was going to be part of this baby's life if he was given that chance, and he was going to do a better job of it than his own father ever had, and nothing on earth was going to stop him.

So he went back to her and sat and watched her sleep, his mind spinning and coming to no conclusion whatsoever.

She heard a *ting.*

It sounded like a message on a mobile, but it wasn't hers. She heard the creak of a chair, then soft footsteps receding down the hall.

Jake. She could hear him talking, his voice quiet and far away, and she sat up, blinking away the sleep. Her water was sitting there on the coffee table, and she sipped it and listened.

Who was he talking to? She hoped it wasn't James, but he had previous for that. Whatever, she was ravenous and she needed to find something to eat pretty soon. She got stiffly to her feet, stretched and padded silently down the hall towards the kitchen, her bare feet not making a sound.

He was sitting on the stool at the far end, propped on his elbows and holding the phone to his ear, but she could hear a woman's voice and she didn't sound happy.

'Hey, you don't need to tell me,' he said, cutting her off. 'I know I'm an idiot. I just needed to offload and I don't need a lecture from you. And no, dammit, it's not a honey trap! She's as shocked as I am.'

She froze, listened to more unintelligible ranting from the other end, then he sighed.

'Yes, I know I don't do that—ever—you don't have to tell me! I'm well aware—and yes, it was just one night. There was no reeling me in, if anything, it was the other way round, but it felt pretty mutual.'

He slid off the stool, opening the oven door as she stood there in the dim hallway, frozen to the spot, unable to walk away without risking him seeing her. She heard more ranting, then Jake cut the woman off, his voice low but furious.

'No, she's not some slag I picked up in a bar!'

She sucked in her breath, and Jake turned and saw her, swore comprehensively under his breath and closed his eyes.

'Stop. Right there. You're way out of order. I'll talk to you later.'

He hung up, threw the phone down and turned to face her. 'Lydia, I am so, so sorry. You really didn't need to hear that.'

She walked into the kitchen and propped herself against

the worktop because her legs were shaking, forcing herself to hold his eyes. 'No, you're right, I really didn't. So who was it?'

'My big sister. She said she wanted to talk to me, and I foolishly told her about us, and now she's…'

'Gone all big sister on you? I heard.'

He shook his head slowly, then met her eyes again. 'I'm so sorry. I just needed to share it, but not like that, not with her jumping to conclusions before I had time to tell her what really happened.' He searched her eyes, and his lips pressed together as if he didn't like what he'd seen, and he shook his head and turned away. 'I'm such an idiot.'

'Jake, it's OK. I have a big sister. I know what it's like.'

His shoulders dropped a fraction. 'Thank you.'

She tilted her head. 'What for?'

He shrugged. 'For not ripping my head off? For not accusing me of shooting my mouth off when you've only just told me yourself?'

'Maybe I hadn't quite got round to that yet, but you seem to have worked it out for yourself. I actually came to find out if you were cooking anything. I'm starving.'

He gave a soft laugh and turned back to her, the regret and frustration written all over his face. 'I've done jacket potatoes. I hope that's OK.'

'With?'

The wry huff of laughter wrapped around her heart and gave a gentle squeeze. 'I hadn't got that far yet. Butter, cheese and/or baked beans—houmous? Or I've got a tin of tuna?'

She felt her stomach recoil. 'Butter.'

'Just butter?'

'Maybe. Maybe cheese, too? Is it cheddar?'

'Yes. And it's a decent one.'

She nodded, needing to eat, not really wanting to sit down with him right then, still angry with his sister but sorry for him caught between them. And still reeling from the shock of the pregnancy test.

How? How on earth had this happened? Why? Why her? And why him? Although if it had to be with anyone, at least he seemed a decent human being. She was just grateful it wasn't Steve's baby. Even the thought made her shudder.

He scooped up some cutlery and put it on the breakfast bar, plated up the jackets and fetched the butter and cheese from the fridge and the grater from a drawer.

'I'll let you put that on. Dig in.'

She did. A slather of butter, a drift of—oh, yes, a really good cheddar—and she picked up her knife and fork and ate.

He watched her, hungry himself but clearly not as in need of food as her.

How—no, *why*—had he allowed this to happen? It went against everything he believed in, everything he'd ever done. He'd learned the lesson his father never had, and he'd *never* had unprotected sex. Until Lydia, and then he'd torn up his rule book and thrown it away. And now he was going to be a father.

He swallowed. A father. Something he hadn't got the slightest clue how to do, but something he was going to do his absolute best at doing well. And that started with owning it.

'We need to tell James.'

Lydia looked up at him in disbelief.

'This soon?'

'Well, when, then, if not now? When you start showing?'

She shrugged, reality dawning on her. 'I don't know. I haven't really thought about it.' Although maybe she should have done. Would have done, given a little time. 'I can't imagine what he'll say, not when I've only just started work here. And anyway, what's this "we"? *I* need to tell him.'

'I think it would be better if it was both of us.'

'What, because you know him so well?'

'No, because I'm responsible, but you're right, of course, I do know him better than you do.'

'You do. You seem to be buddies. He probably already knows we've slept together. You seem to have told him everything else about me.'

She could hear the trace of bitterness in her voice, and it obviously hit the mark.

He frowned. 'Lydia, that's not me, it's not how I do things. Yes, I've talked to him about you, but only what's relevant to your employment.'

'What, like I need counselling?'

'I've never said that, to him or anyone else, not even you, but if he suggested it, it's probably not a bad idea.'

'I think I have bigger fish to fry right now. And anyway, what, exactly, do you want us to tell him?'

'That you're pregnant. Nothing more. And I would like to be with you when he's told. After all, it's my baby, too.'

It was, and he seemed to be taking it very, very seriously, which should have been a relief but somehow wasn't. She didn't know anything like enough about him, so handing control of any part of this to someone who was essentially a stranger was hard.

But necessary?

'Do you think we should tell him how pregnant I am? Because we aren't going to be able to lie about this. It'll be blatantly obvious very soon that I'm much more than "just" pregnant.'

He nodded. 'It will, so I think we're going to have to be honest and tell him what happened.'

'What you say happened,' she reminded him pointedly, and he gave a sharp sigh.

'Well, clearly it did,' he said, pointing out the obvious, and she went back to her jacket potato, stabbing the last bit with her fork before putting it in her mouth and putting her cutlery down with a clatter. She pushed her plate away and met his eyes.

'When?'

'Tomorrow?'

Her heart thumped against her ribs, and she bit her lip.

'What? We might as well get it over with. You need a scan to check everything's OK, and it'll take less than an hour for it to be all round the hospital once that happens. You know what it's like.'

She did, and it was just another complication to juggle. She let out a frustrated sigh. 'I'm so cross with myself.'

He frowned at her. 'With yourself? Why? It's me you should be cross with.'

'No, it isn't, because I didn't let you stop when you wanted to.'

'You believe that?'

'Shouldn't I?'

His sigh was soft and barely audible, but it wrung her heart. 'Yes, you should believe it. I know it can't be easy, but I haven't lied to you once, Lydia, and I won't. You can take that as a given. I owe you that, if nothing else.'

'We don't have to tell anyone you're the father. It's nobody's business but our own.'

He frowned. 'So you want to pretend it was someone

else's?' He looked—well, horrified was a bit strong, but certainly unimpressed, and maybe a little hurt, and she didn't want to hurt him.

'I thought *you* might,' she offered, and he shook his head.

'No. Never. I'm not ashamed of what happened between us. It was consensual, and to deny it is… I don't know, it feels wrong. And if you hadn't had the accident, I have absolutely no doubt that we would have been seeing each other ever since. So no, I don't want to pretend my baby is someone else's, because that night belonged to us, and I know you can't remember it, but if we had to make a baby, that was the most beautiful way to do it. It's my baby—our baby. And I refuse to be ashamed of that.'

My baby. He was claiming it, standing up for it, for her, and for himself, and it brought a lump to her throat. He really was a good man. Kind, decent, caring—and the father of her baby.

She pushed her plate away and met his eyes again.

'I need to go home.'

'Stay here.'

She shook her head. 'No, I can't, I haven't got any overnight things and I have to go to work tomorrow.'

'Then let me come to yours.'

'Why?'

'Because I don't want you to be on your own.'

'Why, because you don't trust me? What on earth do you think I'm going to do?'

'Nothing, I just don't want you to be on your own,' he repeated, and she rolled her eyes.

'Maybe I *want* to be on my own? Maybe I *need* to be on my own?' To cry, if nothing else…

'Is that because *you* don't trust *me*? Because God knows

I've given you enough reasons to doubt that you should, and you've got no concrete proof that what happened between us was the way I've told you.'

There was a world of hurt and disappointment in his eyes, and she felt a wash of guilt.

'I trust you. Of course I trust you.'

'Why? I wouldn't trust me under the circumstances.'

She gave a short sigh. 'Jake, I don't have a lot of choice and, to be fair, you haven't given me any reason not to.'

'Then stay.'

'*No.* I want to be at home, in my own house, curled up in my PJs on my sofa, with a cup of tea in one hand and my phone in the other. I need to ring my parents, my sister— I'm pregnant, Jake. It's not a mental illness, I'm not going to do anything stupid. I'll be fine, I—'

'Just want to be alone…' He gave a defeated shrug and his lips tilted into a rueful smile that made her feel guilty. 'Have it your own way, but promise you'll ring if you need me.'

'I promise.' Her heart thumped again, and she looked away from eyes so unguarded she could see all the way into his soul, and she almost regretted her decision.

Almost. She got to her feet and he followed suit, walked with her down the hall and stopped at the front door.

'Let me walk you home, at least,' he said, ever the knight in shining armour, and she nodded, because giving him that concession wouldn't kill her and it was late now and she hated the dark.

He stopped at her front door, and she put the key in the lock and turned back to him. 'Thank you,' she murmured, and leant in and kissed his cheek. 'For everything.'

And then she went inside and closed the door behind her as the tears slid out from under her lids and started to fall.

* * *

She was right. He really needed to let her take control of the situation instead of pushing her into talking to James before she'd had time to come to terms with it.

He might be the one who'd put her in this situation but, as she'd pointed out, it was her body, her life, her career that were impacted by far the most. He needed to know when to butt out and leave her to it.

However wrong it seemed.

He got all the way home before his resolve weakened. He grabbed a bag, threw some overnight things and clean clothes into it and headed back to Lydia's house.

She'd probably rip his head off, of course, but he could cope with that. What he couldn't cope with was the thought of her alone and scared of what the future held.

He walked up the path, puzzled by the lack of lights on in the house. It was dark now, almost eleven. Maybe she'd gone straight to bed and was asleep.

So soon? And she'd said she was going to ring her family. Maybe she'd decided against that as it was so late. He took a step back, and then heard something—a sob? He bent and pushed open the letterbox and listened, and there it was again, a faint sob in the distance, and he knocked firmly on the door.

Not too firmly, because the lights were out all along the street, and he didn't want the neighbours peering out to see what was going on, but maybe she hadn't heard it. He sent her a text.

Lydia, let me in. I'm at the door.

Nothing. And then the landing light came on, he saw a shadow on the stairs and the door opened.

He took one look at her, walked in, pushed the door shut with his foot, dropped his bag on the floor and gathered her up in his arms.

She'd been lying on her bed, face buried in a tear-drenched pillow, when she'd heard the knock at the door. She'd known it was him before her phone pinged, and she knew him well enough to know he wouldn't give up, so she'd opened the door, swiping angrily at the tears that wouldn't stop.

And now she was in his arms, strong enough to hold her, gentle enough to comfort and reassure, like the curve of a harbour wall keeping out the storm.

She could feel his lips pressed firmly against her scalp, hear the thud of his heart under her ear, feel the warmth of his body seeping into her. And she felt safe.

'Hush, don't cry, it's going to be OK,' he murmured, and she wished she could believe him. Right then, though, she couldn't see how it could possibly be OK, and the tears welled again.

'Hey, hey, come on. Let's go and sit down somewhere comfortable where we can talk.'

He dropped his arms, taking away all that warmth, all that strength, and leaving her stranded. She turned away and stared into the sitting room, nice enough but too exposed, the bay window curtains drawn back, leaving the room visible to anyone passing. And anyway, she was so, so tired…

'I need to lie down,' she said, and headed up to her bedroom. She could hear the tread of his footsteps following her, and she tugged the curtains closed, but she didn't turn on the light, just lay down on the rumpled bedding and patted the space beside her.

She heard a soft clunk, then another as he heeled off his shoes, and then the bed dipped a little and he was there, lying beside her, his face turned towards her in the dim light from the landing so she could hardly make out his features.

'You OK?' he asked gruffly, and she gave a tiny huff of laughter.

'Not really. It's all just so…overwhelming, I suppose.'

His sigh was quiet, and his hand wrapped around hers, squeezing it gently.

'Talk to me,' he said quietly, his voice kind, undemanding. 'Tell me how I can help you.'

Nobody could help her, but… 'You are helping, just by being here,' she admitted. 'I just felt so…alone.'

'You said you wanted to be alone.'

'Apparently not,' she said, another admission. 'I'm just dreading talking to James, dreading what everyone will say. I've got your sister's voice echoing in my head—'

'No! Don't listen to that. She doesn't know you, she hasn't got a clue how it was and, to be fair, I don't really want to tell her that—don't want to tell anyone. It's none of their business, it's ours, and I know you can't remember it, but it wasn't like that at all, and I won't let anyone say it was.'

She rolled onto her side facing him, but she couldn't see his eyes in the gloom. 'So what about James? What on earth are we going to tell James?'

'The truth?' he murmured. 'We met, we really connected, we talked about seeing each other again, said we'd arrange a time once you were home.'

'Is that true?'

'Yes. Yes, it's absolutely true.'

'So why didn't you contact me after I went home?'

He gave a quiet sigh, his breath drifting over her face and teasing her hair. 'Because after the accident you didn't remember who I was, or what had happened between us, and there didn't seem to be a way to tell you. And, to be fair, I thought maybe that was a good thing, because then maybe we could start again when you were back here, but slowly this time, getting to know each other bit by bit, to give us a chance to find out if it was real or not.'

'Only I'm pregnant, which rather blows that out of the water.'

His fingers tightened on hers, and his other hand came up and brushed the hair gently back off her face. 'Yes, it does. And we need to find a way forward. We can still do that—get to know each other properly. Give ourselves a chance.'

To what? To fall in love?

Her heart gave a little thump, and she ignored it. 'What if we *don't* tell people it's yours?' she said tentatively, just to be sure. 'Maybe I could say it's an ex's—let you off the hook.'

She saw his head shake. 'No. We've talked about this. I'll never act as if I'm ashamed of what we did, or of my child, or of you. *Never.* I'm not going to deny it, and I'm not going to walk away. That's not who I am.'

No, she was beginning to realise that, and a gentle warmth spread through her, melting away some of the shock and the fear and leaving her calm and a little less afraid.

'So what now?' she asked, wondering what he'd say, but then he got all knight in shining armour again.

'We *could* get married. My offer's still on the table,' he said, and yet again she wished she could see his eyes.

She sucked in a breath and shook her head. 'That's just silly, Jake. We don't need to get married.'

'You can't be sure of that. Believe me. You never know what's round the corner, what might happen. And the consequences…'

She tried to search his face, but it was in shadow and yet again she wished she'd put on the light. Instead, she squeezed his hand gently and asked, 'What happened?'

He didn't pretend not to understand. He just hauled in a steadying breath, and started at the beginning.

'Mum was a bit of a hippy, a free spirit, flitting through life without a care in the world. She met my father in her first year at uni, in a bar, and she ended up pregnant with my sister. She dropped out of uni, they lived in a series of squats and flat shares with a baby, and then he got a better job and rented a flat, and then after a bit she got pregnant with me. And then he disappeared and she was left alone. Then, three weeks later, his body was discovered at the bottom of a sheer rockface.'

'Oh, no! He didn't—you don't think…?'

'No. His bike was at the bottom, and it had been cold, so his body was well preserved and they could see he had scuffed hands and knees, so the theory was he hadn't killed himself, he'd been trying to climb it and slipped and fallen and fractured his skull. Apparently he'd done a bit of solo climbing in the past, but this time it didn't quite work out.'

'Oh, that's awful, Jake. I'm so sorry. Your poor mum. So you never even met him?'

'No, and my sister doesn't remember him, but Mum was left with nothing. The flat lease was in his name, and she had no way of paying the rent, so she was evicted, and she had to find a home, find a job and put my sister in nursery. Suze started school a few months after I was born, and I went straight into nursery, then to school four years later. Mum had found a job as a classroom assistant in the school, which paid the bills just about and meant she was around in the holidays, and she did an OU degree and ended up as an English teacher, and somehow she held it all together for us, but it was tough, and it needn't have been. If they'd got married, made wills, had life insurance, behaved like responsible adults, it would have been a whole lot easier.'

She said nothing for a moment, then, 'Wow. That was quite a childhood.'

'Yes, it was, but she's now married to someone a bit more responsible, and she's OK.'

'Do you like him?'

'Oh, he's fine. I wouldn't want to be married to him, but he loves my mother and they seem very happy. And he's stable, which is more than my father ever was. That's good enough for me.'

'I'm glad,' she murmured, and then she yawned and muttered a sleepy apology.

He reached across and laid his hand against her cheek, and the urge to gather her up and hold her was overwhelming, but he didn't because now wasn't the time or the place. Well, no, it was definitely the place, but he needed to get the hell off her bed before he did something really stupid.

He leant over and dropped a kiss on her cheek, and moved away, just a little further from temptation.

'You need to sleep,' he said softly, and she nodded.

'I do. Thank you for coming back and talking to me—telling me all that. It explains a lot, and I understand you better now.'

'Good. I can stay if you want, sleep on the sofa? I brought some stuff.'

'No. Go home, Jake, I'm OK. Big girl pants and all that. I'll see you tomorrow. Just drop the latch on your way out.'

'If you're sure?'

'I'm sure.'

He kissed her again, breathing in the scent of her, and dragged himself back before he lost the plot.

'Sleep tight. I'll see you tomorrow.'

And he rolled away, put his shoes on and ran downstairs, scooping up his bag as he let himself out.

The air was cooler now, but not cool enough to put out the fire that was burning inside him. He let himself into his house, poured himself a glass of cold water and went to bed, but he didn't sleep.

Couldn't sleep. It wasn't just the physical longing, that was easy to deal with, but the ache in his heart, the longing for the togetherness they'd had that fateful night—that tortured him for hours.

That, and the fact that if she agreed to marry him purely because she was pregnant it would be for all the wrong reasons and he could be locked in a one-sided relationship for years, unable to love her as he wanted to.

They needed to fall in love with each other—or she did, because he already knew that he was falling in love with her. At least it certainly felt as if he was, or could, and if she never felt the same, then being with someone who didn't love him back could be soul-destroying.

He'd been there with Claire and sworn he'd never get that involved with anyone ever again, but that was then and this was now, and anyway it wasn't about him, it wasn't about love, it was about the security of their child.

Security that he'd never had as a child, with his mother

fighting to provide for them, no father figure in his life, no role-model for parenting or the dynamics of a normal, loving family—he couldn't leave his child as vulnerable as he'd been, leave Lydia as vulnerable as his mother had been.

If his father's example had taught him anything about parental responsibility, it was how not to do it, but he wasn't his father and he wasn't ever going to be, no matter what the financial and emotional cost to him.

No. If he wanted this relationship to work, he had to woo her or accept that she didn't love him. And maybe, given time, she would…

CHAPTER FIVE

SHE SLEPT WELL.

No idea how or why, under the circumstances—exhaustion, probably—but as soon as she woke, she felt the tension creeping back in.

Not about work, she loved her work and she was settling in well, but talking to James—she was dreading that. But she'd done an online self-referral for an ultrasound before she'd left home and as she reached the hospital she had a text telling her to come when she had a break and they'd fit her in.

Good. She'd talk to him after that. When she knew.

Not that she didn't know, of course she did, but it would be the concrete evidence that would confirm it.

She'd been at work for five minutes when Jake came and found her. He gave her a slightly strained smile.

'Hi. Are you OK?' he murmured.

'I'll do. You?'

That strained smile again. 'I'll do,' he echoed. 'Can we have a word?'

'Sure. There's something I want to tell you, anyway.'

She put down the notes she'd just picked up, and they moved away from the desk to a quiet corner.

'So, you go first,' she said.

'OK. I looked up your notes, and they confirm you'd vomited at the scene, and again in the ambulance.'

'So that's the second pill gone, then. Wow. OK. Thanks for confirming that. So, what else?'

'James is in meetings all morning, so we can't talk to him until later. He said he'd be around this afternoon.'

Her heart picked up a little. 'Did you give him any clues?' she asked, and he shook his head.

'No, I just said we needed to discuss something with him.'

She felt an eyebrow climb. 'Discuss? There isn't really anything to discuss, it's more a case of telling him. And I need to know for sure before we see him. I've done an online self-referral for an ultrasound scan, and they've told me to come today whenever I have a break, so I want to do that first.'

'Wow, that was quick.'

'It was. I told them I worked in the ED and I might be exposed to X-rays, which is why they said to come today.' She hesitated, then tacked on, 'If you want to come...?'

'Sure. Let me know when you're going and I'll make an excuse and come with you.'

She finally had a lull late morning, and she sent Jake a message saying she was good to go in five minutes. He pinged back a thumbs-up a second later, and she was at the desk finishing the admin for her last patient when he appeared.

'Ready when you are.'

'I'm ready.' She closed the file and looked up at him, searching his eyes. 'Are you sure you want to go public with this? I could film it on my phone and share it with you?'

'If that's what you'd rather, but by choice I'd be there with you.'

She hesitated, torn, but then she was swamped by doubt. What if there was something wrong with the baby? What if she had to hear news like that on her own? And it wasn't just her baby. She swallowed.

'I'd like you there,' she admitted, although right at that minute she'd rather neither of them had to be there.

He smiled, and the tight knot in her chest eased a little.

'Then let's go before someone grabs us.'

She'd thought she was ready for this.

Ready to see the image of her fourteen-week foetus—*their* fourteen-week foetus—the curl of the spine, the head so big in proportion to the little body, those delicate, skinny limbs already lengthening and clearly recognisable, the beating heart. But it was the profile of the tiny nose and mouth that drew her eye.

The face of their child.

She wasn't ready for that at all, not for the blinding, inescapable reality of the baby growing inside her, the tidal wave of shock and responsibility and, yes, love that engulfed her, and she had to blink away the tears. She gripped Jake's hand tighter, and he squeezed back, his grip almost painfully tight, as if he, too, felt the emotion that was gripping her.

'Can we have a photo, please?' she managed to ask, her voice choked, and she was answered with a smile.

'Sure. Do you want two, so you can send one to family?'

She swallowed. She still hadn't told her parents. Hadn't told anyone since Jake, not even her sister, who she'd been going to call until she'd started to cry…

'Actually, could we have four? Is that all right?'

'Of course. I'll print them now.'

'Thank you. That's lovely.'

She looked up at Jake, and he was still staring at the screen, seemingly mesmerised by that grainy little image of their baby.

She gave his hand another squeeze, and he looked down at her, his eyes glittering with unshed tears.

'You OK?' he asked, his voice a little gruff, and she nodded.

'Yes, I'm OK.'

And she was, she realised. OK, and totally in love with their baby.

They left the room a few minutes later in silence, both wrapped in their thoughts, trying to process their emotions.

But her hand was back in his, and she found she was OK with that, too. More than OK, because it was beginning to dawn on her that it wasn't only their baby she was in love with, it was the baby's father, too.

No, it was too soon to call it love, but it certainly felt as if it could become that, given time, and her heart did a little skip.

'So, what are we actually going to say to James?' she asked, dragging herself back to reality and finally breaking the silence. 'Apart from the obvious.'

His mouth twitched. 'Only what we have to—that we'd clicked immediately, gone out for dinner to celebrate and ended up spending the night together. We agreed to keep in touch and meet up again when our rotas allowed, and then you had the accident and didn't remember me. I think we need to give him that much, because of the date.'

She frowned slightly. 'OK. So, how *were* we going to keep in touch? Did I give you my number?'

'Yes, I put it in my phone and then rang you so you had mine. I had your mother's as well, after the accident.'

'I knew about Mum's, but I got a new phone after the

accident and I don't think the call list was updated. I had to get your number from Mum before I started here, in case I didn't see you at work. She said you'd given it to her.'

'Yes, I rang her on the day of the accident. You'd given me your address, too.'

'My address, or my parents'?'

'Yours—your old one, and then when you were discharged your mother gave me theirs so we could send you flowers.'

Really? She stopped walking and searched his eyes. 'I thought James had organised the flowers?'

'No. I suggested it, and he said good idea and left it to me.'

So it *had* been his idea. His choice, too? Probably. They'd been beautiful, and she'd kept his card on her bedside table until she moved, and she still had it, tucked in a bedside drawer.

All of which was irrelevant right now.

'So, are you going to do the talking? Or am I, since I'm the one who's pregnant?'

His lips twitched into a smile. 'I imagine you'll want to kick it off, but we can share if you like. I'll let you know when James reappears.'

In the end it was easy.

Jake came and found her, and they knocked on the office door and went in. James gestured to the chairs in front of his desk and smiled.

'Have a seat, and tell me what I can do for you. I'm assuming as you're both here that it's something to do with work?'

She was glad of the chair. Her heart was pounding, her mouth felt dry and she had an overwhelming urge to run away, but she couldn't. And even if she did, she couldn't outrun her pregnancy. Didn't want to.

So she squared her shoulders, held her head high, looked James in the eye and said, 'In a way. I'm afraid I'm going to need some time off for appointments and stuff, and then quite a bit of leave.'

She pulled the unmistakable square envelope out of her pocket and slid it across the desk to him.

He didn't even pick it up, just looked at it and then back at her. 'I take it that's yours.'

'Yes. Yes, it is. I'm having a baby,' she ended. Not pregnant, but having a baby, which seemed somehow more significant.

To do James credit, he didn't even blink. He held her gaze for a moment, then his eyes flicked to Jake.

'I take it from your presence that you have a personal interest?' he said, and Jake squared his own shoulders and nodded.

'Yes, I have. And a responsibility.'

James looked back at Lydia, then to Jake again. 'I didn't realise you'd kept in touch.'

'We haven't. Well, only via my parents,' she told him.

James frowned and she could almost hear the cogs turning. 'So…'

'Shall I save you the maths?' Jake said wryly, taking over. 'We spent the night together after her interview. It was late by the time she finished here, she had a long drive ahead, she said she hadn't slept well the night before and I was worried about that so I offered her my spare room. We went for dinner to celebrate her getting the job and—well, let's just say we got on rather better than we'd anticipated. We planned to stay in touch, said we'd meet up whenever our rotas allowed, but then—'

'Then I had the accident,' she chipped in, 'and I didn't know who he was. I just knew that I'd met him, but not for a second did I imagine I knew him that well. And I still remember nothing about it. But somewhere along the line, I suspect the morning of the interview, I missed a pill, and the next morning I'd taken it just before the accident, and I apparently vomited at the scene. I didn't realise for a week that I'd been taking them on the wrong day, but it didn't worry me because I had no idea I could be pregnant. Only I was. I am.'

James leant back in his seat and let out a long, slow breath. 'Wow. That's quite a story. So you're—what, twelve, fourteen weeks, something like that?'

'Fourteen. It's due on the third of February.'

He nodded slowly. 'So how long have you known?'

'Only since last night. I had the scan this morning.'

His eyes widened, and he shook his head slowly. 'Well, at least you're not working in Resus, but you were in there on your first day, and possibly in your last job, too, so you could have been exposed to X-rays.'

'I wasn't in my old job, not after the accident, and I had a lead apron on here and, to be fair, I wasn't in there for long.' Although it was long enough to worry her now, and she wouldn't be happy until she'd seen the anomaly scan at eighteen weeks.

'Well, that's good, it could have been a lot worse. May I?' He picked up the envelope, and she nodded.

'Of course.'

He slipped the photo out of the envelope and studied it, his face softening. 'That's beautiful. Congratulations.' He slipped it back into the envelope and handed it back to her. 'You'll need to tell HR, of course.'

'I will. And I'm really sorry I'm going to mess up your staffing.'

James frowned at her, but he was smiling. 'Lydia, you've got nothing to be sorry about. You're going to have a baby. You concentrate on that and let me worry about the staffing. I have to justify my existence somehow. And naturally I won't say anything to anyone. I'll leave that to you two.'

And that was it—apart from the hug he gave them both as they were leaving his office.

Jake shut the door behind them and smiled at her. 'Well done.'

'He was so nice about it,' she murmured as they walked away from the door, and he took her hand and gave it a quick squeeze and then didn't let go.

'He was. He is nice. I'll see you at the end of your shift, then we can go and get something to eat.'

She was straight back in at the deep end, of course, and it was a while before she realised she still had the photos in her pocket.

In a tiny lull, she took one out and slid the photo half out of the envelope, a wash of warmth and joy flooding over her.

'Lydia…?'

She stuffed it back into her pocket, but not before Laura had seen it.

'Is that yours?' she asked, her voice almost a whisper, and Lydia swallowed hard and nodded.

'Yes, it is,' she whispered. 'Mine and Jake's.'

Her eyes widened. 'Well, he's a dark horse. I had no idea you were together. Congratulations!'

She could feel herself flushing. 'Thank you. You're the first person I've told. Well, apart from James.'

'Oh, the poor man, he must be doing his crust. I'm nine

weeks—I told him yesterday, but he knew we were having IVF, so he knew it was on the cards, but both of us? He'll be tearing his hair out!'

'He said he had to justify his existence somehow.'

Laura chuckled. 'He more than does that, he's a brilliant Clinical Lead. But please don't say anything yet about me. We don't really want it broadcast. We lost the last one at twelve weeks, so I don't really want everyone knowing yet, just in case...well, you know.'

'Oh, Laura!' She hugged her gently. 'I'm so sorry. Of course I won't tell anyone—and ditto, please? Although it won't be long until it's obvious in my case, so I can't hide it forever.'

'I won't tell a soul, but you can tell Jake about me, he knew we were trying again.'

She nodded, and Laura gave her a little hug and went back to work, leaving her feeling even more guilty.

If James had to replace two of his doctors, how on earth would they manage if they couldn't find any? No idea, but it was his problem, not hers, and she didn't need to feel guilty. She'd done nothing wrong, and if it wasn't for the accident, she and the department wouldn't be in this mess.

No. It wasn't a mess, it was a baby, and James had seemed genuinely happy for them.

She just wished she could be sure that Jake felt the same...

Jake thought the shift would never end.

All he wanted was to sit down with Lydia and talk about how they were going to manage things. Who they told, what they told them, and when.

Because he had no idea, and the prospect of fatherhood was suddenly all too real. How the hell was he supposed to do it when he'd had no role model growing up? He didn't even know what a father *did.* It was going to be a steep learning curve for sure, and he just hoped he was up to it.

He found her later, half an hour after the end of their shift. She was about to pick up a file and call another patient in, and he stopped her.

'Come on, you haven't got to do that, you've already worked late and so have I,' he told her, so she put the file down and went and changed.

They ended up back at hers less than an hour later, armed with a quick food shop and some pregnancy-specific multivitamin and folic acid supplements, something she should have been taking since the very beginning—and would have been, had she had the slightest idea that she could be pregnant.

She took one before she put the food in the fridge, and Jake tipped his head on one side and met her eyes.

'You need to make an appointment with a midwife.'

'I do, but I haven't even registered with a GP yet. Where do you go?'

'Lucy Gallagher's practice. Andy's one of our consultants. He only works part-time and they're on annual leave at the moment. Lucy's lovely and she's got a great team. I think most of the staff here use them. Why don't you call them now and I'll do this?'

She did, and five minutes later she had her first midwife's appointment booked in, and Jake was busying himself in her kitchen.

'Here, decaf tea,' he said, handing her a mug, and they went out into the garden and sat on the swing seat in the shade.

'So how did your shift go?' he asked, and she gave him a rueful smile.

'Laura caught me peeking at the scan photo so I had to tell her, but I asked her not to say anything. Then she said James must be doing his crust because she's pregnant, too.'

'She is? Oh, that's great news, I'm so pleased for them. Tom has Retinitis Pigmentosa, hence the IVF because it's carried on the X chromosome, so it'll be a boy, but they lost the last one.'

'Yes, she told me, but I didn't realise he's got RP, that's really tough.'

'Yes. It has been, and his sight's deteriorated to the point that he can no longer work in the ED. He's retraining as a GP, but they wanted another baby so he could see it before he loses the last of his sight. He's only known for about four years, so I guess he's been lucky it was such late onset.'

'It doesn't sound very lucky to me.'

'No, just slightly less bad. They've known each other for years, apparently. He's a really nice guy, they're a lovely couple. He does a lot of the childcare. They've got a little boy, he must be coming up for four soon, and they didn't know about the RP at the time, so it was pure luck that they had a boy.' He tilted his head on one side. 'So, who else have you told about us?'

'No one, only James. I asked Laura not to tell anyone, and she said ditto, but I could tell you as you knew they were trying.'

'Yes, I wondered how it was going.' His eyes searched hers. 'So, what about everyone else? What do you want to say, if anything?'

She rolled her eyes and shrugged. 'Goodness knows. I'm not going to be able to hide it for long, and then everybody's going to talk.'

'So what do you want to say?'

She thought about that for a moment and came up with nothing useful—or at least, nothing she was ready to say to Jake.

'I don't know. What do you want to say? Because we're not really together, are we, not in the happy-ever-after way they'll all imagine,' she told him, trying to keep the wistfulness out of her voice. 'They're bound to ask, and right now I don't have any answers for that.'

Nor did he, but she was right, people would naturally assume that, especially since…

'It's already going round a bit. Oliver said something to me today. You know he's married to Emily?'

Her eyes widened. 'Emily—registrar Emily?'

'Yup. She saw us holding hands, so we must have been coming back from the scan.'

When they were both hanging on for dear life because their theoretical baby was suddenly very, very real…

Lydia closed her eyes and swallowed. 'I thought we might have a couple of weeks' grace.'

'Apparently not. The rumour mill will be in full swing by tomorrow, because she can't have been the only one. She told Oliver that he was the only person she'd mentioned it to, but someone else could have spotted us. And maybe again when we came out of James's office.'

She looked at him, then looked away again, and he watched her fretting at her lip.

'So what now?' she said. 'Since the cat is clearly out of the bag.'

He shrugged. 'I don't know,' he said honestly. 'People by and large are kind, but on the other hand everyone loves a bit of juicy gossip.'

'So when they ask if we're an item, what do I say?

Deny it? Refer them to you? Tell them it was just a random shag?'

He winced. 'It was nothing like that.'

'Well, I can hardly tell them it was love at first sight.'

Except in a way, for him at least, it had been. Or if not love, then something scarily close to it. Was it scary? Or was it just exactly right?

'It wasn't casual. That's not what it was like and I don't want anyone thinking it was. It would feel wrong.'

'Maybe they'll think we've been seeing each other,' she suggested, but he shook his head.

'People asked me if I'd heard from you, and I said no, because I hadn't.'

'But you said we were going to keep in touch, and see each other when we could—so why don't we just start doing that now, and then we don't need to pretend we're not together, they'll just assume we are and have been and that you'd kept it to yourself. Not that it's really any of their business. And it'll give us a chance to get to know each other a bit better, which we need to do. And maybe, if I spend more time with you, it might trigger a memory.'

'It might.' He studied her thoughtfully. Was that what she really wanted?

Was that what *he* wanted?

Hell, yes.

'Let's just go public, then. There's nothing in your fridge that won't keep, so let's go out for dinner. Then if we're seen, that's fine. The gossips can get it out of their system over the weekend, and by Monday it might be old news.'

'And if we're not seen?'

'We will have eaten—and frankly I'm starving because I didn't stop for lunch, so I'm more than ready. And we do need to get to know each other better. It'll give us a chance to talk.'

She hesitated for a moment, then nodded.

'OK, yes, let's do that. Are we going anywhere fancy—do I need to change?'

He felt a pang of regret, because he'd love to take her back to Zacharelli's, where they'd eaten that fateful night, but that was for later, if they ever got to that point.

'No. No, you're fine as you are. We'll just go to the pub, or get fish and chips and eat them on a bench on the prom. Whatever you want. Your call.'

'Pub?'

He smiled. 'Pub it is. There's a good one down by the harbour.'

'So are you sure you're OK with this?' she asked as he pulled up outside the Harbour Inn, and he smiled at her and wished it was echoed in her eyes.

'Why not?'

Why not, indeed? There were a thousand reasons why not, but one really important one why, and as he put an arm around her and led her to the door, he felt a gentle warmth engulf him.

They ordered their food, and then he leant his elbows on the table and ran his finger slowly around the top of his glass.

'So,' he began, looking up and meeting her eyes, 'I've told you about my dysfunctional family—you want to tell me about yours?'

She chuckled, and the sound wrapped round him like a caress and he had to make himself listen.

'Sure—except, to start with, they're not dysfunctional. Dad took early retirement from the Foreign Office and set up his own translation business, so that's why he was in Europe when I had my accident. Mum was a teacher but she now runs the business, and my sister's married to a doctor, they have three children, and she's a midwife.'

'Have you spoken to her, or to any of them? Do they know yet?'

She shook her head. 'No. To be honest, I have no idea how to tell them. Have you told your mother?'

He let out a small huff of laughter. 'No, not yet. I was waiting until after the scan, so I might call her later. And I might call my sister back. She rang me again, apologised, said considering our parents' behaviour she could hardly criticise me for doing the same thing. Except it wasn't really, was it?'

She sighed and rolled her eyes. 'I can't answer that, Jake,' she reminded him.

'Sorry, sorry. But no, it wasn't. We were both… I don't know…a bit shot away by the—oh, I can't describe it. The pull between us? The natural rapport? It was just there, and it blindsided us. I think you were euphoric because you'd got the job, and so was I, and we both thought it would be OK. I wasn't looking for a relationship, not after Claire, but at the time, being with you just seemed absolutely right. And it still does. It's felt like it from the very start.'

She stared at him for a moment, her eyes almost luminous, then looked away.

'It must have done if you told me about her and I told you about Steve. I never talk about him.'

He shrugged. 'I think it was just our way of checking that we were both currently single.'

'Only I apparently went into quite a lot of detail.'

He stifled a snort and nodded, his smile wry. 'Yeah. You really don't like him, do you? I'm sorry I suggested—'

'Don't be,' she cut him off. 'I was just shell-shocked that I was pregnant, and I guess you were, too.'

He was. Still was… 'And now?'

She smiled, and now he could see the warmth in her eyes, and he felt his heart squeeze a little in his chest. 'It's growing on me.'

'Or in you.'

'Oh, very funny. But yes, that, too.'

The smile escaped despite her best efforts, and he leant back to create a little safe distance between them and searched her eyes. 'So, your sister's a midwife. I imagine she might give you a bit of a lecture.'

Lydia shrugged and swirled the slice of lemon around in her glass. 'I don't know. It's not something I've ever had to tell her before so I have no idea how she'll react, or my parents for that matter. To be honest, I'm dreading it—although Mum will probably be delighted because she already thinks you're a wonderful human being.'

'Great judgement,' he said, and he couldn't stop his lips twitching, any more than she could stop one eyebrow from tilting up in mockery. But she was smiling, so he took that as a good sign.

And then she caught him completely by surprise.

'How much do you know about your father? Have you met any of his family?'

He shook his head. 'No, Mum didn't know anything about them. All she knew was his name and the fact that he hadn't got on with his parents, but she had no contact details so she couldn't even tell anyone he'd died. And she couldn't afford a funeral, so the council paid for his cremation, apparently.'

Her brow creased in a little frown. 'Oh, Jake, that's

awful. How sad for your mum. And for him. Have you ever thought of trying to find them? Trying to get in touch?'

'No. Why would I need to?'

'To learn more about him?'

She held his gaze, and he looked away. 'I'm not sure I need to. He wasn't exactly a good role model, by all accounts. That's all I need to know.'

'But it's a whole side of your family that you've never even met. Aren't you even slightly curious? I know I would be.'

She had a point, and for a time he had been curious, but then he'd put it out of his mind. Only now he was going to be a father, so maybe he ought to know?

'Pasta carbonara?'

He glanced up at the server. 'Yes, that's mine. Thank you.'

She set the plates down, asked if they wanted anything else, and as she walked away his eyes flicked back to Lydia's.

'Why do you care who they are?' he asked, curious to understand her motive—always assuming she had one.

She shrugged. 'Because he would have been my baby's grandfather? So it feels kind of relevant.'

'I'm not sure it is,' he said. 'I am who I am, so the only reason would be to know about anything health-wise that could be passed down. I'll ask my mother. She might know something more.'

He picked up his fork, and she reached across and touched his hand, stilling it.

'Jake, I was just curious, you don't have to do anything,' she said softly, as if she could read his mind, and he looked back at her and smiled, but it felt a bit crooked because she'd touched on a sore spot.

'No, you're right, I don't. How's your sea bass?'

'I don't know, I haven't tried it yet. How's your carbonara?'

This time he managed a genuine smile. 'I don't know, I haven't tried it yet,' he echoed, and her gentle answering smile touched his heart.

'Why don't we just eat? And then maybe we should go home and ring our families. Tell them the news.'

He nodded. He'd only known for twenty-four hours, but it seemed like a lifetime. 'Yes, we should.'

But first things first.

He wound some strands of linguine around his fork, put it in his mouth, and as the flavour burst on his tongue he went back for more and put everything else out of his mind.

For now.

CHAPTER SIX

HE PULLED UP outside Lydia's house, got out and walked her to the door.

'I can manage to walk up my path, you know,' she said with a twitch of her lips that made him want to kiss them.

'Just being polite.'

She rolled her eyes, but she was smiling properly now, and she fished her keys out of her bag and turned to him and gave him a fleeting kiss on the cheek.

'Thank you for a lovely evening, Jake. I really enjoyed it.'

'Yes, me, too. We ought to do it again. I'll call you tomorrow.'

Their eyes met and held, and then, despite his best intentions—something that was becoming a habit—he bent his head and kissed her. Not her cheek, but her lips. Just for a second.

Only it wasn't, it morphed into more, and she melted against him, her body up against his giving him all the wrong signals.

His body thought it was a great idea. His mind finally woke up and dragged him away.

'Goodnight, Lydia,' he murmured, and took another step back and walked away before he lost his mind completely.

* * *

It took Lydia a while to psyche herself up to ring her mother.

It had to be done, she knew that, but right now she was sitting on her sofa, her fingers on her lips, reliving that kiss.

For a moment there she'd thought he was going to follow through, and his body had certainly seemed keen on the idea. His reaction had been unmistakable, and the way she'd responded to that shocked her. She'd been more than ready to take it further—and then he'd stopped. And she wasn't at all sure how she felt about that.

A bit of her—a bit that was steadily growing more and more demanding—wanted to know what it would be like to lie naked next to him, to feel the warmth of his skin under her fingers, to feel his hands on her body, his lips chasing kisses all over her—she could almost feel it, and for a moment she wasn't sure if it was a memory, or just her imagination filling in the gaps. She didn't know, but she realised she wanted to.

Too soon?

Not nearly as soon as it had been the first time. Had it really been as earth-shattering as he made it out to have been? Or had that only been for him?

No. Every touch, every look, every tiny brush of his lips fanned the embers of a fire that was burning deep inside her. A fire that didn't seem to want to go out.

Was it—would it be—wise to give those embers any oxygen? To let him make love to her, and fan the flames into a wildfire that could end up burning her as badly as Steve had burned her? Because he certainly had, with his infidelity and total disregard for her feelings, and the bit of her that wanted to be able to trust Jake with her soul was too scared to let her try.

Scared, and scarred.

No. He wasn't another Steve, she was sure of that. But what if he changed his mind and wanted to keep it strictly platonic, to back away from any more physical contact and keep it firmly about their baby?

She had no idea. She couldn't read his mind, and he wasn't giving anything away. The hand-holding, the going out for dinner to the pub—was that all a charade, solely to justify their relationship in the eyes of his friends and colleagues?

In which case, why had he just kissed her goodnight like that, in the shadow of her porch with not a soul around? And there was no way on earth his body had faked that reaction.

'Stop thinking about him and phone your mother,' she told herself crossly. Although she had no idea what she was going to say.

He drove home, only sheer force of will preventing him from turning round and driving back to her, but the want, the need, the ache to hold her, make love to her, feel her body against his again was burning holes in him.

Tough.

He pulled his phone out as he walked through the front door. Ringing his mother and sister would be more effective than a cold shower, he was sure. But in which order? Mother first, or sister?

He hadn't spoken to his sister since he'd ripped her head off for suggesting he'd picked Lydia up in a bar, and he needed to apologise for that—and so did she. But she already knew about the baby and his mother didn't, so he called her first, breaking it to her gently that she was going to be a grandmother.

'I didn't know you'd met anyone! Why didn't you tell me?'

He swallowed his pride and told her the truth, and she gave a heavy sigh. 'Oh, Jake. I thought I'd brought you up better than that! How could you be so silly?'

'The same way you could?'

'Jacob, I was nineteen and so was your father,' she chided. 'You're thirty-two and a doctor, and you really ought to know better.'

Well, that was painfully true.

'You could be pleased for me.'

'Why? Because I don't suppose for a moment you're pleased about it.'

He thought about that for a second, then shook his head. 'You're wrong, Mum. Actually, in an odd sort of way I am pleased. Seeing the scan… I've got a photo, I'll send it to you. It made it all so real.'

'Oh, it's real,' she said bluntly. 'You wait. This is something that'll change the rest of your life and, believe me, you'll find out just how real that is. And you don't have to go through with it, you know. You do have options.'

'No, I don't. I have no options, it's absolutely down to Lydia, but she wants to have the baby, and I want her to, and I want to be part of its life. You could try and be a little bit pleased for me.'

'Pleased? I just hope you realise what you're letting yourself in for. If I'd known—'

'Known what?' he chipped in. 'What life would be like with him? What it would have been like if you'd had an abortion and never had Suze or me? Or if he hadn't died?

We'll never know that, as you're well aware. Anything could happen to any of us at any time.'

'And it sounds like it just did. But…don't go climbing any rocky cliffs, eh?'

Ouch. 'No, I won't,' he said quietly, and then added, 'Am I like him?'

She sighed again, but softly this time. 'A little. You're much more focused, of course, much more self-disciplined, but you look like him, and you got your kindness from him, and he would have loved you. He was a good father, very caring, but always in a slightly random way, but that was no surprise, he lived his life to a different drummer and he could be unintentionally thoughtless. But then he was a free spirit.'

And his 'free spirit' meant she'd been burdened with two fatherless children and an uphill struggle to put food on the table and a roof over their heads.

'I wish he hadn't died before I was born.'

For a long time there was silence, and when she spoke, her voice was soft and thoughtful.

'So do I, but if he hadn't died, I wouldn't have turned my life around and started acting responsibly, and you probably wouldn't be where you are now. Be careful what you wish for, Jacob. Life seldom turns out the way you think it will.'

There was another long silence and then the line went dead, and he stared at the phone, slightly stunned, not so much by his mother's reaction to his news as by what she'd said about his father. She'd never talked about him before in that much detail, and it sounded as if they were very different. Unlike his father, most of his decisions were carefully considered—but not always, or Lydia wouldn't be pregnant and they wouldn't have been having that conversation. So maybe not as different as he'd like to think…

He walked into the kitchen, made himself a coffee and phoned his sister.

'Have you forgiven me yet?' she asked, and he gave a wry chuckle.

'Just about. I was mostly angry because Lydia overheard some of it. It upset her—quite a lot. I'm sorry I ripped your head off.'

'Oh, forget it, I would have done the same to you, but I shouldn't have jumped to conclusions. So, have you told Mum?'

'Yes, just now. She didn't sound overly thrilled. Said I should have known better.'

'Well, you should, Jake, you really should.'

'I know, I know. I kick myself all the time for it, but what's done is done. I asked her about our father—what he was like, if I was like him. She told me more than she ever has, but it didn't shed a lot of light. Apparently I look like him, and I have his kindness, so it could be worse. Do you know any more about him? Have you ever tried to look for his relatives?'

'No. Partly because I might not like what I found out, but also because I know who I am, and I don't need a long-lost family to validate me. I know what Mum told me, that's all. I don't remember anything about him and, to be honest, Jake, it doesn't matter what he was like or where he came from. You know who you are. You're a thoughtful, caring, thoroughly decent human being—even if you were a very irritating little brother—and you'll be a wonderful father. That's all you need to know about yourself. Just live in the moment and enjoy your baby, and concentrate on building a relationship with Lydia—which, as she's the mother of your unborn child, is significantly more important than anything else.'

He was silent for a moment, letting all that sink in, and then he gave a sigh of relief.

'Do you know what, Suze? You're absolutely right. Thank you.'

'My pleasure. So, when's this baby due?'

Lydia was about to phone her mother when it was taken out of her hands by her sister calling.

'Hi, baby sis, how are you doing?'

She laughed softly. 'Firstly, I'm not a baby, Steph, and secondly, I'm—' She hesitated, then sucked in a breath and said, 'I'm pregnant. It's due in February.'

There was a stunned silence, and then, 'Whose? Please, not that awful Steve—'

'Absolutely not. It's Jake's.'

'*Jake?* The doctor Mum met? So—hang on—when, how? I thought you hadn't seen him since your accident?'

'I hadn't. And I don't remember anything about it because it was the night before the accident, but I've had a scan and the date fits with the time of the interview. He took me out for dinner and we got on really well, apparently, and…it just sort of happened. We spent the night together, and I don't remember any of it… And I should, I really should, and because I don't, it's like it's come out of nowhere and I don't know how I feel—'

She felt herself tearing up and sniffed, and Steph sucked in a deep breath.

'We're coming. I'm off all weekend,David's here, so I'll pick Mum up and we'll see you tomorrow morning—'

'Don't be silly, Steph! You don't need to come, I'm all right!'

'We do, sweetheart, we do. We'll be with you as soon as we can.'

'Please. You don't need to do that, Steph. Really, I'm OK.'

'Well, you don't sound OK, and you're my little sister so, like it or not, we're coming.'

They arrived just before ten the next morning, by which time she'd made up the bed in the spare room, put away the hasty supermarket order and had a shower.

She was expecting a load of clucking and fussing, but actually it was really lovely to see them, and by the time they left late on Sunday afternoon she was feeling much less anxious. She hadn't even realised how stressed she'd been, but as soon as they walked in and gathered her up in a big hug she felt the worry melt away.

It was going to be all right. Difficult, maybe, but all right.

And, as her mother said, she could have picked someone far worse than Jake to have as the father. Not that she'd picked him, exactly, but her mother was right. It could have been a lot, lot worse. It could have been Steve, heaven help her, as Steph had thought at first, and that would have been a very different proposition.

Of course, Steph had wanted to meet Jake, but Lydia wasn't having that so she said he might be working. He wasn't, she knew that full well, but the last thing the poor man needed was Steph grilling him, so she felt the little white lie was justified.

And then on Sunday evening, an hour after they'd left, her doorbell rang.

She opened the door and Jake was there, propped against the porch wall, hands in his pockets and a lazy smile on that oh-so-kissable mouth.

'Hi,' he said. 'How are you? Good weekend?'

She dragged her eyes off his mouth and took a step back. 'Lovely, thanks. Are you coming in?'

'If that's OK?'

'Of course it's OK. It's a bit of a mess, I've had my mum and my sister here.'

'I know,' he said, closing the door behind him, and she frowned.

'Have you been spying on me?'

His jaw dropped, and he laughed. 'Why on earth would you think that?'

'I have no idea. So how do you know?'

'Your mother rang me. She just wanted to let me know that they'd be here for the weekend, so not to worry about you.'

'She *what?* Of all the… She didn't tell me that!'

That made him smile. 'No, I don't suppose she did. I thought she might be going to rip my head off, but she didn't at all, she said she was looking forward to getting to know me better at some point. She also asked me to get in touch if I was worried about you at any time. Apparently, you're in the habit of not telling her when things go wrong.'

Like Steve.

She felt her cheeks colouring. 'Honestly, I can't believe her! I'm so sorry.'

He chuckled. 'Don't be sorry, she was lovely, and I was actually quite touched. I'm glad she feels she can talk to me—that she wants to.'

'Well, she would, you're the father of her next grandchild.'

'I am. And I think she'll be a fabulous grandmother. I wish I'd had one.'

'You didn't have a grandmother?'

He shook his head slowly. 'Not on my father's side that I ever knew about, and my mother's mother had died before I was born. Her father was a bit…stern, I suppose. I don't think he was thrilled by my mother dropping out of uni, so we didn't see much of him, and I didn't really like him when we did see him. He died when I was about ten, and I can't say I missed him.'

'Oh, that's sad, Jake, I'm sorry. Can I get you a drink? Tea? Coffee? Or wine? There's some open in the fridge and I won't drink it.'

He shook his head. 'No, I'm OK. It's actually why I'm here. I wondered if you'd like to go out. It's a lovely evening, we could go for a stroll on the prom, get fish and chips?'

'On a Sunday? Are they even open?'

He pulled a face. 'You have a point. There's a nice little pub, we could go there? They've got a deck at the front overlooking the sea. We don't have to eat, we could have a drink—if you want to, that is.'

'I'm not really hungry, but a stroll and a drink by the sea sounds nice.'

So they went for a stroll, down through the pretty residential streets to the seafront, and she found her hand in his.

'Is this for the benefit of the gossips?' she asked, the charade idea still playing havoc with her mind, and he chuckled and glanced at her, a smile on his lips and his eyes soft.

'No, it's for mine,' he said, and her heart skipped in her chest. She tightened her fingers on his, smiled back and carried on walking, a little glow of warmth inside her in the region of her heart.

* * *

The rumour mill was in full swing by Monday morning.

He'd known it would happen, but not so far or so fast. There were sideways looks, subtle nudges, people avoiding his eye. And others more direct.

'What have you been up to?' Sam Ryder murmured in a quiet moment at the desk.

'*Et tu, Brute?*' he said with a sigh, and Sam grinned.

'Chin up, you're not the first and I don't suppose you'll be the last.'

That sounded a bit cryptic, and he turned and searched Sam's eyes, one eyebrow raised in question. '*What?*'

'Guilty as charged,' Sam said with a wry chuckle and walked off, heading back to his patient and leaving Jake staring after him and wondering who would be next.

Emily, of course, who vowed she'd only told Oliver, and he believed her.

'Go on, tell me off,' he said, and she just shook her head and smiled.

'Not me. Or Oliver. I was just going to say I hope it all turns out well for you both. I think Lydia's lovely. I hope you stay together.'

So did he, because with every day that passed he was falling a little bit more in love with her, but there was a lot of water to go under a lot of bridges before he could be confident that they had a future.

If ever…

'Just a heads-up—it seems to have escaped,' Laura murmured to Lydia at the desk.

'Mmm. Everyone's giving me funny looks, but nobody's said anything.'

'Maybe because they don't know you, but I imagine Jake's getting quite a bit of ribbing.'

She saw him over Laura's shoulder, walking towards them, and she gave him a tentative smile as he approached.

'Comparing notes?' he murmured softly, and then turned to Laura, his voice still low. 'I gather you've had good news. That's great.'

'Thanks. And congratulations to you, too. I think it's lovely for you both.'

She walked away, and Jake met Lydia's eyes.

'Are you OK?'

'What, with everyone talking about us? I suppose I'll live.'

'Well, let's give them something to talk about, then,' he said with a lazy grin, and dropped a fleeting but definite kiss on her startled mouth before walking away, humming quietly under his breath and leaving her heart pounding and her lips tingling.

She bit them, stifling a smile, then picked up the next set of notes and moved on.

Two days later she went for her first appointment with the midwife at the surgery. Jake spent the morning wondering how her appointment was going, and it was the first thing he asked when he saw her later.

'All good,' she said. 'She was lovely, and she seemed very happy with the way my pregnancy's progressing, but I'm going to need bigger scrubs soon. I had to buy some new clothes. I'm starting to outgrow things and then they'll all do the maths and work out what happened.'

'Do you care?'

'Not if you don't,' she replied, but he wasn't quite sure he believed her.

However, the next few days ticked by with nothing much more said to either of them, and by the end of the week all the speculation had settled down, to his relief.

It wasn't him he minded them talking about as much as her, because that wasn't fair. They knew nothing about her, and what little they knew was entirely to do with her attitude to work and her ability to get on with her colleagues and her patients.

He didn't want that tarnished by what he'd done, but he didn't need to defend her and, to be fair, nobody said anything about her that wasn't complimentary. Unlike his sister that first night…

The following week their shift patterns changed so he hardly saw her, but he missed her more than he'd expected. He rang her every day, but that just left him wanting her more. He worked a week of nights and then had a few days off, which he used to do a bit of work on the house and the garden, then he cleaned the car inside and out and tried not to think too much about her or the eighteen-week anomaly scan that was coming up.

And then the day came, and his heart was in his mouth.

What if they found something wrong? What if the baby had been damaged by exposure to X-rays on her first day when the biker had come in? Although she'd had the lead apron on, but it didn't stop him worrying.

It hadn't stopped her worrying either. When the scan started, he noticed she was biting her lip and studying the screen, a death-grip on his hand, and he stroked the back of her hand with his thumb to soothe her.

It did nothing to soothe him, but when the sonographer looked up and smiled, he felt the tension drain out of him.

'All good, it's growing well,' she said, and he saw a tear

leak out of the corner of Lydia's eye. She swiped it away and laughed at herself, but he wasn't laughing, he was too busy doing the same thing.

'Would you like to know what it is?'

He looked at Lydia, leaving it up to her.

'Um…no, I don't think so. I'm not sure, and it doesn't really matter,' she said, and looked up at him. 'Does it?'

'Not to me.'

The sonographer nodded. 'OK. Would you like a photo?'

'Yes, please,' they said in unison, and Lydia turned her head and looked up at him and he bent over and kissed her.

'It's OK,' she said, her voice a little choked, and he nodded and took the paper towel the sonographer held out and wiped it gently over the smooth curve that held his child.

He wished he had the right to bend and kiss it, to press his lips to it, but he didn't, and he might never have that right.

Not until things changed between them, and she'd let him into her heart. Was he even ready for that? He wasn't sure, not after Claire. She'd torched his trust well and truly, but Lydia—Lydia was different, and he was different now, but he still had to prove that, and maybe then she'd let herself love him. As much as he loved her?

He could only hope…

They went for a coffee afterwards.

Well, he had a coffee. She had raspberry and cranberry tea, and while it cooled she pulled out the photo and stared at it, and he leant over and rested his head against hers.

'That was just amazing,' she said, and he nodded but he didn't speak, and she realised he must feel just as she did, awed and stunned by the beauty of that tiny person growing inside her.

'It was,' he said, straightening up, his eyes still on the photo. 'Absolutely amazing. And I'm so relieved it's all OK.'

'Just five more months to go,' she murmured, and she felt her heart pick up a little.

Five months didn't seem anything like long enough. She wasn't sure if she'd be ready for it, and there was a bit of her that wondered how she'd manage.

Unless they got married?

No, that was ridiculous. But she didn't want to be alone with a new baby, and she had no idea what exactly he'd meant when he said they could get married. Live together? Share a bed as lovers? Or cohabit, like housemates? Or stay as they were in their two houses, with a yawning void between them that echoed with unspoken feelings too delicate, too new to voice?

Well, they had five months for it to pan out, so she'd just have to wait and see and hope their relationship resolved, because she was beginning to think she really could trust him with her heart, and with her love, but she wasn't at all sure when, how or even if to tell him how she felt.

So she said nothing, and they carried on as before.

Sometimes she saw him at work, sometimes she didn't, and when they could they grabbed a break together, but those times were few and far between.

The evenings, though, were different.

If their shifts aligned they'd go out for a meal, or for a walk along the cliff top, and sometimes she'd eat at his or he'd eat at hers.

But not often, and they were keeping it a little distant, a little platonic, although she wasn't sure whose idea that was, or if it was both of them. Whatever, it seemed to be working, but she was conscious that time was ticking by and she was no nearer to understanding where their relationship was going.

She just knew she wanted it to be forever, and not because of the baby but because he loved her as much as she loved him.

Did he? And did she? Really love him?

Yes. Yes, she really did, but she had no idea how or if to tell him.

CHAPTER SEVEN

SHE WALKED INTO work after a lovely few days off with her parents visiting, and bumped straight into Jake.

'How are your parents?' he asked, and she felt a tiny bit guilty that she hadn't invited him to join them.

'They're fine—I'm sorry, it's probably time you met them—or met Dad, at least, but I didn't know how you'd feel about that.'

He gave her a wry smile. 'That's down to you, Lydia, just say the word—so long as he doesn't want to kill me for doing this to you.'

'Don't be ridiculous, of course he doesn't want to kill you! And you didn't "do it" to me, I did it to myself. It was me who said it was OK, and me who'd forgotten to take a pill. You can't take the blame for that.'

'That again.'

'Yes, that again,' she retorted, but she was struggling to keep a straight face and he just snorted softly and walked away chuckling.

She was about to pick up a set of notes when there was a call over the Tannoy.

'Doctor to Reception—patient collapse.'

'I'll go,' she called to anyone who was listening, and went through into Reception and found a man sitting on a chair and hanging on to the back, convulsing—only not really convulsing, more lurching, while the woman beside him held his hand and had an arm around his shoulders.

She knelt down quickly beside them to assess him, and looked up at the woman.

'Hi, my name's Lydia, I'm a doctor. Has this happened before?'

'No, never. He's had a terrible headache since last night and I was worried so I brought him in, and now he's doing this.'

'I'll get a trolley and we'll move him through into the cubicles so we can have a proper look at him. What's his name?'

'Jon—Jonathan Reynolds. I'm his wife, Sal.'

'OK, Sal, stay there with him and—ah, the cavalry are here,' she said with a reassuring smile as she caught sight of Jake, and she stood up.

'What have we got?' Jake asked, and she shrugged.

'Not sure. Some kind of cerebral event? Headache since last night, then this atypical seizure.'

'OK, let's get him moved through. We're just going to move you onto the trolley, sir, and then we can get you some privacy.'

They lowered the trolley and Jake and a porter lifted him onto it, pulled up the cot sides and whisked him through into an empty cubicle.

Jake looked at her. 'Do you need me, or have you got this?'

'I think so, but are you nearby?'

'Just finishing up. Shout if you want me.'

Always...

She nodded and turned back to her patient.

'Hi, my name's Lydia, I'm a doctor here. May I call you Jonathan?'

'Jon—and this is Sal.'

He closed his eyes, and she glanced at his wife. She looked worried, and she had his hand in a death grip, so Lydia smiled reassuringly.

'So, Jon, you've had a headache, and you've just had a seizure of some sort. Can you tell me how it all started?'

Between them they gave her a brief but worrying potted history of the last twelve hours, starting with the headache that got worse overnight and ending just then with him having some kind of episode.

'So, what did you feel while it was happening when you were in Reception? Can you describe it to me?'

He nodded slightly. 'I had this roaring in my head, a sort of rushing noise, really loud, and terrible headache, and I just started to shake—I was hanging on to the chair. I thought I was going to fall off… I don't know, ask Sal, she saw it.'

Lydia looked at her, and she picked up the story. 'He just started… I don't know…lurching? That's all I can tell you.'

'So, what prompted you to bring him in? Was it just because of the headache?'

'Yes, because he never has them, and this morning he said it was really bad. I rang for an ambulance and they said it would be three hours, so I put him in the car and brought him here because I really didn't like the look of him, and it seems I was right—' She broke off, sounding a little tearful, and Lydia nodded.

'You were, and I think that was probably a very sensible thing to do. Right, the first thing I'm going to do is to listen to your heart, Jon, and do a few simple strength and precision tests. How old are you?'

'Forty-three.'

'And what month is it?'

He looked at her oddly. 'September—is that significant?'

'No, but it's significant that you can give me the right answer. Squeeze my hands—OK, that's fine, and can you follow my finger, please, keeping your head still? That's good. And touch my finger and then the tip of your nose with your right index finger—good, and now the left?'

Deficit. He missed, only by a fraction, but enough to indicate a right-sided event.

'OK. Now, run your right heel down your left shin—that's great. And the other one?'

Again, it was shaky and a bit hit and miss, and while he was doing that, the fingers of his left hand were moving restlessly.

'Mmm. That's a little wobbly. Can you close your eyes and touch your nose?'

Again, the right was fine, the left missed.

It was all highly indicative of a right-sided cerebral event, either a bleed or a clot, so she asked the next obvious question.

'Jon, have you ever been diagnosed with atrial fibrillation?'

'No? What's that?'

'It might feel a bit like palpitations in your chest. It's when the top chambers of your heart don't pump properly, they just quiver, and it can cause little clots which can break loose and lead to a stroke.' She listened again, then went on, 'It's not doing it now, I can't hear anything untoward, but sometimes it can come and go. I'm going to have a word with someone and see if we can get you scanned to find out what's going on. I'll be back in a minute.'

She left the cubicle and spotted Jake on his way into a cubicle.

'Jake, are you free? I'm not sure what to do. I think he needs CT.'

He dumped the notes back on the desk and met her halfway. 'Sure—what do you know?'

'Jon's forty-three, no previous history of AF and his heart's regular, but there was the occasional flutter and he's got some minor neurological deficit on the left. Nothing drastic, but he's not pinpoint accurate and the fingers on his left hand are twitching a tiny bit, as if they're trying to find where to rest, so it's looking like a right-sided event. Can I send him for CT to rule out a bleed?'

'So you're thinking ischaemic stroke?'

She nodded. 'I know he's young, but—'

'—it could be. Sounds very like it. Yup, send him for urgent CT and I'll come and join you when he's back if you want?'

'It could be useful. Not sure what your treatment protocol is here, but I'm thinking if it's not a bleed he needs thrombolysing asap to avoid a permanent deficit, and then a cardiology referral for paroxysmal AF.'

'Sure. Give me a shout if you need me.'

Half an hour later Jon was back, with no evidence of a bleed on the CT report, so she called Jake and they went in to see him together.

'Hi again, sorry I didn't introduce myself before. My name's Jake, I'm a specialist registrar here. We've got the result of the CT scan, and the good news is it didn't show any signs of a bleed. However, that doesn't rule other things out. Lydia and I have been discussing your case, and I'd just like to do a few more tests, if that's OK?'

'Sure.'

He ran through the same tests she'd done and a few more, and then he glanced at Lydia and nodded.

'OK, we both think there's something going on in your brain, Jon, most likely a clot, so we want to start you on an anticoagulant drip, and that should dissolve the clot or clots over the next few hours, if that's what it is. We believe it is, and that that should hopefully prevent any permanent damage, but well done for getting here so swiftly, that was a very wise thing to do and it'll give you the best chance of a complete recovery. I'll leave you in Lydia's hands. She'll sort all that out, and then we'll admit you under observation for a few days. OK?'

Jon nodded and thanked him as he left, and Lydia followed him out and joined him at the desk.

'Thanks.'

He threw her a smile. 'Good spot. That deficit is so slight it would have been really easy to miss, and a strength test would have been useless, he's just lost a tiny bit of precision, and the hunting fingers were highly indicative. Well done for spotting that, it's really subtle.'

'What can I say—I'm a diagnostic genius,' she said, trying to make him laugh and wondering if her face was actually blushing because of his praise or if it was just suddenly hot in there.

His mouth twitched, and he was about to speak when a trauma call came over the speakers.

'Oh, here we go again,' he sighed, and strode swiftly off towards Resus, and she went back to her patient, armed with a nurse and the IV infusion that could halt the damage to his brain in its tracks.

As soon as it was set up, she contacted the bed manager and then sent him to the neurology ward for observation, ECG and and referral to Cardiology if necessary, and called in another patient.

She was a quick one, a simple stitch-up of a stab in the hand with a kitchen knife, trying to get the stone out of an avocado, and then Jake was back at the desk, his face sombre.

'Oh, dear,' she said, looking at him, and he gave a tiny shrug.

'You can't win 'em all. Are you in the middle of something?'

'No, I've sent Jon up to Neurology and then I stitched another self-inflicted avocado injury. People never learn. I'm just finishing up the notes. Why?'

'Because I'm starving and there's enough of a lull to justify escaping. They'll call me if necessary. Fancy a quick trip to the café? I'll treat you.'

'Absolutely, but I think it's my turn. Take it as a thank-you for helping out with Jon Reynolds.'

'It's my job.'

'No, it's not. Technically, we shouldn't be working together. I could have asked someone else, but you were there when it happened and I didn't want to waste time.'

'And there I was thinking you'd sought me out,' he murmured, pulling a sad face, and she punched his arm lightly and closed the last patient's file on the computer.

'Right, I'm done, let's go. You look as if you could do with some fresh air and nourishment and so could I.'

They'd barely sat down on a little bistro table outside the café when they heard the wailing of sirens and the thrum of a helicopter's blades.

'That sounds ominous,' Jake said, and they abandoned

their food and ran, both of their phones pinging. They went straight to Resus and found the teams assembling.

'So, what do we know?' Jake asked, and Oliver picked it up.

'Mass stabbing, and we'll need all hands on deck for this. Lydia, Laura, I'd like you both out there treating the walking wounded, and we need at least three teams in here on the more serious injuries. We won't fit everyone in here, it sounds massive and Theatres are on standby and some of them are being diverted elsewhere. All we know is someone with a knife ran through a crowded amusement arcade stabbing people at random. There are several children, there'll be a lot of stitching up to do, and any puncture wounds will need a depth assessment. We've got Plastics coming down for any facial injuries, so they'll need expert surgery. Anyone got any Plastics experience?'

'I can stitch and glue, I've done a Plastics rotation and Paeds, if that helps?' Lydia offered, and Oliver nodded.

'That could be really useful, we'll put you with the children. Jake, can you triage, please, and we can get through these as quickly as possible and ship them off to wherever they need to go.'

By this time there were two groups of paramedics bringing people in, another from the air ambulance, who went straight into Resus, and the sirens were still wailing.

She attached herself to the Plastics team, and she and Julie, the nurse who'd been so kind to her on her first day, set about cleaning and gluing and stitching the children.

There were some in their mothers' arms, others crying because they'd been separated from their parents, parents frantic because they'd lost their children.

They were all traumatised, particularly a young mother, Sara, with her baby, who'd been separated from her older child. Sara had been slashed on the arm, her baby was uninjured, but she had no idea where her six-year-old daughter was and she was distraught.

'It was just chaos in there—everyone running away screaming, and I lost her—I just lost her—I have to find her!'

'What's her name?' Julie asked.

'Elouise. We call her Lulu. And my husband—I can't get hold of him to tell him, but he needs to find her!'

'Right, give me all the details,' Julie said calmly. 'His phone number, and a description of Lulu, what she was wearing—all of those things will help find her.'

'I need to look for her!'

'No,' Lydia said, gently but firmly. 'Your wound needs attention now, and someone else needs to trace Lulu and bring her to you. If you go off somewhere looking for her, we won't be able to find you to reunite you, will we? And you need medical attention yourself, so stay here and we'll track her down, I promise. Julie will take all the details and get someone onto it straight away.'

'But what if he killed her?' Sara said, her voice rising in panic. 'What if she's dead?'

'Nobody's died, or we would have heard,' Lydia said, hoping that was still true. 'Julie, can you get on it?'

'Sure.'

While Julie did that, Lydia numbed the wound and had a closer look at it. It was fairly superficial, and she managed to distract Sara by asking her to move her fingers, testing her reflexes and sensation, and once she was satisfied that there was no neurological damage, she cleaned it thoroughly and started to bring the wound together with Steri-Strips, lining up the edges before she sutured it.

She got a dressing on it then to cover it until one of the

plastic surgeons had a look at it, and she'd just done that when Julie was back, a little girl with blood in her hair hanging onto her hand like a lifeline, and Sara threw her arms around her daughter and clung to her, sobbing with relief.

'She's not injured,' Julie said quickly, 'it's probably your blood. We've had a good look and she's OK, just a bit scared.'

Lydia looked up at Julie and mouthed her thanks, but she couldn't speak, and tears were prickling her eyes, so she laid a hand on Sara's shoulder and squeezed it gently.

'See? I said we'd find her,' she said when she could speak, and Sara stared up at them, her face streaming with tears of relief.

'I was so worried…'

'We know. And your husband is on his way,' Julie told her.

Ten minutes later the plastic surgeon had checked Sara's wound and was happy with it, her husband had arrived and scooped Lulu up into his arms and hugged her hard, and the family were able to leave.

Lydia and Julie moved on to the next patient, then the next, and somehow they patched them up one by one and either sent them home or to a ward that had been cleared for them.

Finally, hours after they'd started and running on empty, their last patient was sent home and she and Julie came up for air.

'I wonder how they're doing in Resus?' she asked, and Julie shrugged.

'I dread to think. Are you OK? Shall we go and see if we can help, or do you need to eat something and sit down?'

She managed a smile, more or less, and said, 'I'll live. Let's go and see if we're needed.'

* * *

Resus was a bloodbath, and Jake was busy stitching a shallow leg wound on a teenager when he heard the door open.

Please, not another one.

But it wasn't. It was Lydia, with Julie in tow, coming to assist.

'All the walking wounded are done now. Anything we can do to help in here?' she asked him, and he met her eyes over the top of his mask.

'I'm all but done here. This wound's superficial and it's the last on this patient. It needs a dressing on it and then he can go up to the ward. I think we're OK.'

They went out again as he snipped the last suture, and as one of the nurses covered the wound he stepped back, stripped off his gloves and gown and mask and looked at James.

'Right, I'm done for now. Are you OK if I go and grab some food and then come back and help with that?'

'Just go, I'm nearly done. It's time you knocked off anyway, and the night crew are in now. Well done—we haven't lost anyone, and that's a win. Go home—you've earned it.'

He glanced up at the clock and blinked. Nineteen thirty-seven? How? No wonder he was feeling light-headed.

He walked out of Resus and straight into Lydia.

'I'm finished. I'm going to change. I'll meet you back out here, OK?' he said, and she nodded.

She sat down on a bench in her locker room and closed her eyes. She wasn't even sure she could summon up the strength to walk home. She'd been going flat-out without a pause for over seven hours since the first stab victims had been brought in, and the temptation to lie down on the bench and go to sleep almost overwhelmed her, but at least she knew that—so far, at least—no one had died. And that seemed like nothing short of a miracle.

She forced herself to get up, to change, to walk out, and there was Jake, propped against the wall opposite, arms folded and looking as tired as she felt. He shrugged himself away and slung an arm round her shoulders and led her to the door, and they walked back to the end of her road and stopped.

'I'm starving, and I can't be bothered to cook. I need a nice hot shower, and then let's go somewhere,' he suggested.

'Like where?'

'I don't know. Somewhere quick and tasty and close. There's a Chinese restaurant with an excellent buffet just round the corner. Fancy that?'

'Loads of oil and a good old dollop of MSG? What's not to like?' she said, and his mouth kicked up in a weary smile.

'Is that a yes or a no?'

'It's a definite yes,' she said, and he gave a tired laugh, pulled her into his arms and dropped a kiss on her cheek.

'That's my girl. I'll give you a shout when I'm ready.'

Am I his girl?

Maybe. It sounded rather—nice? Was that too bland? Probably, but she was too tired to think of a better word.

She stood in the shower, letting the hot water pour over her head and down her body, washing away the traces of blood on her arms and the scent of it in her nose, leaving her still tired, still hungry, but less tense.

Less tense also because they hadn't lost any of the stabbing victims, although two were critical, Jake had told her, and he didn't sound too hopeful, but at least they'd all done everything they could to secure a good outcome. And Sara and her family were reunited. After the carnage she'd witnessed, she'd take that as a win.

Her phone pinged, and she glanced at it. Jake, saying he was on the way. She found a pair of loose linen trousers with a drawstring tie, pulled on a top, slipped her feet into sandals, dragged her still-wet hair into a ponytail and headed downstairs, just as he arrived at the front door.

'Better?' he asked, and she nodded.

'Much. You?'

'I will be when I've eaten. Shall we go?'

She hadn't realised how hungry she was until they walked into the restaurant and she smelt the food. It was busy, but a couple were just leaving so they were shown to their table and it wasn't long before she was tucking in to the best Chinese food she'd ever had. Bursting with flavour, utterly delicious and oh, so welcome.

'Good, isn't it?' he said, and she mumbled something in agreement and went back for more, and it was a long time before either of them spoke again.

Then, finally, when she'd swiped up the last morsel of loveliness, she met his eyes and sat back. 'I don't think I've ever felt so full in my life.'

'No, but I was ready for it. Shall we go?'

'Sure. Do you want to come back to mine for coffee, or just go to bed?'

He met her eyes and one eyebrow kicked up. 'Would you like to rethink that question before I answer it?'

She ran it back in her mind, and felt her cheeks colour. 'Um…'

'Let me help you out,' he said, his mouth twitching. 'Yes, please, to coffee, and then yes, I will go home to bed.'

Was that really disappointment she was feeling? Or was

it relief? She was too tired to work it out—and, frankly, too tired to contemplate going to bed with Jake and doing anything other than sleeping. Thank goodness he'd had the sense to say what he had.

'Good plan,' she said, and found a smile, but as they left the restaurant she found her hand in his again, and when they got to her front door he pulled her gently into his arms and hugged her, resting his head against hers and sighing quietly.

'I think I'll skip coffee,' he said. 'We're both too tired to do anything but sleep. I'll see you tomorrow.'

He bent his head, tipped up her chin and kissed her, a slow, lingering kiss, before he dropped his arms and pulled away from her.

'Goodnight, Lydia. Sleep well.'

'You, too. And thank you. My turn next.'

He smiled and nodded, then turned on his heel and walked away, and she went inside, locked the door and crawled up the stairs to bed…

When he arrived at work the following day, it was to find that the two critical stabbing victims had died, one in Theatre, the other during the course of the night.

Had he missed anything when he'd been hastily triaging them? Or when he'd moved to Resus to help in there? He had no idea. There had been so many through the doors that he'd lost count, never mind remembering anyone's name. Several of them hadn't had names because there was nobody to speak for them, but his dreams had been haunted by their faces.

Especially the kids, the barely-teens who'd been innocently having fun together and been caught up in a senseless tragedy.

'Any idea yet who attacked them all?' he asked James, and he shook his head.

'Not as far as I know. I think he's still on the loose, and the police are trying to identify him from the CCTV.'

'What kind of a madman could do that? Run through all those people innocently having fun, and slash them all to bits? What for?'

'I have no idea. Maybe he didn't even need a motive. To be honest, Jake, I thought we'd lose more of them than we did, so we've got nothing to blame ourselves for. Everyone did a sterling job in difficult conditions. I'm proud of the whole team. And Plastics are singing Lydia's praises—they were well impressed.'

That was good to know. 'Have you told her?'

'Not yet, but I will. She's not in this morning—she's got an appointment.'

With the midwife. He'd totally forgotten, but he was glad she hadn't. It might have meant she got a lie in, which could only be a good thing. He sent her a message, and she pinged back a reply almost immediately to say her appointment was at nine-thirty and she'd see him after that.

By the time she walked into the ED it was nearly eleven, and she sent a message to Jake to tell him she was in. Two minutes later he appeared, his mouth smiling a greeting but his eyes sombre.

'How did it go with the midwife?' he asked.

'OK—she's very happy with me and she's lovely, so I'm quite relieved. And I bought some new clothes because things are getting tight again.'

'It doesn't show yet.'

'That's because I'm wearing baggy clothes,' she said, and he smiled, but it didn't reach his eyes.

'I'm glad it's all OK. James wants to see you, by the way—he's had some glowing feedback from Plastics.'

'I'll find him in a minute. Jake, what's wrong?'

His face went blank, but his mouth tightened and he gave a short sigh. 'We lost two. A new dad, and a teenager. The ones I told you about yesterday.' His voice was angry, disgusted—and disappointed?

'It wasn't your fault,' she told him.

'I didn't say it was.'

'But you think it could have been. How many did you save, Jake? That's what you need to be asking yourself. Not how many you lost, but how many you didn't. And anyway, they didn't die here in the ED, did they? You said they'd all survived transfer to the other departments.'

'They did, but the man died in the night. The teen was in Theatre and was never going to make it. We knew that, but you never stop hoping.'

'And you think you could have missed something with the man who died in the night?'

How did she know what he was thinking? Right then he wasn't sure he did.

'I don't even know why he actually died or who treated him, but...yeah, I might have done, when I was triaging. I don't know, I can't see how, I was very thorough, but—'

'—you still think you did. Oh, Jake. Cut yourself some slack. You're only human, and you're a great doctor, and I'd trust you with my life.'

He swallowed. 'Well, let's hope it never comes to that.'

'It already did. You were leading when I was brought in.'

He frowned. 'But I didn't save your life, you would have been OK without me. It's not the same.'

'Except you worked on the principle that it could be more than it appeared. I've looked at my notes. I had all the scans, everything. You weren't taking any chances, and I don't believe you did yesterday. And biker Pete is still alive, and doing well, and I know how touch and go that was. You need to have faith in yourself, my love.'

My love? He didn't answer. He couldn't. He just hugged her, hard, and then went back to work feeling just a tiny bit better, those two small but sweet words echoing in his head.

CHAPTER EIGHT

HE FOUND HER at the end of her shift.

'How's your day been?' he asked, and she smiled.

'Oh, you know. Some good, some bad, some funny.'

'Funny weird?'

She felt her smile wobble. 'Funny hilarious, but also really sad. I had a guy in who'd tripped and cut his head. It was quite nasty, but it turned out he'd been running to improve his health, but he'd forgotten his specs and he didn't see the kerb and went flat.'

He frowned. 'Why is that funny?'

'Oh, that isn't, it was the way he told me about it, the way he sent himself up. He was just hilarious all the way through the treatment. He said he'd thought of taking up knitting, but he'd probably fall on the knitting needles and stab himself through the heart. I suggested playing cards, and then he told me his wife died recently so there was nobody to play with, but he might take up solitaire.

'It made me want to cry, and he hugged me when he left. He was so nice, and I felt so sorry for him. He was only trying to make his life better. His children had been nagging him to get out and about a bit more, but he didn't really know how to. I suggested he got himself a dog, and he said he'd been thinking about it, so I hope he does.'

'How old was he?'

'Seventy-eight. Not that old, but too old to hurl himself onto the pavement.'

'We're all too old for that,' Jake said drily, but his eyes were smiling. 'I'm nearly done, just got some notes to finish up. Are you busy tonight?'

She cast her mind over the clothes that needed washing, the house that could do with a dust and a vacuum, and he picked up the hesitation.

'It's OK if you are, but I wondered if you wanted to come round. I've got food in the fridge.'

'Healthy food? Because last night was delicious but it didn't qualify on the health front in any way!'

His mouth twitched. 'It's healthy, I promise.'

'Then yes, please, because my fridge is a bit of a sad event right now. I need to go home and shower and change—what time do you want me?'

Well, that was a leading question. He dragged his mind out of the bedroom.

'Seven-thirty?'

'Perfect. I'll see you then.'

She left with a smile, and he went back to finish off his notes on the last patient. And then, of course, there was a flurry of emergencies brought in, and it was nearly an hour later before he got away.

He walked briskly home, turned the oven on to heat, ran upstairs and showered, towelled his hair vaguely dry, tugged on some jeans and a T and ran back down to the kitchen.

He'd put the salmon fillets in the oven moments before she arrived, and he let her in.

'Sorry, I'm on the drag—we had an influx and I couldn't get away.'

'Par for the course,' she said with a sympathetic smile and followed him back to the kitchen. 'Anything I can do?'

'Yes, sit yourself down and talk to me. I've just got the veg to prep.'

Which, to be fair, took seconds—sugar snap peas, tenderstem broccoli and baby new potatoes, already in the pans to cook in minutes. He put the potatoes on the hob, poured them both a glass of sparkling elderflower and perched beside her at the breakfast bar.

They clinked their glasses, and their eyes met over the top and he felt heat surge through him just like it had on that first night. He turned away and looked down the garden, dragging his mind back into order.

'So, how are you? Apart from growing out of your clothes,' he said, and she gave him a wry smile.

'I'm… I think I'm OK. Having my parents to stay was lovely, and they talked a lot of sense.'

'In what way?'

'Life advice. Take every day as it comes, see how it goes. Nothing is guaranteed, think out of the box sort of stuff. And not to forget that they're there if ever I need them. Have you spoken to your mother again?'

'Yes. She's still less than sympathetic. She told me off again about being thirty-two and a doctor and should know better. Which I already knew, even before she drummed it into me the first time I talked to her about it.'

'Jake, you did nothing wrong.'

'Yes, I did. It's my golden rule—never have unprotected sex. And I broke it.'

'No, you didn't. It wasn't unprotected, I was on the pill!'

'Except nothing is one hundred percent, and I should have provided the backup.'

She rolled her eyes and shook her head. 'I'm never going to convince you it's not your fault, am I?'

He felt his mouth twitch into a smile, and said, 'Probably not. I need to check the veg.'

'That was delicious. Thank you.'

'You're welcome.' He cleared away their plates, peeled the lid off a pre-prepped tropical fruit salad and put it between them. 'Something to round it off,' he said, and handed her a fork.

She stabbed a cube of mango, and wondered what to say. She really didn't know much about him, apart from how he was at work, that he could cook, and that he took his responsibilities seriously. But what else?

Something to break the ice, to help her gain a little insight into this man who was the father of her child. Their child.

Which still seemed odd.

She chewed and swallowed and waved the fork at him. 'If you were having a dinner party, who would you invite? Anyone, living or dead.'

He stared at her for a second, then stabbed a bit of pineapple and quirked an eyebrow at her. 'Any rules?'

'No rules. Start with medical.'

'OK.' He chewed the pineapple thoughtfully, then waved his fork. 'Louis Pasteur, for his contribution to public health. He discovered vaccines and pasteurising milk, both of which have saved countless lives.'

She popped a grape in her mouth and nodded. 'Excellent choice. Who else?'

'Alexander Fleming, for his discovery of antibiotics, which have been and still are invaluable?'

'Anyone else?'

'No, your turn.'

'Florence Nightingale, for raising ward hygiene standards and making nursing a profession? Elizabeth Garrett Anderson, the first British woman to train as a surgeon. You?'

'Christiaan Barnard, for the first successful heart transplant.'

'What about non-medics?'

He speared another bit of mango and frowned. 'Barack Obama? And Michelle, of course. You?'

'Mother Teresa? Oh, and Pope Francis.'

Jake nodded slowly. 'That's really interesting. Can I add Nelson Mandela?'

'You can add anyone you want, there are no rules,' she said with a smile, and he nodded, stabbed a bit of kiwi, ate it and then surprised her.

'Whitney Houston?'

She felt her eyes widen. 'Wow! That's a bit left field,' she said with a chuckle, and he gave a wry smile.

'I grew up listening to my mother singing along to *I Will Always Love You.* I still don't know if she was thinking about my father when she sang it, but sometimes it would make her cry.'

'Wow. That's...oh, Jake... Your poor mum.'

'Yeah. But I was just a kid, and I didn't really get what was going on. I'd never met him, so it wasn't like there was a yawning void, it was just how it was, but not for her. And I didn't understand that.'

'No. I'm sure you didn't.' She laid a hand on his arm. 'I'm so sorry.'

'Yeah, me, too. Anyway, it's your turn.'

'OK.' She went back to the fruit to give herself thinking time, then swallowed and shrugged. 'Um...much more dull, but Martin Luther King? You?'

'He wasn't dull. But…hmm… David Attenborough?'

'Oh, yes! Definitely. He'd be a brilliant guest.' She cocked her head on one side and smiled at him. 'It would be a very interesting dinner party.'

'It would. I wonder what they'd all think of it.'

'They'd have plenty to talk about. I think they'd get on pretty well.'

He held her eyes, and she felt a wash of warmth, of something precious just out of reach. And then he said softly, 'I think we do, too.'

She looked away, the breath trapped in her throat, and the conversation ground to a halt.

She felt her pulse hitch. There was something familiar about it, about those words, this whole thing, and her heart was beating so hard she could hardly breathe.

I think we do, too.

She stopped playing with her fork and put it down and swallowed hard, then looked up and met his eyes. 'Have we done this before? This "Who would you invite?" thing?'

He hesitated, then said softly, 'Yes. Yes, we have.'

'That night.'

'Yes. In the restaurant.'

Her heartbeat picked up another notch, and she looked away. It was either that or kiss him, and the tension between them was palpable, but there on the fringes of her memory was something she still couldn't quite get hold of, some elusive feeling that she needed to understand before this went any further. Because she only had his word for what had happened and, after Steve, she was still struggling to trust.

You can trust him, you know you can.

Do I? Do I know that? Or do I just want to believe it?

She felt his fingers touch her face, turning it gently back to face him, and the raw need in his eyes, the longing, the sheer openness of his expression reeled her in.

His thumb brushed her lips, just a feather-touch, but she had to close her eyes.

'Lydia, look at me.'

His voice was soft, his breath drifting over her face, and she opened her eyes and met his, and felt her body stir into life.

'I want you so much,' he said, his voice a gruff murmur, and the open honesty of his words undid her.

She leant in and touched her lips to his, and she felt the ragged sigh of his breath as he cradled her neck in his hand and kissed her. Slowly, tenderly at first, and then more urgently, fanning the embers that had been smouldering for weeks, ever since she'd kissed him at the end of her first day, right here in this kitchen.

Before she'd known that she was carrying his baby.

'I want you,' he said, the words almost soundless, drifting against her lips, her cheek, down her throat to where the pulse was beating wildly. She arched her neck, and his lips traced her collarbone, the flick of his tongue laden with promise.

And she wanted him, too. So, so much…

'Come to bed with me,' he said, his voice a little ragged. 'Let me make love to you. Let me show you what it was like.'

Her body turned liquid, and his touch was so tender, reeling her in with every brush of his fingers against her skin.

Was this what happened before? This tender seduction? Not an accidental touch of our lips but a deliberate attempt to seduce me?

You don't know him well enough. It could all be lies.

He's not like Steve.

How do you know that?

She squeezed her eyes shut and sucked in a ragged breath as she pulled away.

'I… I don't think that would be a good idea. I think I should go now.'

He dropped his hands, breaking the connection between them that was threatening to push him over the edge of common sense and trying to work out what the hell he'd just done to frighten her away. The kiss? The words? He had no idea.

He swallowed hard and shifted away from her, creating a little more distance. Didn't work. He could still taste her, smell her—

'I'm sorry. I'll drive you home.'

'You don't need to do that. It's still light and I only live round the corner.'

'But it's getting dark, and they haven't caught the stabber yet. So I'll drive you, if you don't mind.'

She hesitated, then nodded, her eyes suddenly wary. 'Yes, you're right. It's probably sensible. Thank you.'

He slid off the stool, picked up his car keys and walked to the door with her close behind him, and when he pulled up outside her house she turned to him and thanked him again.

'You're welcome,' he said. 'I'll see you tomorrow. I'm on a late, so it'll be twelve.'

She nodded and got out, and he followed her to the door and waited until she was safely inside before saying goodnight, his hands rammed in his pockets to keep them under control.

He didn't kiss her—he didn't trust himself to get that close again, and she wouldn't want it, she'd told him that—but he could almost feel the soft press of her breasts against his chest, the gentle swell of their baby making its presence felt, and he ached to take her to bed, to undress her slowly and run his hands over that smooth baby bump. To lay his face against it, to press his lips to it and say hello.

Right before he made slow, sweet love to his baby's mother…

Not going to happen. Not now, and maybe never...

He took a step back, mentally and physically.

'Lock your door,' he murmured softly, and she nodded.

'I will. And thank you for feeding me and bringing me home. I'll see you tomorrow.'

He didn't answer. He just smiled and nodded and turned and walked back to the car, every step rebelling against his good intentions.

They won, and as she closed the door he drove off, reversed onto his drive, cut the engine and rested his head on the steering wheel.

Why had he said that about them getting on well?

What had it triggered in her? Something, for sure.

They'd said it in the restaurant, and that was probably the beginning of the chain of events that led to them ending up in bed. And tonight he'd kissed her. Kissed her, and asked her to go to bed with him.

He'd been so close to losing it. So close to taking her up to bed, and then something, he had no idea what, had freaked her out.

Although it was probably wise, because they *would* have ended up in bed. And he hadn't meant to do that, not yet. There was too much at stake, their relationship was too new, too important, and he couldn't do anything that might compromise it, but it didn't stop him wanting her. And hell, yes, he wanted her.

She was beautiful, responsive, funny, kind, not short of sass if she felt he needed cutting down to size—of course he wanted her! He wanted her so badly it was killing him. But it wasn't just physical, he realised, it was a deep-seated, yearning ache to hold her in his arms and tell her how much he loved her. And, given the chance, he would have done that tonight.

He swallowed.

Did he, though? Did he really love her? Or just want to?

He didn't know, and he couldn't be sure—and before they took that step he wanted to be sure that it was right for them both.

He was pretty sure it was right for him, but her?

Oh, she was responsive, but he already knew that, and all the time he'd been taking her out, wooing her, they'd been growing closer, in so many ways.

But did she love him? No. He didn't think so. Not with all her heart. She was still holding something back, something deep inside that was maybe afraid of being hurt.

Or that had been hurt before—by Steve? He could understand that. Claire's words still echoed in his head, even now.

Or was it just that he was—and maybe always would be—one step ahead of her? He *remembered* that night, he knew just how good it had felt to be with her, but she didn't know that, she didn't remember that—although tonight, maybe, she was getting closer to remembering.

And maybe she was holding back until she did, as if she didn't want to open her heart to him until then, until she knew what had gone before. He could understand that, and she meant too much to him for him to rush her, which was why he hadn't done anything foolish—until tonight.

And tonight, she'd pulled back and distanced herself from him because he'd said that they got along well together—or more likely because he'd lost the plot again and told her he wanted to take her to bed. It was only the truth, but maybe she wasn't yet ready to hear it. Or it had triggered something significant. And he had no idea which, or what.

He got out of the car, slammed the door and locked it, let himself in and went up to bed and lay there staring up at the ceiling and trying to work out where they went next, because right then he hadn't got a clue.

She didn't quite know what to think, but something fundamental had changed tonight.

It had all been going so well, and then he'd kissed her and it had triggered something—a memory of that night? She wasn't sure, and then everything had been moving too fast, and as soon as she'd said she should leave, it was as if a switch had flicked in his brain and he'd retreated.

Probably a good thing, under the circumstances. If they'd ended up in bed—and that was where they were headed, without a doubt—then it would cause a seismic shift in their relationship.

And she wasn't ready for that, she realised.

Not without love, and even if he said the words, she wasn't sure she'd dare to let herself believe them. Steve had told her that he loved her, and look how well that had gone.

Time to cool it—to distance herself a bit from Jake to protect her heart, because she was falling for him hard and fast, and yes, he wanted her physically, but when he'd suggested getting married, it had been a purely practical solution to a problem, not a profession of love.

Or at least it had been then, and without knowing beyond any doubt that he loved her now, she couldn't let herself fall any further under his spell. And until she could remember that night, until she really knew what had taken place between them, she would still feel unsure about him. She wanted to trust him, wanted to believe everything he'd told her about it, but the only way to know if he'd exaggerated her response to him was to go to bed with him.

And that was a minefield she was too scared to set foot on.

At least this way all options were still open, including getting married for all the cold, hard reasons he'd proposed as a way to solve the problem of financial legal security for her and the baby.

But at the heart of the 'problem' that his proposed marriage was designed to solve was a tiny living human being who'd done nothing wrong and hadn't asked for any of this.

That had to be her first and only priority. Love—if it ever happened—could wait.

That night marked a distinct turning point in their relationship.

They were still friendly, but in a very polite and guarded way, and in the next few days there was a distance between them that had gradually been shrinking over the last few weeks, and was now definitely back. With bells on.

They were being careful with each other, taking nothing for granted, with no more going out for meals, no more teasing touches or winks while they were at work, and definitely no more kisses.

He told himself it was better that way.

His heart didn't believe him, but just the fact of the gnawing ache for the rapport and familiarity they'd built up in that short time made him realise just how far and how hard he'd fallen for her.

And now she was distancing herself from him—she obviously didn't love him yet, not in the way he loved her, if at all, and he had no idea if she ever would. Ever could, either because of Steve, or because of not remembering how it had all started, and so not able to trust her feelings. He was almost sure that was what was holding her back, and if he put himself in her situation he'd feel exactly the same.

But he wanted a relationship with his child, he wanted to share his or her life, be an integral part of it, not just someone who rocked up at the weekends bearing gifts in compensation.

And he didn't want a platonic relationship with Lydia, he wanted it all, but if he couldn't have that—if they ended up living in the same house but living separate lives, like housemates, it would be a living hell, and he felt sick at the thought of it.

Yes, he'd suggested marriage, but it had been a knee-jerk reaction for all sorts of practical reasons, and the thought of it now filled him with dread.

And as she'd said at the time, they didn't even have a baby yet. Maybe he was worrying unduly. Maybe she just needed more time, less pressure. Traumatic retrograde amnesia usually resolved in time, so he'd just have to wait, give her time and space and hope that at some point she'd remember enough to trust him with her heart.

Time to take the pressure off.

She'd hardly seen him at work since that night. They'd been on different shifts, or he'd been busy, or—was he avoiding her?

It was her own fault. When he'd said how well they got on she'd felt suddenly scarily overwhelmed, little glimmers of memory hovering there, the emotion swamping her when he'd kissed her. She couldn't make any sense of it. It was all so complicated and confused, and she didn't know what to feel. And instead of talking about it, instead of asking him more about that night, she'd run away.

Or tried to, until he'd insisted on driving her home. And then he'd said goodnight at the door with his hands in his pockets and barely meeting her eyes. Why? It was such a contrast to the way they'd been getting on, and it had confused her even further.

And from that moment, he'd been distant.

Why? Because she'd pulled back when he'd wanted to take her to bed?

They needed to talk. A frank, open, honest conversation about what they felt, but she wouldn't know where to start.

And then her phone rang. Jake.

'Are you busy?'

'No, not really. Why?'

'Can I come round? I think we need to talk.'

For a moment she couldn't speak, and then she told him to come, hung up and swallowed hard, a sense of doom hanging over her.

Her doorbell rang just a few minutes later, and she let him in and her heart sank. His face was strained, that warm, tender smile absent, his eyes avoiding hers.

She led him into the sitting room and sat down quickly on the sofa before her legs gave way. He sat across from her, elbows resting on his knees, his eyes still not meeting hers.

'You said we need to talk,' she said.

'Yes, we do. About the other night.'

She nodded. 'I'm sorry I ran away.'

He looked at her then and searched her eyes, but his were unreadable. 'Why did you?' he asked softly.

She shrugged. 'I don't know. It all felt very familiar, but different, and I wasn't sure what was memory and what was imagination. And it was suddenly… I felt it all closing in on me.'

'I thought you did. Is that because of Steve?'

'I don't know. No—but—maybe. I think he trashed my ability to trust anyone, and I know I should be able to trust you. I'm just not sure if I can, or if I can trust myself. I just know I haven't got the answers that I need, and I don't know if I ever will.'

He nodded slowly. 'That's fine. I'm happy to give you space, I know you need it.'

So that was what he'd been doing for the last few days. 'I don't know if it's space I need, or time, or— Jake, what if I never remember? What have I lost? And how can I be sure that I felt the same way as you said you did?'

'You can't. Only you can know how you felt. And all I can do is tell you how I felt, and how you reacted to me. I can't give you any more than that, and I only wish I could. All I can give you is time.'

'But I don't have time! In four months' time I'll be a single mother, and everything will be different and I don't know how we're going to manage this.'

She blinked back tears and he nodded slowly, his eyes watchful. 'So what do you want me to do?'

She swallowed. 'I don't know. You talked about this getting married thing,' she said, and then ground to a halt.

'And?' he asked, after a heartbeat.

'I don't know what you had in mind…like, being properly married, or just cohabiting but separate, for the sake of the baby, or just… I don't know, just a legal arrangement.'

'What would you want it to be?'

Marriage.

'I don't know. That's why I'm asking you what you meant.'

'I'm not sure I had anything specific in mind. The legal thing first, obviously, and then whatever came naturally.'

'So where would we live? Together? Separately? How much of a commitment are you prepared to make, in terms of sharing the baby? What about night feeds, and walking the baby up and down when it's got colic? What about the school runs, and the nursery drop-offs? And what about leave? You've got critical exams coming up. Realistically, regardless of whether or not we're married, how much time can you give this? Or can't you? Because I'm beginning to think that you can't.'

He met her eyes, and for a long time he said nothing. Then he let out a long, slow breath and said, 'I don't think marriage is the issue here. I think it's more to do with what we feel about each other, and I don't think you're ready yet for more than friendship and support. You don't trust me—you want to, but you can't, and until you can, we won't make any progress.'

Her heart thrashed against her chest, but she lifted her chin and made herself hold his eyes.

'I didn't say we'd get married. I was just trying to clarify.'

'I know, but I'd left it on the table, and—'

'You've changed your mind.'

'No.' He paused for what felt like an age, and then said, 'When I suggested it, it was a knee-jerk reaction, a solution to a problem. And now I don't think it's the right solution for us, or certainly not yet. You don't remember what happened between us, and I think because of that you're holding something back, and that's not fair to either of us.

'I can't do any more to show you or tell you how it really was, and until you either remember or feel you can trust me, it'll always be there between us, that lack of trust, lack of certainty, and I don't think it would be right of us to make that commitment under those conditions, because if we aren't equally committed then one or both of us could get hurt, so I think it's easier and fairer not to put either of us in that situation—at least until and unless we're doing it for the right reasons, and right now I don't think we would be. I can still give you financial and legal security without that, and everything else we can work out down the line.'

He doesn't love me.

That was what he was saying, in so many words, just when she was beginning to think she could trust him. He didn't want to be tied to her. Maybe he just had cold feet, but it felt more than that, and she felt a block of ice settle in the place her heart had been, when all she wanted from him was reassurance.

'OK,' she said. It was the only word she could get out, the only thing she could formulate.

'It won't change my relationship with the baby, I still want to play a large part in its life, but I think for now we should keep it strictly platonic. We'll be in this relationship forever, and we can't afford to screw it up. We need to stay friends, at the very least, until we're ready for more, and I honestly don't think you're ready yet. But I'll still make sure that my pension goes to you if anything happens to me, and I'll draw up a will leaving my house to you, and obviously I'll pay you maintenance and do everything I can in terms of time commitments. Does that sound OK?'

OK? It was light years from OK, but she had no words to express how she felt, so she sat there and looked at him, unable to speak. She gave a small defeated shrug, and he got to his feet.

'I'm sorry,' he said heavily, and the words sounded as if they'd been dragged out of him.

'Don't be. At least I have clarity now. And I think you're right.'

'Good. I'll see you tomorrow.'

And, just like that, he walked out of her house and out of her life.

She held herself together until she heard his car drive away, and then she rolled over, her hands wrapped protectively over her baby, and cried until she could cry no more.

He went home on autopilot, shut the door behind him and dropped onto the sofa. He felt numb inside, hollowed out, his future stretching out in front of him, empty and meaningless.

No. In just over four months there'd be a child to think about, a child to love and guide through life—a child he'd see by arrangement. No waking in the night for a crying baby, no walking up and down shushing it while Lydia slept, because he wouldn't be there. She'd probably go home to her mother.

Would he be there for the birth? For the first word? The first teetering step?

Don't think about that now. Think about what you have to do.

He went into the dining room where he had his desk, and sat at it, downloaded a basic will and filled it in with all the information he could muster, then he printed three copies and put them in an envelope by the door, then went on the NHS pension site and put her down as the person to receive his pension in the event of his death. Then he went back to the sofa, scrolled his phone until he found *I Will Always Love You*, pressed play and turned it up loud.

His chest ached and he rubbed it with the heel of his hand. It felt tight, as if an iron hand had closed around it and was crushing it, cutting off his air supply. He tried to breathe in but his chest heaved, and he realised he was crying—huge, racking sobs that shredded him inside and left him exhausted and bereft.

And cold. So cold, deep inside where his heart had been.

He reached for the throw and pulled it round himself, but it smelt of Lydia, and he buried his nose in it and cried again, while Whitney Houston sang the soundtrack of his heart.

He might have slept. He didn't know. It was five when he looked at his phone, then nearly six. His shift started at seven, so he dragged himself upstairs and had a shower, then went to the basin to shave and clean his teeth. And caught sight of himself.

His eyes were red-rimmed and bloodshot, his mouth was a grim line, and his cheeks were pale and hollow, as if all the life had been sucked out of them.

People would think he'd been on a bender. Tough. He shaved, cut himself and swore, then stuck a tiny bit of tissue on it to help it clot while he cleaned his teeth and dragged a comb through his hair.

He didn't bother to look at himself again, just threw the

comb down and went into his bedroom, pulled on some clean clothes and went downstairs.

Two strong coffees and a piece of toast forced down started to revive him, but his mind was in turmoil and he seriously considered phoning in sick.

Such a cop-out. Anyone would think someone had died.

He slung his phone in his pocket, walked briskly to work and arrived at ten past seven.

James took one look at him and opened his mouth, and he growled, 'Don't ask.'

'OK, I won't, but if you need to go home, just say the word.'

'I don't need to go home. I've got something I want you to witness. Let's go to your office. Sam, I need you, too.'

'What?'

He towed them into the office, shut the door, pulled the envelope out of his pocket and took the three copies of the will out and sat down and signed them, then handed them to James, who looked him in the eye and said, 'Is there something I don't know?'

'No. It's just something I've been meaning to do since I knew Lydia was pregnant. Just sign it, please. It's not something we need to talk about.'

So James signed it, all three copies, and then passed them to Sam, who signed them without a word then gave them back to Jake, looking him in the eye.

'I don't know what's going on, mate, but if you need to unload, I'm here.'

'Likewise,' James said, and got to his feet. 'Right, we need to get to work. And, Jake, you're on cubicles.'

'*Cubicles?*'

'Yes, I'm not having you in Resus. I don't know what's

happened and I'm not going to ask, but I don't need a doctor whose mind isn't on the job.'

'My mind's on the job,' he growled, and turned on his heel and walked out, his teeth gritted. He'd hoped to spend most of his shift in Resus, out of the way of Lydia, but she wasn't on until twelve today so at least he'd have the morning, and hopefully by then he'd be fine and James would let him back in there.

Except he wasn't fine, because at a quarter to twelve a young woman staggered in with a stab wound to her chest.

'Don't let him in here, please don't let him in here—he's following me!' she begged him, hanging onto his arm as he led her through, and he shut the door and hit the button for Security, and all hell broke loose.

The doors were shut, security staff were everywhere, he could hear police sirens coming—and then the woman screamed and he turned to find a man there with a thin kitchen knife, his eyes murderous. He must have already got into the unit somehow, and now he was going to try and kill her.

'He's in here!' Jake yelled, but before anyone could get there the man raised the knife and went for her.

Jake didn't stop to think, he just lunged at him, knocking him off-balance to put himself between them, and then, just as the curtains were wrenched aside and the police poured in, he felt a punch land over his left kidney.

It didn't hurt for a second, but then the pain hit and took his breath away, and he put his hand on his side and it came away covered in blood.

He stared at it numbly, and then felt his legs start to shake.

He'd been stabbed?

The cubicle was full of police now, and one of them looked at him and yelled for help, and James came running.

'He's been stabbed—' the policeman said, and James half dragged, half carried him towards Resus.

'I knew I should have sent you home,' he muttered, and Jake tried to laugh but it hurt too much.

'Let's get him on a bed and get a line in fast,' James was saying, and Oliver was there, trying to look at the wound, and Sam trying to get a line in, Julie carefully cutting away his scrubs to reveal his whole body, just in case there were other wounds, until he was lying there naked, and feeling weaker by the second.

'Is she all right?' he asked, his voice unsteady. 'The woman. He's trying to kill her.'

'Don't worry about her—the police have got him and she's being looked after,' James was saying, and he could hear him snapping out instructions to the others, but his voice was coming and going and Jake realised he was bleeding out.

He heard someone talking about major haemorrhage protocol, and he realised that was for him. 'I'm A-positive,' he said, but he didn't know if they'd heard him.

Julie was holding a mask over his face now, telling him to breathe, and he pushed it out of the way. 'Where's Lydia?' he asked.

'She's not in yet. She'll be OK.'

'Need to see her—tell her things.'

'The police won't let her in, Jake.'

'Need to see her. Please. Quickly…'

'Jake, stay with us.' That was Oliver, his voice far away.

He could hear his phone ringing, then Sam's voice as he answered it, and then someone was slapping his cheek and saying, 'Stay with us,' but he couldn't…

* * *

Lydia arrived at the hospital a little late, dreading bumping into Jake, not knowing how she'd keep going, and then the place was swarming with police and they wouldn't let her in.

'You have to let me in—I'm a doctor here.'

'We can't, madam, I'm sorry, there's been an incident.'

'What kind of incident?'

'I'm afraid I can't tell you.'

So she rang Jake, but it was Sam who answered it, and her heart slammed against her ribs.

'Sam, what's going on—they won't let me in!'

'Let me talk to them.'

She handed the phone over, and the policeman's face paled and he handed the phone back and ordered them to let her through the cordon.

'Sam? What's going on?' she asked as she ran in, and his words took all her breath away.

'Jake's been stabbed. He's in Resus, he's about to go to Theatre. Come quickly, he's asking for you.'

Oh, no, please, God, no…

She ran down the corridor, let herself in with her fob and went straight to Resus, and there was Jake, lying naked on his side, with a knife wound in his flank and James, Oliver and Sam all working on him. There was a drip up and they were squeezing the bag to force the blood into him, and Julie had an oxygen mask and was holding it over his face, telling him to breathe.

And then she was there beside him, stroking his hair back off his face with shaking hands, and he opened his eyes, pushed the mask away and reached out a bloodied hand to her, cupping her cheek while tears streamed down it.

'I…love you,' he said, the words weak, fractured, as he forced them out of his mouth. 'Wrote…a will…last night… You'll be… OK…'

'No! No, Jake, don't talk like that,' she sobbed. 'You can't die—I love you! Don't die, please, you can't leave me, I love you, I love you…'

'Love you…too…sorry…'

Someone took hold of her to ease her away, and she kissed his hand and then he was gone, whisked out of the door with all of them running alongside.

'Don't let him die,' she begged, trying to run after them, but her legs were like jelly and she couldn't keep up, and she turned and found herself in Julie's arms.

'I want to go with him,' she said brokenly, and Julie hugged her.

'I know. I'll come up with you, and we can wait outside.'

'I want to go in!'

'You can't,' Julie said firmly, 'but I'll stay with you. They're doing everything they can for him, Lydia, you know that.'

'But what if it's not enough?'

'He's young and strong and fit.'

'So are half the kids that get stabbed and die! It means nothing. Nothing…'

They reached the waiting area outside the theatre suite, and Julie sat her down and handed her a paper cup of water from the chiller. She sipped it mechanically, on autopilot, and then she saw the blood on her hand—Jake's blood—and she spilt the water all down her front and started to cry again, rocking rhythmically back and forth, her blood-streaked hand over her mouth, until she was too tired to rock any longer, and she leant against Julie, her hand cradled over their baby, and wept silently…

* * *

It seemed like an eternity before the door swung open and someone came out, and she straightened up, her heart racing.

'Are you Lydia?' he asked, and she searched his eyes for a smile, but it wasn't there. She grabbed Julie's hand and clung to it.

'Yes—yes, I'm Lydia. How is he? Is he—?'

'He's alive, and he's come through it well. We've had to remove his left kidney, but the injury was very localised and he'll be all right. He's been very lucky. We're taking him through to Recovery now, so you can come and see him, and then he'll be moved to HDU.'

The High Dependency Unit.

'He's not going to die?'

'Not of this, no,' the surgeon said, and he smiled. 'He'll be all right. He'll be sore, but he'll be all right.'

CHAPTER NINE

WHY DO I hurt so much?

He couldn't think, couldn't do anything except moan with the pain, and then someone was saying, 'It's OK, Jake. It's all over now, we'll give you some more pain relief,' and it all went away…

They moved him to a side room in HDU and Lydia went with them, but it seemed like forever before he woke again.

She sat beside him, holding his hand and stroking her thumb rhythmically over the back of it, a gentle sweep to reassure him and tell him he wasn't alone, and to reassure herself that his skin was warm, his blood—or the blood of several public-spirited donors—was circulating as it should, and she watched the monitor, followed the steady, even beat of his heart, his blood oxygen level a reassuring ninety-eight percent.

Every half hour a nurse came in and checked and made a note on his chart at the foot of the bed, and they always asked if there was anything she needed, but the only thing she needed was for the man she loved to be all right.

And so she waited, as he must have waited beside her after her accident, and she held his hand and watched over him.

She had no idea how long she'd been sitting there, or

what the time was. Someone had brought her a cup of tea, but she didn't drink it because she didn't want to have to leave him for a comfort break, so she waited, and she waited, and then at last the monitor showed his heart rate pick up and start to race.

She stared at his face, and there was a flicker of his eyelids, and he clenched his teeth and let out a low moan.

'Jake? It's Lydia. You're OK, I'm here.'

His eyes flickered open, and he turned his head a fraction and met her eyes, and she could read confusion in that puzzled gaze.

'Side hurts.'

'You were stabbed in the ED. Do you remember?'

His eyes widened, and he sucked in his breath. 'How is she? The woman?'

'I think she's OK. She's certainly better off than you.'

'Good. That's good…'

His eyes drifted shut again, and she let him sleep, and then James appeared.

'Has he woken yet?' he murmured, and she nodded.

'Just, a little while ago. He asked about the woman.'

'She'll be fine, and her partner is now heading for a nice long sentence, with any luck. She told the police he was the one in the amusement arcade, so he's got a lot to answer for. How are you?'

She sighed, and it sounded a little shaky. Not surprising, really. 'I'm OK now—now I know he's all right. I thought he was going to die, with what he said in Resus.'

'I know. It's the weirdest thing. He brought three copies of a will in this morning and got me and Sam to witness them. It's almost like he knew.'

She shook her head, her eyes welling with tears. 'We sort of broke up last night, but he said I'd be OK, he'd make sure I was, and it's not the first time he's talked about that. When he suggested we get married because it offered me security if anything happened to him, I asked him if he was planning on dying any time soon, and he said no, but accidents happen, and then…'

'This wasn't really an accident. He deliberately put himself between them. That's how he got stabbed, trying to save her.'

She shook her head, her eyes filling with tears. 'Idiot. That sounds so like him. It's exactly the sort of *stupid* thing he'd do. He always puts everyone else first.'

Jake's fingers tightened on hers, and he turned his head and gave her a wry smile.

'Why are you two talking about me?' he slurred.

'Because you're the most interesting thing that's happened today,' James said drily, 'but that's fine, we can talk about the weather if you like.'

He gave James a sideways glance and his mouth kicked up in a smile. 'Very funny. Thanks for saving my life, by the way.'

'My pleasure. We can't afford to lose you.' James leant over and ruffled his hair. 'And we would have missed you, even though you're annoying. I'll leave you two alone now.'

He went out, and Jake's eyes met Lydia's and held. 'Did you mean it—what you said in Resus?'

'That I love you? Yes, Jake, I absolutely meant it, from the bottom of my heart.'

'Good, because I love you, too…'

His eyes closed, and he gave a small grunt and his legs moved restlessly.

'Are you in pain?'

'Yeah. I think I need something a bit pokier than whatever they've given me.'

'I'll get someone,' she said, and she stood up and leant over him and touched her lips to his, and he lifted his hand, cradled her cheek and kissed her back.

'I won't be long,' she promised, and she saw the flicker of a smile on his lips before he pressed them together again.

She went out onto the ward and told them, then went back to his side, where she could sit with him and hold his hand so he'd know he wasn't alone, and she would know he was still alive.

Bit by bit, and day by day, he healed.

They removed the urinary catheter on the second day, to his relief, and got him out of bed, which hurt like hell and gave him a better idea of just how lucky he'd been.

If you could call it luck. But he did. He could have died. He hadn't thought about it at the time, but throwing himself between an injured woman and the madman intent on killing her—his baby might have ended up like him, fatherless and with a mother whose heart had been broken.

And that played on his mind. He kept reminding himself that he'd saved the woman's life, but at what cost? And would he do it again?

Maybe. Or maybe do something less dangerous, like hurl a chair at him? That would be wiser. And he needed to think about something else.

Hard, when there was nothing else to do but lie there and think, so he picked up his phone and scrolled through the news, which was every bit as bad.

But Lydia was with him a lot of the time, and his mother and sister came, clucking and fussing and telling him off for not calling them sooner.

'I didn't want them to worry you,' he said, and anyway,

Lydia had been there and he didn't want that precious time with her compromised.

His mother told him off for trying to get himself killed, too, but he brushed it aside and tried not to think about his baby being fatherless, because he was pretty sure he'd do it again in the same circumstances and that scared him.

They came again later in the day, when Lydia was there, and they both hugged her as if they were pleased that she was in his life.

He was glad about that, as he had no intention of letting her go ever again.

And then, to his great surprise, and Lydia's, her parents came. She was there with him, straightening the sheet after helping him back into bed, and there was a knock on the door and they came in.

'Mum, Dad? What are you doing here?' she asked.

'We were worried,' her mother said, and she walked up to the bed, bent over and kissed his cheek. 'How are you, Jake? Are they looking after you?'

He smiled, still slightly stunned that they were there. 'I'm doing okay,' he said. 'It's a bit of a slow process, but Lydia's been here a lot of the time.'

'And he's the most impatient patient,' Lydia said drily, and he felt his mouth twitch.

'I don't know what you're talking about,' he said, and looked up at her father and held out his hand.

'Mr Fraser. Good to meet you at last. I think we need to send the girls off for a coffee, don't you?'

Her father's mouth opened and shut, suppressing a smile, and he shook Jake's hand and said, 'I think that might be an excellent idea. I'd like a black Americano, please, when you come back, ladies.'

'Make that two,' Jake tagged on, and Lydia rolled her

eyes, hooked her arm through her mother's and led her away, and Jake propped himself up a bit better and looked her father in the eye.

'I'm glad you're here. There's something I want to say to you, and she'd probably kill me for it, but here goes. I'm not going to ask for her hand in marriage, as I'm pretty sure she'd say it's her hand and she'll put it where she wants to, but I love her, and I love her more with every day, and I want to marry her and spend the rest of my life with her.

'I know we haven't done anything the conventional way, but if she hadn't had that accident I'm absolutely sure we would have been together now anyway and planning our future, and I'd very much like your blessing for that.'

Her father held his eyes steadily, and then he smiled and held out his hand and shook Jake's again firmly.

'My pleasure. I've heard a lot about you, Jake, and I've been wanting to meet you for some time. We're so grateful that she's found someone who truly loves her, and I believe you do.'

'Oh, I do, I absolutely do. I think I have right from the start. She just took a bit of convincing.'

'She told us you'd asked her to marry you the day she found out she was pregnant, and I thought that was a bit rash and hasty but, having just listened to you, heard what you've said, and knowing how very much she cares for you, I have to say we're both absolutely delighted that she's found someone who'll love her as she deserves to be loved. And she certainly loves you. I have absolutely no doubt about that.'

He stared at her father for a moment, and then looked away, blinking back sudden unexpected tears.

'Thank you,' he said, his voice choked, and he had to swallow hard.

'So, have you asked her again? Because I know she said no.'

He shook his head. 'No, I haven't. I'm… I'm going to save that until I'm up and about again. I want to take her back to where it started, and maybe ask her there, or afterwards, when we're alone so she's not put on the spot in a full restaurant. I'm going to do things properly this time.'

'Just in case you're wondering, I'm pretty sure she'll say yes. She was beside herself when she phoned us after you were stabbed, and she said if she had her way, she'd never let you out of her sight again.'

He was speechless for a moment, then he smiled and said, 'Wow. That's—um… Yeah. Thanks.'

The door opened, and Lydia and her mother walked in armed with a cardboard tray of hot drinks and a bag of something he was hoping were blueberry muffins.

'So, what have you two been talking about?' Lydia asked, eyeing him and her father with a barely disguised smile.

'Oh, just this and that,' Jake said, disarming her before her father could reply, and then jerked his head in the direction of the paper bag. 'So, what's in there?'

'Your favourite,' she said, and handed him a blueberry muffin. 'I'm trying to build you up a bit, but you can save some for me.'

She leant over and dropped a kiss on his lips, and his arm snaked up and caught her so he could kiss her again. Then he let her go with a smile, and tore a chunk off the muffin and handed it to her.

'Is that all I get?'

'For now. As you say, I've got to build myself up.'

It took six weeks to build himself up, bit by bit. The sutures came out after a fortnight, when the skin was properly healed, and he spent the time pottering at home, sitting in the garden and enjoying the late October sun, and he even cut the grass after a week or so of boredom.

Lydia came every day after work, and after they'd eaten they'd lie on his bed and talk and hold hands. One night she said, 'I can feel it kicking,' and laid his hand over the spot, and his eyes welled up. They were doing a lot of that. She would stay until it was getting dark, but then she'd kiss him goodnight and go home, 'So you can rest' as she put it.

After four weeks he went back to work on a reduced shift, and he was working only in Minors, and only in the day, pacing himself until he was fully recovered.

And then, after six weeks, when he was as near to normal as he'd be for a while, he asked her out to dinner.

'That would be nice,' she said. 'When?'

'Friday.'

'This Friday? Won't the restaurants be busy?'

'Probably, but I've booked,' he told her, but he didn't tell her he'd booked it five weeks ago, and he didn't tell her that James had deliberately not rostered her on for the Friday afternoon or the weekend. Nor did he tell her what else he'd done. That could wait.

Friday dawned bright and sunny, and Lydia spent the morning at work, fizzing slightly inside because there'd been something about Jake when he'd asked her if she'd like to go out for dinner that had teased her spidey senses and made her wonder…

Laura was on duty too that morning, now looking nearly as noticeably pregnant as she was, and Lydia told her that they were going out for dinner and she didn't know what to wear.

'I haven't got anything really nice that fits me now.'

'So go shopping. There's a great little second-hand maternity clothes shop in town, and it has lots of really good stuff. Why don't you have a look in there?'

So she did, just as soon as she'd changed, and Laura was right, it was a fabulous little shop and most of the clothes were immaculate. She found an elegant midi wrap dress in a soft silky fabric with a delicate floral pattern, which would go perfectly with the only shoes she had that would fit the bill, because he'd told her they'd be walking to wherever it was.

He still hadn't told her where, and she was gently fizzing with excitement when the doorbell rang. She took one last look in the mirror, checked her lippy and ran downstairs barefoot, her pumps dangling from her fingers.

'Hi,' she said, and ran her eyes over him. He was wearing beautifully cut smart trousers, a white shirt open at the neck and a jacket, and she realised her dress was just right.

'Will I do?'

He smiled slowly, his eyes warm. 'You'll very definitely do. You look gorgeous.'

She felt her cheeks colour. 'Thank you. Will I need a coat?' she added, and he said she might, so she ran back upstairs and came down with a soft cashmere scarf and the only coat that would still go round her.

'Ready?'

She slipped her pumps on and smiled. 'Yes, I'm ready,' she said, and she shut the door and tucked her arm into his. She fell into step beside him and breathed in the enticing and evocative scent of cologne that drifted from his body. It smelt familiar, but she wasn't sure that he'd worn it before.

Maybe that night…?

'So, is it far?'

'Not very—it's just a stroll downhill to the seafront.'

Her heart picked up a beat and she could feel the adrenaline pumping. Was he taking her back to Zacharelli's, the restaurant where it had all started? Would she remember?

Don't overthink it.

They walked slowly down through residential streets lined with elegant Victorian houses, and then they came out onto the seafront and he turned left and walked a little further, past a bistro and a café, and then he stopped in front of a restaurant—Zacharelli's—and smiled at her.

'Here we are,' he said, and she wasn't sure but he'd sounded a little—nervous? He ushered her up the steps and through the door into a bustling space filled with tables, almost all of which were occupied. Someone appeared immediately and showed them to a window table, and she sat down and looked around, a strange feeling creeping over her, and her heart started to beat faster.

'This is our table,' she said, quite sure now, and he nodded, his eyes hopeful.

'Yes. Yes, it is. Do you remember?'

'Maybe. I've been waiting for ages for you to bring me here.'

'It needed a proper occasion,' he said, and her heart skipped a beat.

'So, are we celebrating the fact that you didn't die?'

He smiled. 'That, too.'

'Can I get you some drinks?'

She hauled her eyes off his face and looked up at the server. 'Do you have any alcohol-free sparkling wine?'

'Yes, we do—we have a very nice dry Prosecco which is zero.'

'Thank you. I'll have one of those.'

'Make that two,' he chipped in, 'or actually, just bring us the bottle.'

'Of course.'

She put the menus in front of them and Lydia looked down and scanned the options. She was torn between the risotto and the fish, and she bit her lip and hesitated.

'I don't know what to have.'

'I've been told the *risotto con pollo* is very good.'

'Right, well, that's that sorted, then. What are you having?'

'Ah, well, I'm not sure. Some kind of fish, I think.'

'Mmm. I was debating the seafood skewer, but I love a really good creamy risotto.'

'I think I'll have the skewer,' he said, and he hailed the server.

The drinks came, and she lifted her glass and held it out to him. 'Here's to you not dying,' she said, with a little shake in her voice, and he smiled and clinked her glass with his.

'I'll definitely drink to that,' he said, and then he steered the conversation on.

'So why did you choose Yoxburgh?' he asked, and she shrugged.

'Good reputation, they had the right job at the right level for me at the right time, and I looked it up on the internet and it looked a lovely place to live. Why did you choose it?'

'Oh, very much the same reasons. Good rep, right job, the seaside—what's not to like?'

'Do you have any regrets?'

'No. Not about that.'

She searched his eyes, and he looked thoughtful and a little sad.

'What then? And I don't mean the fact that I'm pregnant.'

'I don't regret that at all. No. It's… I don't know. The time we spent apart, after your accident. I wish I'd got in contact, come to see you in Southampton, taken you out maybe.'

'Would you have told me about that night if I hadn't asked?'

He nodded slowly. 'Yes. Yes, I would. I didn't want to, but—it's only fair you should know what happened. I just wasn't sure how to tell you and I was hoping you'd remember.'

'I had to wring it out of you.'

He winced. 'Yeah. Sorry about that. It just felt so odd, having such clear memories and knowing that it was totally lost to you. I'm still gutted about that.'

'Don't be, it's one of those things. So, we played that "Who would you invite to your dinner party" game here?'

He smiled again. 'Yes. Yes, we did.'

'Any differences?'

His smile became a little sad, thoughtful. 'Not many. I flung in Whitney Houston the last time because that's how I was feeling right then.'

'Oh, Jake… And then I ran away. I'm so sorry.'

They were interrupted by the arrival of their food, and his hanging skewer with its chunks of salmon, monkfish and giant king prawns looked amazing.

'Now I've got food envy,' she said, and he raised his hands.

'Want to swap?'

'No. I want this risotto, it smells amazing, but be warned, we might have to come again.'

His lips twitched, and she picked up her cutlery, took

the first mouthful and sighed with delight. 'Oh, this is just delicious.'

'Good. Want to try a prawn? It's well cooked so it'll be safe.'

He held it out to her on his fork, and she closed her lips round it and drew it off, and his eyes flared.

She was sure that the prawn was delicious, too, but right then all her focus was on the man she loved and the way he was looking at her.

He reached across, scooped up a bit of her risotto, and she couldn't take her eyes off him as his lips closed around it and drew it off his fork. How could he make eating risotto so darned sexy?

She dragged her eyes off him and focused on her food, and the taste of it, the texture, the smell, all coalesced, and she looked up at him, certain now.

'I had this before.'

His eyes flared a little and he went still. 'Yes, you did.'

'And you had that.'

He nodded, and she picked up her drink and took a mouthful and set her glass down with exaggerated care.

'We had a glass of Pinot.'

'We did. And then we walked home.'

She ate the last of her risotto and he finished the skewer, and then their eyes met and he smiled slowly.

'Time to go?' he asked, and she nodded.

'I think it is.'

They walked slowly back up the hill towards his house, and his heart was pounding in his chest—partly because he was still recovering, but mostly because of what was to come. Her fingers were threaded through his and he stroked the side of her thumb with his, just as she had when he'd been lying in the hospital bed after his surgery.

And when they got to his house he opened the door and closed it behind them, and she turned towards him and took his face in her hands and kissed him.

Properly, thoroughly kissed him. Not a tentative peck, a little graze, a teasing linger, but a full-on, let's-go-to-bed kiss.

He lifted his head and stared down into her eyes and all he could see was love.

'Come to bed with me,' he murmured, and she smiled and said,

'I thought you'd never ask.'

He led her upstairs, into the big bedroom across the front of the house, and he closed the curtains and dimmed the lights.

She was glad of that, because it brought an air of romance to the occasion—and it was an occasion. A significant one.

They'd been dancing round this for weeks, and now, as he reached for her dress, undid the tie at the front and slowly eased the sides apart, she watched his eyes flare. His lips parted and he let out a breath and reached out his hand and laid it tenderly over the curve of their baby.

And then he looked up and their eyes met, and he took a step back and slowly peeled off his clothes. It was the third time she'd seen him naked. The first had been in this room, the second in Resus when he was covered in blood and doing his damnedest to die, and now, with an angry scar that curved around his left side between his hipbone and his ribcage.

She reached out and touched it gently. 'Does it still hurt?'

'A little. We might have to be a bit careful.'

'We will.'

She slipped the dress off her shoulders and let it fall to the floor, unclipped her bra and dropped it on top, then the scrap of lace that was the last of her pretty underwear that still fitted, and then he took a step forward, naked now and unashamedly aroused, and drew her into his arms.

She could feel the jut of his erection against her skin, the warmth of his body, the drift of his breath over her face as he bent his head to kiss her again.

'I want you,' he breathed, his voice barely a whisper, 'I've wanted you ever since that first night,' and she cradled his face in one hand and felt his throat working, his pulse thrashing under her little fingertip.

'I want you, too,' she said softly.

'Are you sure?'

'Very sure,' she said, and turned away from him, crossing to the bed and peeling back the covers.

He went round to the other side and lay down carefully, and she reached out and touched his face.

'Are you really OK to do this yet?'

'Much more OK to do it than not to do it,' he said with a wry little smile, and she ran her hand over his chest, over the light scatter of hair that arrowed down his abdomen.

She remembered the feel of it, the hot silk of his skin, the tease of the hair against her fingertips, the ribs under her hand that rose and fell with every breath, his breathing quickening as her hand slid slowly lower, fingers splayed, teasing him.

He groaned as her fingers closed around him, and he grabbed her hand and held it still.

'Don't—I can't—'

She let go, caught his hand in hers and held it against her naked breast, and he cradled it gently and bent his head towards her and kissed it. She could feel the graze of his stubble teasing her skin, the nipple peaking as he moved his attention to the other one.

'They're different. Fuller. And this…'

He ran his hand down over the swell of her abdomen, his fingers splayed, and then his eyes widened and he smiled.

'Hello, little one.'

He bent to kiss it, and then gave a tiny grunt and stopped, dropping back against the mattress and grimacing.

'Are you OK?'

'Yeah, that might have been rather ambitious. Maybe it's a bit soon to do this.'

'Unless I do all the work?'

He searched her eyes, her pupils flared with arousal, and his heart thrashed against his ribs. 'I don't care what we do or how we do it, just so long as I can lie here with you and hold you.'

'I'm sure we can do better than that with a little ingenuity,' she said, and he smiled. And then gasped as she straddled him and lowered herself achingly slowly until he thought he was going to go insane.

He grabbed her hips and lifted himself against her, ignoring the warning ache from his side, and then she started to move. Slowly, tauntingly, driving him crazy. He reached down, his fingers searching, and found his target, and she gasped and clenched her legs around his hips, rocking slowly against him as the tension built and then exploded in wave after wave of sensation.

And then she lay against him, breathless, propped up on her hands as she shifted her weight to the side, and he rolled with her, their bodies still locked together, as the echoes died away and their hearts slowed.

'I love you, Lydia,' he said, his voice breaking on the words, 'so much,' and she wrapped her arms around him and whispered,

'I love you, too.'

They didn't move for a while, he because he actually wasn't sure he could, and she because he was half lying on her and pinning her down.

'Are we just going to stay like this forever?' she said, her breath teasing over his skin and making him want her all over again.

'I'm happy if you are.'

'I don't think you are,' she said, studying his face thoughtfully, and he gave a little shrug.

'Not sure how to move.'

'Oh, Jake—I didn't mean to hurt you!'

'You didn't hurt me, and if I remember rightly, I suggested it, so let's not go there.'

He sucked in a breath, shifted his hips and rolled away from her with a grunt, and she followed him, lying with her head on his shoulder and her fingers splayed against his chest.

'I can feel your heart beating,' she said, and he laughed softly and kissed her.

'That can only be a good thing.' And then he felt his smile die, and he stroked the hair away from her face.

'Can I ask you something?'

She frowned. 'Of course you can.'

He reached out and took her hand in his, pressing his lips to her fingers. And then he asked, 'Why *did* you walk away that night? Was it really just the memories, or was it me? Did I do something wrong?'

'No. I just panicked. I've been steadily falling more and more in love with you ever since I got back here, but you don't give a lot away and every time we got close, you pulled away—and then I did, because I was afraid.'

'Afraid of what? Not of me, surely?'

'No. Not *of* you, but afraid of *loving* you. I think Steve broke something in me, and when I couldn't remember that night, I didn't know if I could dare to believe in you. And then when you talked about us not getting married, I thought you meant you didn't want to be with me, and that broke my heart.'

His hand tightened on hers, his grip almost painful in its intensity, and his eyes glistened with tears. 'Oh, Lydia. I've loved you since that first night, but I didn't think I could tell you that, and I was afraid you wouldn't understand just how beautiful it had been to be together, how perfect it had felt, like we were destined to be together. It wasn't just incredible sex, it was so, so much more, so much deeper. It felt as if we'd reached out and touched each other's souls, and I didn't think I could tell you that, I thought you'd think I was making it up just to get you back into bed.'

'Why would you do that? I don't know you that well, but I know you better than that, and I know you'd never lie to me. And it *was* incredible—and yes, it did feel like you'd reached out and touched my soul, but I didn't know that when you kissed me in your kitchen and asked me to go to bed with you because I couldn't remember, and that scared me, but I felt it now, too, just the same as I did the first time.'

He stared at her, daring to feel a little leap of joy. 'You remember?'

She nodded. 'Only snatches of it—things in the restaurant, like sharing the food, walking back, the feel of your skin against mine, the touch of your hands on my body, the feel of your skin under my fingers, the look in your eyes—so I know we've done this before, I've always felt that, and now I can remember—not all of it, but more than enough to know that our baby was conceived on a beautiful and very special night,' She broke off, swallowed, then went on, 'And I can't tell you how much that matters to me.'

He stroked her face, wiping away her tears, and he cradled her cheek in his hand and kissed her. 'You don't need to tell me. I can see it in your eyes, and I'm so happy for you that you've got it back. I know how important it was to you.'

'It was. It is, and I want to be with you forever. Will you marry me, Jake? Not because I'm having your baby, not to tick the boxes, but because you love me, too?'

His eyes welled with tears. 'That was meant to be my line,' he said, his voice cracking, and she reached out a gentle hand and laid it against his cheek, stroking the tears away.

'So, will you?' she asked, 'Will you marry me, Jake?' and he nodded, swallowing hard.

'Of course I'll marry you, Lydia. It would be a privilege, and I'll do everything I can to make sure that you and our baby are happy,' he said, his voice cracking again, and he gathered her up against his heart and held her there, where she belonged…

EPILOGUE

THEIR WEDDING WAS a small, simple one, held in the hospital chapel surrounded by their families and friends, and the colleagues who'd managed to get away.

His mother and her husband were there, his sister Suze, Lydia's parents and her sister Steph, husband David and their three children, and behind them were some of the people without whom Jake wouldn't now be alive—James, Sam, Oliver, Julie, and some of the surgical team and the nurses on HDU, as well as a smattering of old friends, but not Tom and Laura, because she'd gone into labour this morning.

And in Lydia's mother's arms was Hamish Fraser Warren, born six weeks ago in a blizzard at the end of January and delivered at home by his father because apparently he'd been in a hurry to join them.

Their vows were heartfelt, not a marriage to tick legal boxes but a bone-deep commitment to love, honour and cherish each other till the end of their days, and when he slipped the ring onto her finger and kissed her there wasn't a dry eye in the house.

After the simple ceremony they went to Zaccarelli's, the restaurant that had been such a pivotal part of their relationship, and that held such a special place in both their hearts.

Lydia was wearing the pretty wrap dress she'd worn the night that she'd asked Jake to marry her, not knowing that in his jacket pocket there was a ring that he'd been waiting to give her when they got home. She'd derailed his romantic plans and they'd ended up in bed, but he hadn't complained about that, and he'd given it to her later, lying in bed because, as he put it, going down on one knee when his side ached and she'd already asked him to marry her was a bit pointless.

She looked down at it now, a simple but beautiful ring, exactly right for her, just as Jake was. He turned to her and lifted his glass, and they clinked them together.

'I love you, Mrs Warren,' he said, and she chuckled and said,

'Love you, too, and it's Dr Fraser to you, Dr Warren.'

And he took the glass out of her hand, put it down and leant over Hamish and kissed her, and she could feel his smile all the way down to her toes…

* * * * *

If you enjoyed this story, check out these other great reads from Caroline Anderson

A Vet to Heal His Heart
Finding Their Forever Family
The Midwife's Miracle Twins
Healing Her Emergency Doc

All available now!

THE PARAMEDIC ROOMMATE PACT

JC HARROWAY

MILLS & BOON

To G, my BFF and my everything.

CHAPTER ONE

THE ONLY THING more important to critical-care paramedic Levi Young than being good at his job and helping strangers in need was ensuring the safety of his best friend and paramedic colleague Kaia McBride. This was especially true when she was dangling from the end of a winch wire above a rugged and rocky incline while the rescue helicopter hovered, trying to set her down as close to their casualty as possible.

With adrenaline sharpening his focus, he watched on tenterhooks as fellow crew member Grant lowered Kaia, inch by inch. Only when her feet touched the ground and she radioed in a safe landing could Levi's heart rate settle by a few beats per minute.

'Watch your footing,' he told her through the communication headset, eager to get down there with her and assess their patient. 'I'm right behind you.'

After ten years as a paramedic, experience told him how easily accidents could happen. He didn't want Kaia to be one of those statistics and, second only to the home, he knew, the workplace was where most accidents occurred.

'Okay,' Kaia said, unhooking the winch from her harness.

Their employer, the Southern Rescue Service, provided critical care to remote areas in cases of trauma, accident and medical emergency. Their work was often challenging, their rescue missions taking them to some of New Zealand's remotest corners, from jagged coastlines to lush, bush-clad hills or from snow-capped mountains to vast plains of flat agricultural land. This morning's casualty, a farmer in his sixties, was lying prone on uneven, gorse-laden terrain, where he'd taken a fall while mustering a stray calf. Fortunately, the seasoned farmer had been carrying a personal locator beacon so they were quickly able to find his whereabouts.

'He's conscious,' Kaia told Levi as she reached the prostrate man. 'GCS fifteen.'

The Glasgow Coma Scale score told him their patient must be alert, orientated and able to follow commands. Good news.

'I'm on my way,' Levi replied, clipping the winch to his harness.

While the helicopter hovered in place, Grant lowered Levi and a stretcher to the ground. Levi unhooked the winch from his harness and sent the cable back up to the helicopter.

'All clear,' he radioed the pilot, Mac, leaving him free to find somewhere safe and flat to land the helicopter while he and Kaia readied the casualty for transportation to hospital.

Levi scrambled down the steep slope towards Kaia and the patient, carrying the spider harness and basket stretcher and other medical equipment they might need. He assessed the situation, seeing that Kaia was in the zone. They each took pride in their work, which was sometimes a source of playful competition between them.

'I think his shoulder is dislocated,' she said, glancing up at Levi, the buzz of adrenaline making her deep brown eyes bright with excitement and determination. 'Possibly his ankle too.'

Levi nodded, assisting Kaia to fit a neck brace to immobilise the cervical spine.

'Bill, I'm going to give you something for the pain soon,' Kaia told the patient, who was groaning, his complexion pale. 'Just bear with us.'

While Kaia fitted an oxygen mask over Bill's face, Levi covered him with a foil hypothermia blanket. It was a windy sixteen degrees centigrade today, and Bill was wearing shorts. Levi unzipped his backpack of medical supplies to locate a syringe and painkillers and passed them over to Kaia.

'Thanks,' she said, shooting Levi a grateful look. 'Would you splint the ankle?' She set about inserting a cannula into Bill's arm.

Levi examined Bill's lower legs, grateful that ever since their first meeting, on their first shift together four years ago, he and Kaia had always worked brilliantly as a team. Probably the reason they'd become friends so quickly. That and the fact that when they'd first met they'd each been seeing other people. Kaia was a beautiful woman, but Levi had never had the chance to act on his attraction because she'd been in a relationship with her now ex, Sam. And Levi had been casually dating another paramedic, who'd since left Southern Rescue. But where Levi's relationship had been short-lived, like all his relationships, Kaia had, until recently, lived with Sam. Loved the guy. Assumed he was *the one* until the idiot had broken her heart.

As the pain medication kicked in, Bill's groaning eased. 'My wife…' he said, reaching for Kaia's hand with his good one.

'Don't worry,' Kaia replied, smiling her beautiful smile in reassurance. 'Someone is contacting her. She'll meet you at the hospital.'

'I tried to get back to the quad bike,' Bill said, 'but I couldn't walk.'

'Think you might have a fractured ankle, Bill,' Levi said, having located a tender spot around Bill's right foot. 'Which would explain it. But luckily for you Kaia here is the best paramedic in the country. You just relax while we get you patched up and on your way to hospital.'

Bill gave a small smile, another good sign that his pain was manageable, and Kaia shot Levi a playful wink. All the great things about their relationship were there behind her expression: playfulness, trust, the deep connection of two people who liked everything about the other. The only sticking point…he'd always secretly fancied Kaia.

'*Two* of the best paramedics in the country,' she argued, glancing Levi's way.

Levi smiled back. He treasured their friendship and felt honoured that she'd come to him when her four-year relationship with Sam had imploded.

'Right, Bill,' Levi said, focused on helping Bill instead of the numerous positive attributes of his friend, who was kind and loyal and had recently been through her share of heartache, 'we're going to strap you onto the stretcher so we can get you out of here, okay? Your job is to lie still and let us do all the work.'

With well-practised teamwork, he and Kaia transferred Bill to the stretcher and strapped him in for his forty-minute flight to Christchurch Hospital, a journey that would take close to three hours by road. Getting the casualty the care they needed within the first hour of an accident or injury, or as paramedics called it *the golden hour*, increased the patient's chance of making a full recovery by over eighty per cent and often meant the difference between life and death. He and Kaia were part of a critical-care team that manned over six hundred Life Flights per year in the South Island of New Zealand.

With Bill secured into the stretcher and harness, his injured leg and spine immobilised, Levi radioed for the pilot to return to their location and pick them up.

Levi passed Kaia the winch hook. 'You go first with Bill,' he said as the wind from the rotor blades whipped the rope around despite his firm grip.

Kaia nodded and clipped the rope to her harness while he attached Bill's stretcher to the second hook. When all three of them were safely inside the cabin of the helicopter and strapped into their seats, crewman Grant secured the cabin door and Mac took the helicopter to their cruising altitude of eight hundred feet.

'How are you feeling now, Bill?' Kaia asked a short while later as Levi recorded Bill's vital signs: pulse, blood pressure, heart and respiratory rates and oxygen saturations.

'More comfortable,' Bill said, offering them both a grateful smile. 'Thank you. Thank you both.'

'You're welcome, mate,' Levi said, glancing Kaia's way and smiling while his pulse thrummed. He loved the buzz of helping people and of a job well done. Something of which he could be proud. That he got to do the job he loved with Kaia was an added bonus. And if it meant locking down those feelings of attraction he'd always harboured, it was a small price to pay. He was used to being emotionally self-reliant, after all.

'You guys *do* make a good team,' Bill said with another small smile.

Levi nodded and bumped Kaia's shoulder with his own. 'The best team. You got lucky today,' he told their patient. Then, turning to Kaia, he winked. 'Job well done, McBride,' he said under his breath, wishing he could say more. Such as how beautiful she was or that she deserved so much better than a man who'd strung her along, changed his mind about their relationship and bailed when things became too serious.

But friends was good. Safe. Free from the risks of romantic attachments, which could break down with devastating results, as Kaia's experiences proved. Levi never wanted Kaia to find him lacking in any way or see the dark places in him that others had seen and rejected. He'd rather have her as a friend than her not be a part of his life.

'Same to you, Young,' she replied, smiling as she offered him a secret smile and a discreet fist bump in celebration of another successful rescue mission.

On the windblown helipad on the roof of the hospital, Kaia and Levi helped to transfer Bill over to the hospital stretcher then handed over his care to the Accident and Emergency team.

'Good luck, Bill,' Levi said, resting his hand on Bill's good shoulder. 'Hopefully you'll be back fishing with your grandkids in no time.'

Kaia smiled, her heart clenching with adoration for

Levi, who, underneath his confident, easy-going and competent exterior, was a big softie at heart.

As they watched Bill being wheeled towards the lift, Kaia breathed a sigh of relief. She'd always loved her job. Working with a paramedic as good as Levi, her best friend… Some days that didn't feel like work at all, especially when there was a good prognosis for the patient they'd helped.

She glanced Levi's way and smiled a smile that concealed a mass of complex emotions. He was such a great guy: loyal, smart, funny and attractive. Tall and athletic with sandy hair and blue eyes, he was exactly her type. And now, after weeks of recovering from a miscarriage and her split from Sam, the part of her that had fancied Levi the minute she'd met him seemed to have woken up.

Feeling guilty at the direction of her thoughts after Levi had been an amazing friend and let her move into his spare room when she'd moved out of the home she'd shared with her ex, she looked away.

'Hey,' he said as they crossed the roof towards the helicopter. 'You okay?'

Kaia winced at the concern in his stare. It was the same expression he'd worn ever since she'd come to him for support when her life had disintegrated. The baby had been unplanned. But knowing her own mother had struggled with infertility and considered Kaia, an only child, her *miracle*, Kaia had quickly embraced the idea of being a mother. Of course, she'd done so too soon. Had had to face the possibility that, for her, maybe motherhood just wasn't meant to be after all.

'I'm fine.' Kaia nodded, endlessly grateful for Levi's friendship. But the woman in her longed to have him look at her with something other than concern. She no longer wanted to inspire those sympathetic looks. She wanted to be her old self again, only better. Stronger. Determined that, while she might have chosen the wrong guy in the past, her next relationship, when she was ready for one, would be in pursuit of Mr Right. Next time she'd make sure the guy was sure about her.

'I was just thinking,' she added, trying to keep Levi off the scent, 'that this is the best part of our job: safely delivering the patient to hospital.'

'Really?' he asked, playfully nudging her shoulder with his arm because he was taller. 'You don't think the best part of our job is when we're suspended by a wire over a sheer cliff or being lowered into a freezing river?'

She laughed as they climbed back into the cabin of the helicopter. 'You're right. That can be fun, too, although not the river.'

Levi made everything fun.

'And you and me…we're good at this,' he said, flashing her another killer smile.

'The best,' Kaia said, knowing the competitive part of Levi needed to feel that he was doing a good job. Only for Kaia, leaving the patient to an unknown fate was also the hardest part of her work. Part of her wanted to follow Bill and to see his X-rays and know that her working diagnosis was correct. She wanted to make sure he made a full recovery and was discharged with a rehabilitation plan in place. She wanted to follow up on his progress and see his successful return to farming. Of course, none of that was part of her role. Nor was she ready to discuss her restlessness and the decisions she'd come to recently with Levi just yet.

When they were once more inside the Airbus H145 and strapped into their seats, within seconds the helicopter, affectionately named *Kiwi* after New Zealand's flightless national bird, was airborne again.

'You sure you're okay?' Levi asked again as they headed for the Southern Rescue base at Christchurch Airport. 'You seem…pensive today.'

Kaia sighed, for once wishing Levi didn't know her so well. She had a lot on her mind and finally felt strong enough to make some positive changes. Even so, she kept her stare on her clasped hands in her lap and said, 'I saw Sam last night at the mall. I'd forgotten that he sometimes ventured over to your side of the city for work.'

She looked up, feeling guilty, as if she should have mentioned it to Levi last night. But she was beyond ready for her ex and her grief to be a part of her past.

Levi frowned, that concerned, protective look back in his eyes. 'Did he see you? Did you talk to him?'

Kaia shook her head, reliving the humiliation of having to quickly duck into a shop to avoid bumping into her ex and his work colleague, a woman. 'He was headed for the food court. He might have been on a date with someone from work. I…hid so he wouldn't see me.'

'I'm sorry,' he said quietly. 'Christchurch really isn't that big of a city. I guess seeing him some time was inevitable.'

Kaia shrugged, her stare drawn to her lap once more. 'Yeah. I just wish I'd looked fabulous rather than tired after work.'

Levi winked playfully, his go-to gesture whenever conversations turned too emotional. 'You always look fabulous.' Then he fell serious. 'You could have told me you'd seen him last night.' He leaned close so his shoulder rested against hers, the move letting her know what she already knew: that he was always there for her.

Kaia looked up and stared into his gorgeous and kind blue eyes. 'I've spent the past three months leaning on you. You've been too good to me. Letting me stay in your spare room, listening to all my troubles, mopping up the tears.' She tried to smile but the part of her that had begun to see Levi in a new way since she'd started to crave a change couldn't help but wonder if he'd ever seen her as anything other than a friend.

Even if he did fancy her in return, he'd never have crossed the line while she'd been in a relationship with Sam. But nor had he been anything but a gentleman in all the time they'd been living together since her break-up.

'But that's what friends are for,' he said and Kaia's heart sank at his reminder. 'You can always talk to me, Kaia. You know that.'

'I know.' Kaia nodded, desperate to feel anything other than a failure. She'd believed she and Sam were equally committed to their relationship. She'd thought he was the one. That they'd eventually get married and have a family. But fate had thrown them a curve ball with the unplanned pregnancy and then a miscarriage. And Sam, initially supporting her decision to have the baby, had, after she'd lost it, shown his relief. She'd confronted him and he'd finally admitted that he'd changed his mind about Kaia and forever, right when she'd needed him most.

When she met his stare Levi added, 'You'd do the same for me.'

She smiled playfully, glad to change the subject to *his* love life. 'Except you've never done heartbreak, so I haven't had the chance to console you, tell you that how you're feeling will pass or mop up your tears.'

Not that he was a monk, of course. But all his brief relationships began and ended the same way. An intense period of casual sex, the occasional date followed by the fizzle-out where Levi told the woman of the moment he'd had a great time, but 'just wasn't looking for anything serious'.

Levi shrugged in that easy-going way of his. 'I'm an open book.' He smiled and Kaia let it go, part of her certain that Levi's casual attitude to dating masked deeper issues. At thirty-five he'd yet to find Miss Right, not that he'd seriously ever sought her out even though he was a total catch.

'Anyway,' she said, as they came in to land, 'I'm sick of talking about my ex. I want to be over it.' She'd spent enough time crying over a man on whom she hadn't been able to rely.

Levi nodded, only a flicker of his usual concern in his expression, which was progress. 'Good for you.'

Fortunately, their arrival back at base precluded any further discussion until they'd filed their mission log.

'Come on.' Levi smiled when it was done. 'My turn to buy coffee.'

They headed for the café on base and Kaia took a seat at their usual table in the window, which had views of the snow-capped Southern Alps mountain range. When he joined her with their drinks, Kaia took a hasty sip of her coffee in preparation for breaking some news, one of many changes she'd been mulling over.

'I've, um…got something else to tell you,' she began cautiously, confused by how conflicted she felt over what should have been a straightforward and inevitable decision to move out of her friend's spare room. 'When I got home last night, I did some house-hunting. I think I've found a place I can afford by myself. I've made an appointment to view it.'

Living with Levi was always going to be a temporary, financially motivated solution until she'd got back on her feet. And she felt increasingly guilty for hogging his space, aware that he was probably being considerate by not bringing any women home the entire time they'd lived together.

Levi replaced his mug of coffee on the table and raised his eyebrows questioningly. 'I've told you before, there's no rush. You're welcome to stay as long as you need to.'

Kaia nodded, not quite meeting his stare, because she didn't want to misinterpret his concern for disappointment that she was leaving. 'I know,' she said, 'and I've loved living with you. But it's time I got my life back on track. Time to…move on. And besides,' she continued, 'you'll finally have your place to yourself. I can't cramp your style forever.'

He pressed his lips together as if reluctant to argue. Then he asked, 'So where is this place you've found?'

'Not far from here actually.' She brightened, knowing that he cared but would support her decision. 'It's perfect for work and only five minutes from you. The rental agent can show me around tomorrow.'

'Want me to come with you?' he asked.

Kaia shrugged then shook her head. 'Thanks, but I'm

sure you have better things to do on your day off than house-hunt with me. Besides, you have Lee's football match tomorrow night.'

After his father died when he was thirteen, Levi had understandably been something of a rebellious teenager. He paid it forward by mentoring teens who, for whatever reason, were angry with the unfairness of the world. Lee's father was currently in prison. Levi often took the young man surfing or for a bike ride or showed up to watch his sports matches, providing a reliable male influence when Lee needed it most.

'Oh, yeah,' Levi said. 'I almost forgot. But don't feel as if you have to take this house if it's a dump or rush to move out. My spare room is yours for as long as you need it.'

Kaia swallowed hard against the lump in her throat. He was so wonderful. Not for the first time, she wondered how things might have been different if they'd both been single when they met. But having Levi as a friend trumped being one of his short-term casual relationships. And Kaia was determined that next time she became serious about someone, she'd get it right and make sure he was equally committed to her in return.

'What would I do without you?' she asked, clinging to their playful banter to manage her complicated feelings for her friend. 'Even if you do hog all the hot water.' She forced a bright smile to lighten the mood, although Levi was an awesome flatmate. He cooked, put the toilet seat down and hadn't once brought home a date for noisy sex.

Thinking about that one time she, Sam, Levi and his woman of the moment had gone on an overnight trip together years ago and she'd overheard sex noises through the wall, Kaia flushed and gulped the last of her coffee.

'Well,' he said, leaning back in his chair in a relaxed slouch, shooting her a flirty wink, 'you'll never know.' He spread his arms in invitation. 'I'm right here, baby. And I'm all yours.'

With the return of their usual light-hearted flirtation, Kaia laughed and rolled her eyes. This was their norm. Easy camaraderie. Unconditional acceptance. Just enough harmless mild flirtation to remind Kaia that, despite his good looks and engaging personality, Levi was, and always had been, a free agent.

'I might go ring the hospital,' she said, standing and pushing her chair under the table. 'Check in on Bill.'

He smiled indulgently. 'You really care about our patients, don't you?'

'Don't give me that,' she teased. 'You were the one asking about his grandkids. You care too.'

Levi jerked up one shoulder. 'What can I say? I like kids, but I couldn't eat a whole one.'

Kaia laughed at the joke she'd heard many times. Kids loved Levi. And, considering his own father had died of cancer when he was a teenager, she had no doubt that Levi would make a brilliant dad one day.

'You just need to know your diagnosis was correct, don't you?' he said, watching her with that same indulgent curiosity.

'Don't you?' she volleyed back. 'Don't pretend you don't get a kick from being right. I know you too well, remember.'

Levi loved his career, and, while he wasn't arrogant, he also liked to excel.

'I just like to see a case through to the end,' she said, her mind wandering to the other big change she finally felt strong enough to consider making in her life—retraining to be a doctor. But there was no rush to discuss that right now.

'Still on for drinks tonight?' Levi asked, before she could walk away.

Kaia nodded. 'Of course. I wouldn't miss it, Birthday Boy. Although I still can't believe you chose to work today rather than taking the day off.'

'Are you serious?' He grinned. 'As if I'd let you have all the fun of a rescue alone.' He winked and Kaia's stomach quivered. Was it her imagination or was he extra-sexy today? Maybe there was something in the coffee... Or maybe after seeing Sam last night, she'd finally laid that relationship to rest and was ready to notice members of the opposite sex. And there was no finer specimen than Levi.

'Are you bringing a date tonight?' she asked as casually as the tightness in her chest would allow.

'No,' he said, his smile mocking. 'It's just us and the rest of the Southern Rescue gang. Unless *you're* bringing a date.'

His expression stayed neutral. Kaia found herself wanting to shock him. To say yes. That, like Sam, she was ready to move on. And maybe she was...

'No,' she admitted instead. 'But it's your birthday... You haven't dated anyone the whole time I've been living with you, which is another reason for me to move out, don't you think? So you can have your privacy back.'

He watched her, his expression amused. 'Look at you, worrying about my sex life.'

Kaia flushed, wishing she'd never started this conversation. 'It's more like I'm worried about your love life,' she said, ashamed of her lusty thoughts where her friend was concerned after he'd been so good to her. 'Maybe thirty-five is a good time to start dating seriously,' she said playfully. 'Maybe even settle down.'

That niggle of jealousy that always came when Levi had a new woman in his life bloomed, even as she knew her words would most likely fall on deaf ears. This wasn't the first time they'd had this conversation. Kaia had tried to set him up with several of her single friends over the years.

'You know me,' he said evenly. 'I'm all about the good times. So eight pm, the Runway Bar. Beers and pool.' He raised his eyebrows expectantly.

'Sure.' Giving up, again, Kaia laughed. 'See you later at mountain-survival training.'

But as she walked away, she couldn't help but feel his attitude to casual dating was a smokescreen for some deeper emotions. After all, he wanted a family one day, so he must have a plan for finding a long-term relationship. Or maybe, having witnessed Kaia's heartbreak up close, he sensibly had no desire to expose himself to the risks that came with the search for love.

Feeling both jealous of the future woman who might change Levi's ways and determined to sound him out on why, despite being a catch, he never seemed to take dating seriously, Kaia shoved her feelings for Levi back into the box labelled 'friendship' and headed for the office to call the hospital.

CHAPTER TWO

LATER THAT NIGHT, another patron at the Runway Bar snapped a group photo of the members of the Southern Rescue crew who'd made it for drinks and handed the phone back to Kaia. The gang dispersed into various conversations, but Levi couldn't stop staring at his friend, his feelings sickeningly conflicted. Dressed casually in jeans and a shimmery top, she looked fantastic, happily carefree and sexier than ever. Swallowing down the guilt he felt for offering her a safe space in his home to recover from her heartache and then lusting after her, he tried on a wooden-feeling smile.

'I love the new haircut,' he said, his pulse leaping with both excitement and panic.

Straight after they'd finished work, she'd rushed off to an appointment at the hairdresser's. In all the time he'd known her she'd worn her glossy brown hair long, usually tied back in a ponytail. But now, with at least six inches cut off the length, the tousled, layered cut kissed her shoulders and bounced when she turned her head. And the chestnut colour was shot through with warm reddish streaks that made her gorgeous brown eyes glow in the low lighting of the bar.

'Thanks,' she said, her smile playful as she ran her fingers through the ends. 'It's part of the new me.'

Chugging a swallow of beer to dampen down the surge of forbidden desire he felt for his friend, Levi desperately tried to think platonic thoughts. 'There was nothing wrong with the old you,' he said quietly, hoping she wouldn't sense his inner turmoil.

Until today, until she'd told him she was ready to move out, he hadn't realised how much he'd enjoyed having her under his roof, waking her up with a mug of tea because she wasn't a morning person, sharing the highs and lows of the day over dinner, sitting by her side on the sofa watching some cheesy reality TV show he wouldn't have given the time of day to but for Kaia.

And with her ready to move on with her life, he felt like some sort of caged lion who'd seen a forbidden glimpse of the African Savannah through the bars. As if something he couldn't have was tantalisingly close but just out of reach.

He tuned into the conversation where Mac was regaling Kaia with some story about his latest mountain-biking adventure and the nasty fall he'd taken when his bike skidded on gravel. The guy even pulled up his trouser leg and proudly flashed his nasty graze.

Levi swallowed the irrational surge of jealousy. Mac was happily married with four teenaged kids. What was wrong with him tonight? Was he panicking because Kaia's getting over Sam meant she might be ready to date again? Which meant any opportunity he might have to make something physical happen between them was slipping away? Of course, he shouldn't be thinking of Kaia that way at all. But it was as if the feelings of attraction he'd bottled up for the past four years while she'd been with another man were finally free and screaming in his ear.

'Excuse me,' Mac said when the story ended. 'I'm off to the bathroom.'

Kaia turned to Levi and smiled her lovely smile. 'You having a good birthday?' she asked, ignoring her phone when it pinged with a notification.

'Sure,' he said, wishing he'd settled for a quiet night in with Kaia instead of drinks with the gang, especially given she might soon move out. 'I got to work a shift with my favourite colleague,' he added playfully, 'and now I'm in the pub. What is there to complain about?'

He smiled, trying to act normal when all he wanted to do was step closer and flirt.

'I love you too,' she said, merrily blowing him an exaggerated kiss as her phone pinged again.

That wasn't the first time she'd teased that she loved him. She meant it as a friend because that was what they were: *friends*. But tonight he couldn't seem to tease her back.

'I meant to apologise,' he said instead, leaning close till the scent of her perfume tickled his nose, 'about the kids comment earlier. I hope it didn't come across as insensitive after...you know.'

She'd been devastated to lose the baby, understandably. And since, Levi had tried to avoid any talk of children, preferring to take his cue from Kaia on the subject when she was ready.

'Of course not,' she said, a flicker of doubt in her stare. 'I love kids, too. I just...well, I wasn't sure I could have any,' she went on haltingly, making Levi wish he'd never brought up the subject. 'I guess I'm still not sure.' She glanced down at her feet. 'My mother had several miscarriages before she had me, her one and only miracle. So…maybe it's genetic.'

Levi stepped closer and squeezed her arm. 'I'm sorry. I didn't know that about your mum.'

Kaia shrugged and brightened. 'It's fine. Maybe it wasn't meant to be, for many reasons. Maybe I'm not meant to be a mother. Obviously I wasn't meant to have a baby with Sam. And I'm glad I found out about his doubts before I married him or something…'

Levi pressed his lips together; he'd made his opinion of Sam's not being good enough for Kaia known many times before. Then he said, 'You'll try again when you're ready and in a better relationship. And I'm sure it will happen for you. You're a fit and healthy woman in her twenties.'

She looked down again. 'Maybe…or maybe it's just not worth all the…heartache.'

Feeling another surge of irrational jealousy and panic, Levi was just about to reach out and touch her again when she said, 'Anyway, tonight is about you, not me.' She clinked her beer bottle to his in a toast just as her phone pinged once more.

'Someone really wants to get hold of you,' he said, glancing at the phone in order to appear as if he wasn't staring.

'Sorry.' She winced, looking at the screen. 'I posted that picture we just took on the Southern Rescue socials…'

She stepped closer and showed him the photo, but Levi couldn't concentrate on anything but her closeness, the casual way her arm brushed his, and his body overheated.

'Oh, look,' she said, scrolling through the comments. 'My friend Heidi wants to know if the birthday boy is single.' She beamed up at him as if handing Levi a winning lottery ticket.

'Who's Heidi?' he asked, hypnotised by Kaia's lips, which were slicked with some sort of berry-coloured gloss he wanted to taste.

'I've told you about her before,' she said, playfully nudging him. 'She's a physio. She comes from Waikato, like you, and she might be moving down to Christchurch soon for work.'

'Oh, yeah, I remember now.' Levi's heart sank. He knew exactly where this was going. Over the years Kaia had thrown several 'gorgeous' single women his way, but this was the first time since she'd split up with Sam, and she herself was also single.

But he needed to stop thinking of Kaia that way, if only for his own sanity. She would never think of him in a sexual way and good for her. When it came to relationships and long-term commitment, he wasn't a safe bet. And after the drama with her ex, after losing a baby, she deserved better than Levi…deserved everything she wanted.

'Oh, she's messaged me,' she said, her eyes lighting up. 'She's serious. She really wants your number.'

Levi swallowed and said nothing, trying to pretend he cared about this newest blind-date candidate, Heidi, when really there was only one woman in his head. There had been for months. Kaia thought she was cramping his style by living with him, but he could relax and have fun with her in a way he couldn't with women he dated. With Kaia, there was no agenda. He didn't need to give her the *I'm only really looking for something casual* speech because she already knew his MO. He didn't have to answer questions about his childhood or where he'd gone to school, because he'd already told her part of that story. He didn't have to worry about managing her romantic expectations because he wasn't lucky enough to have her fancy him in return, unfortunately…

Kaia brought up a profile picture of her friend and stepped closer to show him. He leaned in. Her new, shorter hair brushed his cheek, tempting him to turn his face and inhale deeply. Of course, he could do no such thing. He was well-practised at shutting down his emotions *and* shutting down his desire for his friend.

'She's lovely,' she said about Heidi as he thought the same about Kaia. 'You two have heaps in common.'

Again she could be describing him and herself.

'So, do you want her number?' she asked, looking up at him expectantly.

He didn't have the heart to refuse. 'Sure,' he said, with a shrug that made Kaia laugh.

'Don't sound too enthusiastic, will you?' she teased, gently swatting his arm.

Levi tilted his head. 'You know me. I like to keep things…casual.'

She sobered a little, her smile falling. 'Newsflash: you turned thirty-five today. You're not getting any younger. And, as I've recently discovered, finding *the one*—a person who also thinks you're *the one* for them—is trickier than it looks.'

She was downplaying her hurt with humour, but Levi

hated the flicker of sadness in her stare. But, to his relief, her playful mood prevailed.

'I hope you're not holding out for one of those depressing, sexless arrangements with me,' she said, rolling her eyes. 'Where we make a lame pact that if we're both still single at forty, we'll get married. Because I have no intention of settling for so little, let me tell you.'

She laughed again and Levi tried to smile along, but every part of him froze, scared to reveal how much she turned him on. There would be no way in hell he'd survive being married to Kaia without wanting her sexually. It was hard enough fighting the forbidden because of their friendship.

'Next time I enter into a relationship,' she went on, as if oblivious to his treacherous thoughts, 'I'll make sure the guy wants the same things I want and is utterly crazy about me.' She smiled bravely and Levi's heart ached for her.

'He'd be crazy not to be crazy about you,' he choked out, trying to smile but feeling sick with jealousy of this faceless guy. But of course Kaia would get over her heartache and want to date again. Once she'd wanted the whole caboodle: love, marriage, a family. He felt sure she'd want all of that again. And, while Levi had always assumed that one day he'd meet a woman he could see himself committing to, he'd never really needed the love part. In fact, he wasn't sure he was capable of it.

'Don't *you* want to find someone, someday?' Kaia asked, becoming serious. 'Fall in love?' She looked at him with the same flicker of disappointment she'd worn in the café that morning when she'd encouraged him to date properly.

Levi swallowed, his usual glib answer sticking in his throat. He never wanted to let Kaia down. He didn't want her to see through him in case she saw something she didn't like. After all, there was something in him that made his own mother send him away, time and time again. And the one long-term girlfriend he'd had in his twenties had seen through him, seen something she didn't like, as if his best shot at a relationship hadn't been good enough.

'I'm not even sure what love is,' he admitted softly, risking Kaia's disappointment. 'I don't think I've ever been in romantic love.'

'Really?' Her frown deepened and his skin tightened with discomfort. 'Maybe that's because you never give a relationship a chance,' she said, casting him a cautious glance. 'You go into it labelling it *casual*, so it's practically over before it's even begun.'

'Maybe,' he agreed amicably because he didn't want to argue with Kaia or minimise what she'd been through with Sam. The main reason he steered clear of the kind of relationship she thought he needed was because as a teenager, after his father died and he was sent away to boarding school, he'd learned to be emotionally reliant on himself in order to manage the pain of what had felt like repeated rejection. And after that one girlfriend… he'd decided he didn't need all the drama and risk that came with romantic entanglements.

'Maybe you just haven't met the right woman,' she said, smiling hopefully as if he could still be redeemed. 'Maybe Heidi will change your mind.' She raised her phone and laughed softly.

'Maybe,' he said, pushing away all thoughts of the future and the drastic changes he'd need to make in order to be serious relationship material.

Just then, before he could change the subject, a new song began.

'Oh, I love this one,' Kaia said about the background music. 'Let's dance.'

Placing her beer bottle on the table, she reached for his hand and tugged him towards the tiny dance floor next to the pool table, where a few other patrons were dancing.

Not one to miss an opportunity to make Kaia smile, Levi complied, relieved that she'd dropped the Heidi hard sell. But maybe he should take out Kaia's friend. Maybe seeing someone else would stop him thinking about Kaia. Although even her serious relationship with Sam hadn't wholly achieved that…

On the dance floor she took his hand and they did a kind of shuffling close dance with the odd under-arm twirl. Predictably his body reacted to her closeness, to her laughing eyes, her stunning smile, the delicate scent of her perfume and the heat from her body.

'You seem different tonight,' he said, smiling back, his heart thudding with an unsettling mix of excitement and trepidation because, while he celebrated the changes in her, a sign that she was feeling stronger, they also made him nervous, as if his time to make something happen between them was running out. With her moving somewhere else, he guessed it was.

'It's the hair,' she said, laughing and running her fingers through it in a way that left him eager to discover if it was as soft as it looked. If it smelled as good as he suspected.

He leaned close and lowered his voice. 'It's more than the hair.'

She blinked, hesitating. Then she glanced down at her feet. 'You're right,' she said, looking up at him with uncertainty. 'I guess I have been doing a lot of soul-searching recently. I feel like I've been licking my wounds for long enough.'

'That's understandable,' he said. 'And I'm glad to hear it.' Another surge of panic squeezed his throat as he widened his smile. He desperately wanted her to be happy, to move on from the grief and heartache she'd been through in first losing the baby then having her relationship disintegrate in the aftermath. She'd been living with Sam. She'd assumed he was the man she'd spend her life with. Then, as if faced with the seriousness and lifelong commitment of a baby, Sam had changed his mind after the miscarriage and hurt Kaia.

But, for some reason Levi couldn't fathom, watching his friend once more spread her wings in anticipation of flight left him strangely restless and concerned he might be turning into a selfish jerk. Just because he loved her company, that was no reason to clip her wings. But what if she moved out and met another guy and fell in love and Levi missed his chance to—?

He stopped that thought in its tracks. All he could really offer her was sex. And if he so much as suggested that, the risk to their friendship and their working relationship was enormous.

'So...are you ready to start dating again, then?' he asked cautiously, scared of her answer because if she began a new relationship he'd have to stuff all that escaped attraction back into the bottle.

'No...not quite.' She laughed and Levi's panic subsided a fraction. 'But I have been thinking...' Her eyes filled with the doubt that had been rampant after her split from Sam.

'You can tell me,' he said, bracing himself.

She nodded, looking up trustingly. 'I know. We've talked about it before and you've always encouraged me in the past, but I think I'm ready to seriously consider the crazy idea of going to medical school.'

They'd all but stopped dancing now, their feet slowing to a small, shuffling sidestep. Levi frowned, but only because the shift in topic, on top of the other changes today—the new house and new haircut—felt like another rug being pulled from under his feet. They *had* discussed it before. In fact, he'd been the one to insist that she could do whatever she set her mind to.

'I know,' she rushed on, misinterpreting his silence for hesitation. 'It's crazy. Obviously I haven't got all the logistics figured out, but it's something I've wondered about for a long time, as you know. For me, the worst part of our job is the lack of continuity of care. We hand the patients over and our role is done. Unless we chase answers, we never know if they survive their injuries or illness. We never know if our diagnoses were correct or when they're discharged from hospital. I don't know. I... Sometimes I think I could feel more fulfilled in a more direct clinical role.'

Levi's head spun, the panic returning full-blown, even as he nodded in understanding and encouragement. 'I get that,' he said, glancing down to where her hand rested on his arm. He swallowed against the lurch of desire her touch evoked. 'I feel the same sometimes.'

'You do?' she asked, dropping her hand.

'Of course,' he said, drawing her to the side of the dance floor so they could talk in private.

'So...do you think I'm crazy?' she asked, chewing at her bottom lip.

'No, of course not.' Levi wanted to punch Sam for decimating Kaia's confidence that way. 'The opposite, in fact. I've told you before, I think you'd make a wonderful doctor, Kaia. If that's the direction you want your career to take you, then I'll support you any way I can, you know that.'

He loved that she was getting back on her feet after what she'd been through, but everything seemed to be changing so fast. What if she outgrew him and his friendship? What if that part of him others found unacceptable, including his own mother, pushed her away and he lost her forever?

Feeling sick the way he'd felt as a teenager every time he'd had to leave his family at home and return to boarding school, he slapped on his brave face and smiled.

'Thanks, Levi.' As if she'd been waiting for his seal of approval, she smiled gratefully. 'I was a bit worried to tell you in case you pointed out all the downsides, which of course are many. I'm twenty-nine. I'd be a mature student.' She pulled a horrified face then laughed as if she didn't really care. 'I'll have enormous student loans by the time I qualify and that's even if I can pass the entry exams and earn a place.'

'Of course you can,' he said, his heart thudding erratically. She was the smartest, kindest person he knew. And, as if exhausted from years of denial, his mind helpfully added, *and the sexiest.* 'You've just had your confidence knocked, that's all. You should trust your instincts and go for it.'

But how would he survive work without her?

She smiled indulgently. 'Thanks for understanding,' she said, throwing her arms around his neck and hugging him in the same way she had at least once a week for the entirety of their friendship.

With his heart pounding, Levi rested his hand between her shoulder blades and hugged her back. But tonight the friendly embrace felt different. Both precious and precarious, as if he couldn't take it, or his relationship with Kaia, for granted. Something had changed today. A monumental shift in his attraction to her, which, if he was completely honest with himself as only a man who'd had a few beers could be, had always been always there beneath the surface, waiting for the right moment to declare itself. But was this that moment? Or was he just panicking because he didn't want Kaia to forget him when she moved on with her new life, new job, new partner?

He prepared to pull back from the hug as he normally would, but he couldn't seem to resist turning his head so his lips hovered over the skin of her neck, and his nose brushed her hair as he once more inhaled the unique warm scent of her, trying to commit it to memory.

'It goes without saying,' she said, easing back and smiling up at him, oblivious to his desire for her, 'that if I'm successful, if I get a place at med school, I'll really miss working with you.'

'I'll miss you too,' he said, swallowing hard to cover the urge to drag her back into his arms and kiss her. Suddenly awkward in his skin, a new feeling for him, he shoved his hands into his pockets. Otherwise he might reach for again, hold on to her until his world settled back into the comfortable, predictable place he'd made it. A place where he worked hard and reaped the emotional rewards of being good at something rather than a troubled young man who'd been sent away by his mother to be straightened out. Where he relied on himself for his emotional well-being, even if it meant forgoing the kind of serious relationship Kaia thought he needed, the kind *she* needed. The kind he might one day need to figure out.

He would never hurt her by pointing it out, but hadn't her own experience with Sam proved his theory that love was unreliable and often conditional on vague things like a certain kind of behaviour or how you made the other person feel? He'd learned growing up that his disappointing actions and attitude had led to his mother's sending him away, no matter how much he'd begged he would change. After that he couldn't help but feel he'd had to earn his way back into his own family. And even his ex from that first relationship had ended things and moved to Australia, saying Levi obviously wasn't ready to commit. Was it any wonder that he'd become emotionally self-reliant and found contentment without that fickle emotion he wasn't sure existed?

'Come on, Birthday Boy,' Kaia said, tilting her head towards the bar, 'let's grab another beer and I'll put Heidi's number in your phone.'

Levi followed her, his emotions carefully hidden behind an easy-going smile, while inside he wasn't sure which way was up. He knew Kaia meant well, that she cared about his happiness as much as he cared about hers. But the last thing he wanted to do was talk about a date with another woman, when the only woman in his head today was Kaia, his best friend.

And maybe that was where his feelings for her, the temptation to have something more than being friends, needed to stay. Locked away. Never mentioned. Denied.

Resigned that he was in for a long night, he handed over his phone.

CHAPTER THREE

KAIA CLOSED THE taxi door and headed up the path of Levi's place, her emotions a confusing jumble that left her head spinning with more than an alcohol buzz. Poking at some of those feelings, she found the most persistent was the unexpected jealousy she'd experienced the moment Heidi's message had appeared.

Despite Levi's having given Heidi's photo only a cursory glance, his easy acceptance of her number and his casual promise to 'give her a call' had been enough to tip Kaia into new and unforeseen territory, the burn of envy simmering in her chest. She'd ignored it. Levi was a great guy—loyal, dependable, sexy. Every word she'd told Heidi about him was true. And he was her *friend.* She shouldn't be thinking about him in any other way. She couldn't risk ruining what they had—a great working relationship and an invaluable friendship—not when he'd picked her up at her lowest point.

'Great night,' she said, pushing her key into the lock as she tried to reason away her irrational envy.

Maybe because he hadn't dated anyone in the whole time she'd lived in his spare room, as if he was being considerate by not bringing a hook-up home, she'd grown used to his being single. Maybe her jealous overreaction was another sign that she too was ready to move on like her ex. Not that she was in any hurry to start dating seriously. Secretly, she was enjoying that she and Levi were single at the same time. Harmless flirtation with him was helping her regain her confidence, which had been decimated by Sam's change of heart. But maybe she was ready for more than a new haircut.

Telling herself that she simply felt protective of her place in Levi's life as his best friend, and any future relationship he might have would put that under threat, she flicked on the lights and headed for the kitchen.

'Do you want tea?' she asked, switching on the kettle. She needed something to calm her stomach, which, ever since she'd started talking about him and Heidi dating, had formed into a tight little knot she was thoroughly ashamed of.

'Sure,' he said, joining her, that slightly lopsided smile of his on his face that told her he was a bit merry and had enjoyed his birthday.

Because she too was a bit tipsy, she leaned against the kitchen counter and simply grinned at him. He was so handsome, with a great smile. He was a catch for any woman. Shame, then, that he stayed resolutely single. And not believing in love? He'd hinted at that before but she hadn't paid much attention back then because she'd been happy in her relationship. But now she wanted to dig deeper and find out why.

For a few seconds, while the only sound in the room was the gentle rev of the kettle boiling, they smiled goofily at each other. Then a subtle switch infected the atmosphere. Levi's expression turned serious, his blue eyes darkening with intensity as a small frown pinched his sandy-coloured brows.

'I'm going to miss you,' he said, his stare locked to hers so she saw his uncertainty. A rare emotion for her usually confident and self-assured friend.

Kaia's heart rate soared, that thrill of excitement back. There was something different about Levi too tonight. An intensity she'd never before witnessed. It made the attraction she'd spent the past few weeks reasoning away all the more persistent. Of course, she would rather have him as a friend than have more, cross that line and potentially lose him from her life if it didn't work out. Wouldn't she? Because long-term, she and Levi were looking for different things.

She nodded, choked. 'I'll miss you too,' she replied, her voice trailing off to a strangled croak. 'I hope you know that a big part of me wants to stay. You've been… great. I couldn't have survived the past few months without you.'

Everything was easy with Levi. Whether it was stabilising a patient on the side of a mountain or quietly hanging out at home.

'But I've been telling myself that moving out is an important step in my recovery,' she said, resolved. 'It's time to start putting the pieces of my life back together.'

And maybe the way she couldn't stop fancying her friend meant she was ready for something fun and meaningless, too.

He nodded, his eyes bright as if with pride. 'I'll support you in any way I can.' His smile kicked up a notch to the playful one she loved. 'Changing light bulbs you can't reach. Putting spiders you're terrified of outside.

Scaring off creepy neighbours who want your number.' He flexed his arms to show off his intimidating biceps and Kaia laughed.

'Lucky me. I'll have you on speed dial, especially for the spiders,' she teased, trying to get back to their regular playful vibe to help stave off her inappropriately carnal thoughts. 'And the good thing is, I'm not moving far.'

He nodded, but the way he looked at her made her skin tingle on the border between pleasure and pain, as if she were standing too close to a fire. As if he was having the same lusty thoughts as her. But could Levi really be more than a friend? Or was it simply her wishful thinking and the beer? That restlessness nudging her out of her comfort zone? She'd never really been keen on one-night stands, but maybe that was a perfect way to open the door on her new life. The new Kaia.

'We'll still see each other at work,' she added, her pulse flying at the idea of experiencing one night with Levi even as her stomach sank with the realisation that if she went to medical school she'd have to give up her job as a paramedic.

But surely that look on his face must be in her imagination. In all the time she'd known him he'd never once given her any indication that he found her sexually attractive. He was a decent man, yes, and would never have crossed the line while she was in a relationship. But they were both single now. They'd been living together for weeks and nothing. Maybe she was reading too much into his words and expressions.

'This was always going to be a temporary living arrangement,' she finished, trying to convince herself as much as him. 'Besides, you'll finally have your place to yourself,' she added because he'd stayed silent. 'Just think, you can have as much noisy sex as you want when I'm gone.'

She tried to chuckle as she normally would when making a joke, but at the mention of sex even the air molecules around them seemed to still so the noise of the kettle and the rush of blood through Kaia's ears seemed deafening.

He continued to stare, his expression unmoved and unreadable, his chest rising on laboured breaths as if he was seriously upset she was moving out. Drawn to him, she took a half-step closer. 'You must want your life back to normal,' she said quietly, the words emerging strangled by her tight throat.

Levi was a sexual man. The enforced abstinence couldn't be fun. But suddenly it was as if she didn't know him at all and had no idea what he was thinking.

'What if I'd rather have you?' he asked simply, his voice so low she frowned, uncertain she'd heard correctly. Or maybe she'd misunderstood his meaning.

Was he saying he'd rather have her staying in his spare room than sex? Or rather have sex with her? Now sex was all she could think about.

Kaia's heart, which had been poised mid-flutter all evening, because that was its normal state whenever she spent time with Levi, flipped into a new rapid and erratic rhythm. Could he possibly be as attracted to her physically as she was to him? Sometimes, frequently if she was honest, she couldn't help but regret that neither of them had been single when they'd first met. How might their relationship have developed if she'd been free to acknowledge their chemistry? Would Levi have slept with her then moved on, as she'd seen him do countless times with other women? Or might a sexual relationship between them have turned romantic? Only Levi didn't really do romance, nor was she ready for a new relationship just yet. And it was too late to have that with him. They'd become friends instead.

The idea of just one forbidden night bloomed in her head, growing, taking shape, tempting her towards recklessness.

Aware that her mouth was open when his stare dipped there, she dragged in a shaky breath. 'You don't mean that,' she whispered, scared to move from the spot in case she broke the strange spell binding them to this moment.

But what did *her* thoughts mean? Surely they were the wild and thrilling imaginings of a crazy woman. Maybe she'd taken her desire to pivot her life a step too far. It was one thing to want a new look with a fresh haircut, even a new start with a passionate, meaningless night, but another thing entirely to sleep with her best friend and risk losing him.

'Don't I?' he asked eventually. He didn't move a muscle but the scent of his aftershave and the heat from his body bathed her, the dangerous energy coiled in him electrifying the air.

Kaia shuddered. Something had changed tonight, for sure. While she'd prattled on about Heidi she'd been forced to acknowledge that once upon a time Levi might have been the perfect man for Kaia. They had so much in common and shared a particular sense of humour. But hadn't she often wondered why, when he had a very healthy sex life, when they spent so much time together at work and at home, he'd never once crossed that line with her? Hadn't she, in the depths of her loneliest moments since she'd split up with Sam, wondered just how good it would be to sleep with Levi?

Stunned by her rush of mental honesty, by the tantalising idea of briefly exploring this chemistry, she stayed frozen in place. 'I don't know what you're saying.'

Was she seriously considering crossing that line, just one time? With Levi? The man who'd helped her to pick up the pieces when the life she'd thought was hers had disintegrated, piece by piece. The man who, come rain or shine, was always there for her and had never let her down. She literally put her life in his hands on a daily basis at work, safe in the knowledge that he had her back and would never allow her to get hurt. There wasn't another man she trusted more. 'Maybe we've had too much to drink,' she finished, fighting the tightness in her chest and the restless excitement urging her to step closer. To take that risk. To let go for once and have what she wanted.

'I'm not drunk,' he said. Beyond his inscrutable stare shifting over her face, he didn't move.

Warning signs flashed in her peripheral vision. If only he felt the same as she did and could admit they shared some pretty potent chemistry. If only he shared her curiosity of how they might be together and the now insistent and clamouring desire to explore the attraction.

Kaia hesitated, both elated and terrified by this frisson between them, the awareness that she was a woman and Levi was a very attractive man. There was still time to laugh this off and go to bed. *Separately.* But her feet wouldn't move. All those accidental and deliberate touches today seemed more meaningful. As if they'd all been leading to this single moment. This momentous decision.

'Neither am I,' she replied, finally stepping slowly forward.

She had no idea what they were saying, what they were doing, but this conversation felt like an enormous gamble. If she judged it wrong, the way she'd been wrong about her relationship with Sam, she might seriously offend her best friend, who'd never once given her any indication that he so much as fancied her. But if he *did* feel the same, if she was right about his intense looks…? Maybe she could have just this one night.

'You're not making any sense,' she whispered, giving him time to step back or make a joke the way he normally would. But nothing about tonight felt normal, certainly not the way his stare scoured her face, the way he stood as still as a statue, his breathing ragged, as if everything she felt was real and reciprocated.

'Sometimes life doesn't make much sense,' he said, his gaze lingering on her mouth for a few exhilarating seconds during which she became increasingly convinced that he wanted her too. 'It makes no sense to me that your ex would walk away from you.'

A thrilling gasp sounded in her head. 'You're just saying that because you're my friend,' she pointed out, almost from habit, clinging to her last shred of willpower.

Their jokes often bordered on flirtation. But Levi's expression wasn't friendly. It was fierce and searing and raging with what looked like need.

'I *am* your friend,' he confirmed, the look on his face and the few cryptic words he'd spoken flooding her pelvis with liquid heat that slid down her legs so she feared she might actually collapse.

Drunk on the excitement pounding through her body but safe in the knowledge that he cared about her, that she trusted him, she slowly raised her hands to his shoulders.

'Well, on that note, happy birthday,' she whispered.

She rose onto the tips of her toes and pressed her lips to his. Brief. Forbidden. And so tempting she could barely breathe.

But there was still time to pretend this was an innocent peck to mark the end of a fleeting era where for a few months they'd not only worked together but also lived together. Still time to retreat to safety and just be friends.

Only when she looked up his eyes blazed with unfamiliar but definite desire. He'd stopped breathing and she could practically feel the thud of his heart across the small space that separated his chest from hers. Kaia sighed with relief as all illusion slipped away. He felt it too. This chemistry was real and mutual.

'Levi…' she whispered, still torn with indecision. Suddenly the choice, to act or not act, felt equally dangerous. They might never be single together again. This chance to feel attractive again and to know Levi the man as more than a friend might slip through her fingers. She might regret not taking this chance for the rest of her life.

'Trust your instincts,' he said as if he might still be talking about her application to medical school.

But he wasn't. And just like that the fight in Kaia was won.

He moved and she moved. His hands found her waist,

one sliding up her back to rest between her shoulder blades and press her close. Their lips connected once more. Only this time he groaned, his mouth opening hers and his tongue surging and then retreating and then surging again as if he was stunned by the heat of their kiss but also desperate for more.

Kaia, too, was stunned, lunging for him, frantic for another jolt of forbidden lust and euphoric excitement as she kissed him back. But if she'd thought Levi would be hesitant or point out how terrible an idea this was, she was mistaken. His hands slid into her hair and cupped her face, drawing her mouth up to meet his as if he couldn't bear for their lips to part even a fraction. With his eyes open so she saw his determination and desire for her he stepped forward, backing her up against the kitchen counter so he could pin her there with his hips and his hardness as their lips and tongues ravaged any notion of a friendly peck and their panting breaths and daring hands told Kaia that this honest need was most definitely mutual.

'Do you want me to stop?' he breathed as he slid his mouth along her jaw to her earlobe and down the side of her neck, kissing and sucking and tracing the tip of his tongue over her skin.

'No!' Kaia gripped his waist and closed her eyes, aware of his gorgeously sizeable arousal prodding her stomach. Her existence took on a surreal quality. She was kissing Levi and nothing, *nothing*, had ever felt so good. She dropped her head back, a delicious sigh of desire gusting past her parted lips. 'Don't stop,' she begged, panting as she watched his lips glide along her collarbone and over her chest to the tops of her breasts.

Her mind grew foggy, thoughts replaced by wonderful sensations. In all her secret imaginings, she'd hardly dared to dream up this degree of passion. But this was really happening. They were crossing the line. Together.

Before she could verbally encourage him further or argue, primarily with herself, that it was just sex, just one night and she shouldn't get too carried away, his mouth returned to hers, his kisses wilder, his hand cupping her breast, fingers stroking her nipple, turning her on so thoroughly, her knees actually buckled.

'I want you,' he said, his hand sliding under her top. 'But I don't want to hurt you and I still want your friendship.'

'I want you, too,' she said, her arms tightening around his neck. 'Just for tonight.' To show him how much she wrapped one leg around his hips, pressing his pelvis to hers so she felt his erection between her legs where she ached.

'Hold on,' he ordered. With impressive strength, he lifted her from the ground, his hands under her backside, and strode towards his bedroom.

Kaia clung with her arms and legs, taking the glorious opportunity to press kisses down his neck and slide her fingers through his hair, losing herself in lust, knowing she could trust Levi not to hurt her.

They both knew this was simply chemistry and opportunity. Neither of them was looking for a relationship. And they each valued their friendship too much to risk it over sex, no matter how good she feared it might be.

'Do you have a condom?' she asked as he lowered her onto the bed. Ever since losing the baby that hadn't been planned, she'd grown paranoid about contraception. It was still too painful to think about having children in the future, but she certainly wasn't ready now and obviously didn't want any mishaps with Levi.

He nodded and retrieved one from the bedside table. Beyond eager to explore Levi's gorgeous body, Kaia reached for the button fly of his jeans. But before she could get her hands on his erection he joined her on the bed and kissed her once more.

'I've wanted this for so long,' he admitted, sliding his hand under her top as he pressed kisses over her face. He pinged the clasp of her bra and her tingling breast was swallowed in the warmth of his hand.

'Me too,' she said on a moan as he stroked her nipple into a tight, aching peak.

He stilled, shocked. 'Really?'

She nodded and smiled. 'You're gorgeous, Levi. I can't believe it's actually happening.' But she didn't want to stop.

He smiled then, peering down at her with wonder, as if he couldn't quite believe it either. 'It won't change anything between us, you know,' he said with passion. 'I won't let it.'

Kaia shook her head, choked by how much he valued their relationship. 'Me neither.' They would face the consequences of this decision together like adults and protect their friendship.

Because she didn't want any space for doubts to ruin this one time, she tugged at his top and they each paused from kissing to remove some clothes so that they were naked chest to naked chest.

Kaia's mouth dried with lust. She'd seen Levi naked from the waist up before at the beach, but she hadn't been allowed to touch then. Now, she ran her hands over his tight muscles and smooth skin, through the dark scattering of manly chest hair, over his bunched shoulders and down his strong, muscular back. Every inch of him was hard. His skin scorched her. He smelled divine and she was turned on just from the intense way he looked at her naked breasts.

'Levi,' she moaned as he bent his head and took one nipple into his mouth, flicking the tip with his tongue until she writhed under him, her hands shoving at the waistband of his jeans and boxers so she could caress his taut buttocks and shunt his erection harder between her legs where she needed him most.

He trailed his mouth over her ribs and stomach, shifting his weight so he could remove her jeans and underwear, and then lost his own and tossed them aside. For a moment, he sat back on his heels and they stared unashamedly at each other's bodies. Kaia held in a sigh of longing and bit her bottom lip as she took in the sight of his male beauty. All ripped muscles and bronzed skin and power.

Almost reluctantly, their eyes met at last. 'Wow,' Kaia whispered, a smile twitching at her lips. Seeing your friend naked was a monumental moment. She needed the reminder that if this had happened accidentally they'd have laughed it off, such was the playful nature of their relationship. But she was too turned on for laughter.

'Yeah, wow,' he said, his hands sliding up her thighs as if eager to touch as well as look. 'You are so sexy.'

But the moment of levity didn't last long because he reared over her, kissed her once more and slid his hand between her legs, stroking her until she clung to his shoulders, his neck, his face, her entire being burning with need.

'Don't stop,' she said when he let her up for air. She wrapped her hand around his hard length and he groaned, kissing her again, their tongues surging wildly together with wonderful abandon.

When he pulled back, his heated stare devoid of doubt as his touch continued, stroking, teasing, watching her reactions, he said, 'Are you still with me?'

'Absolutely.' Kaia reached for the packet he'd placed on the bed and opened it. She rolled the condom onto him then tugged him on top of her, desperate for more, desperate for everything.

Talking ceased. Laughter became impossible as they kissed and caressed each other's bodies with needy hands and lips and tongues as if starving for this one time.

Finally he was inside her, their hearts banging side by side and their stares locked together in a moment of perfect honesty and ultimate trust.

Levi swept her hair back from her face with both palms and pressed a tender kiss to her lips. 'You're beautiful,' he said.

Feeling safe and treasured, she nodded. 'So are you.' Her fingertips glided up and down his back as she tilted her hips and urged him to move.

'Yes!' Kaia cried as she clung to him, her body moving with his, her hands roaming across his feverish skin, fingers sliding into his hair as they locked stares and breathed in each other's air.

'Kaia,' he groaned, crushing her closer, thrusting

harder and faster, covering her body with his familiar scent and a sheen of sweat.

She climaxed, calling his name, holding him tight as he came too, awash with rush after rush of euphoria that when it was over, and they lay panting in a sweaty heap of satisfied bodies and tangled limbs, made her, absurdly, giggle.

In answer, he raised his head from the crook of her neck, smiled his gorgeous, boyish smile and pressed a kiss to her lips. 'I can't believe you found that amusing.'

'I can't believe we *did* that,' she teased, still too high to regret her reckless decision.

He smiled softly, something sad in his eyes. 'Can we talk about it in the morning? It's late and we're on the early shift tomorrow.'

'Of course.' She nodded, letting him go.

'Don't move.' He kissed her softly then rolled aside. 'I'll be right back.'

Without his warmth, his strength surrounding her, Kaia shivered, pulling the sheets over her body. But as he went to the bathroom to dispose of the condom, all the lovely endorphins drained away to be replaced by those inevitable doubts she'd shoved aside.

Being ready to put her life back together, rocking a bold new haircut was one thing. But sleeping with her best friend? It had been wonderful, but would she live to regret it? Would Levi? Did he regret it already? Was he in the bathroom right now preparing his usual 'let's keep it casual' speech, even though they'd agreed to one night and promised that when it came to their friendship, nothing would change?

Those horrible doubts filled her head until she contemplated sneaking back to her own room before he emerged. But then the decision was made for her. Levi returned from the bathroom, turned out the lights and climbed into his bed, pulling her close.

'Thanks for a great birthday,' he whispered, pressing a kiss to her cheek from behind.

'You're welcome,' she said, sliding her fingers through his and praying he couldn't feel the panicked flutter of her heartbeat.

With her head helpfully supplying all the reasons that could never happen again—their friendship was precious, Levi only did casual flings and next time Kaia fell in love, she wanted it to be for keeps—it took a long time for her to follow him into sleep.

CHAPTER FOUR

THE NEXT MORNING, at the click of Kaia's bedroom door opening, Levi froze mid-stir of his coffee. His entire body felt stiff with nerves and apprehension. He'd awoken at six am to find himself alone in his bed. Both relieved that Kaia had made the decision of how the morning after would go for him and disappointed that she wasn't asleep beside him, he'd jumped into the shower, quickly dressed and made breakfast, pretending that everything was normal. Just any other work day…

Now Kaia emerged dressed in her uniform of grey trousers and a red Southern Rescue polo shirt. She smiled brightly, as usual, sending his pulse into triple digits. Clearly she too was trying to act normal. Except her voice trembled slightly as she said good morning.

'I made you tea,' he said, sliding the mug across the counter as if it weren't the morning after the best night of his life. 'How did you sleep?'

Better to dispense with any awkwardness rather than avoid the topic. He hadn't in his wildest dreams expected last night to happen, but they obviously needed to discuss it.

'Good, thanks.' Kaia shot him a hesitant smile and

took a sip of the tea, obviously happy for him to lead the conversation.

Levi stepped a little closer to her; he couldn't help himself. She looked lovely this morning, her cheeks rosy, her eyes shining and her glossy new haircut framing her heart-shaped face. He cleared his throat. 'Last night was—'

'Incredible,' she interrupted, something in her stare vulnerable.

He smiled and fought the urge to touch her hand, delighted that she'd had a good time. 'I was going to say *unexpected*, but yes, incredible also fits.'

He caught a waft of the shower gel she'd used and fresh arousal heated his blood. But for his doubts, that by selfishly sleeping with his best friend he'd risked the most cherished relationship of his life, his body would definitely be eager for a long, lazy bout of morning sex. He'd fancied Kaia the very first time he'd seen her and he couldn't simply switch that off, not now he knew how explosive they were together.

But they had a shift to get to, and sadly this morning his mind was back in charge. 'I think we should talk about it, though,' he said gently, 'and not just the highlights, of which there were many, obviously.'

When she'd first kissed him chastely last night, he'd considered pretending he couldn't see the desire in her eyes. But, driven by her flicker of doubt as she'd second-guessed the signals he'd been sending, he'd been too weak to resist.

'I agree,' Kaia said, sliding onto one of the bar stools and drawing her drink between her cupped hands like a shield. 'I woke up horrified that we might have officially ruined our friendship,' she continued, her doubt-filled expression intensifying.

'Me too, although I'm not sure there is anything you could do to put our friendship in jeopardy,' he said, rushing to reassure her. 'And we agreed last night that we wouldn't let it change anything.' The sooner she understood that it was business as usual, that they were still friends, the quicker they could each stop worrying that they'd broken the precious thing they'd had.

'Yes, we did.' She smiled a small smile and his lips buzzed, desperate for another taste of their softness and the tiny mewling sound she made when he slid his lips across to her earlobe.

'Just to reassure you,' he went on, forcing himself to sound calm, although he felt anything but, 'I'm as committed to our relationship as friends as strongly as I was yesterday. I really value our friendship. Always have. No one else really gets me the way you do.' Of course, that didn't mean he wasn't more than eager for a repeat of last night. He'd been desperate to take whatever scraps of her he could get. A part of him couldn't believe his luck that she'd wanted him too. But she'd said one night and he would never do anything to put her place in his life at risk.

She nodded. 'Same for me, Levi. I don't regret it one bit,' she added, 'but it's best if we leave it as a one-time thing.'

He allowed himself another sigh of relief that when it came to their friendship, they were still on the same page, even as he swallowed down his disappointment that their incredible night wouldn't be repeated. But he couldn't have the best of both worlds: a casual fling with his friend. That wouldn't be fair to her. They both knew that, long-term, he obviously wasn't the man for her, and he wouldn't insult Kaia by suggesting a friends-with-benefits situation.

'I know you're happily single,' she said, smiling wryly. 'Goodness knows I've thrust enough of my single friends at you over the years to know you're not looking for anything serious just yet.'

He shrugged. She was right, of course. She knew him better than anyone, but her observation still grated for some unknown reason.

'And you said last night you weren't ready to date,' he pointed out because he knew her too. She'd cried on Levi's shoulder over the loss of the baby and the demise of the relationship she'd thought was for keeps. 'I'm glad you're taking your time and not rushing into anything.' Because it was obvious to him that both of those things had badly knocked her confidence.

She nodded. 'I've got enough on my plate with moving into my own place and seriously contemplating a career change.' She looked up from her cooling mug of tea and boldly met his stare, so he saw the same determination to move on that she'd shown him yesterday. 'I guess for me, what happened with us last night was another sign that I'm ready to put the last few months behind me and move on to new challenges, stronger than before.'

'I'm happy for you,' Levi said, seeking that peace of mind that should come with knowing his best friend was feeling ready to make some positive changes in her life, as well as the relief that, despite last night's monumental but incredible blip, she had no unrealistic romantic expectations of him, a man who by his own admission had never been in love.

'So we carry on as usual, as friends?' he asked, confused that he could be both relieved and unsettled by the idea. But maybe it was simply a reaction to being this vulnerable with a woman. Normally, when a physical fling was over for him, he rarely stayed friends with the people he had dated.

'Deal,' she agreed breezily, squaring her shoulders. 'We've done it. It was great. But now we forget it ever happened and go back to being friends and roommates.'

Levi smiled at her pragmatism, nodding through another twisted surge of relief that just left him simultaneously hollow. He'd known it the day he'd met her, but he was so lucky to have Kaia in his life. She was smart and fun and caring. There was no way he wanted to risk the relationship they already had or let her down, just for more, albeit incredible, sex.

Hoping that everything would return to normal after they'd briefly crossed the line before scurrying back to the friend zone, he reached out and cupped her face, his palm tingling. 'You're amazing,' he said stepping closer, a lump in his throat. 'I'll never forget my thirty-fifth birthday. Thank you for making it…special.' He felt his fingers twitch, desperate to slide them through her soft, glossy hair. But he dropped his hand to his side instead, remembering his promises and everything that was at stake.

'You're welcome.' She laughed and stood, draining the last of her tea. 'I had a great time too.'

Finally, the persistent hum of his doubts fell silent. This was for the best. One and done. No risk of dragging out a physical relationship and potentially hurting her when it was over. She'd been through enough, and when it came to the kind of relationship she wanted Levi was a complete novice.

'Is it too soon for a friendly hug?' he asked, desperately trying to re-find that playful, flirtatious vibe of their friendship so he'd know for certain that no lasting damage had been done.

'Of course not,' she said and held open her arms, stepping into his embrace.

Stiffly, because, now that their physical intimacies had caught up with their emotional ones, his body seemed possessed and unnatural, Levi wrapped his arms around her shoulders and tried not to inhale her lovely Kaia scent. She squeezed his waist in a way she'd held him a thousand times before, her head resting on his chest because she was so much shorter than him. But predictably his body reacted to her touch and closeness, his pulse flying, his groin stirring and his muscles screaming to clutch her the way he had last night when they'd been naked and high from their orgasms. Of course, then he'd had a moment's panic that even buried inside her, his arms crushing her while she held him just as tightly, wasn't quite close enough.

But this embrace was over before he could forget himself. Before he'd roused enough conscious effort to let her go, she stepped back and awkwardly glanced at the floor.

'I'm um...going to look at that house after work today,' she said, moving aside to place her mug in the dishwasher. 'Do you mind if we take two cars into work today?'

'Of course not,' he said, irrationally feeling as if she'd kicked him in the gut and told him to get lost rather than simply decided to make her own way to work. 'Do you want me to come with you? Look out for any damp or dodgy neighbours?'

His stomach sank. Was he wrong to think he could pick up their friendship as if last night hadn't happened? Despite the best will in the world, it seemed things were far from normal. Part of him wanted her still, and there had never before been any awkwardness between them when they hugged. But perhaps it would take some time to get back to where they'd been yesterday.

'You have Lee's footie match today,' she reminded him. 'But thanks for the offer. Plus it's your night to make dinner. You'll do anything to get out of cooking, won't you?' She laughed and his insides settled to something approximating normal.

'Busted…' he said amiably, although he secretly loved to cook, a habit he'd picked up from all those school holidays spent living with his bachelor uncle Murray, whose idea of a decent meal was slightly burnt toast.

But this teasing was good. Perhaps he was inventing worries. Perhaps he simply needed to pull himself together and quickly. Forget. Act normal. Fake it until their easy friendship came naturally once more.

'See you there, then,' she said, slipping into her Southern Rescue high-visibility jacket and heading for the door.

Levi stood frozen in the kitchen long after the sound of Kaia's car pulling away had receded. His relief that their first conversation had gone so well was nowhere near enough to overcome the worry that he'd made a colossal mistake last night in indulging his attraction. The trouble was, the sex had been so good, he knew with absolute certainty that, given the same set of circumstances, he wouldn't change a single thing. Unsure where that left him, knowing that they were both set on putting last night behind them, he locked up and headed for work.

CHAPTER FIVE

A BUSY WEEK LATER, Kaia was still trying to pretend that, when it came to her friendship with Levi, nothing had changed. The trouble, of course, was that, no matter how hard she tried, she couldn't forget that amazing night or how being intimate with him had just felt…right.

Every time their eyes met at work or at home her body overheated as she recalled the intense way he'd stared at her when pulling back from a kiss, as if he'd been utterly amazed that it was so good. Every time their arms innocently brushed while they cooked together or took stock of the helicopter's medical supplies at work, it became glaringly obvious to Kaia that everything *had* changed. There was no longer any such thing as an innocent touch. There were no more hugs. No more playful shoulder bumps. And sitting close on the sofa while they watched TV…? Forget it. Touching each other had now become taboo. For Kaia, touching him confusingly meant wanting him again, when she'd promised him that their physical relationship was over, hoped that one night would be the end of their chemistry.

But she was left wondering if the lack of physical contact was deliberate on Levi's part. A sign that, despite what he'd said, he *did* regret that night and didn't want her to misconstrue their usual flirtation. After all, she'd watched him perfect casual hook-ups these past four years, so she shouldn't be surprised that he was clearly more adept at moving on than her.

Kaia concealed a sigh and kept her gaze lowered so that Levi, sat next to her in the helicopter, wouldn't see her turmoil. They were en route to a remote mountain-bike trail in Craigieburn Forest in the foothills of the Southern Alps. A rider had taken a bend too fast and careered off the track, falling down a steep, bush-clad slope, on which he'd found himself trapped by his injuries.

Fortunately his partner had doubled back after stopping for a drink to discover he was no longer behind her on the trail. But the woman had needed to cycle all the three miles back to the car park before she was able to find any mobile-phone reception to call for help.

'ETA three minutes.' Mac spoke to them through the helicopter's comms.

Kaia glanced sideways at Levi, relieved to see an expression of concentration, his usual as he headed into a rescue mission. She gave him a small smile, trying to put her head in the zone.

'This is as close as I can get,' Mac said moments later, hovering in place over the widest part of the bike track closest to the coordinates they'd been given for the location of the casualty. While Kaia and Levi double-checked their harnesses, Grant opened the cabin door and quickly lowered a stretcher to the ground.

Kaia moved into position, ready to be winched down, but before she could descend Levi touched her arm.

'When you get down there, wait for me, yeah?' he

said, his frown of concern for her safety pushing another lump into her throat.

'Of course.' She nodded and gave him a thumbs-up, glad that no matter how awkward things were between them on a personal level, professionally they still had each other's backs. 'Safety first.'

They'd discussed the logistics and rescue tactics on the ride there. Given the dwindling hours of daylight left, the rapidly falling temperatures and the length of time the casualty had been lying immobile with his injuries, time was, of course, of the essence. But it wouldn't do for either her or Levi to also get hurt hurling themselves down the slope on which the casualty had fallen.

When they were both safely on the ground with the equipment they might need, the helicopter moved away to the car park at the start of the trail to wait. Kaia adjusted the heavy backpack of medical supplies and checked the map and casualty's approximate location on her phone. With Levi hauling the stretcher, and after a few minutes of gingerly working their way through the dense bush lining the bike path, they heard someone calling out to them.

'I see them,' Levi said, taking the lead, regularly checking that Kaia was on his tail as they picked their way through dense thicket and over fallen, moss-covered trees, which were slippery underfoot.

When they reached the man and his partner, it was obvious the patient, Alex, was in a pretty bad way. Dressed only in shorts and T-shirt, he was shaking uncontrollably, his complexion ashen with pain and shock.

Kaia performed a quick body scan as she introduced herself and asked Alex what day it was to ascertain his cognitive state. Aside from the obvious cuts and bruises to his face and limbs, he had an open fracture of his right lower leg and was also complaining of neck pain. Fortunately he'd been wearing a bike helmet, which would have offered some protection against head injury.

'Kathy, we're going to need you to carefully step aside so we can help Alex, okay?' Levi spoke to the woman, who, the minute she'd spied them, had dropped her brave facade and was now weeping freely but silently.

'Lie still, mate,' Levi told Alex. 'We're going to stabilise you, give you something for the pain, then get you out of here, okay?'

'Do you think you blacked out?' Kaia asked the man as Levi attached an oxygen mask to his face, a pulse oximeter to his finger and blood-pressure cuff to his arm to record his vital signs.

'No,' Alex said as Kaia scanned the readings. She quickly shone a pen-light in his pupils to test his reflexes, relieved to find them responding normally, another sign that he might have avoided a head injury.

Crouched as best she could at Alex's side, Kaia set about establishing venous access so they could administer painkillers, while Levi unwrapped a hypothermia blanket.

'He's shut down,' she told Levi moments later as she tried and failed to insert a cannula into Alex's right arm. Shock, cold and blood loss meant his veins had collapsed.

'I'll try this side,' Levi said, taking the tourniquet from her, their fingers brushing as they worked quickly and efficiently together.

Kaia removed the cervical spine collar from her backpack and fitted it, then covered the patient with the foil blanket.

'Got it,' Levi said, having more success with the cannula.

Their eyes met and the non-verbal communication they'd shared all the years they'd worked together passed between them: gratitude, teamwork, respect. But there was no time to enjoy the jolt of relief.

As he taped the cannula in place, Kaia drew up some pain medication into a syringe and handed it over. They needed to splint the leg and transfer Alex to the stretcher and carry him out of there. The painkillers would reduce the inevitable discomfort of moving him.

'Let's get some IV fluids up,' Levi said. 'His blood pressure is on the low side.'

Kaia passed him a bag of saline and then opened a sterile dressing. She covered the wound on the patient's leg and carefully applied a splint. With the spine immobilised, she raised Alex's T-shirt and examined his chest for any obvious injuries, deformities or evidence of a punctured lung, although he had no chest pain.

'All good, I think,' she told Levi, handing over the stethoscope. 'Can you double-check?'

'Of course,' he said, taking a second to hold her eye contact. 'Although I trust your clinical skills.'

While the compound fracture was itself a medical emergency, any trauma to the chest could be immediately life threatening. Levi removed the stethoscope and glanced again at Kaia. 'I agree. Sounds good.'

Levi was right. She should trust her instincts more, especially if she hoped to make it as a doctor one day.

'Ready to get out of here?' Kaia asked the man, who'd

stopped trembling now he had some painkillers on board and was a little warmer.

'Ready as I'll ever be,' Alex said with a reassuring trace of humour.

'That's the spirit,' Levi said, positioning the stretcher beside Alex so they could safely log-roll him and slide it underneath his body.

It took a slow and steady thirty minutes to carry Alex back to the bike track, and another ten to winch everyone aboard the helicopter. Although she kept physically fit and weight trained regularly, Kaia knew that Levi had taken more than his share of the load, thanks to his superior size and muscle bulk.

As she caught her breath during a quiet moment on the way to Christchurch Hospital, he leaned over and said, 'Well done. That was physically tough. You did great.'

Kaia smiled and nodded, missing his casual touch and their usually playful interactions. But now that she'd slept with him, she couldn't expect his usual levels of flirtation. He wouldn't want to lead her on or give mixed signals. It was done.

'Thanks for your help,' she said, determined to find some way to stop wanting him. But no matter how she struggled to forget that amazing night, no matter how strained some aspects of their relationship now were, she couldn't bring herself to regret sleeping with him. And if she was honest, she would do it again in a heartbeat.

'Always,' he said, his stare lingering as if he might say something else.

But the moment passed and Alex's heart monitor

beeped, and Levi, who was closest, adjusted his intravenous fluids.

Kaia's chest ached as she racked her brains for a way to make this longing cease so she could have her friend back. Properly. Maybe if she set him up with Heidi this weekend when the woman was in town for a job interview, Kaia would have no choice but to see him as nothing more than a friend again. While the idea still made her feel sick with jealousy, it was worth a shot.

Back at base later that afternoon, Levi retrieved his backpack from his locker and headed out to the staff car park, the cloud that had settled over his head since his birthday oppressive and constantly throwing him off balance.

Despite their agreement to put that night behind them and with the exception of their teamwork when it came to their jobs, nothing about their relationship felt right or normal.

She looked at him differently. All their playful banter fell flat. And it was obvious to him that she went out of her way to avoid touching him, as if she feared he might lunge for her again like some sort of lecherous creep who couldn't control his impulses.

Levi sighed heavily. Why couldn't he shake this preoccupation? Logic, self-preservation and his protective urges all agreed that focusing on Kaia as a friend was the best course of action. They'd even made a deal, and Kaia seemed happy with just one night, which should be a relief to him because he'd hate to risk leading her on. The trouble was, his libido and even his up-and-down feelings clearly weren't operating on logic. And no matter how many cold showers he took, he couldn't stop thinking about her in a way that had nothing to do with their friendship.

Living with her had become torture. Every time he saw her, he wanted to drag her into his arms and kiss away the hesitation on her face. He walked on eggshells when they talked, desperate for her easy, playful company but also scared he'd embarrass himself by reaching for her, driving her to the brink of pleasure once more so she'd sigh his name the way she had that night. So she'd see him as more than a friend. Even his subconscious suffered, his dreams either the erotic kind where they used every horizontal surface in the flat on which to have sex, or alternately eerie nightmares in which he searched in vain for a faceless Kaia, convinced that if he didn't find her his life would be ruined. Psychologists would, no doubt, have loved to poke around in his head.

Disgusted by his weakness for her and by his own selfishness, he emerged from the building to see Kaia waiting at his car, her back leaning against the passenger-side door as she peered at her phone.

Raw need brought his feet to a halt, his body instantly tense and aching. She was silhouetted by the evening sun, her new hair streaked with gold. She'd changed out of her uniform, her skinny jeans hugging her curves, her shirt moulded to her perfect breasts and open just enough at the neck to reveal an intriguing triangle of freckled skin he now knew tasted like heaven. Still a little high from the adrenaline of their earlier mission, he dragged in a shaky breath, preparing for another agonising conversation where the things he wanted to say and the things he was allowed to say locked horns.

'Hey,' she said, looking up and smiling. 'I was just talking about you.' She laughed and waved her phone. 'Well, texting about you, actually. Heidi's confirmed she's definitely in Christchurch this weekend.'

'Great,' he said, in what he hoped was an encouraging way, his stomach sinking as he unlocked the car and they both climbed in. At least Kaia seemed to think things were back to normal.

But even though the last thing he wanted when his mind was stuck on Kaia was to think about another woman,maybe that was exactly what he had to do to get over this…obsession. Because Kaia had obviously moved on. Soon she'd be living somewhere else, changing careers, dating other men who could be what she needed…

Jealous bile rushed into his throat. But he wanted her to be happy. He wanted to protect their friendship above all else.

'Are you still happy for me to give her your number?' she said, facing away from him as she reached over her shoulder for the seat belt.

Happy? A beautiful, intelligent and successful woman wanted his number. *Happy* was all he should be. But the idea of making small talk with anyone other than Kaia left him cold and depressed.

'Sure,' he said in a bare-faced lie, starting the engine. He didn't want her to sense his confusion or the very *un*-friendly Kaia fantasies in his head. She knew him well, after all. He needed to do a better job of acting until he'd worked Kaia out of his system. Because surely that was all this was—the longest, most intense sex-hangover ever. And going along with this Heidi plan might be the perfect cover.

'So how much have you told her about me?' he asked to conceal his lukewarm attitude to her friend. He didn't want to mess this Heidi around. He was happy to meet her, to get to know her, but he'd have to make it crystal clear that he wasn't looking for a relationship. It had been years since he'd had one of those and the only person he wanted to spend time with and have sex with at the moment was Kaia.

That said, she'd made herself clear: for her their one time was over. Pining or fantasising about a replay of that night, a wild fling with his best friend, was pointless and selfish.

'Don't worry… I haven't told her much,' she said, her voice dropping. 'Just what you look like, where you're from and how great you are generally but especially at your job.'

Levi focused on the road but nodded. As long as he'd known her Kaia had always tried to fix him up, perhaps hoping that if she threw enough single women at him one might be Miss Right. It had never truly bothered him until now that they'd had sex. Now that he'd had a single taste of the forbidden fruit he could never have again.

'Remind me what she does again,' he said to distract himself, embarrassed that he'd never really paid attention when Kaia talked about her hot single friend.

'She's a physio with a master's in sports physiology. She worked in professional rugby for a while. Don't you listen to me at all?' she added playfully, a gentle rebuke in her voice.

'Ah, yes… It's coming back to me now,' he muttered, his mind turning to thoughts of dinner and how he would cook Kaia's favourite—healthy chicken parmigiana.

'She's thirty, bubbly and active, and she also loves to surf,' Kaia said, her voice overly bright.

Was it his imagination, or could he detect a strain, as if she was trying too hard to sell this blind date? Huh, wishful thinking on his part.

'So what's her situation?' he asked to distract himself from thoughts of Kaia. 'Why is she single?'

'She worked in Sydney for a while, dated a guy there,' Kaia said. 'But it didn't work out. So she decided to move back to New Zealand. She's nice. Really nice. Not a single red flag, as I see it.'

Except Heidi wasn't Kaia.

'From *your* perspective,' he said, flicking her a smile that almost felt natural.

'Trust me,' she urged, 'she's a catch. Not that she's desperate to get married or anything, although she does want a family one day, like you.'

'That's good,' he said, his pulse surging with discomfort. ''Cos I'm not sure I'm ready to go fishing, as you know.' And the only woman he was interested in spending time with after an intense day at work was the one woman he couldn't have, a woman soon moving out and moving on.

After a few awkward moments, Kaia said, 'You do still want a family of your own one day, though, right?'

There was a definite strain in her voice now, so Levi knew talking about kids was still a trigger for her after the miscarriage.

He shrugged and kept his eyes on the road, desperate to reassure Kaia that it could still happen for her. 'Yeah… I do…'

Another beat of silence passed. 'So how are you going

to have kids if all you do is date casually?' she gently pushed, making an excellent point.

Levi breathed through the vulnerable feeling that came whenever he talked about his emotions. He'd spent so long emotionally distancing himself from his family, and the women he casually dated, that even with Kaia he hated talking about this stuff. But if she could raise the subject of kids after losing a baby, he could suck it up and be honest.

'You're right,' he said, eventually. 'I don't have my personal life all figured out. I guess I just assumed that, when the time was right, I'd meet someone I could feel serious about and… I don't know…take things from there…'

Did that sound as lame to her as it did to him?

The atmosphere in the car changed. Levi scrabbled around for another question about Heidi to change the subject away from his ineptitude at relationships, but Kaia was quicker. 'So let me get this right: you don't believe in love, you're not in any rush to get married but you want kids….' Her voice was low and cautious as if she was secretly horrified. And, hearing it laid out that way, he too heard the absurdity in his words.

'I don't know…' she added quietly. 'You might want to tweak the plan.'

'Maybe you're right.' Levi swallowed, his defences building. Out of the two of them, Kaia was the expert on relationships. But even he could agree that his plan had flaws. She said he was a catch, but what woman would be happy to take a chance on a man offering so little certainty? 'I… Like I said, commitment, forever…it's not my area of expertise.' Maybe he'd never be able to love someone the way they needed to be loved. Maybe that broken thing in him made him unable to love or be loved in return.

Levi's skin crawled as he pulled to a stop at the lights. There were ugly parts of himself he kept locked away, but he hated the idea of Kaia thinking there was something majorly wrong with him, something she would find lacking or a turn-off. 'I did have one semi-serious girlfriend once,' he admitted softly, turning to meet her stare. 'In my early twenties. But… Well, it didn't work out.'

He gulped air, feeling as if he might throw up. Even with Kaia, exposing his emotions this way was tough.

'You did?' she asked, her stare wide with amazement. 'You've never told me about her.'

The lights changed and Levi gratefully focused on driving once more. 'Probably because there wasn't much to tell. We were together less than a year. We didn't live together. She was a nurse. Ambitious. Wanted to move to Australia, where she could earn more money than in New Zealand.'

'So what happened?' Kaia asked, looking at him as if she didn't recognise him. 'How come you split up?'

'She ended it when I wouldn't move with her,' he said, matter-of-factly, desperate to keep that part of him people rejected hidden from Kaia, of all people. He had once tried to be part of a couple, but his efforts hadn't been enough for his ex.

'I'm sorry,' she said, clearly waiting for more information.

'It was no big deal.' Levi sighed and tried to open up, to make himself vulnerable, even though it went against the grain. 'She said our lives were headed in different directions. Said I was immature and not ready to commit.' And she'd obviously had a point.

'Just because you didn't want to move overseas with her?' Kaia asked, frowning. 'That's a bit unfair.'

Levi shrugged, surprised that Kaia hadn't simply agreed with his ex. 'I *was* immature. I was young. And she was right—I wasn't ready to commit to her, not in the way she expected me to. But she was smart. She saw through me.' He tried to smile, but Kaia wasn't laughing. Only staring at him as if he were a stranger. Instead he swallowed past his tight throat.

'Anyway,' he said, 'she obviously saw something in me, in the way I handled the relationship, that she didn't like...' He gave another casual shrug, wishing to draw a line under this conversation. Because to continue was to expose himself to the one person by whom he never wanted to be judged weak or inadequate.

'You wanted different things,' Kaia said with utter conviction. 'Just because you wanted to stay in New Zealand... That's not a character flaw.'

Levi turned and offered her a sad smile. 'I guess not, although that's exactly what happened with you and Sam in the end. You wanted different things.'

'That wasn't the same,' she said, looking straight ahead. 'Sam changed his mind about me, about wanting a family after we lost the baby. I was devastated and grieving but even through that I could sense his relief after the miscarriage. If he'd been honest with me from the start, admitted he wasn't ready for a serious relationship or a family... I could have prepared myself. Or maybe I wouldn't have lived with him in the first place if I'd known we wanted different things from the outset. I might not have even dated him if I'd known our long-term goals were so opposed.'

Levi nodded, feeling sick. He loved that Kaia knew her own mind and what she wanted, but the gap between them relationship-wise only seemed wider now. She still wanted all of those things, and even if Levi wanted them too one day he had no idea how to be that man. She deserved someone ready and able to give her the world: love, commitment, marriage and a family.

'Did you tell your ex you loved her?' she asked, frowning.

Levi shook his head. 'No. Never,' he said, still feeling somehow emotionally inadequate. Scared that Kaia would see his incompetence with relationship stuff, not that it was any great secret. But she was right. How was he going to turn it all around when he met someone he wanted to build a life with? Now that she'd pointed out the flaws in his vague plan, the idea that he would one day wake up relationship-ready seemed preposterous. An insurmountable hurdle. No woman would want a man content to provide security and partnership, be a father to her children, but without messy emotional entanglements.

A tense silence settled. Moments later he pulled the car into the drive and turned off the engine, unsure how to change the subject, because there were no longer any easy subjects between them, sadly.

'Do you regret it?' Kaia asked before he could leave the car. 'Regret not choosing her? Choosing the relationship?'

He shook his head. 'Not at all. We were young. Both starting out in our careers. I didn't love her, and she obviously wanted more than I was able to give.'

And since then, he hadn't really tried to give anyone else more. It was safer to just keep it casual, the way it had been safer to lock down his emotions as a boy and meekly return to boarding school term after term. Because no amount of begging and promising he'd behave better had worked on his mother. And maybe she and his ex had been right—the broken thing in him obviously pushed people away. Maybe it was too late now, after years of shutting down so he didn't feel the sting of that rejection, to change. He certainly couldn't bear the possibility of Kaia's rejection if she too saw a part of him she didn't like.

Kaia frowned, that sickening look of disappointment with him back in her eyes. 'But you might have loved her one day.'

He shook his head, unable to look away from her pensive stare, even though it hurt to see her realisation that he *was* lacking something when it came to relationships. 'I wouldn't.'

'How do you know?' she pushed, impassioned. 'Sometimes love takes time. If you never give it a chance to develop…'

'I know how I felt about her,' he said. 'You can't force it. If the special spark just isn't there…'

Defeated, Kaia nodded, her expression turning sympathetic. 'No…you're right.'

'You're right too,' he said, desperate to get inside the house so this confessional would end. 'Maybe I won't be lucky enough to have a family after all… As this conversation has highlighted very effectively, I'm no good at this stuff and maybe I've put it off for too long.' He tried to smile, to make light of it, but all he really wanted to do was hold her and breathe in her scent, kiss her soft lips and make her moan until she looked at him with wonder again. Not pity and disappointment.

'But you love kids and you're so good with them,' she said, softly. 'Look at Lee. He adores you.'

Despite the burn of fear in his chest, Levi smiled, picturing the special fist-bump greeting the boy had created, just for the two of them. 'Kids like Lee have had it tough,' he said, remembering what it was like to be a hurting young man too small for his feelings. 'If I can help just by giving some of my time and experience… paying it forward.'

'Because you had troubled teens too? After your dad…' she said, looking at him as he were see-through after all. As if all his attempts to be emotionally self-sufficient were pointless.

'I guess…' Levi shrugged, aware he was deflecting and avoiding showing Kaia all of his dark places. The fear that he was irreparably broken. That the broken part of him was not only unlovable, but also pushed people he cared about away. That if he tried to be that vulnerable with someone again after years of shutting people out to stay safe, he might never survive the rejection, especially not from Kaia.

'Mind if we go inside?' he asked, clearing his throat. 'I'm hungry.' Another lie. But he couldn't let Kaia see his worst fears.

'Wait,' she said, reaching for his arm and then thinking better of it and dropping her hand. 'If you ever want to talk about your dad, or anything else, I'm here for you. You know that, right?'

'Sure,' he said, his pulse buzzing a warning inside

his head. He didn't know how to do this, let her in. Let her that close. Even though, for him, there was no one closer. Because what if she too hated what she discovered and walked away? He'd just about survived losing her as a lover after one night. He wouldn't survive losing her friendship.

'I mean it, Levi,' she said, refusing to allow him to brush it off. 'I know things have been a bit…awkward since…you know.' She glanced down at her lap, her hands twisted there. 'But you've been there for me. Over and over again. I've poured my heart out to you many times. I want you to know that I'll always be there for you, too, if you ever need to talk.'

'Thanks,' he said, finally opening the car door. Right then, he'd have rather cut out his own tongue than expose any more of his soft spots. He'd even rather kiss her again and ruin what was left of their friendship.

As he followed her inside Levi vowed to do better to not only keep their friendship intact, but also get a hold of his wildly conflicting emotions. No more pining for Kaia. No more sharing his darkest secrets. He would keep on acting like her friend until things returned to normal. He'd even meet up with Heidi, go through the motions of the blind date Kaia had set up. Who knew? They might even hit it off. And eventually, maybe long after Kaia had moved out, started medical school and moved on romantically, he might even stop wanting his best friend.

He could but hope.

CHAPTER SIX

ALL HELICOPTER-RESCUE paramedics needed to complete mandatory underwater escape training or HUET every two years. The safety training allowed the crew to practise their emergency procedures, escape routes and survival skills. While others in the team saw the training as a break from the norm, escaping a submerged simulation helicopter in cold water was not one of Levi's favourite things. Especially as he knew Kaia always dreaded it.

'I…um… I meant to tell you,' she said as they waited in line for their turn, 'I got that house. I found out this morning that my references were accepted. I can move in two weeks.'

Levi forced a brittle smile onto his face and choked out the appropriate words. 'That's fantastic news. Congratulations.'

'Thanks,' she said, clearly distracted by the test to come.

'I'll make sure I have that weekend off roster if you want,' he offered, feeling sick that his time to enjoy living with her was running out. 'Help you move your stuff.' It might kill him to help her leave him, but he'd have to find a way to keep that concealed.

She looked up as he reached the front of the queue. 'Thanks, Levi. That would be...great.'

Levi hesitated, fighting the instinct to touch her and whisper reassurances about the test. But they hadn't touched since the day after his birthday. And all their talk about relationships the other day had left him feeling paranoid that one wrong move, where he did or said something stupid, would mess this up.

'Young, you're up,' the instructor said, calling Levi forward to take his turn.

Levi dragged his gaze away from a worried-looking Kaia and climbed into the underwater egress simulator. When he was strapped in, he took one final glance at Kaia at the side of the pool and smiled encouragingly. Her face pale, she offered him a nervous smile and a thumbs-up and his gut clenched. She hated this day. Had an irrational, or rational, depending on your viewpoint, fear that she'd get stuck in the simulator and they wouldn't pull her out in time. Not that he would let anything bad happen to her, of course.

'Brace, brace, brace,' the instructor said through the headset. Levi assumed the brace position and held his breath. With a mechanical jolt, the simulator tilted violently as it hit the water. In a matter of seconds, cold water began to fill the fully submerged cabin.

When the movement stopped, and he was fully underwater, Levi opened his eyes, trying to orientate himself in his upside-down position. Part of the training involved not only safely exiting the flooded cabin, but also rescuing an unconscious *casualty* played by a dummy.

Recalling his training and trying to stay calm, Levi

released his seat harness and reached underneath his seat for a life jacket. He looped the life jacket around his neck without inflating it and then, careful not to kick out his legs and injure himself inside the cramped cabin, manoeuvred to the 'casualty', which was strapped onto a stretcher. The sooner he had his turn, the less time Kaia would have to wait in dread.

He freed the straps and, gripping the dummy under one arm, he pushed against the glass pane of the emergency exit and escaped the submersible. With one or two strong kicks, he surfaced and inflated his life jacket, swimming backwards towards the side of the pool with his arm around the chest of the rescue dummy.

A scattered round of applause sounded from the rest of the team. He handed the dummy over to the instructors, who would set up the simulator for the next trainee, and hauled himself from the water, his stare seeking out Kaia once more.

'Well done,' she said, handing him his towel, her face even paler.

She looked so nervous he wanted to pull her into his arms and hold her, but of course he couldn't. 'Good, luck,' he said instead, looping the towel around his neck. 'You'll be fine,' he whispered, just before she took her place on the loading platform.

With nothing more to do but watch, Levi took a seat on the poolside tiered seating rather than head for the changing rooms. He hated the wariness that had developed between them since that night. Hated the way she looked at him with disappointment whenever they talked about relationships. It made him feel as if, despite his best efforts and the sacrifice he made daily to set his rampant attraction aside and focus on friends, he might lose her anyway. But beyond rewinding time and walking away the night of his birthday or being a better man, he didn't know how to fix their relationship.

Kaia climbed inside the simulator and strapped herself in. The simulated fuselage was designed to enter the water at a different angle every time the test was run to prepare the trainees for any eventuality. Levi watched from the sidelines, quickly seeing that Kaia had pulled the short straw. The cabin entered the water tilted on both the horizontal and vertical planes so only one emergency exit was easily accessible, and for the trainee inside there was maximum disorientation.

With his stare flitting between the clock and the submerged simulator Levi clenched his fists, every passing second that she stayed underwater accelerating his pulse and adding to his helplessness.

There were two divers in the water. Their job was to observe the trainee and intervene at the first sign of trouble. Only they didn't seem to be doing anything. Kaia was fast approaching the submerged time limit allowed. Levi knew she wasn't as strong a swimmer as some, and he could tell from the pattern of the bubbles rising that she was still inside the simulator.

Uncaring who saw him react, he jerked to his feet and moved to the side of the pool, panic snatching at his breath. He hesitated a little longer, torn. He didn't want to embarrass her or make a scene in front of their colleagues, but his protective urges were running wild. She was his partner. They always looked out for each other's safety. Frozen with indecision, he watched the water and willed her to appear. After another fifteen agonising seconds, he abandoned his towel and heeled off his trainers, preparing to dive in and help her out.

Then, with a commotion of rising bubbles and a gasping inhale, she broke the surface, triumphantly clutching the dummy casualty under her arm, and inflated the life jacket.

Levi swallowed, his throat so dry it hurt. Adrenaline and euphoric relief rushed through him. She was okay. She was okay.

While she swam away from the simulator he grabbed her towel, talking himself down from a very tall ledge. He was acting unhinged. Paranoid and irrational. Flailing around, neither her friend nor anything more.

He met her at the side of the pool, ignoring the male instructor there to assist, and reached for her hands to help her out of the water.

'That was cutting it close,' he said quietly as she coughed and spluttered and wiped the water from her eyes.

Kaia nodded, clearly unable to speak just yet.

Uncaring if he'd come across as a mother hen, or that the move would necessitate touching her skin to skin, something he'd avoided since *that night*, he wrapped the towel around her shoulders and led her over to the spectators' seats to recover.

'The pocket of my shorts got stuck on the door lever,' she said eventually, still breathless and coughing intermittently.

'The divers should have helped you,' he said, casting them a murderous look. 'A few more seconds and I would have dived in myself.' He took some deep breaths and tried to calm down before she thought he'd lost the plot. 'You were down for too long…'

'Thanks,' she said, gifting him a wobbly smile as she stared at him with curiosity and a hint of confusion.

'No problem,' he said. Shaking inside, he took some deep breaths as his fear for her safety drained away. But it was replaced by other fears. What was happening to him? Was he just emotional because their relationship had changed? Being physically intimate with Kaia was bound to have brought them closer in some ways. And he wasn't used to being that vulnerable with anyone. Kaia knew him well. What if, because of that night, she saw his confusion and desperation and selfish desires and pulled back from their friendship?

That was when Levi realised he still had his arm protectively around her shoulders. Scared to leave it there and equally scared to move it, he offered her a bottle of water, discreetly sliding his arm free before she noticed the heat his body seemed to be generating or heard the excited rush of blood pumping through his arteries. What the hell was he going to do? He couldn't seem to stop this craving. In fact, day by day, it seemed to be getting worse, making him overreact. Making him irrational and neurotic.

'You okay?' she asked after taking a drink.

Levi averted his gaze and shoved his belongings into his bag. 'Yeah,' he said, panicked. 'I need to go. I'm taking Lee to the mall this afternoon. He has a school formal coming up and needs advice on buying a suit. He has a date, so wants to look extra-good.' He looked up to see Kaia watching him with that same curious expression. He wanted to tell her how badly he still wanted her. To crumble and kiss her and selfishly suggest a passionate fling, if only to extinguish this constant need and confusion so he could think straight and go back to just being her friend, as she'd requested.

She smiled, drawing his stare to her lovely lips. 'Okay. Have fun,' she said. 'I'll see you back at home. I'm making tacos for dinner.'

Levi stopped himself from winking playfully. 'My favourite,' he said instead, vowing to pull himself together and try harder to respect Kaia's wishes. 'Thanks.'

And then he fled.

At home that evening, Kaia put the finishing touches to dinner just as Levi walked through the door. Still confused by his lingering looks and his show of protectiveness at the HUET, Kaia smiled brightly in greeting.

'Perfect timing. You must have been able to smell dinner from the mall,' she said trying to sound normal when her body could still remember his casual touch from earlier, his strong arm around her, comforting and thrillingly possessive.

She couldn't help but attribute all kinds of wonderful fantasies to those gestures, those looks. Of course, he *did* care about her but as a friend. And that should be enough. It always had been before. Only now she wanted more. Not just physical things, although the need to relive that night with Levi was constant. She also wanted to understand him better. To help him work through those issues he'd admitted. To see him in an emotionally healthy place where he might be open to a serious romantic relationship. She wanted her friend to be happy.

'Smells great,' he said, looking as if the food might be poisoned.

'Did Lee buy a suit?' she asked, confused by Levi's

obvious distraction and ongoing wariness. By his acts of caring one minute followed by his abrupt change the next, as if he couldn't wait to get away from her.

'Yeah,' he said, his gaze on the meal she'd prepared rather than on Kaia.

'Aren't you hungry?' she asked, suddenly exhausted by the growing distance between them. For the first time, she actually regretted sleeping with him because it had obviously ruined their easy, flirty friendship.

'I...um... I might go for a run,' he said, not quite meeting her stare. 'Clear my head.'

'Okay...' Kaia nodded and took a deep breath. Lucky him that a run would have that effect. Kaia's head hadn't been clear for weeks. Maybe it was time to confront the issue. To talk about the awkwardness and how, instead of bringing them closer, sleeping together seemed to have pushed them further apart, the last thing she wanted.

She swallowed then opened her mouth to speak, but Levi spoke first.

'I'm...um... I'm meeting Heidi tomorrow,' he said. 'I thought you'd want to know.'

Kaia froze, her smile wobbling as she tried to be brave. What with all the pining and craving and lusting, she'd totally forgotten Heidi existed. 'That's...fantastic,' she said, clearing her tight throat. 'I'd forgotten she's in Christchurch this weekend. Good for you.' Feeling nauseous, she looked down and busied herself with squeezing lemon juice into the guacamole she would no longer be able to eat.

Levi shrugged. 'It's just a coffee. No big deal.'

Kaia nodded, unable to ask him any of the questions she normally would, such as, was he excited? Where was he taking her? Did he fancy her? Now, with jealousy hot in her veins, she didn't want to know the details. 'That's great,' she said, her cheerful voice sounding fake. 'I hope you have a really good time.' Of course, it was no big deal for Levi. His relationships never were.

With her heart racing, she began wiping down the kitchen counters. She couldn't let him see her devastation. He couldn't know how secretly, desperate to silence her Levi-obsessed thoughts, she'd hoped they could resume their physical relationship until it had burned out, until they could once more be proper friends as they'd promised.

When she looked up because he'd fallen quiet, his expression was blank. She no longer knew what he was thinking or how he felt. In fact, as the days passed, as her feelings veered wildly between craving his friendship and wanting him physically, the man before her had become something of a stranger. Because she was thinking only of herself. Levi had voiced how valuable their friendship was to him and she wanted more. He'd even started to open up about his past struggles with relationships and all she could think about was her jealousy over a blind date *she'd* organised when she desperately wanted her friend to be happy.

'Do me a favour,' she said, trying to swallow through the lump in her throat. 'Just give it a chance. I know you're not looking for anything serious, and no one likes to feel...emotionally vulnerable, but you're a really great guy and if you let people see the you I see... Well, you just never know where it could lead...'

And if it did lead to happily ever after? If she could never have more of him than that one unforgettable night? If she had to live with this unresolved desire one night hadn't fulfilled, so be it. He deserved to be happy one day, to let someone get close to him again, the way he had with that early relationship, to have that family he craved.

'Are *you* scared to be vulnerable?' he surprised her by asking, a small frown on his face.

'I… Of c-course,' she stuttered. 'I guess…' Maybe if she opened up about her past he would too. 'Sam made me doubt my instincts, as if I should have seen the truth sooner. Seen that we no longer wanted the same things. Sometimes I wonder if I hadn't got pregnant, would he have ever told me he was no longer as committed…? Obviously, I wouldn't want to make another mistake like that, given what it cost me.'

He nodded and their eyes locked. Kaia stopped breathing, that selfish, unreasonable part of her begging him to cancel on Heidi and take her on a date instead. Willing him to want her as badly as she still wanted him. Because, having experienced one night of being Levi's lover, she wanted more than friendship. She wanted impossible things that she obviously couldn't have.

'I'm going to change for a run,' he said, stepping back. 'Save me some tacos for later.'

'Sure,' Kaia said, watching him leave and secretly wishing she'd never made their one-night pact. Because now that he was going out on a date with another woman, one that she'd stupidly instigated, Kaia realised that she might have left it too late to have anything but his friendship, and even that felt somehow tainted and more fragile than ever before.

CHAPTER SEVEN

TWENTY-FOUR HOURS LATER, Kaia was still in a state of self-inflicted wretchedness. Currently home alone while Levi was out on a *blind date* with Heidi and desperate for an effective distraction, she flicked off the TV and picked up the novel she'd earlier abandoned.

While Levi had been gone she'd cleaned the kitchen from top to bottom, taken a long, luxurious shower, painted her toenails *and* called her parents. She just couldn't seem to settle on anything beyond her jealous ruminations.

Seeing that her wine glass was empty, she sighed. The book could no more hold her attention than the TV had. The clock on the wall may as well have been wearing a mocking grin, she'd looked at it so often. Why had she done this to herself? Thrown temptation in the form of a gorgeous single woman in his path when she really wanted him for herself?

Shutting down that dangerous and pointless thought and tossing aside the book in disgust, she marched to the kitchen and poured another glass of wine. He and Heidi were probably having a wonderful time, flirting, figuring out how much they had in common, getting along like a house on fire. And if they hit it off? If Heidi became *the one* for Levi, what then?

Kaia took a massive gulp of the chilled pinot and tried not to seethe with envy. Her twisted logic was selfish. Both Levi and Heidi were her friends. She wanted them to be happy. Only accepting their being happy together was more complicated now that she'd slept with Levi. Of course, part of the problem was that she wanted the same happiness for herself, and ever since the night of his birthday she no longer knew what that happiness looked like.

Once it had been the job she loved and a committed relationship with Sam, even the idea of starting a family, although the pregnancy had come out of the blue. But now…? Now it seemed that nothing in her life was certain. Her job had lost its challenge, her mutually committed relationship had been a figment of her imagination and the baby she hadn't planned but had wanted all the same just hadn't been meant to be. And, despite her attempts to make some positive changes, wanting Levi seemed to be endless and impossible to ignore.

When moments later Kaia heard his car pull into the drive, she took her wine and scurried back to the lounge. She plopped down on the sofa and opened her book at a random page, pretending she'd had a relaxing evening to herself while inside she felt sick to her stomach with nerves.

She waited for him to appear, both desperate to know if he'd brought Heidi home too, and sick with dread at the idea of seeing them together, laughing, flirting, maybe sloping off to Levi's bedroom…

Swallowing hard, she kept her back to the door until he'd entered and dropped his keys into the bowl on the hall table. Then she nonchalantly glanced over the back of the sofa.

'Hi,' she said, trying to keep the clench of her throat from distorting her voice. 'How did it go?' Relief that he was alone pounded through her in time with her rapid heartbeats. She was a terrible, selfish friend to both Levi and Heidi.

Levi kicked off his shoes and sprawled at her side on the sofa, resting one foot on the coffee table so he was all long, sexy limbs and a cloud of delicious scent next to her. Temptation personified.

'Good,' he said, his voice as relaxed as if they were discussing the rugby scores. 'I can see why you two get along.'

Was that it? Kaia swallowed as discreetly as possible and fought hard to curb her curiosity. 'Told you she's great,' she said, needing more from him than a few vague answers.

Questions gathered on her tongue. Did he fancy Heidi? Were they going to see each other again? Had they ditched coffee and booked a hotel room, where they'd had the kind of sex Kaia now knew Levi was capable of? None of that was her business.

As if already bored and moving on from the barely begun conversation, Levi reached for the remote and flicked on the TV, not bothering to adjust the volume, which had been turned down low from Kaia's earlier attempts to take her mind off him and his date.

Kaia sat motionless, the pressure inside her building. She wanted *all* the details. Now. But also couldn't bear to know that he might be seriously interested in Heidi. Not sex-interested, but relationship-interested. Not that it was likely for him or that she had any right to know his personal business, not when she'd recklessly slept with him then slammed into reverse and made some lame and ineffectual attempts to patch up their friendship.

As if he knew she was watching him, and without turning his gaze from the TV, he said, 'I know you want to ask me. Just get it over with.'

'Okay,' she said, her cheeks heating. 'Are you going to call her again?'

That was a legitimate question, since Heidi was her friend. He couldn't read too much into that beyond Kaia's being protective of the other woman, given his track record. Then, because she couldn't seem to control the direction of her thoughts or hold her tongue, she added, 'I kind of thought you might bring her back here. I'd have...made myself scarce if you had.'

He turned, his expression casual. 'Are you saying you'd have been fine with me bringing a friend of yours home for sex?'

Kaia gaped, her face heating. 'I... Yes,' she lied, desperate to know if that had been considered.

Levi looked away. 'Well, as you know, she's in the process of relocating down here for work. So...'

Again he left her hanging, neither confirming nor denying his intentions.

'So you're saying if she did live here you would call her again?' Was it simply the geography temporarily keeping them apart? And why did she need to know so badly? As if his answer might throw as much danger at their friendship as their sleeping together had. With a wince, she realised she'd brought both risks, crossing the line to becoming lovers and throwing a stunning woman in his path, upon herself.

'What's with the third degree?' he asked levelly, his stare moving over her face so breathing evenly became hard. 'What are you really asking me, Kaia?'

The way he said her name, his deep voice all gravelly, reminded her of that night and the way he'd groaned it against her skin. The intensity in his eyes built until she couldn't look away from the spangled blue depths of his irises. And worse, she didn't want to look away. She wanted to drown there.

She opened her mouth to ask one of her many intrusive questions but closed it again when his gaze dropped to her parted lips. Her body flooded with heated memories of that first kiss in the kitchen the night of his birthday, the many passionate ones that had followed, all over her body, the escalation of kissing to the kind of sex she now knew it was impossible to forget.

Because she'd tried. And she knew this man. Trusted him. Loved him as a friend. And with that acknowledgement came the sticking point: it didn't matter how badly she still wanted him or how much she trusted him. One day she wanted a real relationship and Levi was at best lukewarm about commitment. Even if he still wanted Kaia too, he would only be interested in a fling and she couldn't expect more.

As the seconds in which they merely stared at each other in silence passed, the atmosphere around them changed. The hairs on Kaia's arms and the back of her neck prickled to attention. The perfectly platonic space between them on the sofa seemed to shrink as if they'd both leaned closer, which they hadn't. She was overheating as surely as if he'd touched her, as if he'd crushed her naked body to his again. She no longer recognised this manly, sexual man as her friend. What on earth was she doing, setting him up on a date with another woman, when she couldn't stop thinking about him, obsessing over that night, recklessly craving more of him than was allowed?

'You want to know if I fancy your friend Heidi, is that it?' he asked, his voice reasonable, as if unbothered by her curiosity. As if he'd moved on so couldn't for the life of him imagine that Kaia might be jealous. But as she looked closer, thrilling fire glittered in his stare.

'Well, do you?' she asked, her voice a pathetic croak as she battled her feelings: defensiveness for Heidi, guilt that she'd even considered Levi might mess her friend around, and for herself, horrible, debilitating envy. Right then, conflicted and confused, she would take the fling if it was offered. She was that desperate for this longing to end.

For several long seconds he refused to answer. Only stared at her while she squirmed.

'She's very beautiful,' he said finally, looking away so Kaia could draw breath. 'But the answer is no. I don't fancy her enough to want to call her again.'

Kaia's heart thudded wildly within her chest, fresh jealousy that he found Heidi beautiful hot in her veins. Irrational, unfair, petty feelings. But there was also relief that he didn't want to see her again.

Clearly, Kaia was out of control. Jealous and needy and ready to risk their friendship for another night of passion. Preferably several if it took away this agony so she could move on.

'Thank you very much for the introduction,' Levi went on calmly. 'She's a really great person, but if you really want to know, there was just no spark.'

Kaia gaped. No spark? How could that possibly be when, just from sitting next to him on the sofa, she felt as if she might spontaneously combust and incinerate the entire house around them?

'Don't worry,' he said, sounding annoyed with Kaia, 'I let her down gently. I don't think she was feeling it either, if that's any consolation. We agreed to be friends.'

Kaia sat dumb, unsure which of her many emotions she could admit. And the jealousy was still there. How could she be jealous of his and Heidi's potential friendship when their relationship could have become so much more?

'Well, thanks for giving it a try,' she muttered eventually, now drained of adrenaline. 'And thanks for being honest with her.'

He glanced up sharply. 'I'm always honest with women.'

'I know.' Her cheeks warmed again and she nodded. How could she have thought he'd behave any way other than decently? He was a good person. The best. And how could she have forgotten that Levi wasn't the relationship type? All the time she'd known him he'd only dated casually, his upfront honesty with the women he slept with protecting him from relationship dramas or mismatched expectations.

His expression turned serious as he continued to stare. 'Maybe it's time to stop all the matchmaking. Ever since we met you've tried to set me up.'

Kaia frowned defensively. 'Only because back then

I was happy in a relationship and wanted you to feel the same.'

But he hadn't changed. His vulnerability issues and past experiences were still dictating his love life. He was still keeping people, including Kaia, out.

'And yet here we are. Both single.' His stare softened then, his intelligent eyes saying things she wasn't ready to hear, as if he secretly knew she still wanted him and felt only pity.

Kaia swallowed, her pulse skipping a beat. What was he saying? That for the first time in four years they had an opportunity to explore what was clearly a mutual attraction? Or was he trying to tell her that he was happy alone and always would be? Feeling stupid, embarrassed that she'd overreacted to his date, she looked away. When it came to romantic relationships, Levi clearly didn't need or want *her* help, despite his inexperience.

'Okay. No more matchmaking.' She stood, fighting irrational tears. 'After all, what do I really know about finding the right person?' Out of the two of them, s*he* was the one who'd suffered a broken heart. She was the one who'd tried to have a serious committed relationship and failed. She'd been the one who'd needed rescuing when her personal life had imploded. Levi was just the same old Levi. Happy with his hook-ups.

'I guess sometimes,' she said as she carried her wine glass to the kitchen, 'it's just hard to be your friend.'

'What's that supposed to mean?' he asked, frowning.

'It means I don't understand you,' she cried, her bottled-up emotions popping the cork and spilling free. 'You have so much going for you: you're sexy and smart and kind. You own your own home, you're good at your job and you're great with kids. And yet you don't seem interested in prioritising a relationship. I… I just don't understand it.'

He stood and faced her, scrubbing a hand over his sexily stubbled jaw. 'Just because I'm guarded?'

Kaia's heart leapt pathetically at the tiny scrap of information he'd admitted. 'More than guarded. I'm trying to be your friend,' she said, the last word almost sticking in her throat because she was such a hypocrite. 'But every time I try to talk about relationships or try to get you to open up, you make a joke or you say it's no big deal or you change the subject…'

His eyes blazed. After a few beats of tense silence he said, 'It's a habit.' He pressed his lips together, clearly struggling. 'I learned a long time ago to rely on myself rather than someone else for my emotional wellbeing. But I… I *have* let you in. You know me better than anyone, Kaia.'

Moved by his sincerity and ashamed that she'd made such a mess of her own love life, Kaia crumbled. 'I know… I'm sorry. Look, I don't want us to argue. Forget I said anything. I've overreacted. Maybe I'm tired. And we're on the early shift tomorrow. I'm off to bed.'

Maybe Levi's way was the best way. Lonely but safe. And, regardless of her desire and jealousy and relief that he and Heidi hadn't hit it off, Levi could never be anything to Kaia but a friend. When it came to relationships, they were just too different. Kaia may still be recovering from her break-up, still scared to be vulnerable again and make another mistake, but she wanted another serious relationship one day.

'Don't stay up too late,' she said, smiling and trying

to breeze past him. But he reached out and snagged her hand over the back of the sofa.

'Kaia…wait. I… I don't want us to argue either,' he said, seeming uncharacteristically lost for words.

His innocent touch had stopped her in her tracks, chipping away at the resolve she'd only just reached. He looked at her as if he might say something else, something profound or personal, like *I can't forget what we did, I still want you, I want more than friends.* Kaia held her breath, confused by her see-sawing feelings and aching to feel his arms around her again: strong and comforting.

She smiled bravely. 'Friends again, then?'

Something clouded his stare. But then he nodded and let go of her hand. 'Always. Sleep well.'

'You too,' she replied, shuffling off to bed before she burst into agonised tears.

Ever since she'd decided to move out into her own place a part of her had been dreading it, knowing she would miss her friend's easy, uplifting company, his sense of humour and experimental cooking. Tonight, for the first time, she actually welcomed the move. Perhaps with some time away from him, she could stop all this pining and yearning for something one-sided that had no future beyond a temporary sexual fling that only she seemed to want.

Because nothing else seemed to be working.

CHAPTER EIGHT

THE DAY AFTER their late-night disagreement, things between Levi and Kaia seemed to settle somewhat. They were still wary and polite, acting as if nothing was amiss. But neither of them mentioned Heidi again, Levi because he'd told Kaia everything about the date, and Kaia…presumably because she wanted to get their friendship back on track. She'd certainly reminded him often enough: *I'm trying to be your friend... It's hard to be your friend... Friends again...*

Glad to have work on which to focus, Levi listened to Grant relay details of their latest rescue: a multi-vehicle accident on a rural Canterbury road.

'Three vehicles involved,' Grant informed them as they flew to the location. 'Traffic police on scene. Seven casualties. All conscious.'

Levi glanced over at Kaia and tried to smile encouragingly. At least at work they were still a team and could fool themselves that nothing had changed. He could pretend that the oppressive sexual tension wasn't tainting everything, even the air Levi breathed.

She smiled back, her expression the focused one she wore at work.

'One minute out,' Mac said. Levi forgot about his

extreme sexual frustration and the constant craving for the forbidden. Forgot that he couldn't sleep, couldn't eat. That he wanted Kaia even when she threw another woman in his path and was terrified he'd snap and say to hell with their friendship and beg her for another night.

The helicopter touched down in a paddock bedside the road. As soon as the cabin door opened, Levi took off running towards the accident site with his heavy backpack of medical equipment. He heard Kaia running behind him, caught the distant sirens of the fire service and ambulances en route to the scene.

Up ahead, several traffic-police cars were already on site, the road closed. The twisted wrecks of the two cars and a truck that had collided were strewn across both lanes of the carriageway. Levi's boots crunched over shattered glass as he dodged other debris and headed for the traffic officer beckoning them to the most urgent casualty. Levi sprinted over to a mangled car that had clearly collided with the damaged truck a short distance away.

'I can't get the door open,' the police officer said, stepping back to give Levi and Kaia access. 'Fire service on their way.'

The damage to the front of the car had buckled the driver's door and shattered the glass of the driver's window and windscreen. Until the fire service arrived to help cut the man from the wreck, their access to the casualty would be limited.

'Sir, can you hear me?' Levi said, reaching for the man's pulse through the broken car door window. It was alarmingly weak and rapid. 'I'm Levi,' he told the casualty, the driver of the car. 'Can you tell me your name?'

'Cliff,' the patient said, his voice a little slurred and his breathing laboured. 'Cliff Jennings.' He was bleeding profusely from a wound on his forehead. But his being able to talk was a good sign.

Opposite him, Kaia had climbed into the passenger side of the vehicle—an older model, without airbags—and was already staunching the flow of blood from the head laceration with a pad of gauze.

'I've got intravenous access,' he told her, taping the cannula in place.

Kaia nodded as she fitted a blood-pressure cuff and pulse oximeter to measure his vital signs while Levi tested his pupillary reflexes with a torch.

'Blood pressure is on the low side,' Kaia told Levi, her expression full of concern as she passed him a bag of intravenous fluids. 'Sats ninety-six per cent.'

'Where does it hurt, Cliff?' Levi asked, pulling out his stethoscope as Kaia hurried to set up some oxygen.

The man raised a trembling hand to his head. 'And my chest. Can't breathe.'

Levi met Kaia's stare, their eyes expressing what they dared not say out loud. Cliff could have serious internal injuries from the impact with the steering wheel.

'I'm going to examine you, Cliff,' Kaia said, cutting away his shirt so they could observe his chest for any evidence of trauma. She'd barely placed her stethoscope over his lung fields when Cliff slumped back in the seat and became unresponsive.

Levi quickly felt for a carotid pulse. 'He's in cardiac arrest,' he told Kaia, who shifted into the back of the vehicle.

'Recline the driver's seat,' she said, checking the patient for breath sounds then adding, 'Nothing.'

Kaia began delivering rescue breaths with a resuscitator bag. Levi managed to yank open the driver's side rear door, a position that allowed him to deliver chest compressions in time with Kaia's inflating the patient's lungs. Calling to the traffic officer, Kaia passed over the resuscitator bag so she could stick the defibrillator electrodes to Cliff's chest, attaching him to the automatic external defibrillator, which would give them a rhythm reading of the heart and a clue as to why it had stopped.

'He's in EMD,' Kaia said, frowning as they continued CPR.

Electro-mechanical dissociation was the kind of cardiac arrest associated with blood loss and hypovolemic shock, among other causes. The heart showed normal electrical activity but there was no pulse, which meant there was no blood circulating.

'Could be internal bleeding,' Levi said, meeting Kaia's stare. 'Chest or abdominal trauma, perhaps. Let's run through the possibilities: tension pneumothorax, cardiac tamponade, haemothorax.' None of those life-threatening diagnoses had a favourable prognosis.

Kaia continued to frown as they worked in rhythm to maintain the CPR. One of the things that made her such a great paramedic was that she cared so deeply. Of course, that also made her prone to compassion fatigue when they weren't able to save every patient.

That determined look came over her face. 'Keep going,' she said to the officer.

Reaching for her stethoscope, she listened to both lung fields and felt the position of the trachea between the clavicles, her mind likely running through the same list of possible as Levi had considered.

'I can hear faint inflation sounds on both sides,' she said after completing her examination, telling him that a tension pneumothorax was unlikely. The air they were delivering was getting into the lungs.

'Administering adrenaline,' Levi said, flushing the drug into the IV before resuming the chest compressions. 'Could be haemothorax. Cardiac or aortic rupture or tamponade.'

If there'd been catastrophic injury to the heart, the pericardium—the sac around the heart—might fill with blood and compress the heart so it couldn't pump.

'Let's get him to the helicopter,' she said, her expression grim.

With help from the other emergency services which had arrived on the scene, they transferred Cliff to a stretcher and transported him to the rescue helicopter, all the while continuing CPR.

'Keep going,' Kaia pleaded with Levi as they flew towards the hospital, their attempts to resuscitate Cliff so far unsuccessful.

'We won't give up,' Levi reassured her, sweat building in his hairline as he worked hard at the chest compressions. But the desperation in her voice and the sad resignation in her stare told him that neither of them was hopeful for a positive outcome in this case. And, despite the training and the job satisfaction, losing a patient always took a personal toll. It was inevitable. Paramedics were human.

As they handed over a still unresponsive Cliff to the hospital team, Levi's heart sank, knowing from experience that he and Kaia had done all they could, but it might not have been enough to save his life. And all Levi wanted to do was the one thing he couldn't—hold Kaia.

Later that evening, after spending thirty minutes in the shower as if she might wash away her horrible day, Kaia wandered aimlessly into the kitchen. She had no appetite, but she should at least contemplate food. Losing a patient was sadly part of their job, but it never got any easier. And normally after a traumatic shift she and Levi would console each other, laugh together, go for a beer or a long walk or to see a light-hearted movie. Anything to take their minds off what had happened. Instead, as soon as she and Levi had reached home they'd each silently sloped off to their separate rooms like strangers.

Close to tears and deciding that she needed to do something normal with her friend, Kaia marched down the hall and knocked on his door. 'Levi?'

'Yeah,' he called from inside. She pushed open the door just as he added, 'Hold on a sec, I'm naked.'

Kaia froze in the doorway, her apology that she'd walked in on him trapped in her throat. He wasn't exactly naked. But he'd obviously just emerged from the shower and wore only a towel wrapped around his lean hips, a T-shirt clutched in his hand.

'Sorry...' she mumbled, desperately trying to act unaffected by the sight of all his male beauty. Desperately trying not to stare at the droplets of water scattered over his bronzed and ripped chest. 'I...wondered if you wanted to go get something to eat.'

Although faced with Levi's gorgeous body and the ache in her heart, any appetite she might have managed disappeared. There was no use trying to fool herself any longer. She wanted him. Wanted the sexual fling, even if it couldn't go anywhere. It was her last chance to lay their chemistry to rest so that when she moved out next weekend she could start afresh. But was she brave enough to tell him and risk embarrassment or offence?

'Sure,' he said, unmoving, doing nothing to cover up his body.

But then, he was in *his* room, in *his* house. She was the one standing there lusting and internally trying to justify a friends-with-benefits fling.

'Tough day, huh?' he said after a few seconds, a flicker of the old Levi displayed in his sympathetic stare.

She'd missed her friend so much, she almost broke down.

'Yeah…' She sighed, torn between needing him—his unconditional support—and needing to get away from him before she did something stupid again. Before she embarrassed herself and put him in an awkward position. Or worse—pushed any chance of their old closeness further away.

'You did everything right, you know. There was nothing more we could have done for him,' he added, staring in that way that left her nowhere to hide because he knew her so well. 'We tried our best.'

She nodded in agreement, in no way comforted with him so far away and acting as wary as if she were a hungry shark about to strike. But even if she couldn't have sex with him, she still craved his arms around her. She wanted to rest her face against the reassuring thud of his heart. She wanted to secretly breathe in his Levi scent until she felt better. But if he so much as touched her, she knew she'd want more than an innocent embrace. She'd want the fire of before. The darkly dangerous thrill of wanting forbidden things with this man. She'd want any part of him he was willing to give.

'I...' A sigh of frustration blasted past her lips. 'I hate this,' she blurted, tired of pretending that everything was normal. Tired of fighting with herself.

'Hate what?' he asked, as still as a statue. Poker-faced and watchful.

'This,' she replied, gesturing between them. 'Us.'

'What do you want me to say, Kaia?' he asked, his stare holding hers as his breathing sped up. 'What do you want me to do?' There was a chilly tone to his voice that made her hesitate.

'I want us to be normal!' she cried in frustration. Although that wasn't exactly true. There was no part of her that wanted to return to life before they'd slept together. It had been wonderful. No matter how hard she'd tried to forget or how much strain it had put on their easy-going friendship, she still couldn't bring herself to regret it.

'I want you...to be my friend,' she finished lamely, because that was only half the truth. 'I wish... I wish I'd never slept with you.'

His nostrils flared, a hard mask falling over his face. 'I *am* your friend,' he bit out, as if she was asking for too much. 'I'm trying my hardest to be just that. I don't know what more you want from me.'

Confused and miserable, she frowned. Was she being unreasonable? Asking for too much? Selfish and irrational?

'Oh, I don't know what I want from you,' she lied, frustrated that she was a mess and he was just Levi. 'I just know this isn't working. Us. Pretending everything is normal when it clearly isn't. I'm even jealous of my friend Heidi,' she said, disgusted with herself. 'Jealous that you're going to be *her* friend, when I feel like I'm losing you. Even though we promised to protect our friendship.'

His eyes glittered as he dropped his T-shirt onto the bed and stepped closer. 'Why are you jealous, Kaia?' he asked darkly, staring hard, his chest rising and falling on laboured breaths.

'I…don't know,' she whispered, lying again. 'Because I'm stupid… I should never have set you two up.'

Levi glanced down as if disappointed with her answer, his body tensing so every muscle was delineated as if to tempt her further. 'Maybe things will be easier when you move into your own place,' he said quietly, so she could tell this wasn't the first time he'd had that thought. 'Maybe then, seeing less of each other, we can…claw back some perspective.'

Kaia nodded, her throat aching with unshed tears. She didn't want perspective. She wanted their passion. It had been there once, effortless and easy. But he'd clearly moved on and she was being unfair to expect anything else.

'Maybe…' she said, turning to leave the room in utter humiliation and defeat. She'd been the one to kiss him that night. She was the one who'd changed the rules then tried to change them back again. And now…? She wanted to hurl the rule book out of the window. But even that wouldn't change the facts. He no longer wanted her.

'Although,' he said so she froze, 'for me, out of sight won't be out of mind.' He stepped closer, bathing her in the scent of his shower gel and the heat from his body. 'I'll still want you, even when the physical temptation of you is removed. I can't stop wanting you. I'm going crazy. I know I promised to protect our friendship, to not hurt you, but wanting you...it's just too hard to fight.'

Kaia looked up into his blazing stare, euphoria surging through her like an electrical current.

'I've tried everything,' he said, his jaw clenched and nostrils flared. 'Even taking out another woman. A friend of yours. But nothing is working. You might regret sleeping with me, but I'm entranced. You are all I can see. All I think about. Night and day. Every day. Help me. Make it stop.'

At his heartfelt plea, Kaia exhaled what felt like a month's worth of bottled-up longing, her heart beating up into her throat. 'I don't regret it, Levi...'

At the sound of his name he groaned and reached for her, closing the distance. Pressing her body to his. Cupping her face, his lips covering hers, his tongue pushing into her mouth as she cried out in triumph that they'd finally cracked. That he'd felt the same agonising torture all this time. That he still wanted her as badly as she wanted him.

His strong arms crushed her to his naked chest as he backed her up against the wall and kissed her over and over again until she could barely breathe. But nothing could make her pull back, not when she'd spent the past few weeks since his birthday craving exactly this, when in that moment she had everything she wanted and more. She had her friend back, his comforting embrace *and* his wild passion.

'I couldn't fight it any longer,' he said, after releasing

her lips to trail kisses down her neck as his hand cupped her breast and his thumb teased her nipple. 'I tried not to want you. To forget. I've been going out of my mind.'

The anguish in his voice, the defeat, slayed her even as his lips on her skin made her head spin with excitement. 'I tried too. I felt exactly the same. I regretted the friends pact as soon as we made it.' Dizzy with lust, she grabbed his hips and drew them closer, wrapping one thigh around him so his erection prodded between her legs and he would feel how badly she wanted him, wanted this.

She stared up at him, her hand delving underneath the towel to caress and stroke him until he made that sexy growl in the back of his throat and his eyes darkened to black.

'I want you,' she admitted finally. 'I was jealous that you might sleep with Heidi. It's selfish, but I wanted you for myself. I want my friend back, but I want more.' The words felt wonderful to admit, but were still spiced with a hint of danger. He was still forbidden. But maybe this time they could finally work it out of their systems.

'What are we going to do?' he said, brushing his lips over hers, his voice pleading so she knew he was as on edge as Kaia. 'I still want you as my friend.' His fingers curled into her hair as he tilted her face up to his kisses. 'I don't want to hurt you or lose you. But I want this too.'

As if to prove his point his hand delved under her T-shirt, his fingers expertly popping her bra clasp so he could shove both garments up and cover her nipple with his hot, greedy mouth.

'Yes,' she said, panting, desperate to move activities to the bed, ready to promise anything to have him this way.

'We have a fling,' she said, panting because he was sucking her nipple, his hand between her legs, rubbing her through her jeans. 'Get it out of our systems… It can't last and we stay friends,' she reasoned, her mind foggy with arousal. Then, because she didn't want to hear any arguments or contradictory reason, she dropped to her knees at his feet and tugged away his towel.

'Kaia,' he groaned as she took him into her mouth. He braced his hands on the wall above her, his legs, his buttocks and abdominals steely hard as she sucked him, pleasuring him with her mouth. 'You are so beautiful. So sexy.' He cupped her cheek, his stare softening from harsh arousal to adoration. 'I've missed you.'

She looked up, high from the raw emotions in his eyes—desire, relief, trust—as he watched her for a few moments. Then he pulled back, drew her to her feet and hurriedly stripped off her clothes, pausing between garments to kiss her deeply and whisper sexy nothings until she could barely stand upright she was so turned on.

Before she collapsed, Kaia backed him up towards his bed then gently pushed him down until he sat on the edge and thought about searching his bedside table for a condom.

'Come here,' he said, holding her hips and leaning forward to kiss a trail across her belly and down, lower and lower until his tongue brushed her clitoris and she gasped, spearing her fingers into his hair.

'Levi,' she moaned as he filled his hands with the cheeks of her backside and held her to his mouth. 'I've missed you too.'

Kaia braced her hands on his shoulders and tried to stifle her sighs and moans, holding on as he lapped at her with his tongue. At risk of her legs giving way, she finally pushed at his shoulders and then sat astride his thighs.

'Condom,' she said between kisses, her heart squeezing tight with everything she felt for this incredible man. A man who cared for her. A man who believed in her. A man she could trust.

'Drawer,' he said, his hands caressing her back as he stared at her with wonder and admiration and raw need.

Kaia reached over and found a foil packet, sighing when he slid his hand between her legs to stroke her and dived again for her breast, tonguing the nipple into a needy peak. When she had him sheathed, she braced her hands on his broad shoulders and rose up onto her knees. Then, kissing him deeply, she sank onto his length and their arms tightened around each other.

He held her unmoving, his face buried against her wildly thudding heart. She kissed the top of his head, inhaling the scent of him. When he looked up, new resolve shone in his eyes. 'I'll never hurt you.'

She nodded, a tight knot of longing in her chest. 'I know. I trust you,' she whispered. 'And I won't hurt you either. I promise.'

As if she'd touched upon a secret, he flinched infinitesimally. Kaia kissed him. She wanted to know his deepest fears if he'd let her in, but for now she wanted this more.

'You feel so good,' he whispered against her lips as he peered up at her. 'But you're still my best friend.'

A lump formed in her throat as she pressed another kiss to his lips. 'You're still mine, too.'

She sighed, elated that it no longer felt wrong or forbidden to want him this way. It just felt freeing and right, as if there had always been a small part of the Levi and Kaia puzzle missing and this was it.

His hands slid reverently over her skin to her hips, slowly guiding her into a rocking rhythm above him. The tempo built as their kisses deepened. Whenever she rocked down, he thrust up, until soon their gasps and groans and racing hearts dictated the frantic pace.

'Levi!' she cried as he took her nipple into his mouth. Then she was coming, riding him, held so tightly by him they moved as one, still friends but also something more: lovers at last.

CHAPTER NINE

STILL BREATHLESS AND dizzy from his powerful orgasm, Levi relaxed his hold on Kaia but kept his arms around her, kept his face buried against the side of her neck and in her hair, just breathing her in. Kaia caressed his back and shoulders, her fingers gliding through his damp hair as if she too had no desire to shatter this moment of blissful intimate connection.

'I'm very disappointed in my lack of willpower to resist you,' he said, his mind as surrendered as his body as he looked up and smiled.

'I'm glad you finally cracked.' She chuckled softly and tightened her arms around his shoulders. 'I almost did so many times. I just didn't want to be the only one to risk our friendship. I thought you'd moved on.'

Swallowing hard, he tried to show the same honesty. 'I wanted you the morning after my birthday.' He pressed his lips to hers. 'I was just scared to mess up our friendship and lose you. I still am… But you're sure about a fling?'

'I'm sure.' She nodded, smiling as she kissed him once more.

His heart rate settled. They could handle it, separate out their friendship while they waited for this intense passion to burn out. Because surely it would. Kaia wasn't stupid. She'd soon outgrow this inconvenient but undeniable lust and move on, and he had no intention of hurting her or leading her on. But now that they'd found each other again, he wanted as much of Kaia as she would give him. There was no way he'd have survived another day without her touch. If she hadn't found him tonight, he'd have made something happen.

'Give me a second,' he said when he pulled back. 'I need to dispose of the condom. Make yourself at home.'

Kaia climbed off his lap and slid into his bed, her satisfied smile so beautiful his chest tightened. In the bathroom, he took a much-needed second to himself. His overriding emotion now that the he'd snapped and sated his hunger for her was relief that she wanted the same things. To hear of her jealousy, and that her struggles to resist this had matched his own, settled the guilty corner of his mind that had constantly and futilely lusted after his friend.

But then came a fresh rush of fear. He was playing with fire. Friends with benefits was amazing in theory, but she was a relationship person. He couldn't hurt her. Ever.

Determination stiffened his spine as he glanced in the mirror and washed his hands. There'd be no more hiding from this chemistry. No more pretending his need for her was purely platonic. He'd be honest with her and strive to keep their wonderful friendship intact after their physical relationship had burned out.

Because she could never take him seriously as a romantic partner, could she? As she'd pointed out time and time again, he'd spent most of his adult life in casual relationships, never allowing anyone close enough to make him feel vulnerable to rejection. He could no more be what Kaia needed and deserved in the long-term than he could risk damaging their friendship and losing her. He'd never had the kind of serious relationship Kaia would one day want, the kind she'd had before: living together, commitment, love. Maybe even starting a family.

She was understandably scared that she might have another miscarriage, especially given her mother's experiences, but he assumed that she still wanted kids one day. She wanted it all. He wanted kids too, eventually, but, as she'd pointed out, the whole finding someone to love who loved you back thing was a definite hurdle, one he clearly wasn't ready to tackle. If Kaia found the search for 'the one' tricky, what hope would a relationship novice like him have?

Telling himself to stick to the rules so no one, especially Kaia, got hurt, he returned to the bedroom, determined after days of missing their easy friendship that it was the most important thing. 'Can I make you a drink?' he asked, finding Kaia sitting up in his bed with the duvet tucked under her arms.

'I want a cuddle,' she said, pushing back the duvet. 'I've hated the distance between us since your birthday. I've missed my friend. Normally after an emotional day at work we'd hug and have a laugh together.'

Levi slid into bed next to her and drew her into his arms, kissing the top of her head as she rested it on his chest. 'I've missed you too. I just wanted you so badly, I was terrified to touch you in case I messed up. In case you didn't want me back.' With her lying in his arms, her legs tangled with his, he sighed contentedly. 'I kept reciting *be her friend, be her friend* in my head.'

After a moment of just snuggling she said, 'I'm sorry

about what I said last night.' She looked up. 'About finding it hard to be your friend. I didn't mean it.'

Levi tilted up her chin and pressed his lips to hers, the stirring in his groin evidence that this addiction to Kaia was nowhere near over. 'I know what you meant,' he said, stroking his fingers through her hair and down her back, relieved they were talking again. 'And everything you said about me was true. I *have* avoided serious relationships. I… I guess I've always felt stronger alone. Always relied on myself.'

Sadness clouded her stare. 'Why?' she whispered, frowning. 'You said you weren't in love with the girl who moved to Australia, so she couldn't have broken your heart.'

'She didn't,' he confessed. 'I was…emotionally guarded before her, probably the reason I couldn't commit to her the way she expected me to.'

As if sensitive to his emotional discomfort, Kaia glanced down at her hand on his chest. 'Because of losing your father?'

Levi swallowed hard. Now was a perfect opportunity for some of that honesty he'd just promised himself in the bathroom. So why was it so…terrifying, even with Kaia?

'I guess it started then,' he said quietly, the memories he normally squashed bubbling up. 'I was a kid. Thirteen. I loved my dad, and then he was just gone. I guess I expressed my grief by acting out.'

'That's understandable,' she said, sliding her fingers through his chest hair. 'It must have been a horrible time.'

Levi shrugged, so far out of his comfort zone now he might never find his way back. 'Yeah, I guess. I've told you I went to boarding school…'

She nodded waiting for more.

'Well, it wasn't planned. It wasn't my choice. It was a knee-jerk reaction to my teenaged rebellion.'

Her lovely stare soft with sympathy, Kaia pressed her lips together and stayed silent, only nodding with understanding.

'My mother had four other children to care for.' He looked away, struggling to be this vulnerable. 'The last thing she needed on top of my father's death was an angry young man disrupting the home. I can understand now why she sent me away, although at the time…'

She reached for his hand, entwined her fingers through his and finished his sentence. 'It felt like a punishment.'

'Yeah… I guess…' Levi croaked, amazed how intuitively she understood him, perhaps even better than he understood himself. 'I think Mum hoped that the structure and male influences of an all-boys school would help straighten me out,' he went on, 'which it did in lots of ways. I became really good at sport, channelled my energy into football and surfing, and even represented my school at a national level in both of those things.'

She nodded. 'She must have been very proud of you, as I'm sure she still is. You're an amazing role model now.'

Levi shrugged, trying to calculate the last time he'd been home to see his mother. He wouldn't describe them as close.

'Was it just you who went to boarding school?' Kaia asked gently. 'What about your siblings?'

'My three sisters went to the local school. My younger brother went to Charlton College years after me. But he actually wanted to go. It was his choice.'

'Maybe because he looked up to you,' she pointed out softly.

Levi glanced sharply at her, stunned that rebellious and angry teen Levi could have had a positive impact on anyone.

'It must have been hard,' Kaia continued, 'having to leave your family.'

'Of course, especially in the beginning.' He swallowed painfully, easily recalling the tears, the pleading, the promises to be a better son and brother. 'I figured I'd brought it on myself. That I only had myself to blame. Maybe if I'd behaved better, or been good enough, I could have stayed home. So I just…sucked it up and locked down my feelings.'

'I'm sorry you felt that way,' she whispered, her stare full of understanding. 'But I think it was probably more complex than that. Your mother probably didn't send you because she wanted to punish you. She must have been grieving too, feeling the responsibility of being a single parent. She probably thought it was for your own good, which it was in many ways. You excelled there.'

'I guess,' he said. 'Anyway… I realised pretty early on that it was better for me if I managed my expectations rather than riding this emotional roller-coaster every term, hoping that I could behave well enough in the holidays that she'd let me stay home. Not that I visited a lot. I'd spend the school holidays at sports camps or I'd go stay with my Uncle Murray, my father's brother. He lived alone on a small farm near Charlton College, so there was always something outdoorsy to do—chopping wood, fixing fences, mucking out the barn.'

'Was he like your dad?' she asked. 'Is that why you wanted to spend time with him?'

Levi shrugged. 'A bit. He was the strong, silent type. He never enforced any rules or had any expectations of me. Just muttered the jobs that needed doing and left me to it.'

'So you could simply be yourself there,' she said knowingly. 'Maybe you needed that time to process everything that had happened.'

'Maybe.' He glanced down, recalling how a part of him had looked forward to those visits to the farm as a kind of self-inflicted punishment. As if he could work really hard physically and at school and reinvent himself. No more the rebellious, angry teen. Looking back now, it had also been a way to keep people and tricky emotions at bay. And maybe he had withdrawn from his family too.

'Often, when I did visit home,' he went on, 'and spend time with my siblings, I'd feel like an outsider. As if I no longer belonged to my own family, which felt messed up. I worried they didn't like me, or that I'd do or say something wrong and be sent off again. I couldn't ever relax after that.'

She pressed her lips to his. 'I'm sorry. That must have been horrible for you. Although every teenager moves away from being emotionally reliant on a parent. It's natural to some extent. You were also growing up, becoming your own person. Finding your own way to cope with things.'

'That's true,' he said, surprised that he'd never thought of it that way. But had his habitual coping mechanisms to stop being rejected and hurt caused him to keep people at arm's length emotionally? Had he isolated himself too well? Locked down his emotions too effectively so that now, as an adult, he didn't know how to be that vulnerable?

'Anyway,' he said, pushing aside that unsettling thought, 'I got through boarding school. I focused on what I could control—school work, training hard for sports and achieving the tasks Uncle Murray set. Then... I don't know... After school I went to college, trained to be a paramedic and since then work has been my priority.'

Kaia nodded, something close to pride shining in her eyes. 'You're really good at your job.'

'So are you.' He kissed her, a weight sliding from his shoulders at how letting Kaia in wasn't so bad after all.

'So how are things now?' she asked when he pulled back. 'With your mother and siblings? You don't see much of them?'

'We're fine,' he said, stroking her back. 'Everyone is busy with their own lives. My sisters have families of their own and my brother is in the New Zealand Defence Force, so he travels overseas a lot. But we catch up when we can. At Christmas time usually.'

'Have you ever told your mother about how you felt rejected and punished as a kid?' she asked. 'She'd probably be surprised. It must have been a hard decision for her to send you away.'

'Nah... What's the point in dredging it all up?' he said, eager now to change the subject. 'What's done is done, and now that I'm an adult I can kind of understand why she did it. It's like you said; it must have been hard for her after my dad died, and it helped straighten me out.'

'Hard for all of you, I would imagine,' she said, obviously ignoring his attempt to minimise how he'd coped. 'You lost a parent and a role model, just like Lee, only permanently. Then a part of you felt ostracised from the rest of your family.' She looked up once more. 'But I bet your mother would want to know how you felt. You should think about talking to her some time.'

'I'll think about it,' he said, feeling raw and exposed once more.

Her gaze flitted away then returned. 'I imagine you might have felt like you'd done something wrong and didn't deserve the love of your family, but I'm certain they love you, you know. Your mother would want you to be happy and you don't have to deal with everything alone. I'm here.'

'I'm here too and I am happy right now,' he said, brushing her lips with his. 'In fact, I'm ecstatic.' He tried to reach for her waist to pull her closer but she caught his hand and forced him to be serious.

'I understand, you know. I'm scared to be vulnerable too. No one wants to be rejected or hurt,' she whispered, her voice free of judgement. 'And I understand how if relationships are casual, they're on your terms. But nothing worth having is easy.'

Levi nodded, part of him wishing he could be as brave as Kaia. 'That's why I admire you so much,' he said, his heart thudding harder. 'When I see what you went through with Sam… You're so strong. So much braver than me. Putting yourself out there…'

She shook her head. 'I'm not brave. I just don't want to be alone for the rest of my life. I don't want my experiences with my ex to hold me back from something that could be wonderful. Better than what I had with him, which wasn't as solid as I thought.'

Levi's chest tightened. 'See? You're dauntless. And you're right. You deserve so much better than your ex. You always have.'

'You deserve things, too,' Kaia said, cupping his face. '*I* want you. As my friend, my brilliant colleague, and physically.'

Pulling her close, Levi smiled, exhausted from talking about this stuff, even with Kaia, whom he trusted more than anyone else. 'I'm all yours, baby,' he said, rolling her on top of him.

'Lucky me,' she said, smiling and kissing him.

As their kisses became more desperate, playfulness slipping away as passion took over, Levi tried to picture himself being a brave as Kaia. Trying to be the kind of man she deserved. Could he try to be what she needed? Try to give her more than sex? A serious relationship, when he'd never done that before. What if he failed like before and ended up hurting her or pushing her away for good? Losing even her friendship? Could he live with the knowledge that she'd seen through him and found something lacking? Could he survive being rejected by her, of all people?

No. She needed a man who was a safe bet after what she'd been through, and at the moment that obviously wasn't Levi. For now, he'd do what he always did: shut down his dangerous thoughts, ignore his confusing feelings for Kaia and live for the moment. After all, while he had Kaia as a friend *and* in his bed, he was the lucky one. The luckiest man on earth.

Even if all it could be was temporary.

CHAPTER TEN

THE NEXT MORNING, after a blissful sleep in Levi's arms and an exhilarating round of morning sex, Kaia accompanied Levi to watch Lee's football match. They stood hand in hand on the sidelines, shouting encouragement and clapping for Lee's team, who were leading two goals to one.

'Well done, mate!' Levi yelled as Lee successfully tackled the ball away from his opponent and raced into the box. Kaia watched indulgently as Levi filmed the action on his phone, but as Lee took his shot at the goal, Levi gripped Kaia's arm excitedly.

The ball sailed past the opposing team's keeper and into the back of the net. Levi cheered and hugged Kaia, the filming forgotten. 'Did you see that? Brilliant,' he said, his face lit up with pride and excitement.

Kaia couldn't decide which sight was more uplifting—the match and Lee's pride in his goal, or Levi enjoying himself. But, given he was her favourite person in all the world, it wasn't really a fair comparison.

The referee blew the whistle for half-time and Lee glanced over, grinning widely at Levi, who yelled understated congratulations, although Kaia knew he was beyond delighted at Lee's performance.

'What a great match,' he said as he and Kaia found a seat at the side of the pitch.

Content and happy, she leaned against his side. 'It's so exciting. He's playing really well.'

But no matter how hard she tried to be in the moment and enjoy this date with Levi, she couldn't help but relive the heartbreaking details he'd confessed the night before. How it must have felt to feel confused and be missing home, and then feel as if he didn't belong when he visited his family. No wonder he'd become emotionally contained, relying on himself and what he could be good at in order to prove himself worthy. Maybe even show his mother that yes, he'd messed up, but he could turn it around.

'He's trained really hard,' Levi said, casting Lee's team another glance. 'Worked on his fitness levels. He deserved that goal. Look how proud of himself he is,' he said, inclining his head towards Lee, who was in a team huddle on the pitch.

'But trying to play it cool for his teammates,' she added, her heart clenching at Levi's close bond with the young man and all that it represented. Helping other kids who found themselves acting out because they were lost was obviously Levi's way of paying forward for his own turbulent teens. And, while a confused young Levi might have felt he was being rejected or punished by being sent to boarding school, the experience had also given him male role models when he'd needed them most. Just as he was now doing for Lee.

'I'll send him the video,' Levi said, opening his phone. 'He can show it to his dad next time he visits.'

Kaia stared at her friend, her hormones running amok after their emotional night together. How could their relationship have turned around in the space of a few hours? How was it possible for Levi to keep presenting new sides of himself to her when she'd assumed she knew all there was to know? And how could she reconcile this Levi—playful, attentive, unable to keep his hands off her—with man who, through his own habitual acts of self-preservation, claimed he'd never been in romantic love? When he had so much more to give. If only he could face his fear of getting hurt and let people close.

Swallowing hard against the lump in her throat, Kaia watched as Levi sent the video. He looked up, catching her with a smile on her face.

'What?' he asked, sliding closer on the bench seat to put his arm around her waist and nuzzle her neck.

'Nothing,' she said, her heart racing with longing. How could she want him again so desperately after last night and this morning? How could she keep her feelings in check when she already loved him as a friend and knew how wonderful he could potentially be as a partner if only he wanted more than sex?

'You're just amazing,' she said, scared she'd inadvertently found the man of her dreams and he'd been right under her nose the whole time. 'You're really good with him.'

Levi shrugged as if embarrassed by her compliment. 'Kids are easy. You just have to listen and be there for them so they know they can trust you and open up without judgement. All they need is a chance and some encouragement,' he said. 'Someone to tell them it's okay to feel the things they're feeling and give them strategies for constructive ways to deal with those feelings.'

'You see yourself in Lee,' she gently pointed out, aching for the younger Levi who'd been grieving and confused.

'Maybe.' His eyes met hers, and she held her breath as he showed her another glimpse of his vulnerability. 'But if I ever do have kids, I'm determined to listen rather than send them away.'

Kaia nodded, her throat tight. 'I think you're selling yourself short. Kids like Lee are so lucky to have someone like you,' she said, convinced that part of him thought he needed to atone for the way he'd behaved. To prove that he might have messed up as a kid, but as an adult, he was okay—good at his job, a decent guy, helping other troubled kids. 'Someone who understands and cares and shows up for them. I think you have special skills with children that not everyone has. You'll make a great dad, you know.'

If only he wanted a serious relationship… Because what woman would be happy with only part of him? His caring and protectiveness and sense of fun. His physical displays of intimacy but not his whole heart. Not love.

He glanced down, falling serious. 'I had a good role model, too. My dad was a great guy. Fun. Always making time for us. Encouraging us to reach for our goals whatever they were.'

Kaia rested her head on his shoulder and whispered, 'You miss him.'

Levi gave a small nod of acknowledgement. 'Yeah, of course.'

'I think he'd be proud of the man you'd become, just as I'm sure your mother is. I'm proud of you. Losing your father at a tender age was bad enough. Losing him then being sent away to boarding school, however well-intentioned the reasons…' Levi must have felt he'd been dealt a double dose of grief being ripped away from his family like that. 'You know that you didn't do anything wrong back then, don't you?'

Levi swallowed, telling her she'd hit a nerve. Then met her stare, his haunted. 'Do *you* know that? About the baby?'

Kaia looked away, blood rushing to her face because they each knew the other so well. 'I… My head knows it,' she said, facing him again. She couldn't hide, not if she expected him to be open. 'Some days my heart tells me that maybe it happened because it wasn't planned. Because I was careless with my contraception. Or maybe there's something wrong with my body. Some reason I'm not meant to be a mother. I know; it's an unhelpful way to think…'

Levi shook his head, his stare brimming with concern. 'It wasn't your fault, Kaia. It was just one of those things. One of nature's sad ways. We see cruel twists of fate all the time at work.' He slung his arm around her shoulders and pulled her close, pressed a kiss to her head. 'You'll make a wonderful mother one day. Just like you'll be a great doctor.'

Choked and confused by the depth of her longing for him, Kaia nodded and glanced down at her lap, where her fingers were clasped. Seeing him as her friend, she needed to voice her darkest fears to him. But seeing him as the man she couldn't help but imagine having a real relationship with, she also wanted to hide them. 'I don't know… Maybe I can't actually have kids after… last time. Maybe it would happen again…another miscarriage. Like it did for my mother.' Maybe for a man who wanted a family, a man with so much to give, Kaia wasn't a safe bet anyway, even if he wanted her.

'I'm sure you'll be able to have kids,' he said, his arm tightening around her waist and his head dipping closer. 'These things happen, but you're fit and healthy. There's plenty of time. And if it does happen again, you try again. Or you get investigated. There are so many options and scenarios. Don't torture yourself now with what-ifs.'

Blinking against the sting in her eyes, she looked up. He kissed her and said, 'Besides, if you're going to be an amazing doctor, you'll probably want to put off parenthood for a while longer.'

Kaia laughed at his blind faith. 'You're right.' She leaned close for another kiss, her heart soaring that she seemed to have her friend back after the weeks of tension following his birthday. 'Thank you,' she said. 'For saying the right things and always being there for me. I couldn't have survived the last few months without you. Truly.' She held his stare, wanting him to hear her sincerity and not brush it off with humour as he had in the past.

'You're welcome. But remember, everything I've given you, you've given back to me.' He brushed her lips with his and Kaia clung to the kiss, feeling closer to him than ever before, as if everything she could ever want was tantalisingly within reach.

She pulled back and stared into his eyes, wishing this moment, this closeness could last forever. Wishing their solid relationship could evolve from here. How strong and amazing it could be if they took their foundation of friendship and respect and insane chemistry and were able to build on it with something romantic and committed and loving. If only he wanted the same things, Levi would be the perfect man for Kaia.

But Levi was scared to trust in love. Scared to be fully vulnerable with someone and risk the rejection he'd spent his entire adult life safeguarding against. And Kaia needed the certainty that, when she was ready to fall in love again, to let herself be fully vulnerable, the man was equally crazy for her, equally committed to them as a couple and wanted the same things she wanted: a future, a family, forever.

'Second half is starting,' Levi said, pulling her to her feet and cheering as the teams took up their positions on the pitch.

Kaia smiled and clapped her way through the rest of the match, her attention torn between the football and Levi. Maybe if she studied him for long enough, she could figure him out, see him exactly as he was, not how she wished he could be.

At work on Monday, after a weekend of hanging out together, laughing, kissing and more sex than should be survivable, Levi wondered if he'd ever stop grinning at Kaia, sharing secret looks, the deliberate brush of his hand against hers… At one stage, while everyone else had gone to the café for lunch, he'd even pulled her into a deserted office for a sneaky kiss that had almost gone too far.

But all the meaningful looks and knowing smiles stopped the minute a call came in for off on their next rescue mission.

'Our casualty, Peter, is a forty-seven-year-old hiker trapped in the Rakaia River,' Levi told her as Mac flew them to the location indicated by the man's personal locator beacon. 'He was attempting a river crossing with a friend but slipped and got his foot stuck between the rocks.'

'How long has he been in the water?' Kaia asked, frowning with concern as she pulled on her high-visibility drysuit.

Entering cold moving water was always a risk for rescuers and the first rule of swift water rescue was to ensure the safety of the rescue team. Today's mission made Levi nervous because he knew Kaia felt the same. They would not only be thinking of the casualty, but also of each other's safety.

'Forty minutes,' Levi said, checking his watch. 'The friend tried to help him out of the water but ended up getting wet and cold himself. Fortunately he had a change of clothes, so we just have one casualty to worry about. The water temperature is pretty low at this time of year, so if he's trapped for much longer, he's at serious risk of hypothermia.'

The Rakaia was a dynamic braided river spread across the Canterbury plains. Some of the interwoven channels traversing the wide gravel riverbed were deep and some were shallow. The rate of water flow and the position of the channels varied depending on rainfall upstream and were prone to flash flooding.

'There he is,' Mac said through the comms as he hovered the helicopter over the river above the trapped man.

His hiking buddy was on the bank and had thrown his friend a rope.

'Remember the training,' Levi told Kaia as Grant opened the cabin door and readied the winch system. 'And stay close.'

Looking increasingly nervous, Kaia nodded and offered him a small smile that made him feel fractionally better. Clipped to the same winch line for safety, he and Kaia were lowered into the river a short distance from Peter, who was clinging to a boulder in chest-high, fast-moving water with his friend's rope tied around his chest.

Together, arms linked, Levi and Kaia waded through strong currents carrying a buoyancy aid. As soon as they reached him, Levi looped a flotation device and harness over the man's head and under his arms so he could relax against the currents trying to suck him under.

'Peter, we're going to get you out of here, winch you up,' Kaia yelled over the roar of the chopper motor and the rushing noise of the water.

The man was clearly exhausted from fighting the river to keep his torso upright and his head out of the water. His lips were blue with cold, his eyes rimmed with dark circles and his skin alarmingly white.

Levi clipped his harness onto the winch cable, so now all three of them were connected by the lifeline to the rescue helicopter.

'Hold on to each other,' Levi yelled as Kaia and Peter clung to the loops on each other's harnesses. 'And don't let go.' Levi radioed for Grant to take up the slack on the winch cable so they wouldn't get sucked under.

'My foot is stuck in my boot!' Peter yelled back.

'I'm going to have a look and try to free your foot,' Levi said, lengthening the wire to his harness so he could submerge himself in the water. 'Don't be alarmed if I grab hold of your legs,' he told Peter. 'You just keep a tight hold of my colleague, Kaia, here, okay?'

Peter nodded, clinging to Kaia. Levi pulled a small

knife and mini-crowbar from his tool belt and looped their straps around his wrist. Then, with a final glance at Kaia, where he hoped she saw his warnings to stay safe, he pulled down his goggles.

'Be careful,' she called, clinging to the casualty as the water surged around her shoulders.

Levi gave her a thumbs-up, his heart pounding with adrenaline. If he worried about how vulnerable she was, being pummelled by the river, if he surrendered to his fear for her safety, or allowed himself to think she was the most precious person in his life, he wouldn't be able to do his job. All three of them needed to get out of the water and dry as soon as possible.

Taking a deep breath, he pushed himself under the water. Trying to stay under against the force of the river, which wanted to sweep him away, was disorienting. He looked around, seeking out the red of Kaia's drysuit, wrapping one arm around her knees to keep himself anchored as best he could. With his other hand he felt blindly down Peter's calf to the top of his walking boot, encountering the rocks that had him trapped.

Using the crowbar, Levi managed to shift a couple of the smaller boulders by an inch or so. Next he used the knife to cut the bootlaces. Then, just when he thought he'd need to surface for air, Peter's foot worked free of the boot and the currents dragged all three of them a few feet downstream until the winch cable pulled taut.

Levi surfaced, and gulped air, using the winch wire to haul himself upright and find his footing in the fast-flowing water. He looked for Kaia and Peter, but Kaia was nowhere to be seen.

Panic struck him as if he'd run into a brick wall as

he scanned the river frantically. There was no sign of her. Had her harness somehow come loose so she'd been washed away? If something had happened to Kaia on his watch, he'd never forgive himself.

Fighting the water, he made it to Peter, who had his arms submerged, searching.

'She went under,' he said.

Levi crouched next to Peter and felt blindly under the water, his heart in his throat. If he lost her… No… Then, before his mind could go to that truly dark place, something brushed his leg. He grabbed for Kaia just as her head broke the surface and she gasped. Hauling her to her feet, he wrapped one arm around her while the other held on to Peter's harness.

Relief pounded through him so hard he felt dizzy, sick, as if he were outside his body. But she was real in his arms and he clung tighter, desperate to get out of there now.

'Are you okay?' he asked, his own vulnerability an all-over body pain. This was the downside of allowing her to get so close. He might actually be growing emotionally reliant on Kaia, in more ways than as a friend. After all, they were living together, working as a team and sharing a bed every night… He cared more deeply than before, more deeply than he'd ever cared for anyone. And all he could see was the end of them, either this weekend when she moved into her own place or in another week, when she woke up and realised that he could never give her the kind of relationship she wanted. Whichever way he looked at it, he was on borrowed time.

She nodded, clinging to him as she coughed and spluttered and wiped water from her eyes. 'I slipped…went under…couldn't find my footing.'

'Let's get out of here,' he said as they each reached for Peter's harness, drawing him between them so they formed a tightly clinging human sandwich. They needed to get their casualty out of the water and Levi wouldn't be able to relax until Kaia was safe too.

With his stare latched to hers in case she disappeared from view again, he radioed to Grant to haul them up. Slowly, the winch retracted, lifting all three of them out of the river.

Back in the cabin, and while Grant winched himself down to pick up Peter's hiking buddy, Levi tried to drag in some relieved breaths. They still had work to do and Kaia seemed fine, moving into action.

'Peter, we need to assess you for hypothermia,' Kaia told him as she and Levi quickly removed the top half of their bulky drysuits. 'I'm going to cut away your wet clothing. Just try to lie still.'

As the clothing was removed, Levi wrapped Peter in warm towels and a foil blanket, pushing the near miss with Kaia from his mind so he could focus on doing his job. Peter was shivering so violently, he couldn't speak clearly, but he was conscious and alert, all good signs.

'I'm just going to take some observations,' Levi said, attaching Peter to a cardiac monitor and blood-pressure cuff, while Kaia measured his temperature. But every time he paused, his hands trembled almost as badly as Peter's. Not from cold, but from adrenaline and the shock of almost losing Kaia.

'Thirty-four-point-eight,' she told Levi, her stare clearly concerned for their patient.

'You're a bit cold, mate,' he told Peter, glad to have work on which to focus so he didn't once more subside into panic. 'We're going to insert an IV and slowly infuse some warm saline. Get you warmed up.' Chances were, Peter was also dehydrated from being exposed to the river for so long.

Kaia inserted the cannula while Levi set up the warmed saline drip. They worked quickly and efficiently, the in-sync team of old, but after the river incident, the terror that he might have lost her, and the sickening knowledge that he was, despite his attempts to keep boundaries in place so he didn't mislead or hurt her, becoming too attached, Levi could find no comfort in the familiar partnership. He was too freaked out, too scared to probe at his feelings in case they terrified him.

'Just going to change the towels for warm blankets,' Kaia told Peter. Then to Levi she said, 'Help me site these warm compresses.'

'We need to get dry too,' he told Kaia as soon as Grant and Peter's friend were on board. Peter's temperature was slowly increasing, his vital signs stable. He and Kaia weren't sodden, thanks to the drysuits, but they'd both been submerged in the river and they still had their suits around their ankles.

Seeing that they'd done everything they could for their patient for now, Kaia nodded. They stepped aside to properly remove their suits and dry off.

Jittery with shock and desperate to hold Kaia in his arms so he could feel her reassuring heartbeat, Levi handed her a towel. 'I'm so sorry about earlier. Are you okay?' he asked quietly, trying to conceal how volatile he felt, another sign that he'd allowed things to go too far. Allowed her too close. 'I was so worried when I surfaced and you weren't there,' he finished, although *wor-*

ried was an understatement. They were a team. She was as much his responsibility on a mission as their patient.

'It wasn't your fault,' she said quietly. 'My feet just went from under me.' Kaia rubbed her face and hair with the towel. 'I'm fine. And I was worried by how long you were under the water releasing his foot. It felt like a year.'

Aware that they weren't alone and with his back to the others, Levi discreetly reached for her hand. He couldn't stop himself. They were at work and needed to stay professional, but the need to touch her was alarmingly fierce. 'I… I'm so relieved you're okay.'

'Me too.' She met his stare and squeezed his fingers, secretly communicating what they couldn't say. They cared about each other. Deeply. They always had. Yet more reason to lock down whatever the hell was happening to him. Because he never wanted to hurt her or lose their close bond. He was out of control, his emotions all over the place, and if he wasn't careful he'd mess this up and ruin what they had. Fighting the urge to drag her into his arms until he felt like his old self and not this unstable, constantly on-guard person, he dropped his hand and rubbed the towel over his head.

Part of him wished he didn't have to let go. Ever. But as fresh panic slithered through his veins, a resurgence of how he'd felt when he'd thought she'd been washed away, he knew he needed to do a better job of protecting and preparing himself. Their time was running out. Kaia was moving out at the weekend. He would miss living with her. But worse, he was too scared to know if the end of their being roommates also meant the end of the fling.

He wasn't ready. But he would have to face it, just

as he'd had to face the end of the holidays as a kid and return to school.

'ETA Christchurch Hospital two minutes,' Mac's voice sounded through the comms.

Kaia folded away their drysuits. 'We'd better strap in for landing,' she said, shooting Levi a small smile of encouragement.

Levi took his seat, still rattled and confused at how Kaia could seem so calm when he was strung out and had been for days. But of course she was better at this emotional stuff than Levi. He was essentially a serious-relationship novice and there was no flowchart for their route back to being friends. He was making this up as he went along and he was scared it would show. That he'd mess up the way he had as a teen. The way he had when he'd tried to have a relationship with his ex.

Glancing her way, intercepting her smile, he forced himself to be rational and call upon some tried and tested coping mechanisms to lock down his feelings the way he had every time he'd bravely said goodbye to his family.

He wouldn't think about the ticking clock and Kaia moving out. He'd shove all these paranoid and irrational feelings from his mind. And to avoid hurting Kaia, he'd conceal the panic and doubt he felt by stepping outside his comfort zone to begin this highly risky fling and simply enjoy every last second until it was over.

Because the part of him craving her constantly but flailing around with no clue how to deal with this degree of emotional connection was the very part he needed to hide in case it pushed Kaia away.

CHAPTER ELEVEN

LEVI HAD BEEN quiet on the ride home from work, casting her worried glances that no amount of reassurance that she was okay after her dunk in the river would dispel. After a shower and thirty minutes of tossing her few belongings into packing boxes, she sought him out. Finding him in the kitchen looking at his phone, she slid her arms around his waist and pressed her face to his shoulder.

'Want to take me out on a date tonight?' she asked, aware that she'd no longer be living with him after the weekend. 'There's a movie I'd like to see. And after today we could use some downtime.'

He froze, his hand covering hers. 'I can't, sorry. I've literally just promised Lee I'd take him surfing tonight.' He placed his phone on the counter and turned, wrapping his arms around her waist.

Kaia shook her head and smiled, hiding her disappointment and the feeling that something was up with him. 'No problem. I need to finish packing anyway. I was just looking for an excuse to get out of it.' She pressed a kiss to his lips and stepped away, trying not to over-interpret his strange mood.

'Unless…' he said with a small, hesitant frown. 'Do

you want to come? To the beach? You don't have to surf but we could grab dinner on the way home.'

'Would Lee mind if I tagged along?' Kaia asked, trying to be a grown-up when what she really wanted to do was spend all her free time with Levi. She was dreading moving out but couldn't tell him that the idea of leaving almost felt as horrible as when she'd ended her former relationship. He'd freak out and he was already withdrawn and quiet after their mission today.

'I'll ask him,' Levi said. 'But I think he'll be cool.' He smiled, the expression just short of carefree. 'As long as we don't embarrass him by snogging in front of him.'

Stepping close again, Kaia looped her arms around his neck. 'That might actually be pretty tough for me.' She kissed him, moaning softly when he crushed her close, the kiss turning heated.

'I know what you mean,' he said when he pulled back, his stare promising all sorts of X-rated activity when they were alone later.

But, faced with moving out this weekend, oh, how she longed to see more than desire: a sign that he would miss her too, that he more than cared about her as a friend, that he wanted their fling to become a real relationship. She swallowed, her throat dry with fear. Those longings came with a massive risk to their friendship and her own peace of mind. And, given that she'd been so wrong about Sam and missed the signs that he wasn't as committed to her as she was to him, Kaia was terrified to put everything on the line and ask Levi how he felt about her.

Before she could question if he was open to giving the deeper connection they'd found a chance to grow and potentially ruin what might be a lovely trip to the beach, she playfully slithered out of his reach. 'You ask Lee, and I'll grab my coat.'

An hour and a half later Kaia sat on the sand at a local beach popular with surfers, contentedly watching Lee and Levi. She'd even made a doggy friend, belonging to another surfer in the water, who sat beside her and watched.

Out at the back of the waves, Lee and Levi sat side by side on their surfboards. Kaia had watched them do the move so many times that evening that when they lay down on their bellies and began frantically paddling to pick up speed, she knew they'd spotted another unbroken wave they wanted to catch.

She held her breath in anticipation. As the wave broke, they popped up onto their feet, their surfboards pushed along as they both grinned with triumph. Seeing that they were done for now and wading out of the water carrying their boards, she and her four-legged friend walked towards the shallows to meet them.

'That was great,' she said, impressed. 'Well done.'

Lee smiled shyly. 'I've got a good teacher,' he said, glancing up at Levi.

Levi smiled at the lad and stooped to undo his ankle strap. 'We've worked up quite an appetite, haven't we, mate? Think we might need some burgers on the way home.'

Just then, Lee spotted the dog. 'Can I play with him for five minutes?' he asked Levi.

'Of course,' Levi replied, smiling in a way that made Kaia's heart hurt.

Excited, Lee placed his surfboard on the dry sand and threw a driftwood stick for the terrier, who had endless energy, fetching and returning the stick as many times as Lee would throw it.

'He enjoyed that,' Levi said, resting his board next to Lee's and then taking Kaia's hand and tugging her to sit beside him on the sand. The evening sun was still warm enough to ward off the chill of the light breeze.

'You are so good with him,' she said, resting her head on his shoulder as all her doubts coalesced into one big one. What did Levi want and expect to happen after she moved out? Would she be able to miss him and not demand more from their relationship? Sometimes, such as when he'd held her in the river earlier as if he'd never let her go, she felt how much he cared. Then at other times, like now, she wondered if she was simply misreading the signs the way she had with her ex.

'Thanks for waiting for us,' Levi said, his smile the easy-going one. But there was something hesitant in his eyes.

'Are you kidding?' she said, trying to be light-hearted. 'It saved me from packing. I enjoyed watching you and watching the world go by. It's a beautiful evening.' She looked out to sea and tried to be content with the precious relationship they already had, but with each passing day it grew harder.

'Do you want my help with moving at the weekend?' he asked quietly, his gaze trained on Lee as they watched him play with the dog.

Kaia swallowed, feeling a little sick at the idea of no longer living with Levi. 'Yeah, that would be great, if you don't mind. I'll even cook you dinner to say thanks.'

But would he spend the night with her at her new

place, the way they'd been sleeping in each other's arms since their fling began?

He turned then, a small frown on his face. 'You don't have to thank me. We're mates.' He pressed a chaste and salty kiss to her lips and, rather than indulge and linger as she normally would, she pulled back, unable to stay quiet.

'So…what happens after I move…?' she asked bravely, his uncertain and hesitant expression making her feel exposed and a little reckless. 'Will… Friday be our last night together?'

She didn't want to freak him out or push him too far, but it was a logical question. Their fling had no fixed expiry date. They were probably each hoping the intensity would fade with time. But for Kaia, that showed no sign of happening yet.

'I… I don't think it's for me to answer that,' he said, giving little away. 'Do *you* want Friday to be our last night together? Have you finally had enough of me?' He flicked her a smile that reminded her of the jokey, flirty Levi of old.

Disappointed that her fishing expedition had yielded so little, Kaia shrugged, unsurprised that Levi was still guarding his emotions. It made sense he might assume that her moving out would mark the end of their fling… after all, she'd wondered the same thing. But what upset her was how unmoved he seemed by the idea of its coming to an end. Obviously she *was* misreading the signs.

'I didn't really have a time frame in mind…' she said, deflated to discover that Levi obviously wasn't thinking of long-term or forever. Her stomach gave another sickening twist. 'I just wondered what your thoughts were, given we'll no longer be living together.'

'I...' Whatever he'd been about to say, he stopped abruptly as if reframing his words. 'Of course I don't want it to be over,' he said, his fingers stroking hers.

Kaia could practically hear the 'but' at the end of that sentence. She nodded, looking out at the surfers beyond the waves as her eyes stung with tears. How much of her own true feelings could she admit without freaking him out? Without ruining whatever time they had left or discovering confirmation that his feelings for her were still platonic, whereas hers were so much more complex?

'What are your...expectations?' he asked, sounding cagier than ever, as if she'd backed him into a corner.

'I don't have any expectations of you,' she said, lying to protect his feelings and conceal her own.

A big part of her never wanted it to end. This closer relationship with Levi had helped her to put so many things into perspective. What she wanted from her future. What she didn't want. He'd given her a safe space in which to recover from the end of her last relationship and even helped her reconcile the past and her own flawed thinking when it came to losing the baby. Grief could certainly play with your mind. And maybe Levi had never truly processed his own grief for his father, for being sent to boarding school.

When all he did was nod and keep his stare averted, Kaia womanned-up and changed tack. 'I mean, obviously our long-term relationship goals don't align,' she said, her heart thudding from the courage this took. 'I still want a serious relationship one day. And you—'

'And I've never done that,' he supplied, his voice sounding defeated. 'I understand.'

'What do you understand?' she asked, confused and

a little hurt by his withdrawal when, from her point of view, they'd been growing closer and closer these past few days so she'd almost convinced herself that he could change and want a real relationship.

'That you want it all,' he said flatly. 'Commitment, marriage, love. And you deserve all those things.'

Kaia's chest ached with longing for him even as she realised he still wasn't ready to be that man. Not for her anyway. 'I do,' she said, wondering how much of herself she could compromise just to keep Levi comfortable, just to have him for a while longer. 'I do deserve them.'

He looked up so their eyes met. 'I told you I never want to hurt you or let you down.'

She nodded, waiting, willing him to meet her halfway, to say that maybe he could step out of his safe zone for once and build on what they already had. 'Obviously a fling isn't going to cut it for me forever,' she finished when he said nothing more.

'I understand,' he said eventually. 'It would be selfish of me to expect to have the best of both worlds. I just… I'm not ready to lose you yet. Can you…give me a little longer?'

Kaia cupped his face and directed his eyes to hers. 'You're not losing me just because I'm moving out. We'll still see each other every day.' She'd still want him every day too. That was the part that terrified her; that wanting him might never stop. 'And yes…yes, I can.'

But the part of her crushed that Levi still wasn't ready to take a risk for a real relationship with her, the same part that had been let down by Sam and was scared to trust her instincts, scared to make another mistake and be hurt all over again, was still too terrified to ask him outright if he'd ever consider having more with her.

'And we'll always be friends,' she finished instead, hating that what had once been the most important friendship of her life now sounded…inadequate. As if she'd outgrown it. Outgrown Levi. And maybe she had. She'd risked their friendship to have him as a lover and now she had to pay the price that things would never quite be the same for her. She'd stupidly caught deep, deep romantic feelings for him and he didn't, couldn't, feel the same way.

As if he sensed the direction of her thoughts, he leaned close and rested his forehead against hers. 'I… I wish things could have been different with us.'

Her heart pounding with hope, Kaia reared back to look into his eyes. 'What do you mean?'

'I mean I wish I was a different person. I wish I'd met you at a different time, in a different situation.' Anguish dulled his stare and Kaia shivered, certain he was cryptically telling her something she didn't want to hear or should have already figured out.

'I like the person you are,' she whispered, frowning. Couldn't he see that if he could just let her in, open his heart, take that risk, they might have something more valuable than either of them could have ever imagined? Except maybe for Levi it wouldn't be as valuable as his emotional self-sufficiency.

Frustrated, he turned away. 'I know… I just…sometimes I think there's something broken in me and I don't know how to fix it.'

Understanding dawned for Kaia then. He was telling her, in the kindest, clearest way possible, that emotionally, when it came to relationships, they were on different levels. She'd known that very early on in their friendship and nothing, except her understanding of why he was the way he was, had changed. If she'd foolishly expected more from him or imagined he might be able to change for her, that was her fault.

Ignoring her crushing disappointment and humiliation, she spoke candidly. 'You just need time, Levi. Time to figure out what you want from your future. Time to resolve your grief over losing your father at a tender age and your feelings of rejection from your mother. You just need time. And if you want to meet a woman to spend your life with, to fall in love with and have that family you've always wanted, then you'll do that. You'll put in the work for her. But it has to be something *you* want. And right now, as sad as it makes me to admit it for your own happiness, you don't seem ready to want that.'

He looked up, his expression bleak and horrified. Pity tightened her chest, but just then Lee ran over, swinging a piece of seaweed like a lasso.

'Can we go get burgers now?' he said, oblivious to the adults' tension.

'Of course,' she said brightly, standing and pulling Levi to his feet so he didn't see her devastation. 'Come on. It looks like Lee's grown bored of throwing sticks. Time for food.'

As Kaia folded up her towel and Lee went to grab his board, Levi hesitated at her side. 'Kaia…'

She plastered a carefree smile on her face and looked up. 'Let's finish this talk later at home. We don't want to dampen the atmosphere for Lee, not when he's had such a successful surf.' To show him that she was okay with his being unwilling or unable to change for her, she kissed him swiftly, then headed up the beach for the car park, chatting with Lee.

But it was all an act, a lie. She wasn't okay with his rejection. But that was her fault. She'd been here before, more trusting and more invested in a relationship than her ex. If she wasn't careful, if she didn't shield her heart from Levi, she might make another massive mistake and be hurt worse than before, wind up back at square one, all her positive changes undone.

Hoping that her move at the weekend would provide some emotional distance so she could re-evaluate her feelings, she hardened her heart and pretended all the way home.

CHAPTER TWELVE

AFTER DROPPING LEE home the night before, Levi and Kaia hadn't recommenced their conversation after all. Levi had gone for a shower, and when he'd reappeared Kaia's packing boxes were stacked in the hallway. He'd felt so devastated to see them there, so confused and sickened by what they represented and what she'd said at the beach, that he'd found her, kissed her, kept on kissing her until they were both naked and sweaty and driving all memory of their fraught discussion away with pleasure.

Of course, he knew he couldn't hide from the issues forever—his panic over Kaia's looming moving date, his paranoia that she was starting to see through him and knew that he could never be good enough to offer her more than friendship and sex, and the knowledge that what she'd said on the beach about him was true. If he ever wanted a real relationship one day, a family of his own, he had so much work to do…

Because what Kaia wanted from a relationship was a tall order for a man like him. She'd even pointed that out at the beach.

I still want a serious relationship one day. And you... A fling isn't going to cut it for me forever... We'll always be friends...

Feeling overwhelmed, he latched on to his go-to distraction: work. And this morning it was easy to put that first. As their latest rescue call came in, Levi found Kaia in the staffroom.

'Kaia, we're up,' he said, shrugging on his coat and ignoring the memory of her disappointment in him the day before, as if because of the past and his habitual self-reliance he couldn't be the man for her. 'We have a thirty-five-week-gestation female in her early thirties who started labour pains an hour ago while out for a day trip on the Banks Peninsula.'

'Coming,' she said, abandoning her coffee and grabbing her Southern Rescue jacket from the coat hook.

Without further discussion to slow them down, they left the base and ran, heads down, across the tarmac towards *Kiwi,* which was already warming up. Mac and Grant were on board and within minutes they were airborne and en route to their destination.

'Tell me more,' Kaia asked Levi.

Levi scanned the report on a tablet, relaying to herthe relevant details. 'The couple were on their way home from Hickory Bay when the contractions began. The partner kept driving, headed for the hospital, but things were progressing so quickly she made him pull over at the side of the gravel access road.'

He met her stare, searching for that same disappointed look that made him feel as if she was already slipping away, but there was no time now for any personal stuff.

'Thirty-five weeks…' she said, worrying at her lip. 'Do we have time to pick up a midwife from the hospital?' They'd done that many times before in cases where time allowed.

Levi shook his head. 'The partner reports she wants to push, so no. It sounds like the baby will be born in the car, either with or without us. And it's better for all concerned if we're there in time.' They'd delivered babies before, but never one five weeks early.

'Best-case scenario we can transport her to hospital and she has the baby in a labour suite,' Kaia said, looking as nervous as he felt.

He nodded. At least the helicopter was equipped with a small incubator and neonatal resuscitation table in case they got there in time and, if required, needed to resuscitate the newborn.

'We'll face it together,' he said, smiling reassuringly as he reached across and touched her hand. Neither of them wanted to voice the worst-case scenarios, which included a premature baby being born in the back of a car in the middle of nowhere. But he believed in Kaia, and in them as a critical-care team.

Flying directly to their location took nine minutes, a trip that would have been hours for an ambulance by road, given the remoteness and the unsealed road down to the bay.

As soon as Mac had set the helicopter down in a paddock next to the road, Kaia and Levi took off running with the equipment they might need. When they reached the car, Levi took one look at the patient and determined what they'd already known—the second stage of labour was in full swing. Like it or not, this baby was about to be born here and now.

'I'm Kaia and this is Levi,' Kaia said to the couple. 'We're paramedics here to help and take you to hospital, okay?' The couple were in the back seat of the car.

'I'm Jono and this is Lana,' the partner said, looking so relieved to see them, he immediately moved aside.

For a hopeful few seconds Levi wondered if they might, after all, be able to transport Lana to the helicopter.

Kaia pulled on gloves. 'I'm going to examine you quickly, okay, Lana?' She raised the woman's dress and slid off her underwear. After a quick exam, she turned to Levi behind her.

'I don't think we can move her,' she said quietly, frowning with concern.

He squeezed her arm, letting her know he shared the same concerns about the baby's small size. But they needed to make the call.

'What does your instinct tell you?' he asked, his own mind already decided. 'Because I trust that. If you think we're best off preparing to deliver the baby here, then that's what we'll do.'

Looking exhausted, Lana reached for her partner's hand and groaned as another contraction took hold. 'Need to push!' she cried.

Levi handed Lana some Entonox to suck on and Kaia's expression became determined. 'I don't think we can move her until the baby is delivered,' she said, making the call.

Levi nodded. 'Good decision. That was my instinct too,' he said, quickly flicking her a smile of encouragement. 'We can do this.'

Before pulling on his own gloves, he radioed the news to Mac and Grant on board *Kiwi*. Then he took the things they might need out of his backpack.

'Lana,' Kaia said, 'I need to get you positioned better.

Can you slide forward until your bottom is on the edge of the seat, and your legs out of the door?'

With Jono behind, clasping Lana's hands, Kaia and Levi positioned themselves side by side as best they could in the open car doorway.

'Jono,' Levi said, 'keep doing the great job you've been doing. Lana, focus on your breathing, use the gas and air and we'll do the rest. It's going to be fine. You're going to meet your baby soon.'

He looked at Kaia by his side and for a split second saw something in her eyes that made him want to be a better man for her: that trust he'd almost taken for granted. Was his selfish need for her putting her at risk of developing feelings? Could she ever see him as relationship material? Could he risk everything and try to give her more, try to be what she wanted and deserved? Because sometimes, like now, when they seemed so in sync, the idea that this would soon end as she'd said and they'd go back to being just friends, that Kaia would meet another man she could love, was unthinkable.

The look of absolute faith on Levi's face as he'd told Kaia to trust her instincts gave her the calmness she needed to get this job done. Simply knowing he was at her side, that they'd do this together, as a team, was all she needed to know.

Setting her concerns aside and with no time to second guess, she watched Lana breathe through another contraction and prepared herself to deliver this baby. Levi spread sterile towels for the baby to be delivered onto and pulled out a sterile umbilical clamp from their supplies. Kaia reached for a neonatal suction device. If the baby didn't breathe unaided after delivery, they might need to remove mucus from its nose and mouth.

In the zone, Kaia ran through a mental checklist of her obstetric training. If they were lucky, Lana and nature would do all the work and the baby would deliver itself. They'd just need to keep it warm and transport both mother and baby to the hospital as soon as possible.

When the next contraction came, Lana pushed in earnest.

'That's it, Lana. Keep pushing, keep pushing, keep pushing,' Kaia chanted encouragement, while beside her Levi readied a small oxygen cylinder and neonatal mask, calmly preparing for any eventuality.

'I can see the head,' Kaia told everyone. 'You're doing great, Lana.'

As the next contraction began, as she and Levi instructed Lana to push, Levi rested his hand on Kaia's shoulder, letting her know he was there, that he had her back, same as always.

'The baby's coming!' Lana cried, bearing down once more while Jono gripped her hands from behind and kept up a constant stream of reassurance.

The baby's head emerged and Kaia calmly slid her fingers under the baby's chin to feel for the presence of the umbilical cord.

'Okay, pant now, Lana,' Levi instructed. 'The baby's head is out. Well done. You're doing a wonderful job.'

'No cord,' Kaia told Levi, relieved. Then with a final contraction, a final push from Lana, the shoulders and rest of the baby's body were delivered into Kaia's waiting hands.

'Well done. You've done it,' Levi said as the baby took its first breath and mewled. 'You have a baby boy.'

Kaia quickly calculated the Apgar score and and handed the baby straight to his parents. Levi covered the small but healthy newborn in a blanket.

While the couple laughed and cried and welcomed their tiny son Kaia turned to Levi, her relief almost euphoric. 'We did it,' she whispered, smiling up at him.

He smiled back and nodded. 'Great job, McBride.'

But they weren't out of the woods yet.

'You take the baby to *Kiwi*,' Kaia told him as she clamped and cut the cord. 'Get him warm and ask Grant to bring the wheelchair for Lana. I'll stay and get her ready to be moved.' She needed to clean Lana up for the journey and she might need to deliver the placenta.

Levi nodded, and uncoiled the tubing of an oxygen mask. 'Lana, because he's a bit early, we're just going to give your baby a tiny bit of oxygen to be safe, okay?' Gently, as if he'd handled thousands of babies, Levi fitted the nasal cannula to the baby's face and turned on the flow of oxygen from a portable canister.

'Ready for your ride to the hospital?' Levi asked the beaming couple, who nodded, still speechless with wonder.

'If I could take the baby first,' Levi said, 'and get him warm inside the helicopter. Jono, you can help Kaia and our colleague, Grant, get Lana into a wheelchair and across the paddock, okay?'

With proceedings paused until the next contraction, Kaia watched in wonder as carefully Levi took the baby from Lana and smiled down at the wee bundle.

For a second, distracted by the awestruck look on Levi's face and the way her heart clenched painfully, Kaia couldn't breathe. Watching Levi with a baby, his handsome face wreathed in delight, his strong arms protecting the tiny newborn… It was too much. Enough to make her imagine them as a real couple: romantic dates, living together, laughter and love. To make her certain that she could no longer deny her feelings for him and needed to find the right moment to trust her instincts as he'd encouraged and be brave enough to ask him if they could ever have more.

'Does he have a name yet?' Levi asked the parents as he tucked the blanket around the baby boy.

'What about Levi?' Lana turned to Jono, who smiled indulgently and nodded.

'His name's Levi,' Jono told the other Levi, who visibly swallowed, obviously beyond touched.

'Thank you,' Levi said, glancing at Kaia.

'No, thank you. Both of you,' Lana said, happy tears spilling onto her cheeks.

As Kaia watched Levi carefully carry the baby towards the helicopter, she recalled one very important thing that threw her back into confusion and doubt: she might want more of him, want all of him, but Levi wanted a family one day. And, with her mother's history and Kaia's track record, she wasn't a safe bet in that regard. Just as Levi thought there was something broken in him, Kaia had the same fear that she might never get to be a mother.

Now, ignoring that fear and all her others, Kaia helped Lana, no longer certain, despite her gut instincts, that she could have the things she wanted most.

CHAPTER THIRTEEN

THAT EVENING, AS SHE and Levi returned home from work, they were both quiet in the car. Kaia knew she'd have to confront him soon and ask him outright if he saw any kind of future for them. But, feeling paranoid and defensive about her ability to have children, Kaia wasn't sure she could face another conversation about their feelings.

Tuning back into Levi's chatter, she tried to pay attention.

'He's so excited,' Levi said about Lee.

'Is it this weekend?' she asked because he'd been telling her about Lee's school formal.

'Yes, the sixteenth,' Levi said, making Kaia frown with a fresh revelation about the date.

Doing a quick mental calculation, she'd realised with both fear and a flicker of excitement that her period was a few days late. Trying not to panic, she headed inside as soon as Levi pulled up, needing a moment to herself. Automatically, she flicked on the kettle to make tea. Should she tell Levi or keep it to herself? Torn, she chewed at her thumbnail. They weren't a couple. They weren't even dating. No matter how badly Kaia wished they were. And, if Levi was freaked out by the idea of a real romantic relationship, he'd probably lose his mind at the idea of an accidental pregnancy, especially with her.

'Hey…you okay?' Levi asked, joining her in the kitchen.

Kaia nodded, desperately trying to hide the worst of her fears. But he knew her better than anyone and it also concerned him. She should tell him. Maybe just spitting it out would tempt fate so she'd wake up tomorrow, not pregnant after all.

'What a day, huh?' he said, oblivious to her inner struggles as he rubbed her upper arms. 'You were incredible delivering little Levi. I'm so proud of you.' He pressed his lips to her forehead, and for a blissful moment of denial she put her arms around his waist and allowed herself to be held, breathing him in, comforted by his strength and the beat of his heart.

But her reality hit. Her eyes stung as she fought tears. She had feelings for her best friend, a man who'd never really had a serious, committed relationship. She wanted more than a sexual fling with him *and* she might also be pregnant with his baby, although she clung to the fact it was highly unlikely. But even if by some fluke she was, that didn't mean she'd actually have his baby. She might lose this one too.

'Hey,' he said. 'What's wrong?'

When she looked up, all the things she wanted to say to him trapped in her throat, he frowned. 'Tell me,' he urged and Kaia almost told him how she felt about him. How she wanted them to be more than friends, more than roommates, have more than sex. How she wanted a real relationship, and one day, if he could want her back and she was very, very lucky, she also wanted a baby with him.

Conflicted about her late period and knowing he wouldn't know what to do with her feelings for him, and that she didn't want to hurt or pressure him, she said, 'I just realised, when you were talking about the date of Lee's formal in the car, that my period is a bit late.'

Needing distance, she stepped away and pulled two mugs from the cupboard. 'I'm normally pretty regular, but it's probably nothing…'

But even as she tried to reassure them both, her heart flickered with the longing that things could be different if only Levi wanted more.

She kept her back to him as she fished out two teabags, and tried not to surrender to panic. Of course, her fear that she was pregnant, no matter how irrational, was natural after her past unplanned pregnancy and the events that had followed. She couldn't help but imagine the worst-case scenario—that she might indeed be pregnant again and she might lose Levi's baby too.

'Kaia, look at me,' he said from so close behind her she felt the heat emanating from his body.

Kaia turned and tried to be brave, but Levi's concerned frown made her feel sick. There was no way she could be pregnant. No way. But even the remotest possibility was enough to make her thoughts run wild. She and Levi would make gorgeous babies. He'd make a wonderful father. And the part of her that had felt closer to him than ever before these past few weeks craved a committed romantic relationship with him.

'We've been safe,' he reasoned, reaching for her hand. 'You're on the pill and we've used condoms.'

'I know.' She nodded, glancing away from the calm logic and hope in his stare. He was right. But she wouldn't want to see his relief when this scare proved to be nothing. It was too close, too reminiscent of the situation with Sam, and she and Levi was nothing like her and Sam. For one, she wasn't in a romantic relationship with Levi…

'I'm worrying over nothing,' she finished, overwhelmed by the emotional highs and lows of the past few days.

'But you're still worrying,' he said, cupping her face. 'I agree. I think it's over nothing. Of course, I understand why your mind is going there.'

She nodded, but he couldn't truly understand. Yes, he knew she was scared that she might suffer another miscarriage. But her fears were more about her emotional state than the actual one in a trillion chance of being pregnant. Ever since the day of Lee's football match, she'd begun to wonder if she could change Levi's mind about relationships. Sometimes, when she was in his arms or lost in his adoring stare, or laughing with him over some silly nothing, she felt certain that if he could only set aside his fear of being emotionally reliant on another person, and give her all of his heart, they could have it all.

But could Kaia take such an obvious risk when she'd been so wrong in the past? When she was serious about finding that one person who was ready to face anything the world could throw at them by her side, and, by his own admission, Levi wasn't ready to be that man?

She looked up from underneath her lashes, needing to know that he had her back. Not just at work and through their friendship, but in facing the consequences, if any, of their fling. 'And what if I am pregnant?' she whispered, her heart pounding with fear because, while she'd been having feelings, he'd been pulling back.

His frown deepened, as if he'd never before considered the possibility that, if you were lucky, sex led to babies. But then, he was a responsible man who'd never really been in a committed, long-term relationship. He'd never needed to worry about consequences before.

'Then we'll deal with that situation if it arises,' he said, looking uncomfortable. 'There's no point postulating now on something that might not be.'

Kaia nodded and warily stepped away from him. She needed his touch, but needed his reassurances more. 'Thing is… I've been here before. I kind of need to postulate. To play the what-if game.' She met his stare, her breathing tight with all that was at stake.

'Okay,' he sighed as if frustrated. 'Then let's play it. If you are pregnant, although I believe it's highly unlikely, given we've always used contraception, and if you want to have a baby right now, then we'll have a baby. I'll support you and any decision you make. I'll care for our baby while you go to medical school if that's what you want to do. We'll make it work, Kaia. A team.'

A team, not a couple.

Kaia nodded, envious that he could make it sound so simple and hating that, while she had never felt more vulnerable, for Levi it was straightforward. She had no doubt whatsoever that he would love and adore any child of his, but when it came to romantic entanglements he kept his feelings locked down. No need to agonise over sharing a child with her because the complication of romantic feelings wasn't even on his radar.

Whereas Kaia was already too emotionally invested

in him, imagining that she could have everything she'd ever wanted with the best man she knew: a real relationship, commitment, a family. As long as she put everything on the line and told him how she felt, how she wanted all of him: his passion, his fierce loyalty and devotion to those he cared about, his heart.

Choked by longing, Kaia gave a shaky nod. 'Okay,' she said, exhaling slowly so she didn't cry. 'We'll make it work.' She tried to smile as she moved past him. 'That's all I needed to hear. I'm going to take a shower,' she called over her shoulder as she headed for the bathroom, 'then I'll make us dinner.'

As she'd known he would, he let her go.

Alone in the kitchen with his turbulent thoughts, Levi tried to swallow down his rising panic. Not over the idea of a baby. He was pretty certain that Kaia's being pregnant was an impossibility, given how careful they'd been. But because she kept looking at him as if waiting for him to do and say the right thing, and he had no idea what that thing was…

Probing the idea that he and Kaia had made a child together, he waited to freak out. The fear was there, sure, but not as strong as he'd imagined. Thinking of what she'd been through before, and how she felt about perhaps never being a mother, he couldn't leave things there. Couldn't have her afraid and doubting herself.

Minutes behind her, he marched to her room. Finding her bedroom door ajar, he knocked at the en-suite door and strode determinedly into the bathroom. Kaia rubbed away the steam on the shower glass and their eyes met. Hers were full of fear and confusion, as if he were looking at his own reflection.

'I'm coming in, okay?' he said, hurriedly stripping off his clothes and joining her in the shower cubicle. He gripped Kaia's face between his palms and directed her gaze to his while his anxious heart thundered in his chest. 'I know you're probably freaking out after last time,' he said, trying to find the right words and not mess this up. 'But you don't have to be scared. I'll always be there for you,' he said eagerly. *'Always.'*

'I know.' She nodded, her hands sliding to his waist so her touch stirred his ever-constant desire for her.

'I don't know the first thing about the kind of relationships you've been in before,' he said, the rising panic returning, 'the kind you want again. But I never want to hurt you, Kaia. And if you are pregnant, I'll try my hardest to never let you down. I promise.'

Of course, he was fooling himself to think he could possibly be everything she needed. After what she'd been through, she deserved an emotionally healthy man that not only shared her goals and dreams but was also ready to fully commit to her long-term without fear and make her as happy as she deserved. A man that loved her unreservedly, not just as a friend but in every way possible. And he…he was terrified to try to be what she needed and fail. Terrified that he wouldn't be enough. That she'd see that and reject him. That he'd hurt her, lose her for good and have to deal with the horrendous emotional fallout.

'I know,' she said again, blinking as if from the threat of tears. 'I believe you.'

With fear a metallic taste in his mouth, he pressed a swift kiss to her forehead and tried to calm the out-of-control feelings making him irrational and panicked. But her faith settled something inside him, so he went on, making this up as he went to try and reassure Kaia. 'If we have made a baby, we'll raise it together. Love it together. You and me. Won't we?' he asked urgently, his gaze fixed on her beautiful eyes.

Only the idea of his and Kaia's child being also raised by her future romantic partner shoved a fist of envy and helplessness into his gut. But he needed to make her understand how much he valued her, respected, cared. But maybe his unconditional friendship, his promises to protect her weren't enough. Maybe she already saw through him and found him lacking. Maybe those disappointed looks and the way he didn't know what she wanted or how to give it to her meant she actually saw that broken thing in him that had pushed people—his mother, his ex—away in the past. Because he'd let Kaia get closer than anyone else, and her power to crush him was enormous.

Before he surrendered to a fresh wave of panic, she surged onto her tiptoes and pressed her lips to his. 'Yes, of course, we'll do it together.' She pressed kisses over his face, replacing his panic with arousal. 'I'm sorry I freaked out. I just…'

'I understand.' He wrapped his arms around her and held her tight as the water pounded them, needing her touch to calm the storm in his head and chest. Of course, she would feel his thudding heart, see how lost he felt, how poorly equipped he was to deal with this emotional stuff. But his need to console her outweighed his fear to let her in, to see him warts and all.

'You do trust me, don't you?' he asked, his voice tight with need. Not just because she was naked in his arms, but because in that moment, with her scared and anxious, the idea of losing her trust felt like the worst thing that could ever happen.

'Yes,' she replied, looking up at him with certainty. 'I trust you with my life.' She reached up and cupped his cheek, sliding her fingers into his hair so their stares were locked together.

'Then trust me that, whatever happens, we'll be okay. We'll make everything okay. You and me.' He had no idea how to be the kind of man she deserved, but he would always put her needs and happiness above his own, and, if they'd made a child, its too. Now that Kaia had pointed it out, he could see how his mother had acted in what she'd thought were his best interests. That was what you did for your kids, put their needs first.

'Levi…' she whispered, tugging at his neck until their lips brushed.

He was hard now, an inevitable reaction to her closeness. He kissed her fiercely, needing to block out the fears that raged just below his surface. Fears that time was running out. That soon, he'd have to let her go and return to just being her friend. That he'd need to switch off wanting her this way somehow. But the alternative…? To try to give her more than friendship and sex and risk that it wouldn't be enough. And what if it wasn't? He was no good at those things. The past had taught him that the harder he tried, the more vulnerable he became, and the more likely that rejection would follow. What if one wrong move on his part pushed Kaia away and ruined everything? He couldn't risk losing her for good.

Communicating his desperation through his touch, he ran his hands over her breasts, her waist, her hips and backside as their kisses grew more passionate, and Kaia touched him in the same way, as if sealing his promises and her trust with their bodies.

When she stroked his erection he slid his hand between her legs, pulling back to stare at her in wonder. 'I want you, Kaia,' he choked out. 'All the time. I know I need to let you go soon, but…' He wasn't sure how he would do that. She filled his head twenty-four hours a day. He ached for her even when they were together. His need obliterating everything else.

'Don't think about it,' she said, pressing her naked body closer to his. 'Not now.'

Happy to live in denial a little longer, he cupped her breast and took the nipple into his mouth until she moaned and clung to him, slippery in his arms. Before they got too carried away, she turned off the shower. Hand in hand they stumbled into the bedroom, dripping water onto the hardwood floor. But neither of them seemed to care, their kisses frantic, their hands restless as if this might be their last night together after all.

She pulled him down on top of her and he licked the water droplets from her skin, kissing, tasting. He stroked her clitoris, swallowing her moans with his kisses as she twisted his hair between her fingers. He retrieved a condom from the stash Kaia kept in her bedside drawer and rolled it on. Then they were kissing again and finally, as he pushed inside her and stroked her hair back from her flushed face, brushing kisses over her swollen lips, that constant hum of panic he'd experienced for days fell silent.

'I'll never hurt you,' he said, keeping still but for the terrifying lurch of his inexperienced heart. His promise came out a hoarse whisper, the lump in his throat almost choking him. But he was resolved to make her understand that, whether she was pregnant or not, and whether they were lovers or just friends, he was and always would be committed to her.

'I'll never hurt you either,' she said, wrapping her arms around his neck and dragging his lips back to hers.

But, as he lost himself in her, that niggle at the back of his mind persisted. If he couldn't switch off this need for her, if he one day had to watch her fall in love with another man, he feared that would hurt worse than any pain he'd ever known.

CHAPTER FOURTEEN

LATER, AFTER LEVI returned from the bathroom, they lay facing each other in silence. Kaia stroked her fingers through his damp hair and down his neck, over the rounded bulk of his shoulders and down his arm until their fingers entwined. The promises Levi had made in the shower about the possibility of a baby and not wanting to hurt her had sounded to Kaia's ears like important declarations. Ones she was desperate to hear confirmed.

Levi held her face between his palms, staring so deeply into her eyes, she thought she glimpsed the things she wanted to see. That, like her, he had romantic feelings for her and wanted them to have more than just this. Maybe now was that time she'd been waiting for to trust her instincts and ask him outright.

Before she could, he leaned close and captured her lips, kissing her with an intensity that should have sounded an alarm bell in her head. But she was too loved-up, too lost in him and how perfect it felt to be with him, to heed the warning sounds.

'Don't go,' he said fiercely when he pulled back, still holding her face.

She frowned and he added, 'Stay. Don't move out. Live with me.'

His stare was dark with fear and Kaia's heart pulsed painfully, because she knew this man and could see how scared he was to take such an enormous step. She glanced away, unable to look at him in case he saw that she'd fallen desperately in love with him and only pitied her.

'I can't,' she whispered, her palm cupping his face too as she boldly raised her eyes to his. 'I just realised something, Levi. Or maybe I realised it the other day when I saw you hold little newborn Levi. I'm in love with you. Not as a friend but properly in love with you. All of you.'

There was no shame in admitting it after all. Despite how he guarded his emotions and kept people out, he was extremely lovable.

His frown deepened, his stare searching hers, as if seeking the truth.

'I've been trying to ask you how you feel about me for days,' she admitted in a rush. 'To ask if there's any possibility you wanted to try and build a real relationship with me. But I was scared that I'd freak you out. That I'd see the look you're wearing right now, of panic, like that of a trapped animal.'

'No… I don't feel trapped. I… I just don't know the first thing about love and commitment. I don't know how to be the man you want. The man you deserve. I'm no good at those things. But that's why I want you to stay. We've been getting so close. I've tried to let you in. I really have.'

Kaia nodded, her heart cracking open. 'I know you have. I understand why it's scary for you. But that's the thing, Levi, it's scary for me too. I'm scared to put my heart on the line again after last time. I'm scared to make another mistake and care more than the man in my life cares for me. I'm scared that for a man who wants a family I'm not a safe bet, given my history…'

'But I *do* care about you,' he said, impassioned. 'I've always cared and I always will.'

Kaia nodded, her eyes filling with deflated tears. 'I know. And I believed you when you said you didn't want to hurt me. But I am hurting because I want more than this. I want you to love me with every scrap of your heart. I want you to be as sure that I'm your forever person as I'm sure you could be mine. This…what you're offering, us living together… I know it's a big deal for you. You've never lived with anyone before. Believe me, I wish what you're suggesting was enough for me, I really do, because then I *could* stay. I could live a while longer in this wonderful bubble we've created.'

'But it's not enough,' he said flatly, letting go of her face to roll onto his back and stare at the ceiling as if she'd hurt him. But she was hurting too.

Kaia reached out to touch him, then recoiled and simply shook her head. She needed to be strong and trust those instincts. She needed to not settle for half a relationship, one where she could be hurt down the track when Levi decided he'd changed his mind or couldn't love her after all.

'And what if you are pregnant?' he asked, sitting up and swinging his legs over the edge of the bed so his back was to her. 'What then?'

Kaia swallowed hard, refusing to allow the tears to spill until she was alone. 'It's like you said. It's highly improbable that I am. But if we have made a baby and

I can carry it to term… Then we'll both love it. Both raise it.' But apart.

'I'm sorry,' she added, getting out of bed and pulling on the first clothes she came across, sweatpants and a sweatshirt.

He looked up sharply. 'Why are *you* sorry?'

'Because I should have told you how I felt sooner. I was just terrified of shattering the illusion that we had a chance at a real relationship. Too scared to know if, yet again, I'd misread the signs. But obviously I have.' Obviously her instincts were still faulty. Obviously Levi wasn't the one.

She shoved her feet into her trainers, grabbed her bag from the chair and turned to face him. 'It's okay, Levi. Just like I can't help loving you, you can't help *not* loving me. I hope you find the one for you one day. I really do. The woman who makes you brave enough to risk your heart for love. But you can understand why I can't stay now. Not even tonight. I'll let you know if the pregnancy was a false alarm. We're both sure it will be. But if you can give me nothing else, could you please give me some time to work through this?'

He nodded stiffly, his stare bleak and lost.

Kaia glanced around the room, at her possessions packed into boxes and bags. 'Thanks for letting me stay,' she said. And then she left.

By the middle of the following week, Levi was a husk of a man. Kaia had texted him first thing on Monday morning to confirm there was no baby. But she'd also swapped shifts with another paramedic and taken some annual-leave days, so for the first time in four years he'd had to work with someone other than his partner. When he'd arrived home on Monday evening, every single scrap of Kaia had been removed from his house. He'd wandered each room, searching for the tiniest belonging: a stray hairband, a sock left in the dryer, shower gel in the shower. But nothing. It was as if she'd never lived there. Not even the scent of her remained.

To make matters worse, it was a rare quiet week at work. No adrenaline-fuelled rescues as a distraction. Just hour after hour of hanging around base, killing time, waiting for the calls to come in with only his sickening thoughts for company. Kaia's words from Friday night ran through his head.

I want more... I wish what you're suggesting was enough for me...you can't help not loving me...

Staring into space, his fist around a cold mug of coffee in his lap, he tried to decide if it was less painful to think or to feel. She'd finally seen through him, rejected him and his lame attempts to give her more. Her face, hurting and let down, flashed before his eyes. And the pain…physical breathlessness and restlessness that no amount of working out at the Southern Rescue gym could dull… But then, what had he expected? He'd allowed himself to be vulnerable and now he was hurting, just as he'd known he would. Like all those other times in the past.

'Days like these are tough, eh?' Mac said, plonking his lean, wiry frame on the opposite sofa and startling Levi back to the present.

Flinching, Levi placed his untouched coffee on the table and tried to act normal. 'Yeah…killer. I'd much rather be dangling from the winch…'

'Ten more minutes till clocking-off though,' Mac said, glancing at his watch. 'So what's up with Kaia?' he asked after a moment of silence. 'She sick or something?'

Levi swallowed a throat full of razor blades and looked away, ashamed of the way he'd handled that night. The panic that she was moving out. The confusion and doubt he'd been feeling for days that made him want to run, pull back from Kaia in order to protect himself. The certainty that he needed to do something to keep her but might do the wrong thing and mess up, ruin the best thing in his life.

'I'm…um…not sure actually,' he muttered. 'I think she's on a run of late shifts.'

Avoiding Levi, understandably. How could he have done the one thing he'd promised he wouldn't—let her down and hurt her?

'You've been a team for years, haven't you?' Mac asked, clearly oblivious to Levi's grief and self-recrimination. 'Must be tough adjusting to working with someone else.'

Levi nodded, his stomach so knotted he might actually throw up. 'I might have to get used to it,' he choked out. 'We've…um…kind of been seeing each other romantically, Kaia and me, and…'

And he'd messed it up, as he'd known he would. He'd let her get close, been rejected and brought this world of pain down upon himself.

'Yeah,' Mac said, looking remarkably comfortable to talk about feelings. 'Me and Grant had kind of noticed.'

Levi looked up, stunned. 'You had?' He'd thought they'd been so discreet and secretive.

'She's crazy about you, man,' Mac said. 'It's been obvious for months.'

Levi gaped. Months…? Was that true? Had Kaia always fancied him the way he'd always fancied her? Could their fling have been built on more than a tipsy birthday kiss? But of course it was built on more than that. They had the strong foundations of friendship and respect and teamwork and trust and—

He broke off that train of thought as realisation struck. He'd lost more than a friend. He'd lost the kind of rare relationship many people would have envied.

'So have you two fallen out or something?' Mac pushed.

Levi shook his head. If only it were a simple lovers' tiff… He could probably fix that. 'Nah… She's too good for me. She's had a tough time lately. She needs someone…better than me.'

'Is that what she said?' Mac asked, looking surprised. 'Doesn't sound like Kaia.'

Levi shrugged, wishing he could curl in on himself. 'No, not really.' Although her words had felt like a rejection at the time. But now, with some distance, he could agree with every one of them. Asking her to stay living in his spare room had been a knee-jerk reaction to her moving out. She deserved an equally committed relationship and a man who worshipped her. As her friend, he'd tell her to trust her instincts and not settle for so little…

'She's got her life together, you know…' he said lamely, prickles of dread creeping up his spine. 'And I…' He sighed, because without Kaia this life he'd condemned himself to by being scared simply wasn't worth having. 'Well, I haven't,' he finished.

'So you're not even friends any more?' Mac asked, his expression growing increasingly uncomfortable and disbelieving, as if Levi was the stupidest man on Earth for letting a woman like Kaia go.

And he *was* that stupid. She loved him. She'd poured out her heart to him at a time when she'd been most vulnerable—possibly pregnant and convinced she might lose that baby too—and he'd frozen, too scared to let her all the way in or to rely on his own feelings, his own gut instincts.

'I don't know,' he said truthfully, hanging his head. 'I'm giving her time, so…we'll see.'

'Well, don't give her too much time, will you?' Mac said sagely. 'Take it from an old married man—when you love someone, it's best never to let the sun set on a disagreement.'

'Good advice,' Levi said automatically, completely missing the part where he disagreed with Mac because he didn't love Kaia. But as he registered Mac's words he found he couldn't disagree. Because, of course, he loved her. He loved everything about her and probably always had: her playful smile, the way she never let him get away with anything, her sense of humour, her stunning eyes, the way she was the first person he thought about when he woke up and the last before he fell asleep… He loved her. All of her. And not just as a friend.

I hope you find the one for you one day, the woman who makes you brave enough to risk your heart for love.

Piecing it all together, he sat up straight. He'd already found her. She'd been in front of his face this whole time. He wasn't *that* stupid. He'd been scared he couldn't love her properly, but even he could figure out it was better to have Kaia and be terrified of his feelings than to not have her and feel the same way. That was what he should have said on Friday night. Confessed his fears—that he wouldn't be able to make the kind of relationship she wanted work; that she'd see he wasn't up to it and reject him, destroy him; that he'd lose her anyway, her love and her friendship. But wasn't that his exact position now? Wasn't he already destroyed and Kaia still had no clue that he *did* love her back?

Realising that even if she couldn't forgive him for letting her down the other day, he could at least tell her how he truly felt about her, Levi jerked to his feet and strode to the lockers to retrieve his bag.

'Uh, oh…' Mac called after him. 'I've seen that look on your face: a man on a mission.'

Levi couldn't smile at the gentle ribbing from his colleague; there was too much at stake for humour. But, as he watched the last few minutes of his shift tick over, he made a resolution. He might have done the one thing he'd feared the most and pushed Kaia away, but he could still try to win her back.

CHAPTER FIFTEEN

IN HER NEW APARTMENT, Kaia unpacked her box of books and placed them on the new shelf in her new living room, wishing she still felt like the new Kaia. It had taken her most of the day to put the flat-packed piece of furniture together. At one stage, she'd hurled the screwdriver aside and sobbed big, fat, ugly tears all over the inadequate instruction manual.

She missed her friend. If Levi had been there, he'd have helped her decipher the incomprehensible diagrams and decide what screw went where. She could cry on his shoulder and tell him that she'd had her heart broken again, worse than before. But if she couldn't have all of him, she couldn't have her friend. Not yet… Maybe in time she'd be strong enough to see him and not love him. Maybe if she was lucky…

Kaia's phone rang and she ran across the room, scooping it up and answering without checking the caller ID. Maybe it was him, calling to say he missed her and wanted her back at any cost…

'Kaia, it's Heidi Giles. How are you?'

'Heidi,' Kaia croaked, clearing her tight throat. 'I'm good. Nice to hear from you.' Although Heidi simply reminded Kaia of Levi. But then, everything reminded

Kaia of Levi: waking up, the sunshine, even breathing…

'I'm moving to Christchurch next week,' Heidi said, 'and I wondered if you want to grab a coffee some time. I don't know much about the city, so I thought I could pick your brains about where I should live and where to avoid et cetera.'

'Of course, I'd love to catch up,' Kaia said, hoping that by then she might hurt a little less. 'I'll email you my shifts and you can let me know what day works for you. If I'm not working or sleeping I'll be free, so…well whatever works.'

She'd be free because she'd run from her best friend, a man she could trust, the love of her life, because a part of her was still scared to make a mistake, still scared that, despite loving him, she might not be able to give him the family he wanted.

'Sounds good,' Heidi said. 'Hey, thanks again for hooking me up with Levi. He's a really great guy.'

Tears gathered on Kaia's lashes. 'Yeah… I know,' she said, trying to keep the emotion from her voice. The best man she'd ever known. 'I'm sorry you two didn't hit it off. You have so much in common…'

'Kaia…' Heidi said mockingly. 'Are you really that blind? The guy is totally in love with *you*.'

Kaia's jaw dropped and her pulse stuttered. No…

'He talked about you all night,' Heidi went on, oblivious to Kaia's confusion and hope. 'I told him I like surfing and he said, "Kaia would love it too but she's not the strongest swimmer." When I talked about uni and how we'd met, all he wanted to know was what you'd been like at that age. If he wasn't so charming and hot, I'd have tipped my drink in his face and walked out. But I couldn't bring myself to call him out on it because he genuinely seemed to have no idea of his feelings or how to tell you.'

From behind her hand, which was pressed to her mouth, Kaia sobbed. Could he really love her after all? Should she have given him more of a chance to realise his feelings? He'd spent his entire adult life habitually making them smaller to protect himself from perceived rejection. Had she reacted too quickly, scared that she'd made another mistake after Sam? Even if Heidi was wrong, if Levi couldn't love her back, she ached for his friendship. She would rather have him in her life in any capacity than not have him at all. Because he was the only person she wanted to call and talk to about her broken heart, even when he'd been the one to cause it.

Standing, Kaia scanned the room for her car keys. 'Heidi, I...um... I need to go. I'll send you those dates and we can chat when you get here.'

'Sure, take care,' Heidi said and called off.

Desperate to see Levi, Kaia grabbed her keys and bag and without even bothering to look in the mirror at her tear-stained, make-up-less face and wild hair, and yanked open the front door.

And there on her doorstep stood Levi.

'Kaia,' Levi said, dropping his hand—which had been about to knock on her door—to his side, his heart jolting with shock and excitement. 'I know I said I'd give you time, but can we talk?'

She nodded, looking dazed, and beautiful, her eyes red as if she'd been crying. He wanted to punch himself in the face for causing her pain.

'Come in,' she said, stepping back. 'Excuse the boxes… I haven't finished unpacking.'

'I don't care,' Levi said, not even bothering to glance around the sunlit room. 'I just need you to hear me out.'

She nodded warily and dropped her bag on the room's only chair. 'Okay.'

Levi dragged in a deep breath, wishing he could pull her into his arms and hold her until she smiled. But he'd lost that right by being too terrified to tell her how he felt. Maybe he'd lost that power too.

Staring into her eyes, he took a deep breath. 'I know I made a total mess of us, and I don't deserve your forgiveness, but I just wanted you to know that you were right about me.'

'Which part?' she asked, frowning in confusion.

'All of it,' he said. 'What you said about me grieving for my dad and telling my mum how I felt about boarding school and not giving you all of my heart.'

She nodded sadly and dipped her stare.

Levi stepped closer, his words tumbling out. 'But that's the thing, Kaia. My heart, every piece of it, has *always* been yours. Ever since that first day we met. You laughed at my lame joke and then we treated that old lady who'd had a heart attack and you were so smart and kind and funny. I loved you instantly. Bam.' He thumped his chest, the gesture only a fraction of the real feeling. 'Then you mentioned your boyfriend and I realised you couldn't be mine, so I made myself shut down all those new, terrifying feelings so I could be your friend. By that age, I was already so good at hiding my emotions, pretending I was fine alone, self-sufficient. Too good. I did it *too* well. I see that now. You helped me to see it.

I've played it safe for years, telling myself your friendship was my safety net, the only way I could have you in my life. And I *love* being your friend, don't get me wrong. We have the best time together, even when you make me watch those cheesy reality shows. But it's like you said—it's not enough any more.' He took another half-step, drawn to her as always.

'Levi,' she whispered, her eyes filling with tears.

He closed the distance between them and held her face, brushing his thumbs over her cheekbones. 'Don't cry. This is the happiest day of my life because I finally get to tell you how I feel, how I've always felt. I love you, Kaia. As a friend *and* as a lover. You are that woman who makes me brave enough to risk my heart. The only woman. Haven't you felt my love on some level?'

She nodded, her lips trembling.

'It took me so long to admit my feelings but they've been there all along, buried. But I'm ready now to let you all the way in, to be emotionally invested in you, in us. I *do* want a real relationship with you. I want it all, any part of you you'll let me have for as long as possible. I just got scared because I've never done this before—been in love so hard it makes you crazy. I got scared that I'd mess up or my best wouldn't be good enough or you'd see that broken part of me and push me away the way I thought I'd been pushed so many times in the past. But I don't care if you do see my broken parts. I'll love you anyway, because I always have. I realised today that I had a simple choice: love you but never tell you, or love you and beg you to believe me. The only part over which I have no control is the loving you part. So I might as well tell you, even though I'm terrified, even though you might not be able to forgive me for being scared on Friday, for messing up. And if you can't forgive me and you no longer want me or you're holding out for a man who's better at this stuff, then that's fine. I'd be the first person to cheer you on, to tell you to trust your instincts and go after what you want and deserve. You know that. I just wanted you to know that what you said you wanted on Friday, a man ready to love you with all his heart, is right here and always has been.' He rested his hand in the centre of his chest. 'I know you. I know your fears and dreams and you know mine. We're already best friends and that's a good place to build a real relationship on, isn't it?'

She nodded tearfully but her eyes were still rounded with fear and doubt.

'Put it this way,' he said in a last-ditch attempt to persuade her, 'I'm going to love you for the rest of my life anyway, whether you're mine or not. So I've got nothing to lose except you. And I don't want to lose you, ever.'

Her lips trembled as more tears spilled. 'I want to be yours,' she said and his heart soared into his throat so he couldn't speak. 'But...what if I can't give you the family you want?' she whispered. 'Maybe it's me who's broken.'

'No,' he said, shaking his head and dragging her into his arms. 'You're everything. I want you exactly as you are. I know why you feel that way, but if a family isn't meant to be for us, then so be it.' He gripped her shoulders and peered into her eyes. 'I'd rather have you than not. I want *you*, Kaia. Always. For the rest of my life. And a family, *our* family would be a wonderful bonus, of course, but it's not a deal-breaker for me. If it happens, we'll be so lucky and we'll love that kid to death.

But if it doesn't, we'll still have each other. We'll support each other through life. That's enough for me. More than enough.'

Then, because it felt like an age since he'd kissed her, he pressed his lips to hers and poured all the love he'd had to hide all this time into their kiss.

Fully clothed, their smiling stares locked, they lay on Kaia's brand-new bed as the sun set, casting the room in an ethereal orange glow.

'I've always loved you too,' she whispered, her lips tingling because they'd kissed so many times since she'd opened the front door to him.

'I'm so lucky, then.' His eyes crinkled in the corners, his feelings easy to read: adoration, love, the smallest glimmer of fear.

'You were worried about me seeing through you,' she went on, a lump in her throat. 'But I've seen the real you from the start. You're so much more than the easy-going joker and the driven medical professional. You care deeply about people: our patients, Lee, me. You have the biggest heart of anyone I've ever met. Your smile,' she placed her fingertip in his cheek dimple, 'this here…it makes me so happy. But the one thing I love about you above all else is how much you give to others. And you believe in me.'

He nodded, his stare glowing with love. 'I do.'

She nodded. 'And that belief, that support has made me learn so many things about myself. That I can chase my dreams, however crazy they sound. That I can trust my instincts, especially with you. That the things of my past weren't my fault.'

'No.' He shook his head in agreement and stroked his fingers through her hair.

'I literally can't live without you,' she said. 'And I don't want to. I need you. Plain and simple.'

His arms drew her close, his lips brushing hers, his smile growing wider. 'I've told you before, baby, I'm right here,' he said, kissing her again. 'And I'm all yours. You just thought I was joking when I've said that before. Now you know I meant it.'

Laughing with delight, her heart so light it might float away, she wrapped her arms around his neck and kissed him back. Then she reached for his hand and entwined her fingers with his. 'So where shall we live?' she asked, already decided that it wouldn't be apart. 'Your place or mine? Some of my boxes aren't even unpacked, and if I had my way they'd stay like that, ready to be moved back to your place.'

'Our place.' He grinned and nuzzled her neck with kisses. 'You're barely moved in here and this place is just a rental.'

'Okay,' she said, sliding her legs through his and snuggling closer, drowning in happiness.

'We can make an office out of the spare room,' he said, his strong arms around her shoulders and waist. 'You'll need somewhere to study if you're going to med school.'

She leaned back and smiled. 'I love you.' Another kiss.

'I love you, too,' he said, his voice wondrous, as if he couldn't quite believe he was saying those rare words. 'So are you coming back to work in the meantime? I've missed my partner so badly, it's actually become a health and safety issue.'

She laughed again, exposing her neck to the glide of his lips. 'Well, if it's a matter of life or death… I guess I could work with you again…'

Wrapping her arms around him, she looked up. 'About the children…' she said, turning serious for a second. 'I want you to know that, where you're concerned, I do trust my instincts. I know that, whatever happens in our future, you'll be there to hold my hand through any adversity. I've never had that certainty before.'

He nodded. 'I will. Always.'

'And I'll be there for you, too,' she whispered, sliding her hand into his once more. 'Together, hand in hand, we can make our love work.'

'Then let's start now,' he said, kissing her.

So they did.

EPILOGUE

One year later...

ALTHOUGH KAIA ENJOYED being a student again and learning new things, there was nothing better than coming home to Levi after a long day of lectures. Snuggled on the sofa with him, she mused how his belief in her had been warranted. She *had* earned her place in medical school. Of course, she'd kept her job as a critical-care paramedic, too. She'd told Levi she wanted to contribute to the mortgage, but the main reason was that she wanted to keep working with him for as long as possible.

'Right,' he said, untangling himself from her kisses so he could reach for her anatomy book. 'Quiz time. You have to pass your anatomy exams.'

'But I know it all already,' she complained. 'We did most of it for paramedic training.' He too had come a long way in the past year, working on his relationship with his mother, finally understanding that the entire family had been grieving back then and that she'd done her best to meet everyone's needs, his included.

'Then you should get a hundred per cent,' he said, shooting her a stern look then a flirty wink. 'Arteries of the head and neck,' he said from behind the textbook, as serious as one of her anatomy professors.

Kaia sighed dramatically, moving closer to him on the sofa, as drawn to him as ever.

'Superficial temporal artery,' she said, pressing her fingertip to his temple and then climbing astride his lap, the book between them.

'Cerebral, occipital, facial, ophthalmic, maxillary,' she went on, pressing kisses over his face as she named each artery, smiling when he cleared his throat, trying to stay unmoved and on task. 'And I mustn't forget the lingual artery,' she finished, sliding her lips over his, because the lingual artery supplied the tongue. As if to prove her point, she kissed him harder, and when his lips parted touched the tip of her tongue to his in a flirty little tease she felt certain he wouldn't be able to resist for long.

'Kaia,' he groaned when she pulled back, his stare dark with desire and love. 'Are you taking this seriously?'

'Absolutely,' she said, trailing her tongue down the side of his neck. 'Here we have the internal and external carotid arteries,' she said, her lips moving against his skin, 'branches of the common carotid.'

She undid the top two buttons of his shirt and pressed kisses over his upper chest. 'Which comes from the brachiocephalic artery, which comes from the aorta.' By the time her lips reached his pectoral muscle and the thud of his heart, Levi was tense and breathing hard, obviously trying to keep his hands off her.

'You play dirty,' he said, his grip on the textbook white-knuckled.

Kaia smiled seductively. 'I can't help it.' She kept undoing the shirt buttons, one by one, exposing his chest and abs. 'I love you. You're far too distracting.'

With a growl Levi tossed the anatomy book aside, swept his arms around her waist and tumbled her under him on the sofa. She squealed with laughter but quickly turned serious when his mouth covered hers in the kind of kiss that was prefect retribution for her teasing and left her moaning.

Kaia slid her hands up his back and sighed as he trailed his lips across her jaw to her ear. 'I love you too,' he whispered, pulling back to look down at her in that adoring way she loved and never took for granted.

Kaia swallowed from his expression, sliding her fingers through his hair as they stared, their hearts banging side by side. Then, to her alarm, a small frown pinched his brows.

'What is it?' she asked, concerned.

'Will you marry me?' he said, as calm and bold and sure as she could ever have dreamed.

Kaia froze, excitement trapping the air in her lungs.

'I want to spend the rest of my life with you,' he said, unflinching. 'Loving you, supporting you, laughing with you.'

'I want that too,' Kaia said, nodding. 'Yes. Yes, I will.'

She wrapped her arms around his neck and tugged him down for another kiss. But she couldn't stop smiling, and when she released him he too was grinning in delight.

'We're going to have the best time together,' he said as if making a promise, pushing her hair back from her face, his eyes smiling. 'The best life, you and me.'

Kaia nodded, her eyes stinging with tears of joy because he was everything she'd ever wanted and more. 'We are,' she said, pressing a kiss to his lips. 'Because we're the best of friends, too.'

And as they kissed to seal the deal, playfully losing themselves in their wildly passionate love, she'd never felt happier.

* * * * *

If you enjoyed this story,
check out these other great reads
from JC Harroway

Mistletoe Baby Mix-Up
One Night to Royal Baby
One Night to Sydney Wedding
Manhattan Marriage Reunion

All available now!

Coming next month

EXPECTING IN THE ER
Tina Beckett

They got on the elevator, and he pressed the button for the second floor, which was where Mack's office was housed, and they rode up in silence. He didn't try to indulge in small talk or anything else until they reached the confines of his office, and he firmly closed the door and gestured to one of the two seats in front of his desk.

He sat behind his desk, feeling the need to keep barriers between them, including physical ones, to get the point across that they were separate beings with separate lives, despite what had happened in Boston.

'Well, it seems I am to welcome you back to the team.'

'I'm sorry, Mack. I was pretty sure you would have said no, if I had come to you directly with a request to come back to work.'

He nodded. 'Which brings up the question of why you want to come back.'

'Do I need a reason?'

'Frankly, yes. I'm sure it's not because I'm here.'

Her teeth came down on her lower lip for a minute before she answered. 'Not entirely, but it did weigh into the equation.'

'Lainey—'

'No, stop. Before you say anything, I didn't come back in hopes that we'd get back together. That's not what either of us wants. I think we've proved that point. But there is another player in this game. One I just found out about a couple of weeks ago.'

'I don't understand.'

She put her hands in her lap and leaned forward. 'I'm pregnant, Mack.'

Continue reading

EXPECTING IN THE ER
Tina Beckett

Available next month
millsandboon.co.uk

LET'S TALK Romance

For exclusive extracts, competitions and special offers, find us online:

MillsandBoon

@MillsandBoon

@MillsandBoonUK

@MillsandBoonUK

Get in touch on 01413 063 232

For all the latest titles coming soon, visit millsandboon.co.uk/nextmonth